Death or Glory

Michael Asher has served in the Parachute Regiment and the SAS. Together with his wife, Arabist and photographer Mariantonietta Peru, he made the first west–east crossing of the Sahara on foot – a distance of 4,500 miles – with camels, but without technology or back-up of any kind.

He is a fellow of the Royal Society of Literature and has won both the Ness Award of the Royal Geographical Society and the Mungo Park Medal of the Royal Scottish Geographical Society for Exploration.

He has written many books, most recently *The Regiment: The Real Story of the SAS* (Penguin, 2007).

Death or Glory

PART I

The Last Commando

MICHAEL ASHER

PENGUIN BOOKS

PENGUIN BOOKS

Published by the Penguin Group
Penguin Books Ltd, 80 Strand, London WC2R ORL, England
Penguin Group (USA), Inc., 375 Hudson Street, New York, New York 10014, USA
Penguin Group (Canada), 90 Eglinton Avenue East, Suite 700, Toronto, Ontario, Canada M4P 2Y3
(a division of Pearson Penguin Canada Inc.)
Penguin Ireland, 25 St Stephen's Green, Dublin 2, Ireland (a division of Penguin Books Ltd)
Penguin Group (Australia), 250 Camberwell Road, Camberwell, Victoria 3124, Australia
(a division of Pearson Australia Group Pty Ltd)
Penguin Books India Pvt Ltd, 11 Community Centre, Panchsheel Park, New Delhi – 110 017, India
Penguin Group (NZ), 67 Apollo Drive, Rosedale, North Shore 0632, New Zealand
(a division of Pearson New Zealand Ltd)
Penguin Books (South Africa) (Pty) Ltd, 24 Sturdee Avenue, Rosebank,
Johannesburg 2196, South Africa

Penguin Books Ltd, Registered Offices: 80 Strand, London WC2R ORL, England

www.penguin.com

First published by Michael Joseph 2009
Published in Penguin Books 2010

1

Copyright © Michael Asher, 2009

Printed in Great Britain by Clays Ltd, St Ives plc

A CIP catalogue record for this book is available from the British Library

ISBN: 978-0-141-04082-0

www.greenpenguin.co.uk

Penguin Books is committed to a sustainable future
for our business, our readers and our planet.
The book in your hands is made from paper
certified by the Forest Stewardship Council.

To Piggs, Puppi, and Chumo, with love

'The decision of the Axis leaders to allow their African army to cross the Egyptian frontier was in fact the beginning of the end for the Afrika Korps.'

Ronald Lewin, *The Life and Death of the Afrika Korps*, 1977

I

Lieutenant Rowland Green was bleeding to death. He had been hit by a 9mm dum-dum round that had plunged into his armpit and burst out through his back in a shower of gore. Sergeant Tom Caine tore open his shirt and applied a shell-dressing, but it was like trying to stem a dam-burst with blotting paper. Blood soaked into his khaki drill shorts. 'You'll be all right, sir,' Caine said. 'It's not too bad.' He pressed the lieutenant's right hand down on the pad and told him to keep it there. '*Orderly,*' he bellowed. 'I need morphia – *now.*'

Medical orderly Maurice Pickney heard Caine's call, but was focused on another task requiring his full attention. Squatting in a slit-trench a few yards away, he was trying to prize a No. 36 Mills grenade from the frozen fingers of Private 'Tinkerbell' Jones, who had been shot in the act of hurling it. Jones had a critical wound in the abdomen, and was blubbering in shock. Pickney spoke reassuringly to him, holding his wrist in a vice-like grip with one hand, forcing his fingers back one by one with the other. If Jones released the grenade suddenly, Pickney knew, both of them would have about five seconds to live. A moment later he was gripping the steel pineapple tight in his palm, wondering what to do with it. He was about to chuck it over the edge, when he found the pin lying in the dust. He picked it up, slid it back carefully into place, and let out a long sigh. 'We're out of morphia, Sarn't Caine,' he yelled.

Caine swore savagely. From further down the line, he

could hear Corporal Harry Copeland demanding a casualty and ammunition report from each trench in turn. From Caine's left came the booming voice of Gunner Fred Wallace, a six-foot-seven regular soldier from Leatherhead. Wallace was relating his experiences, his words coming out slurred with thirst, while someone else treated multiple shrapnel wounds on his arms. 'I seen a Jerry throwing a potato-masher,' he was saying. 'I shot him and he went down, but I didn't mark where the grenade landed, and just as I was squeezing the trigger a second time, it went off. I didn't feel a damn' thing. Didn't even know I'd been hit till I saw the blood.'

The attack had been over no more than a minute, but to Caine it already seemed like a dream. The Germans, Panzer Grenadiers of Rommel's 90th Light Division, had somehow got through the minefield and crawled up a gully, launching the assault from about two hundred yards. Caine's men – No. 1 Troop, Middle East Commando – had risen to meet them. Hazily, Caine recalled the ferocious clash of bayonet on bayonet, the thump and crack of grenades, the rat-tat-tat of sub-machine guns fired at point-blank range. The fight couldn't have lasted longer than it took to smoke a cigarette, but time had seemed to stand still. Caine's memories of it were a sequence of disjointed images – putting three .45-calibre rounds through a German soldier's chest – three neat scarlet rosettes blossoming on the khaki drill shirt; Lieutenant Green howling as he shot an enemy with a bullet from his Colt; the Jerry snapping off the dum-dum that brought Green down; Fred Wallace dancing madly like a giant marionette, blasting away with his Bren, scything a swathe through the khaki bodies, bringing out his sawn-off twelve-bore shotgun, flaying off Hun faces; Harry Copeland, the battalion's champion sniper, cool as an ice-pick, drilling shots from his .303 into the melee; men falling, men thrashing, men entwined together so you couldn't tell friend from foe, mutilated men screaming for Mother; surly ex-Redcap Todd Sweeney stabbing an enemy in the stomach with a bayonet; a German grabbing Sweeney from behind and Geoff Hutchins shooting him in the head with his Tommygun, so close that half the man's brains spilled out and splashed over them; then Hutchins himself uplifted gracefully on a wave of fire and smoke that whacked his whole body apart.

The desert sky was an open furnace, pulsating raw heat. The stones around the trenches were so hot they scorched bare flesh: inside, the stifling heat lay on the men like a liquid lead; it was too hot to move, almost too hot to think. The commandos had now been awake more than thirty hours, thanks to the huge doses of Benzedrine they'd swallowed, but the amphetamine haze was wearing thin. Caine felt parched, dazed and exhausted. He pulled the brim of his 'soup bowl' helmet down against the lowering sun, then checked that the drum magazine on his Thompson submachine gun was still firmly in place. The gunmetal was hot to the touch. He was the only man in the battalion to use this hundred-round mag, which had a tendency to drop off at inopportune moments. Caine had personally modified the locking mechanism on his magazines, making them secure, and giving his own 'trench-sweeper' more than four times the fire-power of any other. Some of the lads scoffed at what they called his 'Al Capone' shooter, but then few of them had his physique – the powerful shoulders and biceps that were needed to brace the weapon properly.

Caine wasn't much above average height but seemed top-heavy with muscle, as if his chest and shoulders had developed separately from the rest of him. A veteran at twenty-three, his combat experience was reflected in the grimly determined set of his chin and lips, amplified by the cool steadiness of slate-grey eyes that seemed to have been honed by desert winds. He traversed the Tommy-gun's muzzle across the undulating ground in front of the troop's position – shell-holes, bomb-craters, Jerry dead. All the way along the Box he could see palls of black smoke rising from smouldering vehicles – remnants of a supply column that had tried, in vain, to reach them. There were dark circles like black eyes in the desert where Stuka dive-bombers had crashed and burned, shot down by RAF Kittyhawks and Hurricanes. About four miles to the west he could see dust-clouds kicked up by Panzer Army tanks gathering like crows on the edge of minefields that protected the Box. From the ridge behind him there was the continual snarl and crash of twenty-five-pounder field-guns, manned by men of the Royal Horse Artillery. Caine knew that Jerry's 88mm guns would open up any minute.

He felt Green's fingers close on his wrist and glanced down at him. The lieutenant's face was ashen. 'Your fannies, Caine,' he said weakly. 'Ditch them. The enemy will use them as an excuse to execute you.'

The 'fanny' was the combination knuckle-duster-dagger issued only to the Middle East Commando, and Caine saw at once what the lieutenant meant. If the next wave of Germans captured them and found their fannies – not to mention the cheesewire and explosive charges some of the lads had – they would execute them as 'assassins', or 'saboteurs'.

'Don't worry, sir,' Caine said. 'I'll tell the men to bury them.' Green didn't answer, and Caine saw at once that he was dead. Harry Copeland pivoted into the trench and crouched there, his face under the battered helmet a mask of dried blood and dust. He was a gawky, good-looking, gangle-legged ex-Service Corps driver, with a stooping shuffle, a long nose and a prominent Adam's apple, whose profile always reminded Caine of some large wading bird. Cope stared, his cobalt-blue eyes popping at Green's corpse, and at his blood pooling in the sand. 'Poor blighter,' he said.

Copeland settled back on his haunches in the sauna-like heat, sweat-runnels grooving tramlines through the mask of filth on his face. He licked lips that were black and cracked with thirst, doffing his tin lid, scratching at a brush of blond hair that grew stiffly vertical like a field of wheat-stubble. Caine watched his Adam's apple working, and thought Cope might throw up. Instead he laid his precious Short Model Lee-Enfield Mk III sniper rifle on his thighs as if it were a baby, careful not to disturb the zeroing of the telescopic sights. 'You got water?' he begged Caine, his words distorted by a bloated tongue, white with mucus. Caine unslung a felt-covered water-bottle, offered it to him. 'Go steady with it,' he rasped. Cope drank in short gulps, then gave the canteen back. He pulled out two Player's Navy Cut cigarettes and handed one to Caine. 'Wallace is all right,' he croaked, his words coming out more clearly now. 'Hide like a rhino. Took a peppering of grenade fragments, but he's still talking.'

'I heard. To stop that bloke yapping you'd have to run him down with a tank.'

'You all right, Tom?'

Caine touched his face and realized it was smeared with his troop officer's blood. 'Yep,' he nodded, sticking the fag in his mouth. He ejected his last two rounds and swapped drum-magazines on his weapon, snapping the working parts back with unnecessary force. He tilted his head towards Green's body. 'Twenty years old and straight out of OCTU,' he said. 'Hadn't even got his knees brown. Might have made a good soldier – we'll never know. First time in combat and he cops one and lands me with command of the troop.'

Cope lit his cigarette with a Swan Vesta. 'Not new to you is it, mate,' he commented.

'Nope.'

Copeland was one of the few who was aware that, a while back, Caine had been an officer in the Royal Engineers. The corporal didn't know why he had fallen from grace, though. He had never asked, and Caine had never enlightened him.

Caine shook his Zippo lighter out of its protective rubber condom, and lit the squashed fag. 'What's the damage?' he asked.

'Ammo's down to about ten rounds a man, fifty each for the Brens. With Green, we've got another six men dead and three seriously wounded. Not counting the boys on the outpost, the troop's down to seventeen men. Not what you'd call a viable fighting unit.'

Caine had almost forgotten the dozen wounded men posted on a ridge a thousand yards to the west. They had all been hit the previous day, and Lieutenant Green had deployed them on the outpost at first light, on the assumption that the wounded were the most expendable. He had also assured them that they wouldn't be abandoned.

Caine took a glance over the lip of the trench: the sun was like a burnished brass shield, and his eyes narrowed from its brilliance. He couldn't see the men on the outpost, but he could hear the crackle of their Brens and the pop of their .55-calibre Boys anti-tank rifles – proof that they were still holding out. He guessed they were all carrying fannies, and wondered if they would have the gumption to bury them before the enemy overran the ridge.

An 88mm round fried air, droned over the position. Caine and Copcland ducked. 'Here they come,' Cope sighed. The shell burst on the escarpment above them, near enough to shower them with rock fragments that pinged off their tin lids. A moment later another man pitched into the trench and hunkered there, panting and dripping sweat. It was 'Prissy' Hogg, a runner from HQ Troop. 'Where's the boss?' Hogg grunted, trying in vain to wet his broken lips with a bone-dry tongue.

Caine gestured at Green's body. 'I'm the boss.'

'All right, skipper,' Hogg said. 'Orders from the OC. You're to withdraw at sunset, 1845 hours. The whole Battle-Group's being pulled out.' His tongue was so arid and swollen that his speech was a series of small detonations.

Caine glanced at his watch – there was about an hour of daylight left. 'What about the wounded lads on the outpost?' he enquired.

'No instructions,' Hogg said. 'Commando practice is to abandon the wounded.'

Caine jabbed out his cigarette stub, his steady grey eyes glaring at Hogg. 'Don't tell *me* about commando practice, Prissy,' he grunted. 'Mr Green promised them they wouldn't be ditched.'

'Nothing you can do,' Hogg said. 'Leave 'em.'

'I'll be damned if I will. I'm going to pull them out, and I'm coming back with you to get the say-so from the OC.'

Hogg swigged water from his canteen. 'Right you are,' he said. 'We can cover each other.'

Caine turned to Cope. 'Stand the men to,' he said. 'Don't budge an inch from here till I get back.'

Copeland's dust-caked features cracked. 'Where were you expecting us to go exactly? For an afternoon stroll?'

The squadron command-post lay in a redoubt about

two hundred yards along the escarpment. It wasn't far by ordinary standards, but with enemy 88mm guns spewing steel it might have been the other end of the earth. Caine and Hogg zig-zagged along the ridge at a low crouch, taking turns to run and cover. 88mm tracer shells lashed in, splitting in puffs of white and brown all over the hillside. Twenty yards from the redoubt, Caine felt the waft of a bullet against his cheek. The slug that had missed him by a hair's breadth slapped into Hogg, who screamed and sprawled headfirst in the gravel. Caine lifted his weapon and hip-boosted a couple of rounds in the direction he thought the shot had come from. Hogg tried to get up, waving a smashed wrist, pumping arterial blood. Caine was yelling 'Get down,' when he heard another bullet hit the runner's chest with a smack like a massive punch – the impact was so powerful that Hogg hurtled three or four yards.

Feeling sick, Caine crawled over and found Hogg on his back, eyes gaping vacantly at the sky. 'Bloody hell,' he grunted. Another round shaved his tin lid and ricocheted off a boulder near by. Caine rolled, leapt up, and dived maniacally for cover behind a slope. Then, keeping below the brow, he crawled towards the HQ sangar, cursing the big ammo-pouches high-slung from his yoke that prevented him from lying flat. It seemed for ever before he made the sangar and lay prone outside.

A firefight was still going on at the foot of the slope to the north as the squadron's other troops fought off attacks. Caine couldn't see the battle, but he could hear the pop and splutter of small-arms, like a distant squabble between madmen. 'Sarn't Caine, No. 1 Troop,' he bawled.

Squadron Sergeant Major Bill Ramsay crept up to the sangar entrance, hessian-covered soup-bowl shadowing bloodshot eyes. 'I want to see the OC,' Caine told him.

The SSM's head was replaced by that of the OC, Major Kenneth Crawford, a chubby man with spectacles, and a furtive look. 'What's your situation, Sergeant?' he asked.

'We've taken heavy casualties, sir. I don't think we can stand another attack.'

'It'll be sundown soon. Jerry won't be back before first light tomorrow. He doesn't like night-attacks. By that time, God willing, we'll be long gone'

'Very good, sir, but I've got wounded on that ridge to the west.' Caine gestured in the direction of the outpost. 'I want your permission to bring them in.'

Crawford's jaw set. 'Just leave them, Caine. They'll be accorded the rights of war.'

'No they won't. They're carrying fannies, cheesewire and God knows what else. The Jerries don't like 'irregulars'. If they find commando weapons, they'll line them up and shoot 'em.'

The OC didn't seem to be taking in his words. 'You don't understand, Caine. Rommel has broken through the Gazala Line. The whole Eighth Army is in retreat. What do you think . . .'

Caine never found out exactly what Crawford wanted to know, because at that moment the sergeant major's voice shouted, 'Message from battalion, sir.' The major ducked inside the trench, and a second later a shell whistled in, striking the redoubt with a direct hit. All Caine remembered later was a dumb-bell on his chest, a mushroom of earth, rocks and smoke, an expanding flash of orange and black, and several burning bodies being flipped into the air.

He must have passed out, because the next thing he knew he was being shaken by the squadron second-in-command, Captain Robin Sears-Beach, a truculent officer with a game-cock walk, front teeth like tombstones and a disturbing absence of chin. 'You're all right, Caine,' Sears-Beach was repeating. 'Get back to your position.'

Caine did a mental body check: other than the familiar scorch of thirst in his mouth, there was no pain anywhere. Everything seemed to be functioning properly, and he found it hard to believe that he hadn't been hit. Out of the corner of his eye he saw a medical orderly trying to beat out flames on something that looked like a giant black cocoon. The next moment, a round punched clean through the orderly's helmet. He went down without a sound.

Caine tore his eyes away, rubbed split and distended lips. 'You got water, sir?' he wheezed.

'Use your own,' Sears-Beach snapped.

Caine scrabbled for his bottle, uncorked it with shaky fingers, took a blissful gulp. 'The section on the outpost,' he drawled. 'They're cut off.'

'Leave them. Just get the rest of the troop out when the time comes.'

Caine's ashlar eyes smouldered like embers about to burst aflame. 'You don't dump your mates,' he said.

The captain gripped his wrist, and Caine looked into dilated nostrils and bared teeth. 'Don't argue with me, Caine. I'm acting OC, and I said leave them. Now, get back to your troop.'

2

By the time he had crawled back to his position the desert had turned orange and gold, the lowering sun casting strange loops of shadow that gave the whole battlefield a surreal look. The furnace heat was trailing off, replaced by a wind that rose like a scream, driving eddies of dust, rasping faces, sandpapering throats and tongues. The pressure of enemy artillery had eased. The dead had been laid reverently outside the trenches, and Pickney was still working his way back and forth from casualty to casualty. Caine threw himself into his slit-trench. Wallace, who always carried a Bren-gun in action, throwing its weight around as if it were a toy, was in there, bracing the weapon on its bipod legs, in stand-to position. Copeland, brewing tea on a Primus stove, raised his startling blue eyes as Caine crouched against the parapet. 'Prissy's dead,' Caine said bluntly.

'Shit. Was that the HQ position going up?'

'Yep. Whole bunker got wiped. Sears-Beach has assumed command.'

'That turd,' Wallace groaned, waving a saucer-sized hand at the hordes of flies that had invaded the trench the moment the heat had begun to wane. Caine became suddenly aware that his chest and arms were black with the creatures. He started slapping them away but quickly gave up: it was like trying to make a dent in water.

'Tea's up,' said Cope. 'Anyone without his mug can drink out of his arse.'

The tea was hot, sweet and strong, thick with condensed

milk, and they drank it crunching desperately on hard-tack biscuits, flapping away flies. The only good thing that could be said about the heat, Caine reflected, was that it dampened your appetite. When he and Copeland were done, Cope relieved Wallace on the Bren. The big man shifted his gargantuan bulk, squatting next to Caine. With his wrestler's physique, his forest of stubble, his tangled nest of dark hair, his chiselled features black with powder-burns and his intense, black eyes, he looked, Caine thought, like an ogre out of a children's story. Fred Wallace – rugby-prop, champion boxer and the Commando's best Bren marksman – was so enormous that Caine was surprised that any enemy sniper could ever miss him in combat. Subconsciously, he'd come to regard the giant as unkillable – an elemental force of nature. Wallace could usually be distinguished also by the sphinx tattoo on his left forearm – the insignia of his old unit, F (Sphinx) Battery, 4 Royal Horse Artillery – but both arms were now heavily bandaged, adding extra bulk to his already colossal limbs. Wallace gulped the tea and spat it out in disgust. 'Call that tea?' he demanded. 'It would have been *better* drinking out of my arse!'

'That's where you can stick it, then,' Cope said. He noticed that, for all his talk, Wallace didn't tip the tea away.

When he'd finished his tea, the big man drew out his pet back-up weapon – the twin-barrelled sawn-off Purdey shotgun he carried in a homemade leather pouch slung on his belt. He broke open the gun, checked the chambers and started to clean them lovingly with a dry cloth. He didn't try to oil the weapon: he'd long since learned that oil and sand didn't mix.

'I don't know why you carry that thing,' Caine commented. 'It's an illegal firearm. If the Boche find that on you, you really will be for the high-jump.'

Wallace held up the twelve-bore to the light and peered happily through both smoothbore barrels. He took a pair of buckshot cartridges from his webbing, slotted them into the chambers, snapped the gun shut. 'Purdey's got me out of more scrapes than I've had hot dinners,' he said. 'I couldn't part with her now.'

Cope turned back to watch his arc. 'Hey,' he said a moment later. 'A red Very light has just gone up from the outpost. Is that important?'

Caine squeezed next to him and peeped over the brim of the trench, catching the tail-end of the Very flare. 'That's the distress signal,' he said. 'It means they can't hold out any longer.'

The sun had already gone down and the landscape was drained of its wild sunset colours. The furnace wind had dropped, but trails of smoke and dust still drifted languidly across the desert like gossamer veils. Caine pointed out a gully that ran at right angles from the bottom of the salient as far as the outpost ridge. 'I'm going to bring those lads in,' he said. 'I'll work my way up that wadi. It should give me cover from fire, especially after dark.'

Wallace pressed his massive frame between Caine and Copeland. 'I'm with you, skipper,' he said.

Caine shook his head. 'You're wounded.'

Wallace grinned, his teeth pearly white against his powder-blackened face.

'You don't call this wounded, do you? I've had worse than this on a night's boozing in Cairo. Anyhow, you'll never do it on your own.'

Cope released the Bren's stock and sat back on his haunches. His ostrich-like features had taken on a cast of disdainful superiority, as if he were in the presence of a couple of dim-witted pupils. 'I think you may have overlooked one small factor, *mein Herr*,' he said to Caine. 'Some of those boys will be stretcher-cases. What, so you're going to carry half a dozen men each? Pardon me for being a dunderhead, but how's that going to work, then? You're going to ferry them one by one? By my reckoning, that's going to take at least three and a half hours to clear the lot. I reckon the enemy is going to have rumbled it by then, apart from the fact that you're both going to be shattered after a couple of runs.'

Caine nodded. It was true that he hadn't considered the stretcher-cases.

Copeland leaned further over the edge of the trench and pointed down the salient to a knot of lorries that had formed part of the supply column. Most were wrecked and smoking, but not all. 'I reckon there's at least one 3-tonner down there that's in good nick,' he said. 'We could drive it up the wadi and shift the lot of them in one bash. If we've got juice, we needn't head back to the Battle Group RV. We could drive straight to the fall-back at Jaghbub. Can you find the way?'

'Yep, I can find the way,' Caine said, 'but I don't know about "we". I'm not having you getting in the shit for me.'

'What d'you mean?' Wallace demanded. 'It's "commando initiative", innit? If those lads get caught with their fannies, they're dog meat.'

'Sears-Beach didn't see it that way.'

'Sears-*Bitch* is a bonehead – you know that. That chump wouldn't know "commando initiative" if it got up and poked his eye out. He should of stuck to the Shepheard Hotel Short Range Desert Bar-pushers, or whatever crappy outfit he used to be in.'

'Yeah, and if we *do* get in the shite," said Cope, grinning, 'we'll just say you ordered us to do it.'

Caine gave in. He knew he shouldn't be putting their lives at risk like this, but their loyalty moved him almost to tears. 'This calls for a sacrament,' he said. He brought a crumpled brown cnvclopc out of his brcast pocket, and offered it solemnly to the two men.

'What's this?' Cope enquired.

'Bennies,' Caine said. 'We'll need them if we're going to get away with a stunt like this.'

3

There were still a few minutes of light left when they made it to the 3-tonner. Before leaving, Caine had passed command of the troop over to Corporal 'Todd' Sweeney, the next most senior non-com after Copeland. He told Sweeney to extract the unit the moment darkness fell, and to make a tactical withdrawal to the Battle Group RV behind the ridge. There would be transport waiting to take them back to Jaghbub. Sweeney, a tight-lipped, balding ex-military policeman with a barrel chest and a head like a football, didn't seem happy with the order. 'What am I supposed to say if Captain Sears-Beach wants to know where you are?' he demanded. 'I don't like bullshitting my superiors.'

'You ain't got a problem, then, have you?' Wallace grinned. 'Sears-Beach ain't your superior: he's a bloody moron.'

'Tell him the truth,' Caine cut in. 'Say we're missing in action.'

As an afterthought, the three of them had handed over their fannies to Sweeney for safekeeping, and Caine had felt an unexpected reluctance to part with his dagger. True, being captured with an unorthodox weapon would hamper any attempt to present a cover story, but on the other hand, it was the commandos' symbol – both their cap-badge, and the mark of their 'specialness'. Caine had had to tell Wallace to relinquish his fanny twice before the giant pressed it reluctantly into Sweeney's hands.

As they reached the wagon, the RHA battery on the ridge launched a walloping barrage, splitting the darkness with seams of blinding white light. They hurled themselves flat with their hands over their tin lids and didn't move until the bombardment stopped. There were answering booms and flashes from the German 88mms, but Caine judged the elevation too far above them to worry about.

He sloped off to make a quick inspection of the vehicle, and was back in five minutes. 'Looks like the driver took a round in the head,' he said. 'Sniper job. Ten to one he stalled the engine. I doubt that the lorry was hit, because she's carrying a load of "flimsies". If she had been, they'd have gone off like a rocket.'

Copeland nodded. 'Flimsies' were four-gallon cans of petrol, packed two to a wooden crate, so called because of their notorious tendency to leak. Cope could never understand why the Allies hadn't adopted the German-pattern 'jerry' can, which was so much more efficient. 'That'll solve the juice problem, anyway,' he said.

'Yep, but we'll need to get rid of some if we're going to fit the boys in.'

They moved to the lorry, where Copeland and Wallace started passing flimsies out of the back. Caine removed the dead driver and laid him in the sand. He jumped into the cab and examined the starter, gear lever, pedals. Just as he'd guessed, the gear lever was stuck in first. The fuel gauge showed that the tanks were almost full.

He jumped down, checked the tyres, then took a peek under the bonnet. The engine looked sound. He closed it, hurried round to the tailboard and found that the others had dumped enough flimsies. 'You take the tailboard,' he told Cope. 'Fred, there's a hatchway up in the cab roof, with a pintle-mount. Can you fix the Bren there?'

'I'll have a look.'

'How many mags did you get?'

17

Wallace had collected .303 ammo from the rest of the troop, but still had only three full magazines. 'If we get into a contact,' Caine said, 'fire only singles.'

Caine was in the driver's seat and about to hit the starter when Cope banged on the back of the cab. 'How are they going to know it's us?' he demanded urgently. 'They'll be on a hair trigger up there. We don't want 'em opening up on us.'

Caine cursed himself silently. He fumbled in his haver-sack for the Very pistol he'd brought. 'Thanks, Harry,' he said to the back of the cab. 'Talk about dunderhead – I completely forgot. The signal is a blue Very light. I'm firing it now.'

He stuck the pistol out of the open window and squeezed the trigger. There was a bang and a pop, followed by a flash of brilliant blue light. Caine and Wallace sat frozen until it faded. As if in answer, there were more crashes of artillery fire from the top of the escarpment. Caine noted that the interval between salvos was getting longer and guessed that the gunners were covering themselves as they limbered up. They must be almost out of shells by now anyway.

Caine reloaded the Very pistol in case it was needed. Then he toed the starter and the engine burst into life. Close up it sounded like thunder, and Caine had to remind himself that in the vastness of the theatre, with hundreds of vehicles lumbering about and big guns firing all over the place, the enemy would never pinpoint its location. 'I'm keeping her in first,' he told Wallace. 'We're going without headlights, so mind you keep your beady eyes on the road.'

Caine was the scion of generations of village blacksmiths, and had fire and steel in his veins. He had been at home with motor vehicles ever since he had learned to drive a tractor at the age of twelve. An apprentice mechanic in

Civvy Street, he prided himself on his ability to handle them. Managing a big lorry in the desert at night wasn't all that easy, but as a Sapper mechanic he'd been attached to 7th Armoured Division – the 'Desert Rats' – from the start of the war. He had as much desert driving experience as anyone, and more than most.

He nursed the vehicle slowly into the gully, his eyes pinned on the way ahead. Daylight had faded out completely, and there was no moon – he drove by feel and starlight. Potholes, rocks and sudden drops were the main threats, but there was also the danger that Jerry had mined the area or sowed it with thermos bombs. The one thing he fervently hoped was that there was no enemy night-patrol hidden in the darkness. Once the lorry was spotted they would be damned lucky if they got out – with all that petrol in the back, a single round could turn them into a fireball.

He gripped the wheel hard, hunched over, his heart throbbing, his breathing rapid. Every yard covered safely was a small victory. The lorry bumped and rattled over the stones. Occasional flashes of cannon fire ripped the night sky open above them, making Caine wince. Once again he had to remind himself that the artillery duel was nothing to do with them.

'Stop!' Wallace growled suddenly. Caine's heart bumped. 'What is it?'

'Something down there.'

Caine put the gear lever in neutral and applied the handbrake, while the giant dropped from the cab, landing on hands and feet like a big black panther. He disappeared into the darkness and shortly reappeared on Caine's side, his tiny black eyes holding pinpricks of starlight. 'Step in the wadi bed,' he said. 'About two feet. Can you make it?'

Caine told him to stand back. He put the truck in gear

and inched her over the edge of the step. There was a second's hiatus before the front wheels dropped and the big balloon tyres bounced on the hard surface with a wobbling of suspension. Caine moved the lorry forward until her back wheels had cleared the step. He applied the brake, dropped out of the cab and shouted to Copeland. The three of them set to work collecting boulders to build a ramp so that they could take the step easily on the way back.

It took only a few minutes. Back in the hot seat, Caine drove forward slowly, all his senses alert. The truck rocked and grated over rough boulders. Occasional 88mm shells whizzed overhead. The ridge was only a thousand yards from where they'd started, but it seemed an age before they arrived. Then, while Wallace and Cope covered him from outside, Caine made a three-point turn, expecting shots to ring out from above every second. He cut the engine and joined the others in the lee of the escarpment, where they crouched close together for a moment, taking slow sips of water from their canteens. Though the air had cooled slightly since sunset, the ground still throbbed with the heat it had soaked up in daylight hours. They watched enemy shells star-bursting on the Box behind them. Return fire from the RHA was desultory now, and Caine guessed there was only one gun left, firing for effect. That meant the entire Middle East Commando – or what was left of it – had gone. They would soon be joining the defeated remnants of the Eighth Army from the entire length of the Gazala Line, limping back to Egypt in a vast motor fleet – the worst defeat the British had suffered since Dunkirk. For a moment an unexpected loneliness engulfed him. He found himself thinking about Todd Sweeney, and hoping the rest of his troop was safely on its way to the fall-back RV.

He put it out of his mind. 'All right,' he said. 'We go up

spread out five yards apart, and carefully does it. We don't want any accidents.'

The ridge was loose shale, no more than thirty feet high. It was an easy enough climb, but far too noisy for Caine's liking. What if the lads had failed to spot the Very light? What if they were walking into an ambush set up by their own men? Caine broke over the ridge and spotted a movement, a faint flutter of white in the darkness. He fell flat just as a weapon cracked. A bullet soughed past his ear. 'Don't shoot!' he screamed. 'Don't *anybody* shoot. It's Tom Caine, No. 1 Troop.'

'Caine?' a reedy voice came out of the darkness. 'Hell's bells, about bleeding time.'

Caine moved forward cautiously and almost bumped into Jake Campbell, a wiry corporal formerly of the Highland Light Infantry. Campbell looked to be in a bad way – his face was covered in concussion cracks, like old porcelain, and both his head and his left arm were swathed in bandages – hence the white flash Caine had glimpsed in the darkness. Campbell held a .45-calibre Colt automatic pistol in his right hand.

'You never could hit a barn door at twenty paces, Jake,' Caine said.

'Lucky for you, brother.'

Cope asked if he'd clocked the blue Very light. Campbell nodded shakily, and Caine saw that he was on the verge of collapse. He put his arm round the corporal's shoulders to steady him. 'Thank God,' Campbell whispered. 'Mr Green promised, but we thought you wasn't coming.'

'Where are the rest?'

Campbell pointed weakly to a low rise only a few yards away. 'In all-round defence,' he cackled.

'Listen, Jake,' Caine told him gently. 'Go down the slope,

and you'll find our 3-tonner in the wadi. Get in the cab and rest. You've done enough. We'll take it from here.'

'Aye, well you'd best put a move on, because we spotted enemy patrols creeping through the minefield just before last light.'

Campbell staggered off. Caine and the others moved to the bank, where half a dozen commandos sat or lay on ground like the surface of a cheese-grater, in a rough semi-circle. They had abandoned their slit-trenches at sunset, re-assigning them to the dead, whom they'd buried there in sand and gravel as best they could. The ridge-top was grooved and pitted by enemy rounds, and the thicket of thorn-trees that had once ringed the position had been reduced to a nest of groping, skeletal claws. Of the twelve men Green had posted on the ridge that morning, only these six were left alive: many were barely conscious, others begged through swollen lips for water their rescuers couldn't give them. Some were shockingly wounded. Private Dick Grafton's leg was a raw mass of bloody pulp from which the bones protruded. Private John Pearson's right arm had been shattered, the bones crushed, the blood vessels hanging out. Private Arthur Norris sat holding a shell-dressing to the side of his skull, a good proportion of which appeared to be missing.

'Jesus Christ,' Wallace gasped. 'What the hell happened here?'

'Hell happened,' someone gasped, and Caine recognized 'Quiff' Smithers, the section medical orderly. He was lying in a huddle on the ground, his khaki drill heavy with dried blood. 'I tried to patch 'em up,' Smithers said, 'till I took three rounds in the leg.'

Caine gulped, realizing that Smithers was virtually paralysed. 'You've done a cracking job,' he said. 'You deserve a medal for this. You all deserve a medal.'

'They can stuff their medals,' Smithers groaned. 'Just get us out of this shit-hole.' He squinted at Wallace and, noticing the giant's heavily bandaged arms for the first time, exploded with hysterical laughter that turned quickly into racking coughs. 'You don't look too bloody good yourself,' he spluttered. 'Talk about the blind leading the blind.'

'Yeah, well, we're the best you're going to get, mate,' Wallace grunted, slightly miffed. 'You can either put up with us or stay here.'

They had no stretchers, but they scoured the dead men's haversacks for ponchos and used them to ferry the wounded downhill, worst cases first. To spare Wallace's arms, Cope and Caine did the carrying, while Wallace covered them with the Bren. As they ferried the last casualty – Smithers – over the brow of the ridge, the giant said softly, 'There's a light.'

Caine and Copeland laid the wounded man down and hunkered next to Wallace, peering into the night. Caine was just beginning to think that the big man had imagined it, when he spotted the faintest flicker of flame. 'A match,' he said.

Copeland nodded and fingered his sniper rifle. 'Lighting fags,' he said. 'Ideal sniper bait.'

'Forget it,' Caine said. 'Let's get this man in the wagon.' They moved the medical orderly downhill, with Wallace walking backwards, covering them. While Cope was making Smithers comfortable with the others, Caine pulled out of his haversack a small surprise he had been saving for this moment. It was a No. 76 Hawkins grenade – a flat canister of explosive like an oversized brandy flask – with a time-pencil attached. He half-buried the bomb in the sand and crushed the time-pencil. The fuse gave them five minutes to clear out.

Caine hauled himself into the driver's seat, noting that Wallace was already positioned at the hatch above, his Bren fixed on the pintle-mount. 'Here we go,' he said.

He hit the starter. There was a dead click. He tried again: the mechanism failed to respond. He tried and failed a third time, then hurled himself out of the cab, head swimming, wondering what twisted logic had persuaded him to plant the Hawkins grenade before he'd even started the engine. The time-pencil was set to five minutes. If he couldn't start the lorry within that time, the bomb would blast the wagon and the wounded men to kingdom come.

For a split second he hovered between decisions – whether to try and remove the time-pencil, to clear everyone out of the lorry or to fix the problem. He took a deep breath and realized that he knew what the trouble was. He'd been working with engines all his adolescence and adult life, and had an instinctive feel for them. For him, motor vehicles were dependable creatures that would perform any duty required of them so long as they were treated with respect, and their needs supplied. He decided to trust his instinct: at once he felt calmer.

He opened the bonnet, stared into the gaping darkness and took another deep breath. He didn't need a torch to deal with a 3-tonner engine: over the years he'd trained himself to inspect them by touch. Knowing there would be no second chance, his fingers walked deftly from spark plugs to carburettor, radiator, fan belt and engine block, feeling for faults, testing connections. Finally, he felt the battery. Exactly as he had thought: one of the leads had come loose. As he strove to tighten the screw, he heard Wallace shout, 'Enemy on the ridge!' There was a clatter of sub-machine-gun fire, still out of range, but getting closer. Caine closed his eyes, praying that no stray round would hit the petrol in the back.

He finished screwing, slammed the bonnet, rushed back to the cab. He hoisted himself into the driver's seat, hit the starter. The engine roared.

He had just shifted into first gear, when something hard clunked stone not ten yards from his window. 'Grenade!' Wallace yelled from the hatchway. Caine rammed down the accelerator and the lorry jerked forward, just as the grenade erupted in a whoosh of fire. 'Enemy coming down the ridge!' Wallace bawled.

Caine revved the engine and changed into second gear, dimly aware of the rat-tat-tat of Schmeisser 9mm sub-machine pistols, the pop of Gewehr 41 semi-autos. He twisted the steering wheel, desperately veering left, then right, already going faster than was safe in this terrain. There were screams from the wounded men in the back. Above him, Wallace had started firing a steady stream of single shots. Caine noticed the pause as he changed magazines, and knew his ammo wouldn't last much longer. At the tailboard, Cope was punching off aimed rounds as steadily as was possible from the bucking vehicle. 'They're nearly down,' Wallace roared.

Right then, Caine heard a stomach-churning whine of air like a high-pitched siren, followed by a detonation that seemed to lift the world up and flip it over, ripping the night into a million brilliant shards. The lorry jiggered as a blast wave belched over it and Caine gripped the steering wheel so hard his knuckles turned ivory. He was just thinking that it was an awfully big blast for a Hawkins bomb when he heard another rasp like a giant razor slicing through canvas, and a second shattering explosion sent the night wobbling, followed by a third, smaller one. For a moment there was no sound but for the droning engine, then Caine heard Wallace yell. 'Yaah! The Gunners! God bless the Horse-Gunners!'

It struck him like a slap in the face that they had just been saved by shells fired by the Royal Horse Artillery, from the last 25-pounder on the Box. The third explosion had been the Hawkins bomb going up. If he had ever in his life made any disparaging comment about the Artillery, he begged silent forgiveness. The gun crews up there must have seen them from the start. He didn't know how the hell they'd done it in the dark, but it was the finest damn' gunnery he'd ever seen.

The truck roared down the wadi, and Caine strained his eyes to make out the step where they'd built the ramp. It came up in less than a minute, and Caine slowed down and changed to first. The lorry took the step without a hitch. Caine changed back to second and was just accelerating, congratulating himself on his foresight in preparing the ramp, when something big and soft thunked on the bonnet. Caine's eyes popped out in disbelief. It was an Afrika Korps soldier, his face pressed hard against the windscreen and twisted into a horrific leer. He was struggling to bring a Schmeisser to bear with one hand while holding on desperately with the other. Caine, blinded by the obstruction, felt the lorry's wheels shuddering and fought to right her. He shot a sideways glance at the now-comatose Jake Campbell in the passenger seat, and as he did so noticed Wallace's twelve-bore sawn-off leaning against the gear lever. He didn't know why the giant had left it there: he remembered Wallace loading it, though, and was certain he hadn't used it since. He grabbed it, cocked the hammers one-handed, pointed it at the ghastly face only inches away from his and fired both barrels The windscreen shattered; the German's face seemed to burst into flames and was gone. Caine kept his head low, ducking glass shards, almost lying on the steering wheel. For a moment he thought she was going over. Then the big balloon tyres got a purchase. Caine took the curve in second, changed up to third, and accelerated onwards into the desert night.

4

Lieutenant General Sir Claude Auchinleck, Commander-in-Chief, Middle East Forces, stood under a lazily circling fan in his war room, in shirt-sleeve order against the heat, studying one of the huge maps tacked to his wall. The defeat of the Eighth Army on the 'impregnable' Gazala Line was the worst reverse he had suffered in his thirty-year military career. Allied forces were now in full retreat, and the Axis would soon turn its attention to Tobruk, the last Libyan port in British hands.

The 'Auk' had been up until two o'clock that morning, presiding over an agitated conference on the fate of Tobruk. Now, though, his gaze was focused on what appeared to be a green blob on the vast blue expanse of the Mediterranean – the island of Malta. The more he thought about it, the more convinced he was that Malta was the key. 'Force and fraud are in war the two cardinal virtues,' he recited to himself.

'Thomas Hobbes,' a voice grated behind him. The Auk swung round to see Major General 'Chink' Dorman-Smith, his Deputy Chief of the General Staff, waiting by the conference table. 'I didn't hear you come in, Chink,' he said.

Dorman-Smith saluted and removed his field-cap. A lean Anglo-Irishman with a pugnacious face that many a staff officer longed to punch, he and Auchinleck had been close since they had served together in India. Chink could be charming, but he was disliked at GHQ because of his caustic wit and his ability to pinpoint a fool at a thousand paces. The Auk considered him the most original strategist of his time.

'I was just thinking about Malta,' the C-in-C said.

'So I gathered. Is it to be force or fraud?'

'This may be the time for fraud. Why? What do *you* think Rommel will do?'

Dorman-Smith glanced at his chief, trying to assess his state of mind. Most commanders would have been bowed by the traumatic defeats of the last few days, but the Auk still stood poised like Horatio on the bridge – cool, imperturbable, fighting fit. With his immense physique, stone-carved head and electric-blue eyes, he had always seemed to the cerebral Chink someone larger than life – an exile from an epic tale of gods and heroes. He could well imagine the Auk in breastplate and plumed helmet, marshalling the phalanx at Thermopylae.

The DCGS took a step nearer the map and surveyed it with a penetrating gaze. 'He'll take Tobruk,' he said incisively. 'We won't stop him now. But then he'll be faced with a dilemma. Does he go for Malta or for the Nile? He can't do both, because Malta is a job for the Luftwaffe, and he doesn't have the airpower to execute two operations at once. The Malta option would leave the Panzer Army twiddling its thumbs, and if there's one thing Rommel cannot stand, it's inaction. His successes have all come from speed and aggression – remember the dash for the Wire during Crusader? No, he'll race for the Nile like a bat out of hell, and try to catch us with our pants down. I'm sorry to say, sir, that judging by the current state of the Eighth Army, he may well succeed.'

The Auk nodded: as usual, Dorman-Smith's reading of Rommel's character coincided closely with his own. He was about to add something when three staff officers entered. They were Brigadier Francis de Guingand, Director of Military Intelligence, Lieutenant Colonel Dudley Clarke, chief of the Deception Service – 'A' Force, and Captain Julian Avery, of the Special Operations Executive's G(R). wing. Auchinleck glanced at his watch. 'Is it that time already, Tom?' he asked de Guingand.

The brigadier, a tall, black-haired officer with humorous features, nodded. 'I'm afraid so, sir. *Runefish* is outside – shall I wheel her in?'

'By all means – I'm looking forward to meeting her.'

Auchinleck sat down at the head of the conference table, but the others remained standing. Dorman-Smith shifted uncomfortably, aware that he hadn't got round to saying what he had come for, and unsure if he was still welcome. 'Do you mind if I stay for this one?' he asked.

The Auk considered it for a moment. The DCGS had been indoctrinated to a low level in the *Runefish* project, but the C-in-C didn't want him making any untoward comments during what would be a sensitive meeting. He decided to risk it. 'No, stay if you wish, Chink,' he said. 'You might find it interesting.' Before he had finished the sentence, *Runefish* glided into the room.

To full-blooded men largely deprived of the company of women, First Officer Maddaleine 'Maddy' Rose, Women's Royal Naval Service, was a provocative sight. She wore an immaculately starched khaki drill uniform that only served to enhance her striking figure – high, firm breasts, long legs, lean shoulders, lithe hips carrying not a gramme of surplus weight. As graceful and supple in her movements as an acrobat, she possessed an air of elegance that was set off by the blue officer's rings on her shoulders, the blue chiffon scarf and the blue and white tricorne hat cocked jauntily on her boyishly cropped golden hair. Her features were strong but pliant, her full lips expressive, her eyes – an almost super-natural shade of aquamarine – seemed to conjure depths of solemnity beyond her years. Her hands and feet were surprisingly small and delicately formed. On a webbing belt at her waist she wore a .45-calibre Colt automatic, holstered on the right for a left-handed draw. She gave the C-in-C a brisk naval salute, and the faintest whiff of perfume drifted by.

'Good afternoon, First Officer,' Auchinleck said. 'It's a pleasure to meet you at last.' He sat back in his chair and looked her up and down. Maddy endured the appraisal patiently, wondering if the C-in-C was a ladies' man. He was certainly handsome, and looked far younger than his fifty-eight years. She'd been told that he was a loner who never went to cocktail parties, and that he had a young and pretty American wife at home. Maddy was accustomed to men undressing her mentally, but she felt that the Auk's appraisal was not of that kind. He was interested only in whether or not she was right for the job. 'My dear,' he said finally, 'you are far too charming to be a Jack Tar.'

For a moment Maddy wondered if this was a criticism, but the sniggers of the other officers told her it was a jibe against the Senior Service. Dorman-Smith pointed to the weapon she was carrying. 'That's rather ambitious for a lady,' he said drily. 'Can you use it?'

Rose gave him a shy smile, showing two front teeth with a minuscule but rather fetching overlap. 'I'm close-quarter-battle trained, sir. I did the Grant-Taylor course at Jerusalem.' Her voice was a girlish contralto with a husky edge. There was, the C-in-C noted with approval, no trace in it of either nerves or cockiness.

Dorman-Smith raised a single eyebrow. 'And?' he enquired.

Maddy blushed. 'I qualified as marksman,' she said. She made it sound as if her accomplishment were a random event that astonished her as much as anyone else. There was little that was in-your-face about Maddy Rose, Auchinleck decided – she was wistful without being aloof, modest and yielding without being feeble: a willow tree, he thought.

Dorman-Smith seemed impervious to her charm. 'I see,' he commented, 'and what else can you do that an *ordinary* officer can't?'

Maddy glanced appealingly at Dudley Clarke, a small, rotund Gunner whose unassuming exterior concealed the gifted and unorthodox mind that had created the commandos. It was Clarke who had selected Maddy for the *Runefish* mission, and her training was his responsibility.

Clarke looked daggers at the DCGS. 'Now, General,' he said, in a manner that was borderline insubordinate, 'I think you can safely assume that First Officer Rose is up to the job. She is a qualified parachutist, she's trained in signals and medical skills, she's au fait with infantry small-arms, including foreign weapons, and she speaks German, French and Italian fluently.'

Dorman-Smith shot him an amused glance. 'Really?' he said. 'And all that just to escort some dispatches to London?'

'Excuse me, sir,' Clarke said acidly. 'I think we should do well to remember how vital this job is. First Officer Rose is a volunteer, and is exposing herself to considerable risk.' He turned his eyes to the Auk, and there was a twinkle in them now. 'After all, even the best-laid plans of mice and men go oft astray.'

The Auk waved a massive hand, making a mental note never to invite the DCGS to such a meeting again. 'Quite, quite,' he said. 'Point well taken, Dudley.'

He gestured to a chair. 'Sit down, Miss Rose.'

As Maddy posted herself beside him, her starched trousers crackled, and she worried for a moment that opting for trousers instead of a skirt had been too risqué. All sartorial thoughts were dismissed from her mind, though, when the Auk leaned towards her. At close quarters he was every bit as impressive as she'd been told. There was a dignity about him that was almost regal. Outside, in the offices and corridors of GHQ, there was suppressed panic, but in here, around the Auk, tranquillity held sway.

'You've been briefed on the current situation?' he asked.

'Yes, sir,' she said. 'Colonel Clarke briefed me earlier.'

'You realize that this is a first. I have never entrusted such a mission to a woman before. A great deal depends on you. Colonel Clarke tells me that you are fully dedicated to your assignment. Is that so?'

'Absolutely, sir.'

'Excellent. The attaché case, Tom.'

De Guingand produced a slim leather case and slid it along the table-top towards Rose. 'This contains the dispatches,' the Auk said. 'You are to take them to London and present them to Prime Minister Winston Churchill himself. They are for his eyes only. I have seen to it that you have the highest clearance, and I am sure I have no need to repeat that Operation *Runefish* has the top security classification. Not a word of it must be breathed to anyone outside this room.'

'I'm fully aware of that, sir.'

'Good. Now, you have been prepared for every eventuality. If for any reason the documents are endangered, you are to destroy them – the attaché case has a self-destruct mechanism that Captain Avery will show you how to initiate. If necessary you will repeat the message verbally to the Prime Minister. I understand that among your many accomplishments is a retentive memory, therefore I am going to say it only once and I expect you to memorize it perfectly.'

'Very good, sir.'

'You will tell Mr Churchill that there is no longer any chance of holding Tobruk, either in isolation or as part of a defensive line. The Eighth Army has been more fragmented by its recent defeat at Gazala than the Axis knows. Our armour has been destroyed or put out of action. Our infantry divisions are wheeling aimlessly through the desert with no safe harbour. More than half of our aircraft are missing. We have lost more than eighty thousand men, large numbers of guns and vehicles, and tons of fuel and supplies. Our logistical system is in ruins. Worst of all, Eighth Army's morale has reached rock bottom. The men have lost confidence in their officers, and officers are now openly questioning the decisions of the High Command. More than twenty-five thousand men have deserted, and the Army is a hair's breadth from mutiny. Our assessment is that Rommel is likely to push into Egypt immediately, following up his Gazala victory. If so, the Eighth Army will almost certainly be destroyed. You will say that the Commander-in-Chief therefore requests permission to evacuate Egypt forthwith. He wishes to withdraw to Palestine or even up the Nile to Port Sudan. That completes the text of the message, Miss Rose. The dispatches are coded in a cipher known only to the Prime Minister's office. They contain the casualty figures and damage assessment as accurately as we know at present, but the final figures may be much worse. Now, repeat the message, please.'

Maddy repeated it flawlessly – it wasn't much, after all, compared with some of the massive texts she'd had to memorize in her time.

When she'd finished, she found Auchinleck and the others staring at her sombrely, as if the gravity of the message had sunk in for the first time. 'Very good, First Officer,' the Auk said. 'Now, what are the arrangements, Avery?'

Julian Avery stepped forward, looming over Auchinleck's shoulder. As tall as de Guingand but much slimmer, he was twenty-six years old, with a pale moustache and wayward straw-coloured hair. The most junior officer present, he was also the only one wearing full service-dress, complete with Sam Browne belt, the red collar-tabs of the General Staff, and parachute wings on his sleeve. He smiled encouragingly at Rose, and she beamed back – while Clarke had been in charge of her training, it was Jules Avery who had been her instructor. A close bond had grown up between them during the course, but it had never transcended the teacher–student relationship. Maddy was aware that Avery was attracted to her, but had her private reasons for remaining distant.

Avery produced a clipboard and glanced at his watch. 'We're running a little late, ma'am,' he said, 'but no problem – we left a wide margin. A staff car will be here to pick you up within the hour.' Maddy's eyes widened slightly at the formality of 'ma'am', but she put it down to the presence of the C-in-C, and the fact that, technically, she outranked Avery – a Wren first officer was the equivalent of an army major. 'Your aircraft, an RAF Bombay of 276 Squadron, is waiting for you at Helwan,' Avery went on, 'and is due to take off at 1830 hours. You've already met your pilot, Flight Sergeant Orton, who has been fully briefed on the mission. If there is still time you can go through the emergency drills with him. You will find on board everything you might need in an emergency – parachute, medical kit, survival kit and a biscuit-tin transmitter with details of an emergency SOS frequency. Your personal code, as you know, is *Runefish*. Do you have any last questions?'

Maddy thought it over for a second. 'Yes. If I am asked why this message was delivered in person, what am I to say?'

Avery nodded with approval to indicate that he'd anticipated the question. 'You will say that we have reason to
believe all wireless messages from GHQ are being intercepted by the German "Y" service, and that our codes have
been compromised. In view of the grave nature of this
message, we could not risk it to the airwaves.'

'Thank you.'

'Anything else?' Auchinleck enquired.

'No, sir.'

'Well, then, I have one final duty to perform.' He took a
small cardboard container like a jewel-box from his shirt
pocket and placed it on the table. He opened it and picked
out what looked like an ancient and slightly yellowing molar.
He held it up for her inspection. 'Potassium cyanide,' he
said. 'Inside a hollow tooth made of bakelite, fitted to your
gum by gutta-percha. Bite hard on the tooth and the poison
kills instantly.' He replaced the authentic-looking tooth
gingerly into the box. 'If, God forbid, the worst came to the
worst, you might wish to do the right thing, rather than let
such secrets fall to the enemy.' Auchinleck fixed his clear
blue eyes on her. It was, Maddy thought, a superb performance. 'Should you wish to avail yourself of it, there is a
Medical Corps dentist downstairs who can do the job. However, I am not ordering you to take it, Miss Rose. That
choice is yours.'

The other officers, she noticed, were all standing stiffly
now, their eyes riveted on her. She supposed they were
wondering if she would be shocked. In fact, she'd accepted
death as her wages for this job the moment she'd volunteered for it. She picked up the box and put it away without
ceremony. No one made any comment. If they hadn't been
in the presence of the C-in-C, she felt, they would have
cheered.

The C-in-C rose. Maddy took the attaché case and followed suit. She was about to salute when the Auk put his hand out. She shook it, feeling her own hand small and frail in his larger one. 'The message you're carrying is of crucial importance to the future of the Eighth Army, of the North African campaign, and ultimately of the war,' Auchinleck said. 'I can't tell you, Miss Rose, how much I appreciate your commitment or how greatly I admire your courage. You set an example that many men would envy. Thank you, God speed, and the very best of luck.'

For the first time, Maddy felt a lump rise in her throat and had to fight back the tears. She forced herself to think of Peter Fairfax, tortured and murdered by the Gestapo in France, and was quickly filled with the rage she knew would soon disperse them. She saluted the C-in-C, then turned and marched out of the room, flanked by Avery and Clarke.

Auchinleck watched them until they were out of sight. 'A remarkable woman that, Tom,' he said to de Guingand. 'Think she can pull it off?'

'She seems a pussycat on the surface, but underneath she's got steel claws. She was engaged to an SOE agent, Peter Fairfax, who was dropped into France last year. His network had been infiltrated by the Nazis and he was betrayed. The Gestapo gave him the full works – electric shocks, burning cloths on the genitals – horrible business. When he wouldn't talk, they shot him and cut his hands off. Rose is carrying the cross.'

'In times like these, it helps.'

'She won't be overlooked, sir, that's for certain. She stands out like the fairy on a Christmas tree.'

5

Less than a mile away, the man who called himself Hussain Idriss, was leaning on the radiator of a beaten-up Standard, with a hand-scrawled sign reading, 'Taxi' in the windscreen. Hussain had been many things in his life, but today he was a taxi driver. He had borrowed the banger from a friend, and it had been parked at the junction of a side-street near GHQ for the past ninety minutes. He was dressed in cheap European clothes and shoes so old that the soles were almost worn through. His thick dark hair was ruffled and there was a blue shadow on his chin. He must have looked the part, Hussain told himself as he lit up his sixth Cleopatra, because he'd already had to turn down two prospective fares.

Hussain could pass as a Cairene anywhere, even though he did not possess a drop of Egyptian blood. In fact, he was a German and his real name was Johann Eisner. Born in Cairo of German parents, his mother had been widowed early and had remarried a wealthy Egyptian business-man, who had raised Johann as a Muslim. Eisner's education at English schools in Egypt had alternated with spells at boarding school in Germany. When war broke out and he was called up for military service, the Abwehr – German Military Intelligence – realized they had a unique asset – a German who could pass undetected as an Egyptian, and who knew Egypt like the back of his hand. Eisner had passed all tests with flying colours. Not even his closest instructors had divined the one serious flaw in his character that might clash with his excellence as a field agent.

The previous night Eisner had been playing a role that suited him better – a millionaire Egyptian playboy, at the exclusive Kit-Kat cabaret on the Nile Corniche. His main reason for going there was to catch the floorshow of his friend, the belly-dancer Hekmeth Fahmi, but the club was a magnet for GHQ staff as well as officers on leave from the front, and a place where he frequently picked up snippets of information. It was astonishing how rapidly British officers dropped their guard in the presence of half-dressed young women, especially after a couple or four of the Kit-Kat's special cocktails.

One of the cabaret girls, a sensuous French blonde called Natalie, was in his pay. She had no idea that he was German. Last night, after the tumultuous applause for Hekmeth Fahmi had died down, Natalie had sidled up to his table in the subdued light and asked him to buy her a bottle of champagne. When the Veuve-Cliquot was duly brought and opened with a flourish, Natalie folded her long, sinuous legs, fitted a cigarette into an ivory holder, and graciously accepted the light Eisner offered her from his gold Ronson. 'You know I have many lovers?' she said in French.

Eisner, whose French was as fluent as his Arabic, peered at her from behind the dark glasses that were de rigueur for rich Egyptians in Cairo nightspots. He nodded. '*Mais naturellement*,' he said, 'you are the most charming girl in Cairo, Natalie.'

'Earlier tonight,' she purred, 'I was entertaining one of them in my flat – a young and amorous captain from British headquarters. I think he had already had many drinks before he arrived. He was upset, so I gave him more whisky and coaxed the problem out of him. He said that he'd been given a most important assignment carrying papers to London, but at the last minute the job had been given to another officer – a woman officer of the Royal Navy.'

Eisner's ears pricked up with genuine interest. He had a spy's passion for anomalies, and this certainly sounded unique. He poured Natalie a second glass of bubbly. 'Did he mention the nature of these papers?' he asked.

She brushed back an unruly lock of blond hair with a movement that was enticingly seductive. She picked up the glass, sipped her champagne and smiled. 'He did not say,' she said, 'but he told me that they were for the British Prime Minister himself. That is why he was so angry – he felt that his work might have been noticed at last. It would also be his first chance to get back to England since the start of the war. I asked if this was the only thing that angered him, and he admitted that the woman was young and pretty and that he suspected her of being the lover of his superior. I myself suspected that he liked this woman – perhaps she had been *his* lover, and the real reason he was angry was because she had betrayed him. I did not tell him this of course.'

'Of course.'

'Later he fell asleep in my bed, and I went through his brief-case. Most of the papers were of no interest, but among them was a schedule entitled *Operation Runefish*. I copied it down.'

Natalie paused, opened a small sequinned handbag, and extracted a neatly wadded sheet of paper. She handed it to him. Eisner unfolded it and squinted at it in the dim light. It was, as she'd told him, a schedule:

1300 hours – lunch
1330 hours – Runefish to draw personal weapon:
.45 Colt auto with spare clips

1400 hours – private briefing with Runefish
1430 hours – Runefish to meet C-in-C and collect
dispatches. Cyanide pill to be issued
1530 hours – Runefish to leave GHQ in staff car
1630 hours – Runefish to arrive Helwan airstrip.
Aircraft, Bombay of 276 Squadron
RAF, to be fuelled and ready.
Runefish to go through emergency
procedures with pilot, Flt Sgt
Orton, Peter, RAF. Runefish to
find emergency equipment on
board: 1) Parachute 2) Medical Pack
3) Survival Pack 4) Emergency
transmitter, packed in haversack,
with SOS frequencies
1830 hours – aircraft takes off

Eisner read it carefully. One item of information caught his attention in particular: *'Cyanide pill to be issued'*. That alone suggested this was no ordinary assignment. And Natalie had mentioned 'Mr Churchill'. *Cyanide* and *Mr Churchill*: together they indicated that something of significance might be happening here. He realized that an important item was missing from the schedule. 'Where is the date, my dear?' he enquired.

Natalie grimaced. 'I am an imbecile. I have forgotten to write it down. The date was tomorrow, 12 June 1942.'

'You're sure?'

'Yes, I am sure.'

'Excellent. I don't suppose your lover told you the real name of the woman involved?' he asked.

She blew out a stream of cigarette smoke and shook her head provocatively. 'No, but I found out *his* real name. He calls himself Richard Ross, but he is really Captain Julian Avery.'

Eisner had made a mental note of the name, and had realized suddenly that this talk of Natalie's lovers had unleashed an urge he hadn't experienced in months. He had glanced back at her appraisingly, surveying her sleek legs, supple figure and gently pouting lips, and pictured her tied to his bed, naked and whimpering – an image so chillingly vivid that it had him fingering the hilt of the razor-sharp stiletto he carried concealed at his waist. He'd been sorely tempted to invite her back to his houseboat that night, but had fought off the compulsion. To bring his 'extracurricular activities' home could have been fatal in more ways than one, and Natalie was far too valuable an asset to lose.

6

Eisner had never heard of Captain Julian Avery, but after leaving the club he had telephoned his two contacts at GHQ – Egyptian clerical workers with Axis sympathies who had slipped through the British screening net. The first didn't know the name Avery, but the second, a woman, did. She told him that Avery's department was G(R) – the Cairo wing of the Special Operations Executive. She was also able to confirm that a First Officer of the Women's Royal Naval Service had been seen at GHQ, but was unable to give her name or to describe her. It wasn't much, but it was enough to convince Eisner that this case was worth the investment of a little time and effort.

Now, leaning on his 'taxi', he was beginning to feel nervous. He had been hanging around in Garden City too long, and a Military Police jeep had already passed once. Sooner or later it would come back again, and the MPs in it would wonder why he was still there. He'd brought a brand-new Leica camera with him in case there was an opportunity for a shot of the girl. It was in a bag on the back seat of the car, and he didn't relish the idea of having to explain to the MPs why a down-at-heel taxi driver should be lurking near GHQ with a camera worth more than he was.

He squashed out yet another Cleopatra butt with one decrepit shoe, and looked at his watch. It was half past four, which meant that, if Natalie had been right about the date, *Runefish* was an hour behind schedule. But had she been right? Perhaps the schedule had been dated yesterday,

11 June, and the bird had already flown. For all he knew it might have been dated last week.

He was about to give up, when a Humber staff car rumbled past. Eisner looked up in time to get an impression of a figure in the back seat – blue shoulder-rings, rich blond hair under a blue and white Wren's hat. He jumped into his vehicle, started up, and followed the staff car into the stream of traffic. Luckily it wasn't as busy as usual – the news of Rommel's victory at Gazala had cleared the streets. Shops had been hurriedly closed down, and, there had been a 50 per cent drop in the value of foreign currency on the black market. This was a great embarrassment to Eisner, who had smuggled in cash in sterling pounds. The only way he could now obtain its true value was by applying to the British Army Pay Corps office – an establishment he had good reason to avoid. He felt ambivalent about the prospect of Rommel's arrival in Cairo. On the one hand, he hoped for a German victory, on the other, it would mean an abrupt end to his luxurious amoral life as Rommel's spy.

The Humber turned left on to the Corniche opposite Roda island, following the dark waters of the Nile upstream. It was the right direction for the airstrip at Helwan. GHQ cars normally beetled through the city at breakneck speed, but even if the occupant of this car was late, she seemed in no hurry – the vehicle dawdled along at a steady thirty miles an hour. He tagged on behind, staying a hundred and fifty yards to the rear, allowing other vehicles to overtake him but never losing sight of his quarry. Roda fell away and as the minutes ticked by Eisner became increasingly confident that he hadn't been spotted. The driver made no attempt to go faster, never turned off the main road and never halted or slowed down to let him pass. Soon, the road veered away from the Nile into the narrow, tortuous streets of Maadi.

Teetering tenements lined the road, with lines of washing fluttering from the balconies like strings of flags.

The traffic slowed as the road became congested with donkey-carts, donkey-trains and flocks of goats and sheep marshalled by broad-backed fellahin in turbans and tobacco-coloured shifts. Women in black headscarves with gold pins in their noses peered down from the balconies, and urchins in tattered striped gallabiyas ran along the gutter. Eisner was so intent on not losing the Humber that he only just noticed the flash of brake lights in time. He jammed his foot hard on his brake pedal, evoking a cacophony of honks from behind him. He leaned on his horn in response, craning his neck to see what was happening. Two vehicles ahead of him, the staff car had been brought to a standstill by a vast horde of goats and sheep.

It occurred to Eisner that this might be a good opportunity for a photograph. He applied the hand brake and fished in his bag for his Leica. Balancing it on his knees, he turned sharply out of the line of traffic and pulled forward in first gear until he was abreast of the staff car's back windows. He glanced ahead to make sure nothing was approaching from the opposite direction: fortunately the oncoming traffic had also been halted by the sheep. To his right, he could see the woman through the back window of the Humber – khaki drill shirt, blond hair, perky Wren's hat. He took a second to check that the Leica was ready, aware that he was taking a chance – if he were spotted photographing a GHQ staff car, it could land him in very hot water indeed.

He was about to lift the camera for a quick shot, when the woman turned her face towards him. He almost dropped the Leica in shock. It lasted only a split second, but he was certain that he had seen her face before, and in a context that couldn't have been more different. It was the face, not of a Wren officer, but of an exotic dancer he'd once seen in a Cairo nightclub.

Eisner looked away instantly, his pulse racing. Their eyes hadn't locked, and he was almost sure she hadn't noticed anything unusual. He waited a fraction of a second before chancing another peek. She was gazing straight ahead now, and the sheep-flock was thinning. He raised the Leica, and without bothering to frame it properly, clicked off a shot. He placed the camera back on the seat next to him. The column of traffic was stirring, and he let the Humber pull away. With a great deal of bellowing, gesticulating and honking of his horn, he managed to squeeze his car back into the traffic.

In a few moments he was out of Maadi and back on the Nile. His pulse was returning to normal. The staff vehicle was toddling along at the same unvarying pace, displaying no sign that he had been made. As he drove he strained to dredge up a name and a background for the face he'd seen. His first impression had been of a cabaret girl – a hostess or a dancer – but he tried out several times and places and none of them seemed to fit. It was as if his memory was deliberately blocking him, and he felt exasperated. He normally had an excellent recall of faces, especially those of pretty girls, but the more he pondered it, the less sure he was. He knew the mind sometimes played tricks, and he had glimpsed the Wren for only a fraction of a second, from some distance away. Perhaps she had one of those faces that always seem familiar, or perhaps she only *looked* like someone he'd seen before. What he could not get over, though, was that spontaneous and instinctive sense of recognition he'd felt.

He snapped out of this mental tug of war to see that the Humber was slowing again, this time for the Military Police checkpoint outside Helwan airstrip. He was aware that it was the first of several. Security here was tight, and though

his papers were in order there was still the camera to consider. He came to a halt and turned his vehicle round slowly
enough to make sure that the staff car had passed through
the barrier.

As he headed back towards the city, he decided that,
whoever the woman was, her mission was worth reporting
to his Abwehr controller. Eisner belonged to the Abwehr's
Abteilung No. 1, the department handling special military
intelligence, which, in North Africa, was commanded by
Major Heinrich Rohde. Rohde was a martinet – no, Eisner
corrected himself mentally, he was a thug. He felt apprehensive about handing him incomplete data, yet he had no
choice. For now the girl's identity would have to remain
uncertain: he could not commit himself without a name or
something more definite than a hunch. He had the photograph, though, and one never knew what a little discreet
investigation might turn up.

Eisner drove mechanically, preoccupied with his rumi-
nations, and it was a good five minutes before he became
fully aware that he'd acquired a shadow. A small saloon – a
black Vauxhall – was trailing him one car back, maintaining
her distance at a rock-steady pace. Eisner knew he'd registered her presence subconsciously in the rearview mirror
just after he'd turned back at Helwan: he could have kicked
himself for his amateurish behaviour in changing direction
in sight of a military post. It would have looked suspicious
anywhere, and these were dangerous times. British Field
Security would be keeping their eyes skinned for actions
like this.

Turning round at a checkpoint, and carrying an expen-
sive camera for no good reason: these were enough to get
him bagged. Once he was in custody the Field Security
swine would develop the film, find the shot of the female

staff-officer in the GHQ car, and his goose would be well and truly barbecued.

Eisner was too seasoned a hand to panic, though. First, he had to be certain that the Vauxhall really was a tail: he began to work methodically through his list of surveillance-spotting measures. He speeded up: the Vauxhall accelerated. He slowed down to a crawl: the Vauxhall slowed. He took the next right abruptly, without indicating: the small car stayed with him. He pulled up by the side of the road: the Vauxhall stopped a discreet distance behind. Peering hard in the mirror, he could just make out the driver. He appeared to be a lean-faced, tight-lipped Egyptian in a dark jacket, but that meant nothing: at least half the strength of British Field Security were Arabs. Eisner put the car in first gear and moved off hastily into the traffic. The Vauxhall followed.

They were in the back-streets of Maadi, full of jostling crowds in ragged pyjama-cloth, goats, sheep, donkeys, hand-carts, squint-wheeled push-bikes, smoky, backfiring motor-cycles, down-at-heel vans – a ponderous procession of humanity streaming through alternating blocks of shade and molten gold from the lowering sun. It was an area Eisner knew well – but then he knew most of Cairo well. As a boy he'd spent much of his time wandering around the city on foot or riding trams and buses: with its successive waves of the oriental and the western, its continuous surge of life, the city had never ceased to fascinate him. Now, the detailed mental map he'd acquired as a youth paid off. For ten minutes he played hide and seek with his pursuer, hanging sharp lefts and rights at the last moment. The man in the Vauxhall stuck doggedly on his tail. Finally, having created an interval between them he judged long enough, Eisner turned sharply down an alley he knew to be a derelict cul-de-sac.

His tyres crunched on rubble, broken plaster, glass shards, torn newspaper. The place was lined with derelict tenements that had been due for demolition for decades. Vacant windows stared down at him like blank eyes. He drove as far as he could go, stopped the car, checked that the place was deserted. A glance in the mirror told him that the Vauxhall hadn't yet entered the alley. He cut the engine, opened the glove compartment, pulled out an ordinary-looking length of wire. He jumped out of the car, and leaving the door unlocked and the Leica on the passenger seat, sprinted for the shadow of the nearest broken-down doorway. He had just made it when he heard the purr of the Vauxhall's engine behind him.

The small black car pulled up about six yards from his Standard. The door opened and the driver emerged – a slope-shouldered, spindly-limbed man with a sad face and a drooping moustache, whose oversized dark suit flapped loosely on his lean limbs. He was carrying a .38-calibre Enfield six-shooter, cocked and ready. As Eisner watched, Spindle-shanks moved cautiously over to the Standard, peered through the side window. Seeing no one inside, he tried the door on the driver's side, opened it, and bending over the driver's seat, groped with his left hand for the Leica.

It was all the opportunity Eisner needed. He was on the man in three silent bounds, looping his wire garotte round the Egyptian's throat and pulling tight. The man tried to scream but only a sickening gurgle emerged. He dropped his pistol, attempted to get his fingers under the wire that was already digging a quarter of an inch into his flesh, and failed. Eisner jerked him backwards, wrenching him to the ground, driving his face into the dirt. Getting his knees in the pit of the man's back for purchase, he heaved on the wire with all his weight. The Egyptian tried to push himself up, his legs thrashing frantically, but Eisner held on as if riding a bucking horse. He strained on the wire until an artery in the man's neck popped, shooting spritzes of blood four feet along the road surface. The Egyptian's eyes became red gashes, his legs ceased thrashing: the gargling sound in his throat stopped. He went limp.

Eisner didn't relax his grip until he was certain the man wasn't faking. Then, leaving the garotte in place, he got up, panting, siezed the dead man by the armpits, and dragged him over to the Vauxhall. He opened the rear door, flung the body on to the back seat, and trotted back to his own vehicle. He picked up the dead man's pistol, stuffed it into a pocket, then opened his boot and took out a tin of petrol.

He scurried back to the Vauxhall, flung the Enfield revolver on top of the corpse, then sprinkled the interior of the car with petrol. He doused the tyres and bonnet, then laid a ten-yard trail across the uneven ground. Moving fast so that the petrol wouldn't have time to evaporate in the heat, Eisner returned the empty tin to his boot, got back behind the steering wheel, gunned the engine. He drove past the Vauxhall to the end of the petrol-trail, opened his door, struck a match, dropped it on the dark stain. He waited a second to see that it had ignited, then slammed the door and sped off. Just as his car turned out of the cul-de-sac, Eisner heard the whoosh of the Vauxhall bursting into flame, followed almost at once by the ear-splitting karump of her gas tank going up.

Forty minutes later, as Eisner was tapping out a coded message to Heinrich Rohde from the hidden cubicle in his houseboat off Zamalek, an RAF Bombay, with First Officer Maddy Rose on board, took off from Helwan.

7

By day, Jaghbub bore little resemblance to the ideal of a desert oasis – it was a sandy depression with a few palms, straggling clumps of acacia and tamarisk, and the ruins of a monastery that had once been the stronghold of the Senussi Islamic Brotherhood. It was flyblown and mosquito-infested, its water so brackish it might have been the in-spiration for Epsom salts. By night, though, when Caine's 3-tonner limped in on three good tyres at the tail end of a 50th Division convoy, none of this was apparent. It was as teeming as Piccadilly Circus on a Saturday night, and twice as rowdy – men caterwauling, engines churning, gears grating, wheels spinning, as a score of Allied units milled around trying to lick themselves into some kind of shape.

Thankfully, Caine had no need to locate the Aid Post, because he had long since transferred his wounded to the 50th Div. convoy's field ambulances. Of the half-dozen men they had snatched from the ridge, only five had made it. The sixth, medical orderly Quiff Smithers, had been last on the lorry, and had been hit twice on the break-out in the wadi. The man who had helped save the lives of his com-rades was now buried in a nameless grave on the gravel plains.

Caine's only task was to locate Middle East Commando lines, and surrender to the blessed luxury of sleep. Until they had run into the convoy, he'd stayed awake almost continuously with the help of the Benzedrine, navigating by dead-reckoning while Wallace and Copeland took it in turns at the wheel. He reckoned he'd had four hours sleep in the last forty-eight. Now, he had Cope stop the lorry while he asked at a Military Police post for the whereabouts of the Commando. 'You'll find them over by the monastery,' the Redcap on duty said. 'What's left of 'em. Poor sods took a hammering, and no mistake.'

Dog weary, they had almost given up looking when they came across the leaguer – a dismal assembly of lorries, jeeps, AFVs and tents, pitched in the lee of the ruined wall. They reported their names to the duty NCO, then unrolled their 'flea-bags' and slept off their Benzedrine hangovers for fifteen hours.

Heat and flies woke them at mid-day. Caine found himself wolfishly hungry and began to sort through their compo rations. He came up with tea, sugar, Carnation milk, oatmeal, margarine, tinned jam, tinned bacon and hard-tack biscuits, the size of saucers. While they were eating, Todd Sweeney appeared with a couple of the boys from No. 1 Troop, bringing back their personal kit and fannies. Caine was delighted to see them, but despite the yells of recognition and back-slapping the cheerfulness was pumped-up, over-shadowed by the loss of so many comrades. Sweeney said he'd withdrawn the remnants of the troop to Battle Group RV without a hitch, until, waiting to get on the transport, Sears-Beach had appeared and demanded to see Caine. 'I told him you were missing in action,' Sweeney reported, 'but he wasn't convinced.'

'Just how hard did you *try* and convince him?' Wallace demanded.

Sweeney shrugged. 'I did my best, but he didn't believe it. He said he was going to report you to the commanding officer when he got back.'

'That bonehead,' Wallace swore. 'They should never of

allowed a berk like him in the commandos. Rear-echelon pen-pusher if ever I saw one. Ex-Pay Corps or sommat – God's gift to us mortals, you know.'

Sweeney's face stayed deadpan. 'He's ex-Military Police,' he said. 'Like me.'

'Oh I *see*,' Wallace drawled, beaming with mock surprise. 'Now, how *could* I have forgotten that? Oh, *I* remember now. Weren't you one of them ex-Redcap boys that Sears-Beach insisted on recruiting for the Commando, even though the CO said he didn't want the ranks full of dirty, snooping ex-coppers?'

'You'd better watch it, Private Wallace,' Sweeney growled, his cheeks scarlet.

'Or what? You going to put me on Dixie? This is the Middle East Commando, mate, not the bleedin' wooden-tops. Maybe you ain't heard, but we don't have no bowin' and scrapin' here. And it's *Gunner* Wallace to you, anyway.'

Sweeney stuck out his chin, squared his oil-barrel chest, glowered at Wallace through pinball eyes. He weighed up the big man's colossal proportions, his dark-stubbled jowls, his jungle of matted hair. He let his eyes drop, pivoted on his heels and walked away, his thick arms swinging, matching his rolling, simian gait.

Harry Copeland watched him until he was out of sight, then turned back to Wallace. 'What was all *that* about?' he enquired.

'The blighter never even *tried* to cover up for us,' Wallace scoffed. 'Too busy brown-nosing Sears-Beach.'

'What's that chap got against the skipper, anyway?'

Wallace grinned at Caine, who caught his eye and snorted. The giant glanced back at Cope. 'It was before you come to the Commando. See, when Sears-Beach first arrived he got hisself a servant – big chap called Dennis Twigley.

Ex-Gunner. Nice bloke. Sears-Beach used to call him *Sylvia*, and when they was up the Blue, in winter, he used to have Twigley bring him a hot-water bottle every night. Wouldn't sleep without it. *'Where's my bottle, Sylvia?'* he used to say in this hoochie-coochie voice. If I'd have been Twiggers, I know where I'd have stuck the bloody bottle. Anyway, you soon put the kibosh on that, didn't you, skipper?'

Caine couldn't help chuckling at the memory. During a regimental 'chunter session', when anyone was allowed to bring up any subject, he'd asked about the propriety of officers in a commando unit having servants in the field. A master–servant relationship didn't sit right with the commando ideal of comradeship between officers and men. In reply, Sears-Beach had stood up and awarded Caine a disdainful glare. 'You of all people should know, *Sergeant* Caine,' he said pointedly, 'that as an officer, one has to be liberated from such trivial duties as cleaning one's own kit, so that one's mind remains free for making the decisions that save lives.'

Caine resented the barbed reference to his terminated commission, and amid cheers of approval from the enlisted men, asked, 'Does cleaning kit include preparing hot-water bottles, sir? And perhaps you'd kindly explain to the lads here just how many lives *your* decisions have saved?' Sears-Beach had never forgiven him for that. He had been doubly incensed when, the following day, the commanding officer had posted a notice on regimental orders, declaring that the practice of officers having servants in the field was henceforth forbidden.

After lunch, Medical Orderly Maurice Pickney arrived with his magic chest. A mildly spoken ex-merchant seaman from Birmingham, Pickney was noted for his kindness and compassion: he had a reputation for being as ready to help

Axis wounded as his own. He wasn't much older than thirty, but he looked like someone's granny, his face as lined and wrinkled as an old prune.

Pickney examined Wallace's shrapnel wounds and told him that they were already healing nicely. He advised him not to keep them bandaged up, and gave him sulphenamide ointment. Feeling as if he'd just been paroled from a long jail sentence, Wallace went off happily to hunt down a Royal Army Ordnance Corps field workshop. He was back thirty minutes later, rolling a spare balloon tyre with his foot and carrying a replacement windscreen unit. He, Caine and Copeland stripped down to their shorts and set about restoring the lorry they'd picked up at the Box. After the way she'd got them clear of the Boche that night and brought them home safely, they'd acquired a certain affection for her: Caine had christened her *Marlene*, after Marlene Dietrich. He fretted that she would now be returned to her owners – the King's Royal Rifle Corps – until Wallace scrounged paint and a stencil, painted out her KRRC insignia and stencilled in the ME Commando's 'fanny' badge.

They had completed the truck repairs and had just sat down to clean their weapons when they were confronted by the ramrod-straight figure of HQ Squadron Staff Sergeant, 'Frosty' Greaves – a sallow-skinned Scotsman, wearing battledress tunic with khaki drill trousers, desert boots, light web-order.

'Morning, Frosty,' Caine said.

'Afternoon, *Sergeant* Caine,' Greaves replied.

Caine noted the emphasis on *sergeant*. He stood up, flexed cable-like pectorals, flipped strapping shoulders, tensed hardball-sized biceps. He knew what was coming. The Commando, being an irregular unit, had no provost-staff like a line-infantry mob: whenever internal discipline was required they sent along poor old Frosty Greaves, who lacked the truculence of the natural policeman. Caine often thought that Greaves and Sweeney should have swapped places.

'Sears-Beach survived, then,' Caine said. 'Pity.'

Greaves suppressed the flicker of a smile. 'No disrespect to officers, Sarn't, if you please. You are to present yourself at the battalion command post forthwith. That means now.'

Caine regarded the staff-sergeant with his steady, sand-blasted eyes. For a moment it looked to Wallace as if he might refuse. Then he fished in his haversack for the black Tankie beret he favoured, put it on, slung his supercharged Tommy-gun over his shoulder. 'No rest for the wicked, is there, Staff?' he said.

Greaves' face did not relax: the skin was immaculately shaved and shone as if it he'd scrubbed it with sandpaper. 'No facetiousness please, Sarn't. You're in deep enough shit as it is.'

An HQ tent of sorts had been erected against a White command vehicle inside the monastery yard, but the commanding officer had set up shop in a derelict room opening off it through the blanket that served as a door. Camp tables, chairs and oil lamps had been arranged, and a tarpaulin slung over the gap where the roof should have been. An enormous map of the theatre of operations had been pinned on one wall, illuminated by shafts of light from cracks in the wall. It was this map that the CO, Lieutenant-Colonel Hilary St Aubin, was scrutinizing as Caine and Greaves marched in. Behind a table on Caine's left stood Sears-Beach, very erect, displaying his prominent front teeth, holding a brass-tipped swagger-stick stiffly under his arm as if on inspection parade. To Caine's right stood a sandy-haired subaltern wearing the Royal Horse Artillery badge on his field-cap. Caine had never seen him before.

The CO turned towards them, but neither Caine nor Greaves saluted. It was one of the formalities that the commandos had long ago abolished, with a view to encouraging the comradeship between officers and soldiers which a lot of people had gabbed about, but which had never quite been achieved. St Aubin was unshaven, bareheaded, and clad in a threadbare woolly-pully, with corduroy slacks and desert boots. He wore a lime-green silk scarf around his neck, a webbing-yoke with small ammo-pouches, and a pistol in a low-slung holster secured to his leg.

Caine knew that the colonel was old-school – a Great War veteran with a hearty manner that was partly contradicted by his expressionless roastbeef face. He was said to be immensely proud of the Commando, but on the few occasions Caine had spoken to him previously, he'd had the impression of something inscrutable beneath the cheerfulness. Caine's nose for people was usually good, but in this case he couldn't have said whether St Aubin was a man of genuine warmth, or the type who could cheerfully commit his men to a kamikaze mission.

The CO took a lit pipe out of his mouth and pinched the bowl between finger and thumb. 'Sarn't Caine,' he said. 'You are Acting Troop Commander of No. 1 Troop, is that right?'

'Yes, sir.'

'Captain Sears-Beach has put you on a charge for disobeying a direct order in battle. That is a very serious breach of discipline – one that could land you in front of a court-martial. Are you aware of that?'

Caine squared his brawny shoulders, shot Sears-Beach a piercing glance. The officer caught the look and flared. 'Don't dare deny it, Caine. We have an eyewitness. Lieutenant Edwards here was with the Horse Gunners on the Box and he saw everything – didn't you, Edwards?' He gestured towards the other officer, a wiry-looking man with a pink face and a blond bum-fluff moustache. Caine judged him to be about twenty – a good three years younger than himself. Edwards shifted nervously and his face grew pinker. 'Yes I did, sir,' he stammered, 'but I have to say that I reported the matter only because I thought the sergeant here deserved a medal. It was the bravest thing I've ever seen in my life.'

Caine realized with a gush of gratitude that it was Edwards' crew whose last salvos had saved them. 'That was no mean gunnery, sir,' he said. 'How on earth did you do that in the dark without scragging us?'

Edwards' blush grew deeper. 'It was nothing really . . . well, we spotted your blue flare from the 3-tonner and guessed what you were up to. After dark we saw muzzle-flashes from the ridge and identified them as enemy weapons. We already had a range on that ridge in case it was overrun earlier, so we lowered the elevation a fraction and put our two last shells down at its base. It was a gamble, of course, but I'm glad it paid off. We spotted the lorry coming back a few minutes afterwards, so we guessed you'd survived.'

'We did, sir, and now I know who we have to thank for it. You're the one who should have a medal . . .'

'*Excuse me*,' Sears-Beach cut in furiously. 'This is *not* a mutual-congratulations session. Caine is here to answer a charge.' He turned to the CO for support, but St Aubin replied with an irritated look. 'Well, then,' he said, 'perhaps you two gentlemen would be good enough to retire and let me get on with it.'

'But sir . . .' Sears-Beach protested.

'Dismissed, Captain. Escort them out, Staff Greaves, and make sure I'm not disturbed.'

'Very good, sir.'

Caine fought back a wry smile. He had been marched in like a prisoner, but now it looked for all the world as if Sears-Beach was being marched out in his place.

8

After they had gone, St Aubin stuck his pipe in his mouth, knitted his bushy eyebrows and fixed Caine with a firm stare. 'Well?' he said.

Caine explained that Lt Green had promised the wounded lads that they would not be abandoned, and his conclusion that, left with identifiable commando weapons, they would be executed. 'I know standard operating procedure is to ditch the wounded, sir, but this was a special case.'

St Aubin looked doubtful. 'It's my fault that they were carrying commando paraphernalia,' he said. 'I should have given the order to leave it behind. I agree with Lt Edwards that you deserve a medal, Caine, but there's still no way round the fact that you disobeyed a direct order.'

The colonel pulled at his pipe while Caine waited in suspense. 'I know you, Caine,' he said. 'I've seen your conduct sheet. You have an excellent field record. It is a fact that commandos are expected to use personal initiative – the way we were deployed at Gazala, for instance, was a damn' waste. We're meant to be a raiding unit, not a bunch of woodentops. I've lost a lot of good men, and I don't want to lose another one now. So I am prepared to make you an offer, Caine. It happens I'm looking for someone to lead a search-and-rescue mission behind Axis lines. Do that for me, and you have my assurance that the court-martial business will be dropped.'

Caine searched St Aubin's face with his wind-scoured eyes. He was about to speak when the CO interrupted him, holding up the stem of his pipe. 'I know you're going to ask what the mission is, but I can't tell you. It's classified. I must have your commitment before I reveal anything about it. I can only say that it is hazardous and that your chances of survival are about even.'

Caine gasped: the odds weren't encouraging. 'You mean I have to take it "blind", sir?'

St Aubin nodded. 'Take it or leave it, but bear in mind that if you refuse, Captain Sears-Beach will press for a court-martial.'

It was blackmail pure and simple: for all the colonel's blarney, the choice boiled down to either taking the mission or ending up on jankers. For him there wasn't a choice because, whatever the job was, it couldn't be worse than the five years' hard labour he would probably end up with if Sears-Beach had anything to do with it.

There was a silence that went on for ever, broken only by the drone of flies, and voices from outside that seemed to drift to his ears from the dark side of the moon. St Aubin glared at him. 'Well?' he demanded.

Caine swallowed hard. 'All right, sir,' he said in a rush. 'I'll take it.'

The marble face didn't relax, but Caine saw, or imagined he saw, a glimmer of triumph in the colonel's eyes. 'Sit down,' St Aubin said. It was the first time since getting busted Caine had been asked to sit in the presence of an officer. He pulled up a camp chair and sat down with his overweight Tommy-gun between his knees. The CO had moved over to the map again, and faced Caine with his pipe poised as if about to conduct an orchestra. 'What I'm going to say is for you only,' he said. 'You will need to tell your men something, of course, but what you tell them should be governed by the "need to know" principle.

'Understood, sir.'

St Aubin grunted and pointed the stem of his pipe at the Cyrenaica area of northern Libya. 'Last night an RAF aircraft crossing the Gulf of Bomba was hit by Italian ack-ack fire and went down in the desert here, south of the Jebel Akhdar – the Green Mountains. The sole passenger, a Royal Navy officer, baled out by parachute before the crate went down. The officer, codenamed *Runefish,* was a courier bound for Blighty, carrying top-secret documents for the Prime Minister. If the documents or the officer fall into the hands of the Boche, there will be hell to pay. These secrets are so crucial, they could change the whole course of the war. This is where you come in, Caine. I want you to take a section of twenty-odd men from what's left of the Commando, and whatever you need from the stores and the MT Pool, and snatch *Runefish* from under the Hun's nose.'

Caine let out a low whistle. 'It's going to be like finding a grain of sand in the Great Sand Sea, sir. In any case, there are tens of thousands of Axis troops between here and Cyrenaica – we'll never get through.'

St Aubin blew smoke and coughed. He laid the pipe in a pot ashtray on the table with a small, pudgy hand. 'Locating the officer shouldn't be difficult for a man of your calibre. We have a good idea where *Runefish* went down, because the Bombay was being trailed by a Royal Navy Albacore spotter, whose pilot recorded the coordinates. *Runefish* must have landed within a few square miles of that point, and can't be far away even now. *Runefish* was issued with a biscuit-tin wireless set and given an emergency frequency on which to transmit an SOS signal. There aren't many Royal Navy officers swanning about behind enemy lines at this juncture, and this one is rather special. As to your second point, you're right about the concentration of enemy troops, but in fact there couldn't be a better time for a small patrol to get through. Axis and Allied forces are mixed up in confusion all over the desert, each using the other's captured transport. In my opinion, it's most unlikely that you will be noticed.'

'I see, sir.'

'However, I'd be a fool to pretend that this assignment is going to be a pushover. It's not. We have word from our agents that a company of the Brandenburg Special Duties Regiment has been deployed in the area. It's possible that they've been sent after *Runefish*.'

'You mean the Jerries know about *Runefish*?' Caine cut in.

'We have to assume it's likely. The German "Y" Service regularly intercepts our signals traffic, and there are almost certainly enemy informers in GHQ. It's even possible the aircraft was deliberately targeted.'

'That's going to make it a lot more interesting.'

'Precisely. So you see, getting in there is one thing. Snatching *Runefish* and getting out again, evading the Brandenburgers, the entire Panzer Army and the Luftwaffe is quite another. That's why I give you no more than a fifty-fifty chance of survival.'

'No point me asking what these documents are, is it, sir? I mean, it's "need to know", isn't it?'

St Aubin's forehead crinkled. 'It wouldn't be violating the "need to know" rule to tell you a little about what you would be risking your life for. It might add a little incentive, and in that sense you might be construed as "needing to know". He took a deep breath. 'These documents concern some trials for a weapon the navy has been working on for some time – *Assegai*. *Assegai* is a new type of glider bomb that can be launched from a submarine. It's guided to its target by a combination of radio and radar, and has a range of two hundred miles. The *Assegai* bombs have already been tested, and only the trial results are needed for the green light. These results are outlined in the documents being carried by *Runefish*. You can imagine the devastating effect of this weapon if used on Rommel's tanks, but I'm saying too much. Of course, what I've told you is merely a thumbnail sketch, and even if you spilled the beans under interrogation, it would mean nothing without the technical specifications. I don't need to tell you what is likely to happen if the Jerries get those specifications. Not only will they be forewarned, they will effectively be able to abort the attack. They might even be able to reconstruct the glider bombs and use them against us. So there is your incentive, Caine. If you fail in your mission it could tip the whole balance of the war.'

For a moment, Caine stared at his commanding officer in disbelief. He was flattered that the CO had chosen him, but the sceptic in him groped for an ulterior motive. 'Why entrust such a crucial mission to me?' he asked. 'Why not send a senior officer? I'm just a humble sergeant, after all.'

Caine thought he saw a flash of irritation in the colonel's eyes but, if so, it was quickly extinguished. The clipped voice went on, even-keeled and infinitely patient. 'Believe me, Caine, other plans have been considered and rejected. A Long Range Desert Group patrol might do the job, but they're all deployed on crucial tasks. The Cherry Pickers or the King's Dragoon Guards might do it with an AFV squadron, but they'd be too conspicuous and, anyway, they're desperately needed to cover Eighth Army's retreat. The only special-service troops available are what's left of my poor old Middle East Commando. As for officers, I've precious few left, and none of them could match your skills and experience. You're mustard as a vehicle mechanic, a class-one land navigator and a combat veteran with several years clocked up in the desert. Besides, you were an officer once, and you displayed remarkable leadership skills. If it weren't for your peculiar penchant for taking orders as a basis for discussion, you'd be a major by now. You could say that I'm getting an officer's skills for the price of an NCO. Cut price, if you see what I mean.' St Aubin chuckled at his own joke, but his eyes stayed cold. 'When all's said and done about obeying orders, Caine, you've proved yourself more resilient than most, not to say more courageous, and that's what the commando principle is all about – the ability to adapt to changing conditions.' Suddenly and unexpectedly, St Aubin winked. 'We're both members of the desert club, Caine. Unlike *some*,' he nodded towards the door through which Sears-Beach had disappeared . . . 'we have both got our knees brown, and we both know that the best way to survive up the Blue isn't necessarily by adhering rigidly to the rules.'

It was St Aubin's final pitch, and Caine had never heard anything quite like it. In so many words, if he'd read them right, the CO had vindicated his action in retrieving the wounded men and tacitly condemned Sears-Beach as a hidebound fool. That particular sentiment chimed with Caine's own feelings, but the rest of the speech was so unexpected it set his internal alarm bells ringing. It had to be flannel. He had a nagging hunch that St Aubin had left out something vital, and was prepping him for a mission quite different from the one he'd been briefed about. Caine was tempted to tell him where to stick the assignment, but he was aware that he had already given his word. There was no going back on it now.

The colonel was bending over the table, scribbling in a field message pad with a stub of pencil. He tore the page off and handed it to Caine. His manner had become businesslike. 'This is a note to the Regimental Quartermaster Sergeant Major, authorizing him to give you anything you ask for in terms of kit, rations, weapons, fuel and transport. The RQMS will stick to everything like glue, of course, but don't take any nonsense. You'll need three or four soft-skin vehicles and some armour. You can pick your own men – you'll want some specialists, such as a medical orderly and an interpreter. You start an hour before first light tomorrow, and you have seven days to complete the stunt – I've written down the grid reference of the point where the aircraft piled, and another for the RV where you're to be in a week's time – the head of a pass on the Maqtal plateau. A Long Range Desert Group patrol is being assigned to escort you from there back to the Wire. They'll be waiting for you: your recon signal is a blue Very flare. And don't be late – the LRDG boys are in demand these days.'

Caine stood up and slung his heavyweight Tommy-gun over his shoulders. 'I'll file a mission plan with the HQ Squadron office, then, sir,' he said.

St Aubin smiled crookedly. 'Let's keep this one off the books, shall we?'

Caine gave a start. No mission plan meant that if anything happened to St Aubin in the meantime, no one on earth would know where they were. He gulped. 'Very good, sir,' he heard himself saying. Then it occurred to him that he knew nothing at all about the officer he was being sent to look for. 'You said *Runefish* was "special",' he said. 'What exactly did you mean?'

St Aubin chuckled again, and this time there was real feeling in the sound. 'Of course, of course,' he said. 'I've forgotten the most important thing of all. Stupid of me. *Runefish* is special because she is a woman. Her name is First

Officer Maddaleine Rose, WRNS – twenty-three, blond and, I'm told, shapely in all the right places.'

Caine felt his face drop in surprise. 'And there's one other thing I haven't mentioned,' the CO went on. 'If you are unable to extract First Officer Rose, then your orders are explicit: you are to execute her. Is that clear?'

Caine stammered a 'Yes, sir', and stumbled out through the blanket stunned, unable to decide which appalled him most: the idea of a young woman lost and alone in the endless Sahara, or the prospect of having to put a bullet through her head.

He was about to pass through the gap in the monastery wall when a dark figure barred his way. It was Sears-Beach, and he did not look happy. His tombstone teeth were bared in a humourless grin, and he was slapping his shin with his swagger-stick in an aggravated manner that Caine didn't like. 'What did the CO say to you, Caine?' he demanded.

Caine was forced to halt. 'With all due respect, sir,' he said, 'that's none of your business. Now, would you mind letting me pass?'

Sears-Beach's normally pale face flushed crimson. He lowered his head like a bull ready to charge and took a step forward, jabbing Caine hard in the chest with the brass tip of his stick. 'You had better be careful what you say to me, Sergeant,' he growled.

A wave a fury burned through Caine: he'd just returned from days of hard front-line combat in which, thanks largely to the incompetence of officers like Sears-Beach, more than half his unit had been scragged. A minute ago, he'd laid his life on the line, taking on a mission he had only a flea's chance of surviving. He was damned if he was going to stand being poked in the chest by a nincompoop who hadn't even got his knees brown, no matter what his rank. Growling with rage, he grabbed the swagger-stick, twisted it easily out of Sears-Beach's grasp and tossed it hard against the monastery wall. As the officer reeled back in astonishment, Caine raised his chin and clenched his fists. 'Next time you try that, *sir*,' he said softly, 'I will ram that thing so far up your arse you will need to put your hand down your throat to polish it. If you want to know what the colonel said to me, I suggest you ask him. He won't tell you, but you can ask him anyway.'

Sears-Beach took a step backwards, swallowing hard, and a fleck of spittle appeared at the corner of his mouth. He wiped it away with a long finger. 'I don't know what deal you struck with the colonel,' he hissed, 'and I don't care. I've got a long memory, Caine. By God you'd better keep your nose clean from now on, because long after the Commando's disbanded and the colonel's posted, I'll still be watching you.'

He bent down, picked up the swagger-stick, jammed it under his arm, and with as much dignity as he could muster, swivelled round and marched away.

9

It took Caine twelve solid hours to get everything ship-shape for the *Runefish* mission. Wallace and Copeland volunteered, as he'd known they would – Wallace immediately, Cope after a few minutes' soul-searching. Caine had appointed Copeland second-in-command and quartermaster, and Wallace his gunner and general minder. Together, they collected another twenty-one volunteers, mainly from the fractured Middle East Commando, but also odd stragglers from other units. One prize addition was a pear-shaped lance-jack from the Royal Corps of Signals, a loquacious Welshman named Edward 'Taffy' Trubman, who was said to be a whizz at wireless communications. Of Caine's old No. 1 Troop, Todd Sweeney had joined them, together with medical orderly Maurice Pickney, and an ex-Rifle Brigade lance-jack named Robin Jackson, who, like Fred Wallace, was a champion machine-gun shooter. Caine had managed to find two more specialists, both ex-51 Commando. Lance Corporal Moshe Naiman was a German-born Palestinian Jew who spoke Italian, Arabic and German. His comrade, Lance Corporal Gian-Carlo 'Janka' Cavazzi, was a short but savage-looking Corsican, ex-Free French airborne, who'd also served with the Foreign Legion, and was a trained demolitions instructor. Finally, Caine had persuaded an ex-Royal Army Ordnance Corps fitter, Lance Corporal Henry 'Wingnut' Turner, to join them. He knew that 'up the Blue', their lives would depend on vehicle maintenance.

By midnight, most of the stores had been loaded, and the

seven wagons grudgingly assigned to them by the RQMS, 'Pop' Tobey, were lined up along the monastery wall. The oasis was quieter than the previous night. Though retreating Eighth Army units had been shambling in from the Gazala Line all day, most had already pulled out towards the next 'sticking point' – a station called Alamein on the road to the Nile Delta.

The desert cold had set in under a creamy, moonlit sky, and the commandos had donned greatcoats, sheepskins, leather jerkins and corduroy trousers. While the lads were brewing up tea with condensed milk and spooning down bully-beef stew with ship's biscuits, Caine made a final inspection of the transport with Turner, a cadaverous-looking non-com with ears like windsocks. Apart from the newly acquired 3-tonner, *Marlene*, there were two other 'long-bonnet' Bedfords, christened *Vera* and *Judy*. Caine was happy not to have been palmed off with 'snub-nosed' Bedfords, whose access to the engine was more awkward. There was a six-wheel US-built Ford Marmon Herrington 6-tonner, nicknamed *Gracie*, with a water-bowser, a Daimler armoured car and White and Dingo scout-cars. Caine had ordered all insignia and recognition-symbols removed, and in the case of the soft-skinned vehicles, bumpers, radiator covers and mudguards stripped, as well as anything else expendable that would economize on weight and allow easier access for repair.

Caine and Turner checked that all the wagons had been fitted with condenser-tanks for overheating, sand channels and sand mats for extricating them from 'stickies'. The three AFVs carried sun compasses, and *Gracie* boasted a winch. The Dingo and Daimler armoured cars were fitted with No. 11 wireless sets.

Caine would have liked the little snub-nosed Dingo as his

command-vehicle for the operation, but as she carried only two men, he'd reluctantly settled for the White, which had room for seven. Standard Whites were open-top, and boasted a 'skate-rail' around the open rear body, on which a .50-calibre Browning machine-gun could be traversed 360 degrees. Caine was happy to see that this one had been modified: the skate-rail had been removed and an armoured roof had been welded on. The solid tailboard had been replaced by rear doors of half-inch steel plate, and there were two hatches in the roof of the cab with pintle-mounts for heavy machine-guns.

While the White was a traditional armoured car based on an ordinary lorry chassis, the Dingo was a state-of-the-art fighting vehicle, of which only a handful were on issue in the theatre as yet, undergoing combat trials. Caine hadn't even seen one close up before, and he couldn't resist running a hand along her armoured skin. 'Beautiful bit of engineering,' he commented.

Turner grinned, recognizing a fellow enthusiast. 'Six cylinders, 55hp, 30mm of armour,' he said proudly. 'She's got four-wheel drive, and a pre-selector gearbox with a fluid flywheel – five gears forward and five reverse.'

'No spare wheel, then?' Caine said, not seeing one.

'She doesn't need one – she's got hollow "run flat" tyres.'

'I'll bet that makes her a bit rough.'

'No, the wheels have independent suspension – she's a lovely ride. We'd better look after her, because Pop let slip that she's "experimental" and they want her back. I'm amazed you managed to prize her away from him, skipper.'

Caine laughed. True to form, the RQMS had proved obstructive, sneering at St Aubin's note, cavilling over every item on the shopping list as if it were his own life's blood.

Caine knew that this stinginess was in the nature of all 'Q' staff, and experience had taught him the correct response. He had charmed, coaxed and cajoled Tobey into ceding item after item, until he'd ended up with exactly what he wanted. Well, *almost* exactly, because all four lorries had Lewis guns mounted on their observation hatches, which bothered him. He thought the Lewis obsolete, as it carried an open magazine of only forty-seven rounds and was easily jammed by sand and dust. 'Good for anti-aircraft work, though,' Turner observed when Caine pointed out the problem. 'When I was with the motorized infantry, I saw a chap bring down a Messerschmitt 110 with a Lewis. Bloke called Crow. Emptied the whole mag as she blew over, and actually saw the rounds tearing up the fuselage – she dumped not half a mile away.'

Caine had wanted to mount Vickers 'K' aircraft machine-guns on all the vehicles, but as only four 'Ks' had been available, he'd had two pairs installed on the Dingo and the White – the Daimler didn't need extra armament as she had a turret hefting a 20mm gun. Caine knew the Vickers was designed to be air-cooled by an aircraft's slipstream and tended to overheat if used on the ground, but with a hundred-round mag, and firing almost a thousand rounds a minute, it was the most devastating weapon in its class. 'We should test-fire these weapons,' he told Turner, 'but I don't think the MPs would relish us breaking the blackout regs. We'll have to do it in the field.'

Caine saw Copeland gliding out of the darkness with his camelline stride, his SMLE sniper rifle slung over his shoulder. He was waving some papers. 'Here's the list of volunteers, skipper,' he announced. 'By the way, I've found a crew for the Daimler: Lance Sergeant "Flash" Murray, and his oppo "Shirley" Temple, from the Armoured Corps.'

'Good work, Harry. How's the loading doing?'

'It's done.'

'All right, let's get everyone together and let them know what it is they've volunteered for.'

While the volunteers were gathering, Caine scanned the list, which noted only name, rank and parent unit:

Bramwell, Victor	Gdsmn	1 Coldstream Guards
Caine, Thomas	Sgt	Royal Engineers
Cavazzi, Gian-Carlo	L/Cpl	51 Commando
Copeland, Harold	Cpl	Royal Army Service Corps
Floggett, David	Bdr	Royal Artillery
Graveman, Augustus	G/Mate	Royal Navy Commando
Hanley, Richard	Gnr	Royal Horse Artillery
Jackson, Robin	L/Cpl	Kings Royal Rifle Corps
MacDonald, Ross	L/Cpl	Black Watch (Royal Highland Regt)
Murray, Alastair	L/Sgt	Royal Armoured Corps
Naiman, Moshe	L/Cpl	51 Commando
O'Brian, Robert	Pte	Royal Ulster Rifles
Oldfield, Michael	Tpr	Inns of Court Regiment (RAC)
Padstowe, George	L/Cpl	Royal Marines
Pickney, Maurice	L/Cpl	Royal Army Medical Corps
Raker, Albert	Pte	Pioneer Corps
Rigby, Martin	Pte	Duke of Cornwall's Light Infantry
Shackleton, Barry	Cpl	Royal Scots Greys
Sweeney, Charles	Cpl	Royal Military Police
Temple, Paul	Tpr	Royal Armoured Corps
Trubman, Edward	L/Cpl	Royal Corps of Signals
Turner, Henry	L/Cpl	Royal Army Ordnance Corps
Wallace, Frederick	Gnr	Royal Horse Artillery

He counted off twenty-three names including his own: it was a good mix, he thought, a nice balance of cavalry, infantry and specialist-corps men. It was slightly biased towards NCOs, of course, but he trusted that, thanks to the equalizing nature of commando training, this would boost the quality of the unit rather than creating an 'all-chiefs-and-no-Indians' situation.

Copeland touched his shoulder, announced that the muster was complete. Caine scanned the bodies before him. Unshaven, clad in their motley coats, with silk scarves, stocking-caps, black berets or balaclavas, carrying personalized Tommy-guns, Bren-guns and Lee-Enfield .303s, they looked like a rag-tag mob of partisans – pitifully few against the might of the Panzer Army. Caine reminded himself what two years in the desert had taught him – nothing, not weapons nor tanks nor artillery, counted a damn against the quality of the men behind them. And these were good men: mostly commando trained, all battle hardened, accustomed to the harsh discipline of the desert: combination individualists and team-players, confident but not reckless.

Caine introduced himself to the lads he didn't know, including the group's sole Bluejacket – Gunner's Mate Gus Graveman, a regally whiskered sailor from the Royal Navy Commando who reminded Caine instantly of the sea-dog on the Player's Navy Cut packet. He also met the new Daimler AFV commander, 'Flash' Murray, a sandy-haired little bruiser from Belfast with scarred fists like mutton chops and the guarded look of a street-fighter. Murray's driver, Trooper Paul 'Shirley' Temple, bore no resemblance to the child star after whom he'd been nicknamed. He was a gawky, big-boned clodhopper of a man with outsize hands and feet: Caine found himself wondering if he'd even fit into the confines of the little Daimler. Neither Shirley nor Flash was commando trained, and it was for this reason,

Caine explained, that, though Murray was a lance sergeant and second in rank only to Caine himself, it was Copeland who'd be occupying the second-in-command slot.

Caine launched into his briefing, and the men listened in grave silence until he mentioned that *Runefish* was female. This brought whoops and catcalls. 'Who's she, then?' some wag demanded. 'General Ritchie's squeeze?'

'For all I know, she could be,' Caine beamed, the crow's feet at the corners of his eyes crinkling, 'but as they say, "It's not ours to reason why."' He resolved quietly that, whatever St Aubin had said, the men needed to know why they were being sent to extract a Wren first officer, when even captured generals were left to rot in Axis jails. He decided to initiate them into *Assegai* – for what it was worth – as soon as possible after they'd left the oasis.

Caine had divided the execution of Op *Runefish* into four phases – move out, advance to target area, withdrawal from target area, final RV back to base. 'Friendly forces,' he said. 'None, except for perhaps a few Senussi Arabs. They're generally friendly to us, but you can never tell – it has happened that they've shopped Allied troops to the enemy. Enemy forces: as if the Panzer Army wasn't enough, we know that a company of the Brandenberger Special Duties Regiment has been deployed in our target area. We can't be sure whether this has anything to do with *Runefish*, but whatever the case, it won't make life any easier for us. If they *have* been sent to find her, then we'll just have to make sure we get to her before they do.'

'How are we going to recognize her, then?' asked Maurice Pickney. 'Have you got a photo?'

It was a question that Caine had already put to himself. 'No photo, I'm afraid,' St Aubin had said when he had returned to inquire at the office. 'All I can tell you about her is that she's a left-handed, green-eyed blonde who speaks fluent German, Italian and French.'

Caine shifted to a discussion of tactical considerations, and finished up with a few generalities. 'Remember lads,' he said, 'it's desert rules. Every man carries a map and compass and knows the next RV. No one is ever left on his own. No one goes anywhere without a full water-bottle, not even for a piss at night. Every wagon carries three days' rations of food and water. If a wagon breaks down, you stay with it. If a wagon gets stranded, you stop and work out your position, or wait till someone comes for you. Whatever happens, stay focused. Anyone left alone without a clear grasp of where he is on the map is likely to feel an urge to keep moving. Don't give in to it – the Blue is a damn' big place.'

He stared round at them, seeing only shadows like gathering spirits in the darkness. Above them, familiar constellations trooped out in full royal panoply: Caine recognized the sparkling cluster of the Pleiades, the three bright studs of Orion's belt 'All right,' he said. 'That's it. You're volunteers, and I know you'll do a good job. The best of British to us all.'

Before dismissing the boys, Caine ordered Copeland to issue a rum-ration all round.

While Cope was doling out rum, Caine and Wallace unrolled their flea-bags by the White scout car. A pair of bats looped-the-loop over the monastery walls, and an owl hooted softly in the darkness. Copeland arrived a few minutes later, carrying a jar that was about two thirds full of Navy-issue rum. They squatted down in the cold sand by the White's wheels, arranging jerkins and coats around them, and Cope poured three fingers into each of their mugs. 'That ought to warm the cockles of your heart,' he said.

Caine sipped the rum and felt the first drops setting his stomach on fire. 'That's *good*,' he announced. 'Consider my heart well cockled, Harry. Say what you like about the Bluejackets, you can't fault their rum.' He held up his tin mug and proposed a toast. 'Here's to all Jack Tars, especially First Officer Maddaleine Rose, wherever she may be.'

The three of them lit cigarettes, cupping them deftly in their hands to prevent the glowing tips from showing and breaking blackout regulations. They could just make out each other's faces in the starlight. 'We aren't exactly a fearsome crew,' Copeland grunted, 'but we *do* pack a punch out of proportion to our size. There's a Bren for every two men, Thompsons and SMLE .303s. Every man's been issued with a .45 Colt pistol, and a twenty-two-inch sword-bayonet. We've got ten boxes of Mills grenades, five Boys anti-tank rifles, Long Yoke attachments and blanks for grenade throwing, three two-inch mortars, thirty No. 2 landmines, six boxes of Nobel's No. 808 gelignite, and time-pencils, instantaneous fuse, detonators, four Lewises and two pairs of Vickers 'K's, and that's without the two-pounder on the Daimler. There's even some No. 76 Hawkins grenades.'

'You want to watch them things,' said Wallace, gulping rum. 'That crush-igniter system they have is unstable. We only need one to go up and the whole convoy'll be fried.'

Cope ditched his cap-comforter, running a hand through his bog-brush blond hair. 'Just the ticket for tanks, though,' he said. 'One seventy-six will whack the tracks right off a Mark III panzer.'

'Only trouble is, Jerry'll shoot your arse up before you get near enough to throw it.'

'Maybe you didn't see how Tom used that Hawkins when we pulled the boys out the other day?'

'For your information, Mister "Hostilities Only", it wasn't

the Hawkins that saved our bacon, it was them Horse-Gunners. God bless the artillery.'

Copeland raised a hand as if he were a timid schoolboy asking a question. 'Please, sir,' he piped in a mock-childish voice, 'does "hostilities only" mean I'm not one of those cretins who sent millions into mass suicide in the trenches in 1914?' He paused and resumed his ordinary voice. 'Maybe it means that, unlike some, I'm capable of thinking for myself,' he said. 'And by the way, it's *Corporal* "Hostilities Only" to you.'

Wallace snorted. 'You practising to be Todd Sweeney?' he said, ''cause for a minute there you sounded just like him.'

'Leave it out, Fred,' Caine cut in, frowning. Disagreements like this between Cope and Wallace had been known to erupt into fistfights. 'There's no "regulars" and "hostilities only" in the commandos,' he said. 'We all volunteered to get away from all that bullshit – officers and other ranks, regulars and territorials, us and them. We're all fighting the same war, aren't we? Or are you two fighting a different one?'

Cope and Wallace blinked at him, and Caine grinned back, exasperated. His two mates were as different as Laurel and Hardy, but he liked and valued both for their distinctive qualities – Wallace for his staunch and unswerving loyalty, and Cope for his precise and analytical mind.

Wallace had been his mate almost from the day he'd arrived at Middle East Commando, still smarting from his swift descent from lieutenant to private soldier. As the 'crow' in his troop, he'd been assigned a bed-space next to the door of his tent, despite the fact that there were other spaces: the old lags told him these were 'reserved'. He hadn't understood the dirty trick they'd played on him until

78

next morning, when he'd woken up to find his blanket soaked in piss. Almost everyone in the tent got up to urinate during the night, and instead of going outside to the latrines in the cold, would pee from the door-gap. If there were any 'blowback', it was the man sleeping by the door who copped it.

It had been Wallace who had decided that enough was enough, taken him firmly by the arm and shown him a space as far away from the door as possible. When the others ganged up on him, Wallace growled that 'the crow' had had his 'christening', and that anyone messing with Caine in future would first have to deal with him. As he was currently the heavyweight boxing champion of the Commando, no one bothered to take him up on the challenge.

Wallace had joined the Horse Gunners straight out of school, and was proud to have served with the celebrated 'Sphinx' Battery. A born Tommie, he was a good practical soldier, but not the type ever to rise above the hallowed rank of private, which, according to him, was the best rank ever made. He was solid and reliable, but even the army hadn't taught him to curb his violent temper, which, coupled with his physical strength, could make him truly formidable. He had appointed himself Caine's protector, but the tables had turned several times when Caine, with his diplomat's manner, had managed to get Wallace out of hot water. The most notable occasion had been when the Regimental Sergeant Major had shot a dog Wallace had become attached to. The RSM's claim that the dog had rabies hadn't prevented Wallace from knocking him out cold in the NAAFI. It had taken all Caine's rhetoric to save the giant from a court-martial.

When Harry Copeland had joined the troop from the Royal Army Service Corps later and become friendly with

Caine, Wallace had been frankly jealous. Cope was everything the ex-Gunner wasn't – handsome, educated, cultured. He'd taught history at a boys' school and was a superb organizer, with a mind like a seven-carat-diamond drill-bit. Rumour had it that he had turned down a commission because he was a 'communist', and although this was absurd, it was true that Copeland despised the callous and unimaginative regulars whom, he thought, had bungled the Great War.

The thing was, almost everyone agreed with him, even the regulars. Caine, a regular himself, had an axe to grind against the military establishment for its unforgivable slowness in adopting new technology. Wallace explained away Caine's friendship with Copeland as a case of shared hatred for 'the officer class'. This might have been an exaggeration, but it was a feeling Wallace himself could identify with. He'd seen too many young officers turn up in North Africa with what he called 'ten-pound-note' voices and an inflated idea of their own importance. The good ones were, in his opinion, few and far between, and it didn't surprise him that Caine had been ejected from their number. Caine was simply too good to be an officer, Wallace thought.

For a long time, Copeland and Wallace had loathed each other. Cope felt physically challenged by Wallace and regarded him as a muscle-bound thug. Wallace was the first to admit that he wasn't an educated man, but he resented Cope's insinuation that he was somehow retarded. They had recently reached an uneasy truce, though, under the influence of their mutual loyalty to Caine.

'So who *is* this tart we're supposed to be snatching from under Rommel's nose?' Wallace demanded. 'Seems an awful lot of trouble to go to just for some snooty bint.'

Even before the words were out, Wallace knew he'd

blundered. If there was one thing Caine was touchy about, it was women. Not that he didn't like them, but he never referred to them as 'bints', 'tarts', 'judies' or 'crumpet'. To him they were always 'ladies'. One of the few times Wallace had seen him nettled was in a Cairo bar when two drunken Australians had started abusing a young hostess. The girl couldn't have been more than sixteen. Caine had watched them in brooding silence for a minute, then, without any prelude, marched over with his rope-like chest-muscles heaving, and floored both, one after the other, with a volley of snapping knuckle-bones delivered so fast that Wallace remembered only a blur. When the Ozzies had picked themselves up, Caine made them apologize to the young lady before having the doorman kick them out. Wallace had been shocked: he'd been giving Caine the benefit of his protection for months, never dreaming how smartly the ex-Sapper could handle himself – in fact, Wallace had never seen anyone faster in his life. He'd made a mental note that night never to abuse women, even verbally, in Caine's presence. In the heat of the moment, though, he'd forgotten his vow.

Caine was staring at him, his eyes flecks of mercury in the starlight. 'There aren't any tarts or bints on this job,' he said. 'The woman we're after is an officer of the Royal Navy. Let's just call her *Runefish*.'

'Right you are,' Wallace muttered, avoiding his gaze.

Caine guessed his mate was recalling the fight in the Cairo bar, and regretted it. His reputation as a brawler wasn't something he relished. It brought back too many unpleasant memories of the time he'd broken his stepfather's jaw with a one-two punch in the living room of their cottage in the Lincolnshire Fens. There was no doubt in his mind that the Butcher had had it coming – he'd tormented Caine for four years, and abused both his mother and sister – but it had appalled him to discover that he was capable of such an attack.

Caine's real father, Frank – a blacksmith – had died when he was twelve, from complications arising out of a kick in the head by a maddened horse. From the time Caine was old enough to lift a hammer, though, he'd been helping his father in the forge, and had developed spectacular shoulders, arms, and chest muscles. Even at twelve, though, he'd been astute enough to realize that horse power would soon be a thing of the past. A year later he'd left school and apprenticed himself at a local garage, where he'd taken to tinkering with motors like a trout to a torrent, awed by the ingenuity and power of the combustion engine. He'd also talked a retired pugilist named Earl Marsh into training him as a boxer. Marsh had noticed and developed his spectacular one-two punch.

It had been the move he'd relied on the night he'd heard his sister May's terrified screams for the last time. He recalled breaking in on the six-foot, fourteen-stone Butcher, who had pinioned May on the couch and was slobbering drunkenly over her. Though Caine could never remember actually hitting his stepfather, he clearly recalled the snap as his jaw broke.

The Butcher had vowed to get his own back, and had reported the assault to the police. Caine had been arrested. The charge was a serious one, but the constable assigned to his case grasped the circumstances and was sympathetic. He decided that justice wouldn't be served by Caine going to Borstal, when it was obvious that his stepfather was the more guilty of the two. If Caine agreed to join the army, he said, he would not only keep a careful eye on the Butcher, but would also make sure the assault charge was quietly dropped. Caine felt that he was betraying his mother and sister, but there was nothing else for it. A week later he visited the nearest army recruiting office, lied about his age and enlisted in the Royal Engineers. His mother committed suicide five years later, writing that she could no longer take the Butcher's conduct. Caine was an NCO by that time and loved the army, but his failure to be there, to help her when she most needed him, was something for which he could never forgive himself.

10

A torch-beam flashed in their faces, and the three men ducked instinctively. Wallace drew his sawn-off Purdey, cocked a hammer, pointed it at the torch. His black eyes narrowed to pinpricks. 'Put that bloody light out,' he boomed.

The light vanished, and they made out the carp-headed hulk of signaller Taffy Trubman twitching in front of them – a corpulent figure of intersecting ovals, like a dark snowman, his leather jerkin unbuttoned to display a pot belly. Everything about Trubman was overblown, except for his hands, which were as slender and delicate as a girl's. His double-chinned, fish-shaped face was unshaven, his eyes goggling behind thick spectacles. 'Sorry, boys,' he stammered.

'You will be next time,' Wallace grated. 'You're lucky I didn't put a pound of buckshot through your guts.'

Caine groaned. 'When are you going to ditch that weapon, Fred?'

Wallace eased the shotgun's hammer back, looking surly. 'Don't say a word against Purdey,' he grated. 'She saved your arse when we pulled those boys out.'

Caine nodded to Trubman, 'What is it, Taffy? he asked.

'I've calibrated both the No. 11 sets, skipper. We've got comms with Group HQ.'

'Good work.'

'Right you are. The No. 11's a good set – its range is only supposed to be twenty miles, but they've found it can work at a thousand or more. Skywave, see. Bounces sigs off the ionosphere. But bear in mind that the desert plays hell with the links – 'specially sandstorms. These are very sensitive transmitters – you've got to nurse them like babies. One bad bump can ruin a set, and without a link, we'll be up the creek without the proverbial . . .'

Caine caught the expression on Wallace's face and put a warning hand on his arm in the darkness. 'Very good,' he said placidly. 'I'll remember that. You want to join us for a snort?'

Trubman shifted, eyeing the rum jar. 'No thanks. I'm teetotal – good Welsh Presbyterian, see. Anyway, I need to get some kip.'

'All right. Just watch that torch – blackout regs are in force and I don't want you getting nabbed by the Redcaps.'

As the Welshman trudged back into the shadows, Caine held up his hand to arrest the inevitable rhetoric from Wallace. 'All right, he's not commando material,' he said, 'but he's a volunteer, and I'm damn' grateful to have him. Good signallers are rarer than balls on a she-camel.'

Wallace grunted and drained the last of his rum. 'Well, it's about time to hit the sack,' he said.

'Right,' Copeland said, stubbing out his Player's Navy Cut carefully in the sand. 'But Fred's question is still valid, skipper – just why *is* this *Runefish* . . . "lady" . . . so special that they're launching a search-and-rescue op for her? I mean, maybe that joker was right. Maybe she really *is* Ritchie's sweetheart or something.'

Wallace chuckled. 'It's "need to know", innit?' he said.

Caine paused, wondering if he should tell them. He'd already resolved to brief the unit fully once it was on the move. He decided that he could trust Cope and Wallace to keep their mouths shut until they had left base. He explained the details of *Assegai* as St Aubin had revealed them to him.

When he'd finished, he wasn't entirely surprised to find Copeland eyeing him dubiously. '*Assegai*,' the corporal repeated, as if weighing up the merits of the name. 'That's a Zulu stabbing-spear. A rum name for a long-distance-missile system.'

'So what?' Wallace honked. 'Our top brass ain't exactly famous for its imagination.'

'So why does the whole spiel sound like a fantasy? Remote guidance to long-range targets? That's far in advance of any gear I've ever heard of.'

Wallace snorted. 'Perhaps Mr Churchill had so much on his plate he forgot to brief you on the latest top-secret gadgetry. That's a shame – after all, as a *corporal* you must have been well up on his list.'

Caine snickered. Cope clunked down his mess tin. 'All right, Mister Clever Dick,' he said. 'If it's top secret, maybe you can explain why St Aubin revealed the details to Tom here just before we set off on a dodgy mission with a fifty-fifty chance of getting bagged. Where's the need to know? None of us need to know – we're buckshee foot-sloggers on a search-and-rescue op. The whole yarn's as full of holes as a tart's knickers – sorry, skipper, but it is. Why would GHQ choose a Wren for the job when there are a thousand pen-pushers of the 'Barstool Desert Group' in Cairo that would have done? A bint like that – I mean a girl – would stand out like a sore thumb at a bachelor party. Just what you need if you're carrying top-secret documents, eh? And isn't it a bit late to be ferrying specifications round, anyway? I mean, last time *I* looked, the Eighth Army was in retreat. The whole story sounds like something out of H. G. Wells.'

'Who?'

'That science-fiction writer – you know, *The Time Machine*? *War of the Worlds*?'

'Never heard of him.'

'Why doesn't that surprise me? Don't suppose they've got past "Jip the cat went up the hill" in Leatherhead.'

'Maybe, but at least we're savvy enough to know that having a corporal's stripes don't make you God's gift. You're so brainy, astonishin' you ain't been invited to join the planning staff by now.'

Cope's reply was nipped in the bud by a guffaw from Caine. 'All right, boys,' he said. 'I think I've about had it.' He shook the drops out of his mug and started cleaning it with sand. 'You're right, Harry – my first reaction was that this was all cock and bull, and as far as I'm concerned the jury's still out. But as I said, we're just cogs in the wheel. We believe what we're told, and we follow orders. The *Assegai* story might be above board or it might not, but one thing is certain: whatever *Runefish* knows, it's the real McCoy – so vital that, if we can't get her out, we have to execute her.'

Leaving the other two staring at him in astonishment, he slid his mug back into its pouch, lurched to his feet and marched off towards his sleeping space.

Caine had often tried to imagine how big 'the Blue' actually was. The part of it that concerned the Eighth Army – the so-called 'Western Desert' – was itself as large as the whole of India, and that was only one region of the Sahara. It was an ocean – a sea of undulating rock and gravel and sand that stretched unbroken to the west for an incredible distance of three thousand miles. And, as at sea, you had to navigate by the sun, the stars and the moon across a vista without fixed points.

Not that the move-out required any navigation at first, because the track leading north-west from Jaghbub was marked with oil drums every half-mile, bobbing in front of the White's windscreen like harbour-buoys. They had a Military Police motorcyclist to pilot them the first ten miles, and Caine watched his red tail-light, almost mesmerized. He'd been impressed to note the quiet sense of purpose about his men when they had mounted the wagons an hour before dawn – the absence of raucous jokes and nervous chatter. It was cold for a June morning, and the commandos were swaddled in coats and stocking-caps, their breath coming out like smoke. Dressed in his officer's duffel coat, Caine had taken the passenger's seat in the White scout-car next to Cope – the designated driver. Wallace shivered over the twin Vickers 'K's on the double observation hatch above, crooning a Vera Lynn song in a surprisingly melodic baritone. Trailing the lead vehicle came the Dingo with fitter Wingnut Turner at the controls, and Taffy

Trubman doubling as W/T operator and gunner. The six-wheeled Marmon Herrington, *Gracie,* followed, towing the water-bowser. *Marlene, Vera* and *Judy* crawled behind her at well-spaced intervals. The Daimler AFV, crewed by Flash Murray and Shirley Temple, brought up the rear.

When they reached the ten-mile marker, Copeland stopped and let the engine idle while the Redcap turned his bike around. As he skidded to a halt by the side hatch, they saw a demon mask leering out of the darkness – motorcycle goggles on a face luminous with white dust. 'That's as far as I go, lads,' he said. 'Just stay with the bollards till first light, then you can use your sun-compass. I don't know what crazy mission you're on, but I hope you make it.'

'There goes the only living witness that Operation *Runefish* ever left base,' Cope said, teasing the wagon into gear. 'I notice his nibs wasn't present to see us off.'

Caine had also noted St Aubin's absence, and it irked him. 'Not that I missed him personally,' he told Copeland, 'but if anything happens to him, no one at GHQ will have a clue where we are, or what our orders were.'

'That happened to a mate of mine on a Jock column,' Cope grinned. 'They were up the Blue for a month, covered about two thousand miles – bumped Mekili and bagged God knows how many Axis wagons – even aircraft. When they got back, there was no one left at HQ who remembered them. No mission plan – the movements were all in the head of some half-colonel, who'd copped one and was six feet under. When they whaled into Abbassia barracks, all puffed up with what they'd done, the Adjutant said, "Who the bloody hell are you?"'

Caine cackled with laughter. 'I can just see that happening to us.'

Copeland flashed a quick glance at him. 'You know,

skipper,' he said, 'you always look as happy as a pig in shit when you're up the Blue – don't you find all this emptiness gives you the willies?'

Caine shook his head. 'Nope. The first time I was in the desert, two years back, I had the feeling that I'd returned to a place I'd known long ago. It was as if I'd finally come home.'

'Not surprising in your case,' Cope snorted. 'I mean your stomping ground – the Fens – it's not much different, is it? I went there once – desolate, flat land going on mile after mile – you can drive all morning and never see a tree.'

Caine grinned at him. It wasn't exactly what he'd meant. He wasn't a religious man – as a child Sunday school had been the misery of miseries for him. Yet the desert had a sense about it that he could only describe as *holy* – a sacredness that had nothing to do with going to church on Sundays. 'What about you?' he asked.

Copeland shrugged, without taking his eyes off the dark piste. 'Me, I come from a big family – second of five children. We made our own world wherever we were, and I suppose that taught me to feel at home anywhere, as long as I have friends around me. I can see what you mean about the desert, only if I was stranded here on my own, I'd go crazy.'

Caine nodded. In the desert, panic always lurked close to the surface. That was what desert rules were designed to combat. He'd learned his lesson during an early trip up the Blue, when he'd left his leaguer by night to relieve himself. He'd walked no more than fifty yards from the camp in pitch darkness, but on attempting to return had realized with a surge of alarm, that he wasn't even aware in which direction it lay. He could have shouted to his comrades, but the humiliation would have been unbearable. Instead, he'd decided on a plan. He would walk fifty paces in the most likely direction, marking the way with the shovel he'd brought with him. If he failed to find the leaguer, he would retrace his steps to his start point and take fifty paces in another direction, continuing until all four directions had been covered. Luckily his first choice had been the correct one, but Caine had never forgotten that momentary terror of disorientation, and had resolved that in future he wouldn't make even the shortest journey without knowing exactly where he was.

They were silent for a moment, then Copeland said, 'You know, Tom, the chances of picking up *Runefish* are about 5 per cent. I reckon they've sent us on a snipe hunt.'

Caine was about to agree, but stopped himself, clutching the door strop with his left hand, staring dead ahead. 'Just think of that girl alone in the emptiness, lost, confused, powerless to do anything, surrounded by the whole bloody Panzer Army.' He turned and stared at Cope. 'Whatever bullshit story we've been fed, we can't leave her there, Harry. No. I'm going to get her out, if it's the last thing I ever do.'

Caine's words cheered Copeland, and went a long way to dispel his misgivings. It was good to be with a leader who was committed.

The stars were already fading, the eastern horizon edged in fire-washed ochre. A quarter of an hour later the sun burst through riffling dust-clouds, a gleaming fire-opal, painting bizarre shadow versions of the wagons in the sand before them. Caine waited until the sun was high enough to provide a clear shadow for the sun compass, then instructed Cope to give three short blasts on his horn – the prearranged signal for 'general halt'.

Caine found his prismatic compass and jumped out of

the wagon. The desert lay featureless to every horizon – even Jaghbub oasis had been swallowed up by the vastness. The mission's projected 'landfall' was a point just over two hundred miles to the north-west, near the Italian post at Msus. Caine had already worked out the grid bearing with map and protractor – now he had to convert it to a magnetic bearing and transfer that to the sun-compass. Land navigation was a meticulous business, but one in which Caine had excelled from the beginning. He was good at it, yet he'd never become blasé, never lost the thrill of gratitude he'd experienced the first time he'd brought a convoy to within a stone's throw of a point in the middle of nowhere, merely through his own calculations. It had given him a satisfying illusion of mastery over the wilderness.

What had been worrying Caine since they'd left Jaghbub, though, was the fact that he was the only qualified navigator on the op. If he went down, there would be no substitute. He'd decided to train up Copeland and Wallace, and when they'd grasped the basics, they could pass it on to the other lads.

Calling his two mates to accompany him, he moved about ten yards from the scout-car. 'You have to get far enough away from the wagon so that its metal doesn't affect the prismatic's magnetic field,' he explained. 'You can't use a prismatic in a vehicle because the constant gear-shifts and varying speeds are impossible to compensate for.'

He fixed the bearing and held the compass out to them. 'Now,' he said, 'all you have to do is manoeuvre the vehicle until the shadow of the sun-compass is aligned with this bearing, and drive in a straight line, keeping the shadow in the same place.'

'Wait a sec,' Cope protested, wearing his disdainful 'clever-boy-of-the-class' expression, 'the sun doesn't stay in one place, so doesn't that mean we have to keep on shifting the vehicle?'

Caine smiled. 'Full marks, Harry,' he said. 'That *would* be the case, except that we have Bagnold sun-compasses with a calibration disc. Instead of constantly shifting the wagons about, we simply adjust the disk every thirty minutes, according to our azimuth tables. Apart from that, it's just a matter of logging the distance between each adjustment so you can calculate your position by dead-reckoning.'

Wallace looked mystified at the mention of 'azimuth tables' and 'dead-reckoning', but Caine wasn't worried that he was out of his depth. Wallace was a practical soldier who needed to grasp things with his hands rather than his mind, but once he'd mastered the lesson, he would never forget it.

When Cope had the White pointing in the right direction, Wallace took his post at the hatch and went on humming Vera Lynn. Caine resumed his seat beside the driver. As they set off into the open desert, he felt a surge of euphoria. The Sahara never failed to give him this thrill. Time was meaningless here – a year was the same as a thousand years. Once you were clear of 'civilization' it was as if you'd cut yourself loose in time and space, entered a freefall dimension whose hugeness reduced the war to a skirmish between colonies of ants. In the Blue, you broke free of normal human limits, engaged with nature's raw dynamics in a way you could never do in a city. Caine felt privileged to be here.

His eyes worked constantly over the surface: sheets of flat, hard sand, crusts of shattered shale, hard gravel beaches, oval playas glittering with salt crystals. He picked out paths through the void, urging the driver left or right, balancing the compass-shadow against the wagon's speed, against the going. The drive was punctuated only by halts to adjust the sun-compass, but Caine was glad of these short pauses, as opportunities to feel the earth beneath his feet, taste the intensity of the almost ceaseless northerly breeze, feel the wax and wane of the sun's heat. Once he spotted a red admiral butterfly, coming from nowhere, going nowhere, and it seemed to him that the creature had been put there solely for his delight.

On the good going the wagons sped along at forty miles an hour. Caine had instructed the drivers to fan out into 'air formation' – a rough arrowhead whose object was to present a more difficult target to marauding aircraft. On standard runs Caine would have taken a 'jinks' – a detour – every few miles, to throw off any spotters locked on their tracks, but time was short, and he decided to risk not taking one.

By ten o'clock the desert was an inferno. The commandos doffed their outer layers, stripping down to shorts and socks and donning their special-issue footwear: Indian-style sandals known as *chapplies*.

They had just halted for an azimuth adjustment when Caine heard the snarl of engines and the distinct grating of gears from beyond the horizon. He knew there was a convoy out there somewhere, but he couldn't see it. Caine had experienced this strange desert phenomenon of sound amplification before but had never been able to explain it. The curious thing, he'd observed, was that as soon as the convoy became visible, the engine noises would cease entirely until it was up close. Now, sweeping the landscape with his field glasses, he picked up a string of black beads on the edge of the world, apparently motionless among a glittering quicksilver mirage of pools and lakes. Caine got back into the wagon, pointed out the vehicles to Cope and told him to drive towards them. As his wagons approached, the convoy seemed to remain stationary – Caine spotted

94

Union Jacks and formation-pennants that identified it as an Eighth Army column. Oddly, not until Caine's vehicles were within a couple of hundred yards of it did the column seem to unfreeze and explode into life – another optical illusion that Caine had become familiar with.

Close up, it was a sorry sight – mixed-up British, Indian, New Zealand, South African and Free French wagons, driven by men with the hollow eyes of mummies, their faces gaunt and ghost-like under a film of chalky dust. There were limping trucks with shell-holes shot through their canvas covers, crippled AFVs being towed by mobile cranes, damaged field guns, broken-down Bren-gun carriers, trackless tanks and the skeletons of aircraft on transporters, wounded men crammed like sardines in the back of captured Axis lorries, who bounced on looking neither left nor right, like men possessed.

'The face of defeat,' Caine commented.

Copeland stared after the disappearing column. 'Jesus wept,' he said.

Just before noon, Wallace called Caine up to the observation hatch and pointed out another convoy approaching. It was perhaps two miles away, but even at this distance Wallace was certain it was the enemy. Caine watched it with his binos, marvelling at the acuity of Wallace's naked eyes. The convoy was a large one – a dozen big Italian Breda lorries, at least one of them carrying a 90mm self-propelled gun, and some Fiat Triple-Sixes. It was being led by an Italian A41 armoured car. 'Ities, by the look of it,' Caine said.

'Let's scupper them,' Wallace suggested. 'They'll never know what hit 'em.'

Caine was sorely tempted. These six-wheel Bredas were masterpieces of Italian craftsmanship, specially designed for difficult terrain. Beside them, British trucks were crude, mass-produced jobs. A couple or three Bredas would be ideal for the *Runefish* mission. Sadly, he shook his head. 'We can't afford to take prisoners,' he said.

'Who said anything about prisoners?' Wallace smirked, patting the quilts on the Vickers 'K's.

In commando training they'd been encouraged to go into action with what the instructors called the 'killing face'. That was the expression on Wallace's countenance now. Caine saw it, and shook his head. 'Listen,' he said. 'If those Ities surrender, I'll be faced with a choice of letting them go or shooting them down in cold blood. And that's a choice I wouldn't want to make – would you?'

Wallace sniffed. 'I suppose not,' he said.

Caine scoped the area around them. Fifteen miles to the south-west was a dune field, no more than a shimmer of varnished light on the skyline. It was too far away to reach quickly, and instead he picked out a low escarpment not more than a mile away, bristling with camel-thorn. 'Head for that ridge,' he directed Copeland. 'Left – nine o'clock. There's enough shadow there to hide in, and we can sling the scrim nets.'

Minutes later, from the shelter of a camouflaged scrim net, Caine watched the convoy with his field glasses as it rumbled past a quarter of a mile off. There were no flags or pennants this time, but he clocked Allied 3-tonners among the Italian trucks and noticed that some of the wagons were being driven by men wearing the insignia of the Royal Army Service Corps. He let out a slow breath. 'It's one of ours,' he said. 'Captured vehicles.' Wallace whistled, and Caine grinned at him. 'It doesn't pay to be hasty, mate,' he said.

At high noon sun-compasses were ineffectual, so Caine made use of the halt to let the men brew up tea, to open tins of sardines and peaches in the shade of tarpaulins they'd rigged up under the scrim nets. At the previous night's briefing he had instructed drivers and co-drivers to check their engines and tyre pressure at every major stop and to top up with petrol and radiator water. He was pleased to see the two-man crews going about these tasks with practised ease.

Caine realized that he hadn't had time to give Taffy Trubman a signals brief, and after posting two lookouts to watch the flanks, he walked over to the Dingo, where the signaller was erecting a rod aerial. 'Don't get comms with Group,' Caine said quietly. 'Maintain complete wireless silence unless we hit an emergency.' The Welshman considered him over his thick glasses: his puffy face took on a bemused expression. 'That's not standard operating procedure, skipper,' he said. 'SOP is to get comms at every stop.'

'You'll find a lot that's not SOP on this job – we have our own rules. There's too much risk of getting dee-effed, and we can't afford that.' He handed Trubman a page from a message pad with numbers scrawled on it. 'What I want you to do at each stop is to tune into this emergency frequency and listen for *Runefish's* SOS signal. She's got a biscuit-tin set, and if we pick up her transmission it'll solve the problem of locating her. Only, if you do pick up anything, whatever happens, don't acknowledge it. When you pack up the set, tune it back to zero, so there's nothing to betray the frequency if we get bagged.'

'Right you are,' Trubman sniffed. He adjusted his glasses and returned disconsolately to his aerial-building.

Caine had Copeland call the rest of the boys over, intending to fill in the gaps in the briefing he'd delivered the previous night. He had only just begun, though, when one of the sentries, a clean-cut ex-Guardsman called Vic Bramwell, arrived back, out of breath. 'There's a column coming directly towards us, skipper,' he gasped. Caine glanced west, but Bramwell shook his head and pointed in the opposite direction. 'No, it's coming up behind us,' he said. 'Looks as though they're following our tracks.'

'Who the hell is that?'

'It's not any of the ones that passed us this morning. I'd say it's British, though. Four 3-tonners, one towing a 25-pounder – maybe a Jock column?'

Caine scratched his head. Jock columns were mobile units combining small packets of infantry and artillery. They'd been used extensively in the first year of the desert war, but he hadn't heard of them being deployed since. 'What are they doing heading west?' Copeland enquired.

'Maybe we're not the only ones on a special mission,' Caine said, but he felt doubtful. He was certain St Aubin would have warned him about a parallel operation – the CO had said that the only special-service troops available were the ME Commando. He pondered whether to stand the men to, but instead told them to stay alert in the cover of the nets and tarpaulins. He sent the sentry back to his post and told Flash Murray to man the Daimler's 20mm and cover the visitors. He called Wallace to join him in the open.

The 3-tonners were on them within minutes, coming like strange lumbering animals out of the paste-white landscape, carrying veils of dust and sunlight reflected on their windscreens like silver banners. Caine squared his wide torso towards the wagons, cradling his outsize Tommy-gun in the ready position. Wallace looped the sling of his Bren-gun round his neck. They stood their ground, though Caine was acutely aware that if there were any shooting, they'd go down in the first volley.

The convoy halted a hundred yards from them, and a tall,

sandy-haired officer dropped out of the leading wagon. Caine saw faces behind the windscreens and heads popping out of the observation hatches. The officer marched up to them as if he were on a parade ground. Close up, Caine saw that he was wearing captain's pips on his shoulder straps, a peaked service cap bearing the badge of the Scots Guards and khaki drills that seemed impossibly well pressed for desert service. He carried a .303 slung over his shoulder.

The captain was obviously expecting a salute. Though they never saluted their own officers, Caine thought it best not to risk being identified as commandos. He threw one up, and the captain returned the gesture languidly. 'Captain Broderick, 201st Guards Brigade,' he said.

Caine noted the 'bar of Shepheard's' drawl. 'I thought your lot was at Knightsbridge, sir,' he said.

The captain grimaced. 'Knightsbridge, alas, is no more. Jerry overran us yesterday. One hell of a scrap – never seen anything like it: men screaming, burning guns, wrecked lorries, tanks everywhere.'

Caine's heart sank. He knew that Knightsbridge was the last defensive box on the Gazala Line, and that its fall meant that the Eighth Army's rearguard action had failed. 'So Rommel will be going for Tobruk,' he said, shaking his head.

'Yes, one has to say the Desert Fox has done us up. All our brass-hats have demonstrated is that they're a bunch of incompetents.' He chortled. 'There's a rumour going round that Mr Hitler telephoned Mr Churchill the other day and offered to remove Rommel from his command. His only condition, he said, was that Churchill left all *his* generals in place.'

Caine tittered politely, but was secretly surprised to hear this mutinous sentiment expressed by an officer of the socially elite Guards Brigade.

'And you are . . . ?' the captain enquired, glancing at Caine's black tank-beret, searching in vain for a cap-badge.

'Covering the withdrawal,' Caine said, meeting the officer's eyes unflinchingly.

A shadow passed across Broderick's clean-shaven face. 'I see. Look here, you wouldn't have a medical orderly with you, would you? Only we have a chappie with a rather bad wound in the chest, and no one to do the works. Wouldn't trouble you, of course, but he's in a bad way.'

Caine weighed it up. He didn't want to waste time doing other people's jobs for them, but he couldn't refuse to save a dying man.

'How'd that happen, sir?' Wallace demanded gruffly.

The officer favoured the giant with a friendly smile. 'Oh, bit of a shoot-out with Jerry. Almost nabbed us, you know.'

Wallace pointed west with his massive, shrapnel-scarred, sphinx-tattooed arm. 'Yeah, but Knightsbridge is in that direction, and you're coming from the other.'

Broderick screwed up his face in an expression of mock imbecility. 'Oh Christ,' he said. 'Don't tell me we're lost?'

Caine and Wallace exchanged a brief glance, and Caine was almost certain he heard the big man whisper 'Wooden-tops' under his breath.

The captain didn't seem to have heard it. 'About that orderly?' he said.

'Very good, sir,' Caine said. 'You can bring your man into the shade over there, and my orderly will have a look at him, but we can't take him with us. We're heading for the front. And sir, ask the rest of your men to stay in their wagons – only the stretcher party, please.'

'I understand perfectly,' Broderick cooed. Caine sent Wallace to fetch Maurice Pickney, while the captain bawled orders as shrill as parade-ground commands. A moment later four men dismounted from the back of the leading lorry, easing out a stretcher carrying what looked like a bundle of blood-smeared white rags. Taking a handle each they shuffled towards the little group, walking in step like a solemn funeral procession. The soldiers were tall and almost uniformly fair-haired, dressed like the captain in well-pressed khakis, and carrying Lee-Enfields slung from their shoulders. Even after they had laid the stretcher under the nearest awning, they remained po-faced and silent, accepting the cigarettes Wallace doled out but resisting his attempts to make conversation.

While Broderick looked on, Caine and Pickney examined the wounded man. He was putty-faced, gasping for breath. Lifting his crudely applied dressings, Pickney saw bubbles of blood oozing from a gaping puncture in the chest. He shook his head. 'It's a sucking pneumothorax,' he said. 'He needs surgery. All I can do is seal up the wound and leave a valve so that air can escape, but it'll only be a stop-gap. You'll have to get him to an aid-post right away.'

Pickney delved into his medical chest and produced a gauze pad and a bottle of petroleum jelly. He smeared jelly on the pad and crouched down next to the patient, who looked only half conscious. 'Come on,' the orderly said. 'I just need you to take a deep breath and let it out slowly. You'll be all right, mate.'

At the word 'mate' the soldier's eyes opened wide. He took in the scene with a terrified expression. Focusing abruptly on the gauze pad in Pickney's hand as though it were poison, he swiped it away with a croaking yell. 'Jerries!' he roared. 'They're bloody Jerries!'

For a split second the little group stood frozen. Caine, unsure whether the soldier was delirious, took a step back, and in that moment saw Broderick's eyes flickering right and left. The captain's hand made a move towards his rifle, and in a flash, Caine brought his Thompson to bear on him. Broderick seized the barrel and tried to wrestle it from him. Caine stepped forward, squeezed iron. The weapon spat, working-parts thumped forward, gas belched from the muzzle with an ear-spattering crack. A .45-calibre round punched into the left cheek of the captain's arse. 'Broderick' let out a roar, cursed in German, jumped sky-high as if bitten by a snake.

Caine never saw how he landed. At that moment there was a kettle-drum bump of ordnance that seemed to shake the very ground they were standing on. Like everyone else, Caine fell flat on his face. There was a second boom, followed by a ruckle of Bren-gun fire. Caine was seized by a fit of coughing and clicked that the area was shrouded in billowing white smoke, under whose cover the stretcher party was scrambling to its feet. Caine saw Wallace shift his huge frame, going for his twelve-bore sawn-off. Before he could draw it, one of the stretcher-bearers dealt him a crunching blow over the head with a rifle butt. In an instant the strangers had scooped up their screaming captain and were making off towards their vehicles. Caine raised his Thompson to fire after them, then let it fall.

The Bren-gun rattle came again, followed by the clatter of Tommy-gun and .303 fire from the men under the scrim nets. 'Stop shooting!' Caine yelled.

An instant later came the gear-grating sound of the enemy 3-tonners moving off rapidly. From his left, Caine heard the hum of the Daimler's turret engaging, realized that Flash Murray was about to put a two-pound shell up the bum of the escaping wagons. 'Don't fire,' he shouted.

A moment later the smoke cleared, and it came to Caine

that Murray must have lobbed a couple of smoke grenades from his tubes at the first sign of trouble. It had been the only thing the RAC lance sergeant could do, because if he'd let rip with a high explosive round it might have dobbed them all. He sensed Wallace at his elbow. The big man was staggering, a great knobby hand in his tangled mop of hair, covering a head wound that was dribbling blood. 'You all right, mate?' asked Caine.

'It's nothing – only a scratch.'

'Some scratch,' Caine said. He shook a cigarette out of a crushed packet, stuck it in Wallace's mouth and lit it for him with his Zippo lighter. Wallace took a long drag and removed it with his left hand. 'Why did you let them get away, skipper?' he demanded. 'We could have had them.'

Caine's polished granite eyes remained steady. 'We could,' he said, 'but it would have delayed us. It would only have been a pain in the arse, Fred.'

Wallace gurgled with laughter, despite his wound. 'Nothing to the pain in the arse that bloke's going to have tomorrow morning. See how he jumped? Could of made the Olympics.'

Caine chuckled, then a thought struck him. 'You realize they risked their lives to save one of our own men?' he said. 'Would we have had the guts to do it? We'd have let the blighter peg out.'

'They might as well have done,' Wallace said, pointing with his cigarette to the patient on the stretcher. Pickney, leaning over him, glanced up desolately. 'Didn't make it,' he said. 'Asphyxiated – that last effort was too much for him.'

Wallace swore under his breath. 'I *knew* there was sommat wrong with that joker,' he growled. 'Knightsbridge, my hairy arse.'

Pickney stood up and faced him, tugging his blood-smeared hand away from his head wound. 'Better let me have a look at that,' he said.

While Wallace was graciously allowing the orderly to doctor him, Copeland came raking over with his sweeping strides, blue eyes glittering like ice cubes, his sniper rifle held at the ready position. 'That's us blown,' he said calmly. 'They'll have alerted the nearest Luftwaffe squadron by now. We can expect visitors any minute.'

Caine detected a hint of reproach in his tone.

'I didn't see any wireless aerials on those wagons,' he said. 'They were all captured lorries.'

'We can't be sure they didn't have a set. In any case, they'll inform the first Axis unit they come across and they'll be after us quicker than axle grease.'

Caine shaded his eyes and swept the horizon. 'We'll change direction,' he said, pointing south-west. 'See that dune chain over there? We'll head for that then wheel round back on to our course. They won't be expecting us to go that way, and it might at least buy us some time. Come on, let's get saddled up. Maurice – take two men and bury that poor sod. Cope – make sure everything is stowed. Let's move it.'

12

The going was classed on the map as 'soft' – an undulating plain of sand like a padded flesh-coloured quilt, as far as the barrier of the dunes. This was the most difficult surface to drive on, apart from a full-blown sand-sea, because it was booby-trapped with *mish-mish* 'stickies' – pools of dry quicksand that could virtually swallow an armoured car in a single gulp. Copeland was at the wheel again, and Wallace had insisted on retaining his place as spotter, despite his knock on the head. Caine tried to persuade him to take some rest in the back of one of the trucks, but he shrugged it off, declaring that with the risk of air attack, they needed his 'Mark 1 commando eyeball.'

Cope drove at a steady thirty miles an hour, to the soothing rasp of the tyres, while he and Caine mulled over their encounter with the bogus Guardsmen.

'Funny,' Copeland said, 'I was talking to some blokes from 50 Div. last night, and they warned me the Boche were up to tricks like that. They said they were using captured wagons, just attaching themselves to our convoys, cool as cucumbers, and as soon as there's a stop – bang, they nab the nearest vehicle.'

'It's a rum old war,' Caine said, shaking his head. 'More like piracy on the high seas. Another minute and they'd have nabbed *us*. Lucky that chap came round and saved our hides.'

'That "officer" spoke damn' good English, though. Very la-di-da. Must have been at British public school.'

'Had me fooled,' Caine said, chortling. 'When he got nailed in the arse and shot up yelling *Gott im Himmel* or whatever it was . . . well, that's a story I'm going to tell my grandchildren.'

'Hold your horses, skipper,' Cope chuckled. 'You haven't got any *children* yet . . .'

'*Sticks!*' Wallace belted out suddenly from the observation hatch. Cope eased the White to a halt, aware that hard braking would dig the wheels into the sand. They hopped out to find *Gracie*, with Todd Sweeney at the wheel, buried up to her rear axles in mish-mish. Sweeney had the lorry in first gear and was revving the engine hard, but her two pairs of back wheels were spinning. The harder he revved, the deeper she was digging herself into the sand. 'Stop revving, Corporal Sweeney,' Caine shouted. 'Your back wheels haven't got traction. If she goes any deeper, we'll have to unload her.'

Sweeney scowled at Caine through the windscreen, but desisted, letting the engine idle. Caine turned and walked directly in front of the lorry for about ten yards, testing the sand with his feet – these pools rarely extended more than a dozen paces. He'd been told that mish-mish lay in places where there were minute air-pockets between the sand-grains, causing them to collapse like a house of cards under pressure. He marched to the back of the lorry and tested the sand in the opposite direction. 'You've got solid ground about seven yards behind you,' he told Sweeney, 'so you'll need to put her in reverse.'

Sweeney stuck his bullet head out of the window. 'That'll be really easy,' he snapped, 'with the bloody bowser yoked.'

Caine gave Sweeney a hard look, then told his co-driver, Gunner Dick Hanley – a bulldog-faced, rugby-playing old mate of Wallace's from the Royal Horse Artillery, to unyoke the bowser. He ordered the rest of the truck's crew – Pickney, the Corsican, Cavazzi, and an ex-private of the Inns of Court Regiment named Mick Oldfield – to pull out the sand channels. As they were sliding out the five-foot steel ramps, the other crews gathered round. Caine appreciated their team spirit, but realized it left the column wide open. 'I want all drivers and spotters back to their wagons,' he said. 'You're our eyes and ears, so stay alert. Everybody else, help to push the bowser out of the way, then grab a shovel or help with the sand channels. This will be SOP every time we get a *stick*.'

The men were soon at work with shovels and bare hands in the scorching sand, digging out deep grooves behind the truck's wheels, deep enough to feed the sand channels under them. It was hard graft in the blazing sun and they were quickly panting and sweating – the sand was so hot that it scorched their hands and knees. Caine paused from his shovelling and wiped the sweat off his forehead with his silk Tank Regiment scarf. 'All right, lads,' he said. 'That's deep enough.' He supervised the placing of the sand channels, then had another pair brought from one of the 3-tonners. 'Any dab-hands at channel-throwing?' he asked.

Co-driver Dick Hanley, who'd once played prop-forward for the army, put up a ham-like mitt. 'Yep, I'll have a bash, skipper.'

'We need two – anyone else?'

Private Martin Rigby, a small red-bearded Cornishman from the Duke of Cornwall's Light Infantry, volunteered. When Caine asked him jokingly for his qualifications, Rigby said he played bowls for his village. The steel ramps were so hot the two 'throwers' had to put on gloves to carry them to the rear of the truck, where they got ready to hurl them in place when she reached them. Once moving, it was crucial to keep the wagon's momentum, so the channel had to be thrown with precision and timing. There was only one chance, and it needed a good eye and a steady hand.

Caine gave Sweeney the order to start up, and the lorry roared into life. 'Just take it steady,' he told the driver. 'Don't hit the gas too hard.'

Sweeney scowled again, and lamped her into gear. The truck lurched backwards, her rear wheels bracing the sand channels. The steel sank several inches, but the wheels got traction, the engine screamed and the men cheered as she belted in reverse along the channels. Caine watched Hanley and Rigby slap the second lot of channels in place with perfect accuracy. The spectators hollered as if they'd just watched a goal scored by their favourite football team. Caine gave the two throwers a broad grin and the thumbs-up. 'Well done, lads!' he shouted. 'Now we're going to have to winch the bowser out.'

When they were ready for the off again, Caine looked at his watch and realized that the 'unsticking' had taken almost an hour. Even though it had been complicated by the water-bowser, this was too long, but he knew it would get quicker and smoother with practice. The two channel-throwers were worth their weight in gold, but he had his doubts about Sweeney as a driver. Ground-feel was essential to a good driver up the Blue, and Sweeney was too hasty and aggressive: he just didn't have it.

Caine was about to give the signal to move out when Cope said. 'Where's Wallace?'

Caine's heart missed a beat as he realized that they'd almost left without him. He jumped out and scanned the area around the convoy. 'There he is,' Copeland yelled suddenly, pointing ahead through the windscreen. The giant was lumbering slowly towards the convoy from the direction of some low sand-hills, his Bren-gun slung underarm. He appeared to be carrying something, and his wide, granite-carved features puckered with a smile. Caine jogged out to meet him. 'You all right, Fred?' he asked.

Wallace lifted up the small bundle in his arms, and Caine saw to his astonishment that it was a baby gazelle – a fragile, elegant creature of brown and white, with enormous eyes, a slender head and long spindly legs. 'Abandoned by the mother,' Wallace rumbled. 'We must have frightened her off. It ain't more'n a week old.'

Caine raised his eyebrows. 'What are you going to do with it?' he asked.

'I'm taking it with me, of course,' Wallace said. 'Can't leave it here – poor thing'll die.'

Copeland's face dropped when he saw what Wallace had brought. 'You're not bringing that stinking animal in here,' he bawled.

Wallace's dark eyes narrowed. 'There's one stinking animal in here already,' he said.

Cope looked to Caine for support, but the sergeant shrugged his broad shoulders. He knew from the incident of the dog shot by the RSM that Wallace was attached to animals, and hadn't the heart to tell him to ditch it. Instead, he allowed the gazelle to take up residence in an empty petrol crate in the back of the White, until its fate could be decided.

Cope gave a short blast on his horn: the convoy breezed off. Caine turned his attention back to the going and the shadow on the sun-compass, directing Copeland to the left of the dune field that was now looming up close – a wall of interlocking cut-glass facets with knife-blade crests hundreds of feet high. Caine knew there was no chance of getting through it at this point, but he was confident that they would be able to go round – there were no major sand-seas marked on the map in this area. Sure enough – and to Caine's relief – a plain of wind-graded gravel opened up on the southern side, allowing Cope to accelerate to forty – the column's maximum speed. They trolled on silently for an hour, the wagons playing around each other jubilantly in loose air formation. Caine told Copeland to stop for a compass adjustment. The White was just about to slew to a halt, when Wallace roared, '*Aircraft. Three bombers at twelve o'clock. We got about two minutes – maybe three.*'

Caine's blood ran cold. He squinted through the windscreen, making out three planes raking over the horizon, sinister dark insects against the flawless azure screen of the sky. This was the direct consequence of his decision to let the enemy go, he thought. As Cope had predicted, 'Broderick' had contacted the nearest Axis air-unit in double-quick time. His diversion hadn't put them off the scent.

Caine drew a long breath, and in the instant it took to expel it, made a sober assessment. At the briefing the previous night they had discussed four alternative actions on air attack: run for cover, halt, open fire or scatter. There was no cover nearer than the dunes, so that was out. Stationary wagons were hard for fast-balling pilots to clock from the air, but he guessed they'd already been seen. The utility of shooting it out depended on the bombers' altitude, and he reckoned these were out of range of his Lewis guns. 'We'll scatter,' he told Copeland. 'When you see the strike pattern, turn sharp out of its path.'

Cope gulped grimly, his large Adam's apple working. He hooted five times – the agreed dispersal signal – then flipped off his cap-comforter, ran a nervous hand through his thatch of blond hair and reached for his tin hat. He tilted it on and hunched forward over the wheel, his eyes like gas-blue jets in the starched face. Caine knew that this manoeuvre required stone-cold nerve from the driver: he also knew Cope would deliver. He ramped on his own tin lid and stuck his head and shoulders through the hatch. Wallace had removed the dust quilts on the twin Vickers and was traversing them, his eyes like ink spots, glaring at the raiders over the sights.

'Hold your fire,' Caine said. He eased himself into position near by, then swivelled round and made hand signals to the spotters poised on top of the other vehicles. The action was interrupted by the ear-crushing drone of aero-engines. Caine half turned to take in the great silver mosquitoes careening towards them – it was a moment of complete and terrifying powerlessness. He didn't see the bombs, but he heard the whine as they fell, scatter-gunning along the desert surface directly in front of the wagon. Sand and stones heaved up with a noise like ripping steel, burst in fountains of foul smoke and debris. The earth vibrated: the air quivered. Hot pressure seared Caine's lungs.

He watched the strike pattern approaching with almost detached interest. Just as the crisis point arrived, Copeland swerved out of the bombs' path, so sharply that Caine and Wallace had to grip the hatch covers to stay upright. As the White bumped and shuddered, Caine took a quick dekko over his shoulder to make sure the spotters on the other wagons had understood his signals. He was satisfied to see that all but *Gracie* had dispersed to the four winds, each vehicle taking a separate course. None of them had taken a hit. There was a startled yell from Wallace. '*Blenheims!*' he bawled. 'They're *ours*.'

For an instant Caine didn't believe it. He watched the dark bombers fade into the distance, bank with the grace of seagulls on a thermal, dump altitude, brace for another approach. With a sinking feeling, he recognized the profile of RAF Blenheim light bombers. 'They're out of bombs,' he hissed. 'They're dipping into a strafing run.'

Caine knew that, while bomb strikes were always inaccurate, strafing was likely to be far more deadly. He ducked back into the cabin. '*Stop*,' he ordered Copeland. The driver stomped the brake-pedal, and the White jerked to a halt, sending Caine sprawling over the seat. 'It's the RAF,' he told Cope, picking himself up. 'Fred, get down here. Get those recognition panels out. *Now*.'

He shoved open the side door and half tumbled out on to the sand. He waved at the nearest wagon – *Gracie* – clocking the drawn face of Sweeney as he pulled up. The other vehicles were still speeding away in every direction.

'They're *ours*,' Caine bawled to Sweeney. 'Someone help us with the recognition panels, fast.'

Heart bumping, he watched the Blenheims completing their turn. Wallace clattered out of the White with a Bren-gun slung backwards from his shoulder, grasping a bundle of recognition panels in one hand and a Very pistol in the other. He thrust the pistol at Caine, and together they jogged clear of the convoy, the panels flapping like flags behind them. An instant later they were joined by Sweeney's co-driver, rugby-player Dick Hanley. Caine spun round to see the planes swooping down on them like giant bats: 20mm cannons ratcheted, shells kicked up spurts of sand, stitched ladders of dirt and rock fragments across the desert floor. He heard the whine of shrapnel spinning off stone, clocked the other four men from *Gracie* proned out around the lorry, heard ricochets as rounds fizzled and snapped over their heads. The air reeked of scorched chalk dust and smoke.

Caine reminded himself that the recognition signal was one white Very flare. He lifted the Very pistol, squeezed metal. There was a dry click: the weapon misfired. '*No.*

Christ, no!' he swore. The shadows of the bombers lifted overhead in a concerto of screeching engines and shrieking guns: Caine and Wallace dropped and rolled, ate sand and gravel. Hanley stood his ground, shaking his ham fist at the soaring aircraft. A second later his body split apart at the seams, exploded in a gush of blood and tissue, grilled skin, dismembered limbs, mushed body-parts that splattered the desert for twenty yards.

The shadows passed. Wallace leapt to his feet, his face a pallid death-mask of fury, gimlet eyes blinking at the gory mess that had been his mate. He swung the Bren-gun into his scarred arms, cocked it with a clank and lifted the stock to his shoulder, sighting up on the receding planes. 'You bastards!' he roared. 'I'll have you, you Brylcreem bastards.' Caine flung himself on the giant, grabbing the Bren's muzzle, jerking it down. 'Fred,' he said. 'Fred. They're *ours*.'

Wallace struggled, brushing him away, his eyes fixed on the swiftly vanishing bombers. '*Ours?*' he rasped, his voice strained and distant. 'Maybe you ain't been with us, Tom, but they just blew my mate to pieces. If I get hold of those Brylcreem Boys, I'll show them who's *ours*.' He tried to yank the Bren away but Caine held on tight. 'It was a *mistake*,' he gasped. 'You won't make it right by shooting them down.'

Wallace gave a last jerk, and Caine let the weapon go. 'All right,' he said. 'They're out of range. Go on – waste ammo.'

Wallace stared at the Bren in his hands, glanced at Caine, flashed a glare of pure hatred after the aircraft, then let the weapon drop. A moment later he doubled over and vomited furiously into the sand.

Within minutes the convoy had regrouped. The troops poured out of their vehicles and rushed over to see what had happened. Cavazzi and Oldfield from *Gracie* had been grazed by shrapnel, but apart from Hanley there were no major casualties.

They buried all they could find of the ex-Gunner's remains where he had fallen and built a cairn of stones over the grave. Caine noted its latitude and longitude so that the body could be retrieved later. As he turned away, he felt the boys' eyes on him, some of them smouldering with resentment, as if he himself had been responsible for Hanley's death. He wondered if that could be true. If he had recognized the aircraft as 'friendlies' earlier, would it have made a difference? Would it have mattered if the Very pistol had worked? He doubted it – it had all happened too fast.

He stopped in front of them and passed round a tin of Player's Navy Cut cigarettes. 'It's hard,' he said, feeling a lump growing in his throat, 'but you can't blame the RAF. We're going in the 'wrong' direction, and we don't have ground-to-air recognition markings: if we had, the enemy would be down on us like a ton of bricks. The RAF can't know the positions of every friendly patrol, and in any case, our mission is secret. It's one of the risks we have to take.'

Several of the vehicles had shell-holes punched through their bodywork, and tyres and fuel tanks had been punctured. One of *Gracie's* coil-springs had been damaged, but otherwise there seemed to be no serious mechanical problems. The lads set to work changing wheels, repairing punctures and treating fuel tanks with soap – a temporary measure that would do until a longer stop. There were no spare coil-springs, so Caine instructed the crew of the damaged lorry to jack her up on the 'high-lift', and collected an inner tube and some wire. Caine called Wingnut Turner to help. 'What are you going to do, skipper?' Turner asked.

'It's a trick I learned with my Sapper squadron. An inflated inner tube will pass muster for a coil spring until we can do a proper job.'

The two of them crouched under the truck, and while Caine held the tube between the axle and the chassis, making sure it was clear of the exhaust system and the driveshaft, Turner wired it firmly into place. Caine called for the air pump to be attached to the lorry's engine. He clipped the air line to the tube's nozzle and shouted to Sweeney to start up. 'Give it forty pounds,' he told Turner.

When the boys let the jack down minutes later, the truck seemed as stable on her springs as if they were all factory-new. 'That will last for hundreds of miles,' Caine told the fitter, glancing in Sweeney's direction. 'As long as the lorry's driven carefully, that is.' Turner grinned and gave him two thumbs-up. They were startled by the sound of hands clapping, and turned to find that almost the whole unit had gathered to watch. From the men's admiring looks, Caine guessed that they no longer held him responsible for Hanley's death.

13

Johann Eisner, aka Hussain Idriss, was sitting at the bar of Madame Badia's nightclub with a whisky and soda in one hand and a cigarette in the other. Tonight he was neither Hussain nor Eisner but Captain Sandy Peterson, an officer of the General List. No one would have recognized him as the taxi-driver who had shadowed Maddaleine Rose only two days earlier. He wore immaculate khaki drills, his hair was dyed blond and cropped military-style and he sported a trim moustache of fine horsehair attached with gum to his upper lip.

The club was dimly lit by lamps held within potplants, and the air was fuggy with tobacco smoke. Eisner sipped his drink slowly and stared at the half-dozen young women on the stage, clad in diaphanous pseudo-Arabian Nights costumes, swaying sensuously to the swirling percussion of an Egyptian band. The club was by no means packed – a few couples, the usual smattering of wealthy Greeks and Turks with their entourages, knots of prim staff-officers in uniform and others on leave from the Western Desert. Club hostesses gathered expectantly at their tables like exotic birds around a water-hole.

Eisner finished his whisky and set the glass down on the bar, nodding to the barman for a refill. 'Don't drown it this time,' he said. The barman, a mild-faced Armenian in a spotless white shirt and black bow-tie, sported a genuine handle-bar moustache that shamed Eisner's false one. He held up a bottle of Dewar's White Label. Eisner nodded again, and watched him as he poured out a measure, then added a squirt of soda from a siphon. 'Nice set of girls you've got here tonight,' Eisner said.

The Armenian pushed the glass towards him and winked. 'If there is one you fancy, I can introduce you, sir.'

Eisner winked back. 'The night is yet young, my friend – what's your name?'

'My name is Joseph, sir.'

Eisner took a deep breath. 'I wonder if you could possibly help me, Joseph,' he said. He slipped out of his wallet a two-by-three-inch copy of the photo he'd taken of the blond Wren officer in the GHQ staff car. He had trimmed the shot carefully so that the Wren's hat and scarf had vanished and only the face remained. 'I'm looking for this girl,' he said. 'Her name is Betty, and I think she may have worked here.'

The young man held the shot close to the bar-light, and Eisner looked on, trying not to betray his anxiety. He'd been obsessed with the idea that he knew this girl from the moment he'd glimpsed her at Maadi, but it was only after he'd developed the shot in his darkroom that he'd been forced to admit what part of him had been trying to deny: her name was Betty, and she was a cabaret girl at Madame Badia's. He had never spoken to her and didn't even know her full name, but he did know that she'd witnessed an unpleasant event that had occurred here one night, twelve months ago. The only other living witness to that event was himself.

This was his first visit to the club since that night, and he had returned with some trepidation. In fact, for the past two days he'd been fighting a desperate rear-guard action with himself. His instinct for self-preservation told him that returning to the scene would be suicidal, yet he'd been egged on by the same ruthless force of curiosity that had made him a spy in the first place. Betty's transformation from cabaret girl to Wren officer was intriguing enough, but the fact that she'd been assigned a mission worthy of a suicide pill was a mystery he was powerless to resist. The club was his only lead.

He knew deep down, though, that it wasn't these facts that had tipped the balance: what had ultimately brought him here was the terrifying discovery that she was the woman he had locked eyes with that night. It was terrifying because it seemed that, despite his lifelong denial, there was some unseen power that was inexorably forcing him to confront his own fate.

In the end, he'd deployed the rational thinking that had always been his saving grace. One of the first lessons he'd learned in security work was the difference between threat and risk: a threat was constant; a risk could be modified. He had modified the risk by assuming the identity of a British officer – a guise he hadn't used since his early days in Cairo. He had retrieved his khaki drill uniform and his service cap with the nondescript badge of the General List. The General List touch was ingenious, he told himself, because it didn't tie him down to any particular unit, and the fact that many GL officers had grown up abroad would explain any slight 'strangeness' in his accent or behaviour. If asked, he was one of dozens of Egyptian-born Englishmen whose fathers worked in the cotton trade.

The club was in Zamalek, a former private house in its own grounds with a terrace overlooking the Nile. As he strutted in through the open door with an air of propriety he didn't feel, the giant tuxedo-clad doorman had asked him to deposit his Smith & Wesson at the reception. Eisner had handed it over with every sign of resentment, though the truth was that he'd never expected to be allowed to take it into the club. He'd worn it only to distract attention from the viciously sharp stiletto strapped to his leg.

Once through the inner door, his confidence had returned. No one had given him a second glance – and why should they? After that night the police had been looking for a well-dressed, clean-shaven Egyptian wearing a tarboosh and dark glasses. There was no reason to identify that man with a respectable, fair-haired British officer on a night out.

The barman was shaking his head. 'I'm sorry, sir, but this is not a good shot – a little out of focus. As far as I can say, I've never seen this girl. I'm sure she doesn't work here, but she may have done in the past. I wouldn't know – I've only been here a few weeks. The name Betty does ring a bell, but you'd have to ask someone who's been here longer.'

'I see. And who might that be?'

Joseph pointed to one of the scantily dressed girls in the floor show – a lithe, fair-skinned beauty with glistening black hair. 'Her name is Sim-Sim,' the barman said. 'She's been working here the longest of all the girls. When the performance is over, I'll call her.'

Eisner nodded and sat back with his drink to enjoy the rest of the show.

Ensconced with Sim-Sim at a table minutes later, though, he began for the first time to feel uneasy. Close up, she proved even more of a jewel than she'd appeared on the floor: her pale face, made slightly sultry by the frame of rich tresses, possessed what he thought of as an aristocratic cast. He regretted the fact that she'd covered her sleek figure with a black cloak. From a distance he'd guessed she was an Egyptian Copt, but she turned out to be a Lebanese Christian from Beirut, and spoke both English and French.

Sim-Sim smiled at the champagne he bought her and at

his compliments on her dancing. All was going well until he produced the photo of Betty. Then her black eyes seared him. 'Why are you looking for Betty?' she demanded.

'So she did work here, then?'

'Yes, she did work here, but not any more. Why do you want her?'

Eisner related his cover story: they'd met at an Embassy party a year ago and had fallen for each other. They'd spent the night together, and in the morning she'd vanished, leaving only this photo behind. 'Like Cinderella's glass slipper,' he chuckled. He'd never forgotten her, and now, after a stint of active service, he was trying desperately to get her back.

He was a good actor, and the story was eased down by a couple of glasses of champagne. By the time he'd finished, he hoped that she'd be less hostile. She wasn't. 'You must be a very special man,' Sim-Sim said drily, 'because when she worked here, Betty was the only cabaret girl who didn't date clients. She was popular, but she never went with anyone.'

Eisner sighed. 'I'm not special, just lucky,' he said. 'That's why I've got to find her.'

Sim-Sim drew the cloak around her more tightly. 'I'm sorry,' she said, 'but I can't tell you anything about Betty.'

'Why not? Where's the harm? I only mean her well.'

She swept back her silky hair and put down her champagne glass, leaning forward and fixing him with a black stare. 'Betty witnessed a terrible crime here,' she said. 'Perhaps you read about it in the newspapers?'

'I don't think so.'

'The middle-aged wife of a very high-up British diplomat was raped and murdered in the ladies' room. Her murderer was an Egyptian who'd been her lover, to whom she'd betrayed her husband's secrets. He was selling them to the Germans. When she discovered that he was having an affair with another woman at the same time, she denounced him publicly, right here in the club. He followed her into the ladies' room, raped her in an obscene way and cut her throat. Betty came in while it was happening – she was the only witness. The man might have killed her, too, but he heard the doorman coming and jumped out of the window. The police investigated it, of course – British Intelligence, too. They asked Betty a lot of questions, but up to now, no one has ever discovered the murderer's identity. He wasn't a regular at the club – no one had ever seen him here before.'

'That's a horrible story,' Eisner said. 'It must have been terrible for Betty. Excuse me, though – what has it got to do with me?'

The girl sat back, looking down at her hands. 'Nothing,' she said. 'You are a nice, respectable British officer, but there's at least one person out there who has good reason to want Betty dead. That's why I can't tell anyone about her.'

Eisner shifted in his seat, weighing possibilities. He noticed that Joseph, the barman, was watching him from the shadows, and he could see the immense mass of the doorman through the connecting door. He pushed his chair back, sighing again. 'I understand,' he said. 'You've been a loyal friend to Betty. I'm sorry to have bothered you.'

He got to his feet. He was just about to leave when Sim-Sim said, 'Tell me, Captain, have you ever been in the club before?'

He whipped round and met the deep black pools of her eyes. 'No,' he said. 'This is my first time. Why?'

She shrugged. 'Oh, it's just that there's something familiar about you, that's all.'

He bowed slightly, and forcing himself to walk with dignity, made for the door.

From behind the bar, Joseph saw him go. When he was out of sight, he picked up the telephone and dialled. 'Is that Major Stocker?' he asked quietly a moment later. 'It's Corporal Tankien here. You asked to be kept informed if anyone came in asking about *Runefish*? Well, someone just has . . .'

Beyond the partition, Eisner was strapping on his Smith & Wesson by the reception desk. A little to one side, there was a dark tunnel that he knew led to the ladies' room. He glanced in that direction, asking himself why its proximity should make him feel nervous. After all, whatever horrific crime had been committed there twelve months ago, it had nothing to do with him.

14

On the third morning out of Jaghbub, Caine's commando hit the Targ al-'Abd, the ancient slave route that cut across the bulge of Cyrenaica. This, Caine knew, was the frontier of the Axis heartland, and it marked the start of the advance-to-target phase of the op. This was the area where Maddaleine Rose's plane had gone down.

Caine's crews had been driving all night on Benzedrine, partly because Caine wanted to broach the track in daylight, but mainly because of a stroke of bad luck they'd run into just after last light. Clearing a ridge at full speed, they'd hit an enemy leaguer – an Afrika Korps 88mm anti-tank battery, with about ten trucks and half a dozen guns. The German gunners had evidently just bedded down, but the camp was directly in front of Caine's column, only a few hundred yards away, and there was no chance of avoiding it. His mind racing full throttle, Caine ordered Cope to give three long and two short honks on the horn, the signal to form into line abreast and assume action stations. There had been no time to stop and discuss it. Copeland slammed closed the forward and side hatches. Caine grabbed his Tommy-gun from the seat bracket and lodged himself in the observation hatch next to Wallace, who was already hunched over the Vickers. The wagons were ranged into a rough-dog's leg, and Caine saw Flash Murray, at the hatch of the Daimler, manoeuvre the AFV forward. 'Charge!' Caine yelled, but the order was drowned by the crump of a two-pound shell from the Daimler's gun. A gush of yellow lightning torched the half-light: a Jerry truck whamped up in flame.

Caine's wagons were reeling down on the leaguer at forty miles an hour. The machine-gunners opened up almost at the same moment: their guns line-squalled, doled out blinding sabre slashes of crimson fire, wove a deadly web of orange tracer that dusted the desert surface, sliced into Axis vehicles. Two more enemy trucks went up in sears of red and black. Next to him the Vickers 'K's shuddered and clunked, dead cases plinked into gunny-sacks: Wallace pumped through mags at light-speed, whomping drumfire.

In seconds they were into the leaguer, into a bedlam of enemy shrieks and howls, into a muzz of flaming wagons and toxic gas, crashed into madly turkey-trotting men, pulped bodies under wheels. Caine squeezed iron, tippled streams of .45 calibre left and right at anything that moved. Tracer flew, Jerry small-arms stuttered, rounds blipped across the White's bonnet, bounced at angles from her armour, whanged and fizzled into the night. Caine saw a German gun-crew working frantically to bring an 88mm gun to bear. He tack-tacked a dozen .45 calibre rounds at it, then it was lamped by a 20mm incendiary: the shell bang-flashed, swiped crew and gun to shreds with a blinding light, a heart-stopping swish of flame. Then, suddenly, they were through the leaguer, zooming into darkness and open desert. The guns went silent one by one, the clamour eased to the tap and rattle of fire from the German survivors. One mile clocked up, then two, then five, until the German column was a chain of bright bonfires along the skyline behind them. Caine told Copeland to give the general halt signal. Slowly his nerves let go as the adrenalin tension evaporated. As they rolled out of the wagon, arms round each other's shoulders, he and Copeland collapsed in fits of hysterical laughter.

There had been no serious damage to the wagons, and no casualties. For a few minutes the commandos couldn't believe that they'd got through. The only one who didn't share the general hilarity was Fred Wallace, who stood watching the others with a mournful face. When Caine asked him what was wrong, the giant showed him the carcase of the baby gazelle he'd found earlier. Her neck had been broken by the jolting of the armoured car during the contact.

They had pressed on all night, hoping to put as much distance as possible between themselves and the enemy. Once his glee at being alive had faded, Caine recognized grimly that Axis patrols would be after them at first light. They'd had no choice, but their presence was now well and truly known to the enemy.

Caine was glad not to have blundered over the old slave route in darkness, though, because it was riddled with thermos bombs, sown as a deterrent to Allied traffic. The bombs were hard to see, as they lay in the dust just below the surface, like flocks of venomous serpents. Caine joined Wallace on the hatch to get a better look at the way ahead. 'Bloody lethal, those things,' Wallace said. 'I had a mate in the mechanized infantry was on a wagon that hit a thermos bomb in this area. Ripped the wheel right off, set fire to the cab. My mate hops out to stop hisself getting fried, lands smack on another one. Blew his flippin' leg off, didn't it, poor bugger.'

Caine shuddered, making a mental note to be doubly cautious. As a Sapper he'd been trained in mine-laying and lifting, and privately considered landmines vicious and inhuman weapons. One of the most traumatic experiences he'd ever had – far worse than being bounced by Stukas – was when he'd been assigned to a mine-laying troop in Tobruk. There hadn't been enough mines to complete the perimeter, so his OC had had the idea of 'stealing' mines from the Germans. One night they'd slipped into an enemy minefield and lifted no fewer than five hundred mines before one of the troop had made a wrong move and got his leg demolished. The pressure of that patrol – the danger of a mine going off any second, as well as the ever-present menace of being spotted – was something Caine would never forget.

Caine told Cope to give the three-blast general-halt signal, and instructed Turner to take the Dingo ahead as pathfinder. A thermos bomb might blow the wheel off the scout-car, but its thick armour would at least protect the occupants. When the snub-nosed scout had covered about a mile without mishap, Caine had the rest of the wagons follow on, hugging her tracks.

Caine stood at the observation hatch, his eyes riveted to the surface. 'Keep her steady,' he told Copeland. 'No more than five miles an hour. There might be something the Dingo missed.'

They were within a hundred yards of the scout-car when he called to Copeland to stop. Taking a mine-prod out of his kit, he climbed cautiously from the cab and knelt down in the hard sand a few yards ahead. He probed into the dust, keeping the prod at an angle of 45 degrees. A moment later it came into contact with metal. 'Here's a naughty one,' he told Wallace, who was watching from the hatch. 'Thank God I spotted it.'

Clearing sand away with his hands, he uncovered not a thermos bomb but a large, flat anti-tank mine. He let out his breath slowly – these things packed a punch big enough to destroy any of the vehicles in his convoy, but at least they were relatively easy to clear. He smoothed away sand until the whole dish shape of the mine was exposed. Then, laying down his prod, he took a deep breath and lifted it with both hands out of the tiny depression, rising very slowly to his feet. Wary of straying from the blazed trail, he moved the mine only three or four paces, then laid it tenderly on the surface. He stepped back, let out a sigh of relief, wiped the sweat off his brow with his hand, and got back in the vehicle. Cope gave him thumbs-up. 'Good show, skipper,' he said.

They were heading north now, towards the Jebel Akhdar, the 'Green Mountain' massif, where the great sand waves of the Sahara broke against reefs of foothills, covered in moorland and dense acacia scrub. The convoy passed relics of former battles – huddles of trackless tanks peppered with shell-holes, AFVs charred and blackened, wrecked Bren-gun carriers, the scorched skeletons of trucks, the hulks of air-craft in loops of blistered earth. Caine avoided approaching these mementoes of death.

This pre-Saharan belt was the country of the Senussi – Bedouin descendants of the great Islamic brotherhood that had once controlled the caravan routes across the whole of Libya from their monastery at Jaghbub. Their camps and semi-permanent hamlets lay scattered through the foothills, often sited so cleverly that they remained unseen. The Senussi were hostile to their Italian colonial masters and therefore classed as friendlies by the Allies. Their hostility ensured that, unless on a punitive raid, Axis forces mostly stayed close to their garrisons.

There was plenty of cover here. Before the heat had begun to kick in, Caine halted the convoy for breakfast in a shallow wadi sheltered by rock overhangs and groves of camel-thorn. There was a gentle breeze, carrying the scent of juniper and wild thyme from the mountains. Caine sited sentries with Bren-guns on every vantage point, then sat down to eat the breakfast Wallace had whipped up – tinned sausages and tinned bacon in a stew with fresh onions, ship's biscuits and tea. As Wallace ladled stew from the dixie into their mess tins, Cope made a face. 'What do you call this?' he enquired. 'Talk about stew. Looks more like pigswill. Pity you didn't save Bambi. We could have had a couple of gazelle steaks.'

Caine saw Wallace's huge fists bunch on the ladle, and thought for a moment Cope was going to get it round the ears. 'Guess what,' he growled, making an obvious effort to restrain himself. 'It *is* pigswill. That's what I usually serve to pigs.' They were none of them in the best of humours, thanks to Benzedrine withdrawal. 'This is damned *good*,' Caine cut in hastily. 'I don't care what they say about compo-rations, this grub is better than you'd get at Shepheard's.'

Wallace held up an onion that looked no bigger than a golf-ball in his massive hand. 'This is the secret,' he said. 'Best way to stop desert sores.'

Cope snorted, but Caine nodded seriously. Desert sores were the bane of the Eighth Army, but they had nothing directly to do with the desert. They were a form of scurvy resulting from a diet lacking in vitamin C, very similar to the affliction suffered by sailors in olden times. Caine was just thinking that this was yet another parallel between the desert and the sea when Copeland said, 'Something's burning.'

'It ain't the stew,' Wallace growled.

Cope was sniffing the breeze. 'No, really,' he said. 'I smell burning.'

Caine inhaled air, taking in the distinct odour of fire-ash and smoke.

'We'd better have a look,' he said.

They finished their breakfast, then scrambled up the escarpment behind them. Lying flat on the top, Caine spotted a pall of black smoke rising perhaps three miles away. He dug out his binos and scoped the source of the fire, making out an Arab settlement – a sprawl of mud-brick buildings sited on a steadily rising convex masked by furrows, hillocks and thick acacia groves. He caught the flash of sunlight on the windscreens of trucks.

'There's a Senussi village down there,' he said. 'Looks like they've had a visit from someone unpleasant.'

They crawled off the lip of the hill, sat back among the rocks. 'I think we ought to do a recce,' Caine said. Copeland made a face. He had half guessed what was coming, and saw a whole new Pandora's box of complications being opened up. 'It's none of our business,' he said.

'It *could* be our business,' said Caine. 'This is the area where *Runefish* went down. Anyway, we ought to know the dispositions of enemy troops. One little shufti won't hurt.'

Cope read the grim determination on Caine's lips and jaw and clocked the faraway look in his stone-burned eyes. 'Famous last words,' he said.

They left the rest of the group in the wadi and went off in the White scout-car. Hugging the available shadow, Cope managed to get the wagon to within half a mile of the village before judging it too hazardous to proceed. Caine told him to stop under a low butte, and leaving Wallace with the wagon, the two of them climbed to the top.

For the second time, Caine swept the village with his field glasses. What he saw appalled him. The settlement consisted of twenty or thirty wattle houses, some of them with black tents erected in the yards. Many of them were on fire. The

German troops in the streets were in at least platoon strength, and they were rousting Arabs – men, women and children – from their dwellings, and marching them at gunpoint, with prods, kicks, and rifle butts, to the village square. It was there that most of the activity was focused. Caine lingered over the scene for a moment, swearing avidly under his breath, then handed the binos to Copeland. 'Take a look at that,' he said. 'The village square.'

Cope could hear the disgust in his voice.

He took the glasses and zeroed in on the square. 'Jesus wept,' he exclaimed. 'They've erected some kind of gallows. They're hanging the villagers one by one, they've got them herded together – oh *Jesus* . . . they're even doing the *children*.' His voice quavered. 'I can see three, no four corpses – they're hanging the dead ones up from the walls of the mosque.'

When Caine took the binos back, he saw that Copeland's face was as drained of colour as it had been when he'd ordered him to evade the bombers. They stared at each other for a moment. 'We've got to do something about this,' said Caine.

It suddenly occurred to Cope that they might be skylined, and he yanked Caine's arm, pulling him back off the top. They lay side by side in clumps of esparto grass just below the brow. 'Skipper,' Copeland said urgently, 'there's bugger all we *can* do. This isn't in our brief.'

Caine snatched off his black beret and rolled it in his palms. 'We'll have surprise on our side,' he said. 'If we go in with the AFVs, all guns thundering, they'll never know what hit them.'

Cope shoved his body backwards to get a better view of Caine. 'Let's just think about this, Tom,' he said. 'Whatever happens, we'll take casualties. Even if we stop what's going on, it will only focus the enemy's attention on us. They're already after us for hitting that gun battery. They'll know we're here. They'll hunt us down with aircraft and big battalions. Any action we take can only jeopardize our mission, you *know* that. Why did you let those bogus Guardsmen go the other day? Why did you tell Fred we couldn't attack an enemy column?'

'That was different. That would have meant lumbering ourselves with prisoners. There are civilians down there – women and children. They're powerless.'

'All right. Let's call in an air strike.'

Caine shook his head. 'It's not going to happen, Harry. We're five hundred miles behind enemy lines. Even if the RAF had the capability, they'd never get here in time. No, we're here. It's down to us.'

'Consider what's at stake,' Copeland said, his voice almost pleading. 'If we don't get to *Runefish* before the Hun, it could jeopardize tens of thousands of lives – maybe millions. It could change the whole course of the war.'

For a moment, Caine's determination seemed to waver. It was an impulse like this, he remembered, that had cost him his commission in the Royal Engineers. Then his jaw set firmly again, and he regarded Cope with his rock-steady gaze. 'I'm not giving up on *Runefish*, Harry,' he said, 'but this is happening *now*, and we can stop it. Sometimes you have to follow an intuition that's deeper than orders, not just blindly do as you're told.'

Cope snorted. 'They warned me about you, Tom. They said you think orders are a basis for discussion.'

'Yet here you are,' Caine said. 'You volunteered to come with me.'

He replaced his beret, pulling it tightly down to one side. 'Look,' he went on, 'I don't deny that I've dropped myself in the shite over stuff like this before, but in the end – if we survive – we've got to live with ourselves when it's all over. That's why we pulled out our wounded mates the other day, wasn't it? We knew we might get in deep crap, but we did it because if we'd abandoned them we couldn't have looked each other in the eye.'

Cope shook his head in exasperation. 'These aren't our mates. They're not even really our allies.'

'They're people,' said Caine gently. 'Just women and children, caught up in a war that's none of their bloody business.' He paused. 'I'm going in, Harry. I'm not ordering you to go with me, but whatever happens, I can't leave this. Not women and children, not even for *Runefish*. I'd have it on my conscience for the rest of my life.'

Cope let out a long sigh. 'All right,' he said. 'I'll do it, but on the condition you tell the lads that anyone who objects isn't obliged to go.'

Caine let a sad half-smile play out. 'No one will object,' he said. 'You know that as well as I do.'

It took only minutes to get back to the leaguer. Caine called the lads together and explained the situation in the village. He added that this was strictly a 'volunteer' job, and that no one was obliged to take part. Not a single voice was raised in objection.

In normal circumstances, Caine would have made an immediate plan and a fall-back plan. There wasn't time for this, however – he was aware that every minute they delayed meant another innocent life lost. He traced a rough map of the village in the sand. 'It's laid out like a cross,' he told them. 'There's a sort of main street that runs north–south, meeting a narrower west–east street in the square. Most of the Jerries are concentrated in the square, and we didn't spot any pickets out. These boys aren't watching their backs –

and so much the better for us. We estimate they're in about platoon strength, but we'll have surprise on our side. Our target is the square, and we'll go in hard. It's crucial that we take out at least two thirds of the enemy in the first three minutes. Don't give them a chance to counter-attack. Heavy weapons: we saw one Schmeisser MG30 mounted on a truck in the square – it'll be on our right. There are three soft-skins, no AFVs. Lance Sergeant Murray, your task is to take out the Schmeisser MG30 with 20mm rounds and destroy the lorries. Our other two wagons will engage enemy personnel with Vickers 'K's. I need the best gunners we've got . . . that will be Gunner Wallace on the Dingo, and Lance Corporal Jackson on the White. No wild shooting – if we hit any civvies it'll spoil the whole show. The rest of you will ride the AFVs. As soon as we hit the target area, you'll deploy and advance to contact. Bren-gunners take up tac positions in doorways or behind walls, others engage the enemy hand to hand if you have to. Lump the blighters with all you've got in the first three minutes. Our aim is to kill or capture *all* the enemy – don't let anyone get away.'

The barrel-chested ex-Redcap Todd Sweeney was watching Caine as if he'd have liked to find a flaw in the plan, but couldn't. 'We're going to need cut-off groups, then,' he said sourly.

'Yep, I've got that thought out. We can't spare groups, so I want one man on each side of the village. I need four good shooters who can take out escapees from a distance.' He considered it for a moment, and chose Trooper Mick Oldfield, a hatchet-faced ex-bank clerk from the Inns of Court armoured-car regiment, Lance Corporal George Padstowe, a seasoned ex-Marine, Vic Bramwell, the eighteen-year-old ex-Coldstreamer, and Private Albert Raker, a squat and powerful ex-Pioneer Corps man.

'What about *our* trucks, skipper?' enquired Robin Jackson, the ex-King's Rifle Corps machine-gun champ.

'They'll stay in leaguer here, under camouflage scrim. Lance Corporal Turner, I want you to keep with the wagons – pick three good men to stay with you.'

The skeletal RAOC fitter twisted one of his spade-sized ears unhappily. 'Aw, skipper,' he protested, 'I wanted to go in with the lads.'

'You'll see plenty of action later, Wingnut,' Caine said. 'I need you here in case there are any problems with the transport.' He didn't add, 'if I become a casualty,' but Turner knew what he meant, and resigned himself to a passive role. 'When the action's over,' Caine continued, 'I'll call you in with a red Very light. Any questions? All right, ladies, let's saddle 'em.'

As the lads climbed aboard the three AFVs minutes later, Caine was proud to note that there wasn't a hint of the bravado that to him denoted 'windiness'. These men were steady – that was the highest compliment you could give soldiers in the British Army. They had all seen combat before, and no longer nurtured illusions. 'Crows' always wanted to prove themselves in action, and that could lead to stupid recklessness. He knew what it was like from his own initiation under fire. At first there was an exciting adrenalin rush – you saw your mates get killed but somehow it didn't matter because it wasn't you, it didn't seem real. You felt that you were special, invulnerable, different, and what happened to them would never happen to you. For Caine, that sense of immunity had been ruptured the first time he'd been wounded – by shrapnel from an 88mm shell that had written off his lorry and left him with steel fragments in his shoulder and scalp. After that, the feeling of being 'special' had begun to evaporate and he'd started to understand that, if he didn't shy from battle, it wasn't because he was 'brave' but because he was terrified of letting down his mates, and of showing his fear.

Caine had realized later that this factor was the very glue of the martial spirit. An army was drawn together by the notion that its members would rather die than admit their fear. This was why, just as he'd predicted to Copeland, no one had objected to joining this hazardous side-mission: it was the reason men volunteered for dangerous missions in the first place. If Caine had learned anything in his time as a soldier, it was that heroes were ordinary men who found themselves at the right place, at the right time. If you survived it was mostly down to luck.

15

The hanging in the Senussi village of Umm 'Aijil, had been halted by the sudden appearance of the village sheikh on a balcony overlooking the square. The old man, grasping a Mannlicher rifle, had demanded the release of all the prisoners. For platoon commander Oberleutnant Ernst von Karlsruhe, of No. 2 Company, the Brandenburg Special Duties Regiment, it was an exasperating delay in a job that should have taken no more than a couple of hours. If Karlsruhe had had his way, he would have rounded up the Arabs in the square and shot them down with his Schmeisser MG30, but his battalion commander's instructions had been specific: he was to make an example of this village. His plan was to burn most of the place down, leaving some of the corpses hanging from the walls of the mosque as a grisly reminder to any other Senussi who might be ready to harbour the enemy.

This was the second delay von Karlsruhe had had to put up with. The first had occurred when a young woman had stabbed one of his men in the groin with a little knife. This had so inflamed the troops that they'd raped the girl savagely, and then raped a few others for good measure. Brandenburgers weren't known for ill discipline, but it had taken some time for him to restore order.

The Oberleutnant had found the belligerence of these civilians unexpected. They fought back. Even now, when most of them were being confined by a cordon to the opposite side of the square, under the muzzle of the Schmeisser

MG30 machine gun mounted on one of his trucks, he could hear them screeching and spitting at his men. Some were even attempting to attack the Germans with stones and bits of wood, and were being fought off with kicks and rifle butts.

The Oberleutnant, a squat, knob-like officer with a predatory pike's face and a swaggering walk, was aware that his platoon's situation wasn't tactical. Too many of his troops were concentrated in one place, and he'd put out neither sentries nor forward pickets. This nagged at his sense of professionalism, but he told himself that there wasn't much to fear from the Allies. If the reports were true, Eighth Army was now scuttling back behind the Wire with its tail between its legs. The desert skies were so thick with Axis planes that an air raid was improbable.

When the old man had first appeared on the balcony, Von Karlsruhe's reaction had been to guffaw at the Santa Claus figure with the wizened face and long white beard in his tattered Arab shirt, hooded cloak and tightly bound head-cloth. His laughter was quickly stifled, though, when the sheikh promptly shot off the face of a corporal standing right next to him. The round mashed the corporal's jaw and bulldozed into his brain, spattering the Oberleutnant with fragments of bone, grey matter and teeth. For a moment Von Karlsruhe stared incredulously at the corporal's twitching body. Then he drew out a handkerchief and began to wipe off the blood, remembering suddenly that the Mannlicher was a hunting rifle of celebrated accuracy, and that he was probably the next in its sights.

Von Karlsruhe agreed to negotiate. While he was pretending to do so, raging inwardly at the waste of time, two hefty Brandenburgers sneaked up to the balcony and overpowered the old man. The weasel-faced Feldwebel in charge of the hanging detail came over and pointed out that the sheikh's daughter was among the prisoners. He suggested that before stringing the old man up, they should first gang-rape his daughter in front of him, then hang her. It would be a fitting revenge for the corporal he'd shot. The officer recoiled in disgust. 'Are we animals?' he raged. 'There's been too much of that already. Hang her, yes, but keep it clean. Let's be done with it.'

The girl accepted her fate with remarkable dignity. As the Feldwebel drew the hood over her head, her father, pinioned by the two Germans on the balcony above, tried to look away. One of the soldiers wrenched his head back, forcing him to watch. Another private was just looping the noose around her neck, under the Feldwebel's supervision, when a .303 ball-round hit him smack in the centre of the forehead. It had been fired at a distance of five hundred yards by champion sniper Corporal Harry Copeland.

The soldier dropped without a sound. The Feldwebel turned with bulging eyes to see three enemy vehicles roiling down the street in fumes and dust, engines churning, machine guns stabbing out long spears of blood-red flame. Two twin Vickers 'K's thunked and drummed at a thousand rounds a minute, tick-ticking tracer and ball, weaving patterns across the road, skewering parked lorries, carving up the troops guarding the prisoners. The Germans reeled in shock, crashing, rolling, jiggering like puppets, flapping at gunshot wounds. Some dropped their weapons, others leap-frogged for the shelter of doorways and walls. The Senussi prisoners wormed through them and hared off down the street. The Schmeisser MG30 crew on the cab had just swivelled the gun to scythe them down when a 20mm shell shrieked and split open among them, shredding the gun to shards, whacking the crew apart in a searing flash of red, orange and black. The lorry guffed into crackling flame.

The AFVs creased to a halt. Helmeted, stubble-bearded commandos in bleached khaki shorts hopped off and scattered, fixing bayonets, whaling Mills grenades, hammering rounds as they ran. Bren-gun crews made cover, lay prone, snapped out bipods, cocked working-parts, spritzed double-taps. A dozen or more Germans went down in the first wave of fire.

Still on the armoured cars, Wallace and Jackson, their faces powder-black from the rounds they'd already fired, pivoted twin Vickers, frenetically pulling iron. They sling-shotted tracer, boosted bullets at moving targets. Flash Murray, in the Daimler's turret, welted another two-pound incendiary at the enemy trucks. The shell scraped air, stonked a cab, detonated: glass flew, steel slivers shivered, the fuel tank mushroomed up in a bubble of molten gas.

Copeland, in cover behind the Dingo's rump, clocked the two enemy on the balcony trying to heave the old man over the rail. He zeroed-in his sights, got the first of them in his cross-hairs. He held his breath, eased the trigger. He saw a scarlet blister swell just above the soldier's ear and watched him collapse, spewing blood. He sighted in on the other Jerry, cracked a second .303 slug through his chest, saw a smile frozen on his face as he piled over the rail and dropped into the street. Murray's two-pounder kettle-drummed, whomphing flame. A third shell scorched air. Another truck whiplashed fire and gas.

A knot of commandos was advancing through smoke and dust, Tommy-guns blipping, Lee-Enfields cracking. Caine found himself looking down the barrel of Von Karlsruhe's Walther P38, and felt a round whirr past. He fired his Tommy-gun, sowing the officer's broad chest with blood and lead. Von Karlsruhe felt his body go numb, felt the earth come up to meet him, saw his world go black.

A round slugged Caine's helmet, ramming him clean off his feet. A German goliath loomed over him with bayonet fixed. In slow motion, Caine saw the Corsican, Cavazzi, take the Jerry in a bearhug, one hand behind his shoulder, jerking him on to the razor-honed fanny in the other. Caine saw the knife bite hilt-deep into khaki drill, saw the point emerge from the Jerry's back, saw the two of them – the huge German and the tiny Corsican – locked in eternal embrace.

A Jerry tried to brain Cavazzi from behind with a rifle butt, but the Corsican dodged, taking the whack on his helmet and shoulder. He let go his fanny, wriggling free to find Private 'Bubbles' O'Brian, ex-Royal Ulster Rifles, dragging his assailant off him by the belt. O'Brian swung the German round, and Caine, back on his feet, punched a .45 calibre round through his head, point blank. Another Jerry came from nowhere, hitting O'Brian like a tornado, slashing his throat with a bayonet. Caine saw the wound gape like a red mouth and felt his comrade's blood drenching his shirt. He shot the German through the chest, clocked the bullet blast out of his back in a sluice of burned flesh.

Some of the enemy had taken cover behind a low wall around the mosque and were knocking loop-holes in the brick, laying down fire with Gewehr 41 semi-automatic rifles and Schmeisser sub-machine pistols. Caine, riding an adrenalin wave, saw the weasel-faced Feldwebel dragging a Senussi girl away with a bulging arm crushing her throat, and recognized her as the girl under the gibbet. He was going after them when he heard the punka-punka-punka of a Schmeisser MG30. He wheeled around, saw 'channel-thrower' Martin Rigby, ex-DCLI, gunny-sack over with a pattern of machine-gun wounds stitched at two-inch inter-vals along his thigh. Blood squirted from one of them in yard-long squidges. Caine whirled round with an 'o' of surprise on his mouth, just as Todd Sweeney, to his left, screamed, '*Armoured car.*'

Caine blinked in disbelief. He saw the German AFV wheeling through the whorls of smoke and dust, clocked the goggle-eyes of the driver through the open hatch. He registered starbursts of fire from the mounted Schmeisser MG30, the razor-slash grin of the gunner behind it. He felt its fire shave air. He fell flat, his mind ransacking itself for clues as to how they could have missed the AFV, knowing this was the critical point in the scrap, knowing the surviving Jerries would now be poised for a counter-attack.

The drumfire from the twin Vickers on the Dingo and the White faltered at the same time, and Caine thought Wallace and Jackson had both been knobbled by MG30 fire. Jackson was lying sprawled over his Vickers with a gunshot wound in the chest, but Wallace was wrestling with a jam. The giant unloaded and cleared his guns, smacking drums back in with huge hands, while Taffy Trubman stuck his double-chinned face out of the hatch to see what was up. Truman's fishy eyes fixed on a German at a window pointing a 7.92mm Gewehr 41 semi-automatic rifle at Wallace. The signaller poked his SMLE tentatively over the hatch and squeezed off a .303 round. The rifle smacked, and the Jerry at the window vanished. Wallace's mouth dropped open. He said nothing. He went on clearing the stoppage.

On the White, Copeland perched over the still-conscious Jackson. He slapped a shell-dressing on his wound and barked at him to hold it in place. Cope scanned the scene through shifting smoke. He took in commandos hitting the deck, the enemy AFV rolling towards them, the Germans behind the mosque wall prepping a reprise. He heard the thud of the Schmeisser MG30, saw its muzzle sunbursting. He shouldered his rifle, gauged the range, lined up his sights, centred the MG30 gunner in the cross-hairs. He held his breath, greased the trigger, heard the Lee-Enfield crack, saw the gunner slump. At almost the same moment the Daimler rolled forward, her turret grating as it rotated. There was an ear-splitting wallop as a tongue of fire and gas licked out. Cope saw the enemy AFV going up like a rocket, coming apart in steel slivers and black smoke. He moved Jackson out of the way and braced the twin Vickers. On the Dingo, Wallace cleared the stoppage, reloaded, boosted fire.

Caine felt the crump as the German AFV went up and saw the gunner's body spiral in smoke. He heard the resumed thump-thump of fire from the Vickers and took in the commandos skirmishing forward out of doorways, pumping Thompsons, firing Brens from the hip. Electric patterns of tracer bee-lined in, and Caine saw the enemy behind the mosque wall caught in crossfire, puppet-dancing, dropping weapons, squelching blood. Two commandos lobbed grenades that volcanoed up in V-shaped detonations of brickdust and mangled body parts. The Daimler loomed in closer, punching off an HE shell that dashed the wall into a million little pieces.

As Caine picked himself up, he heard the girl shriek. He spotted the Feldwebel lurking at an open doorway, holding a Mauser pistol to her head. Caine ran towards him, shooting deliberately wide with his Thompson to suppress the Hun's fire without hitting the girl. He felt his breech-block clump on an empty chamber. The Feldwebel fired, the slug nicking Caine's knuckles. He saw the girl's features contorted. Furious, he went into a crouch and scrabbled for a spare magazine with his wounded hand. He brought it out slick with his own blood but couldn't fix it in place. Another round whizzed off his tin lid. He dropped his Thompson, drew his Colt .45. The girl shrieked again and flopped down in a dead faint, giving Caine a clear shot. He squeezed iron, shot the Feldwebel smack through the temple.

Small-arms fire was fizzling out. The Vickers had gone silent. Murray was rotating the Daimler's turret left and right with nothing to shoot at. The village was still blazing, but the wind had changed, and in the square the smoke had begun to clear. Todd Sweeney realized that there hadn't been any return fire from behind what was left of the wall for the past two minutes. He crept up and lobbed in another No. 36 grenade. The grenade cracked off. The commandos waited. Lance Corporal Moshe Naiman, the Jewish-Palestinian interpreter, called out in German, ordering anyone left to come out with his hands up. There were no takers. 'I don't think there's anyone alive behind there,' Naiman said.

'They fought bloody hard,' Sweeney said. 'Who the heck *were* those blokes anyway?'

16

Caine holstered his .45 and helped the girl to her feet. The old man with the Father Christmas beard he'd seen on the balcony came running up and took her from him. He said something in Arabic, pointing at Caine's hand, still dripping blood. Caine had almost forgotten the wound. He nodded, then slid a field dressing from his top pocket, knelt down and tried to apply it. This was difficult with a single shaky hand, and a moment later the girl took the dressing from him. Her hands were gentle and astonishingly steady for someone who'd just dodged death more than once. She was, Caine couldn't help thinking, a European's dream of an oriental woman – the long jet-black hair, the smooth café-au-lait skin, the high-bridged nose with its hint of pride, the large round eyes, the full figure. He turned away from her, crushing these thoughts from his mind.

The old man kicked the Feldwebel's body with a sandalled foot, then, apparently satisfied that he was really dead, picked up his fallen Mauser .38 calibre and stuffed it into his belt. He retrieved Caine's Thompson and laid it reverently at his feet – an action that looked remarkably like a tribute. 'I am Sheikh Adud,' he said in fractured English. 'Sheikh of this village. This is my daughter, Layla.' The girl nodded slightly, showing tiny crow's feet around her eyes. 'Thank God you came,' the sheikh went on. 'You saved us . . . my daughter . . . thank God.' He broke off, evidently overwhelmed by emotion, and Caine looked away, embarrassed. When the field dressing was in place, he thanked Layla, picked up the

Thompson with his good hand, and stood. To the south, the houses were burning ever more fiercely: Caine could feel the heat on his face. 'You have to evacuate the village,' he said. Adud shook his head blankly. Caine shrugged and pointed to the mosque, where his men were gathering. 'Come over there,' he said.

The square was a snapshot of hell on earth, redolent with the smells of blood, cordite, charred flesh and scorched engine oil. It was littered with enemy dead, lying like beached dolphins in dark patches of their own blood, their faces ghostly blue. There were, Caine noticed, some unspeakable wounds. The Jerry armoured car was still crackling and hissing from the 20mm incendiary: over to his right, he saw the skeletons of the three German trucks melting down in smoke and flame. His own vehicles were manoeuvring into defensive positions by the mosque, and Caine was pleased to see that the Bren-groups had formed a perimeter.

There were figures trawling among the enemy dead – Senussi women in rainbow-coloured dresses. He wondered if they were looting the corpses, but a flash of steel told him otherwise. He raced over and caught hold of a tall woman with plaited hair and face tattoos who had just slit the throat of a German soldier, already badly wounded in the belly. The Jerry's jugular spurted gore. Caine grabbed the woman's wrist, tried to wrestle the dagger away from her. She resisted, cursing him roundly, her eyes wild – it was like fighting a hank of twisting cable, Caine thought. More women closed around him, screeching and yelling. He saw interpreter Moshe Naiman dashing over and let go of the woman abruptly, as if she were something poisonous. 'What's this about?' Caine asked the interpreter.

Naiman, a lightly built, energetic, olive-skinned youth of about nineteen with a hooked nose and alert eyes, talked with the woman for a moment. 'This soldier was one of those who raped her,' he told Caine.

'Tell her we don't murder wounded men,' Caine said.

When Naiman translated this, the women shrieked back at him like a flock of disturbed crows. 'They say these men dishonoured them,' Naiman said. 'They claim the right of revenge – unless we're taking them with us, in which case the wounded are under our protection.'

He watched Caine with a puzzled half-grin on his face. Both he and Caine knew that they couldn't take the wounded Germans, but killing them was a war crime that might one day come back to haunt them. 'Just tell them to stop,' Caine said, turning away. 'Anyone found killing a wounded man will be shot.' He knew at once that it was a punishment he'd never be prepared to carry out.

Caine found Todd Sweeney coming towards him, gesturing impatiently at the burning AFV. 'Where the heck did it spring from?' he demanded. 'You said there weren't any armoured cars.'

Caine detected the barely suppressed anger in his voice and felt his face glow, knowing that Sweeney was right. The success of the action had depended on the enemy not being able to regroup, and the appearance of the AFV might easily have cost them the battle. There was no one to blame but himself. He realized that in his impulsive rush to play white knight there'd been a lot of factors he'd overlooked: what to do with enemy wounded, what to do with his own wounded, what to do if his unit lost so many men the *Runefish* mission was no longer viable. 'They must have been hiding it,' he answered lamely. 'There was no sign of it on the recce.' Another thought struck him. 'Did you see any wireless aerials?'

'Nope,' said Sweeney tersely, his eyes falling suddenly on Caine's bandaged hand.

'You all right?'

Sweeney seemed so interested in his wound that for a minute Caine wondered if he might be estimating grounds for having him declared a casualty.

'Just a graze,' he said, shrugging it off. He remembered how Bubbles O'Brian's throat had been slashed in the melee. 'How's O'Brian?' he enquired.

'He'll be fine,' Sweeney said. 'Pickney got a shell-dressing on him before he bled to death, and the wound wasn't that deep. Jackson copped it in the chest, but it's a cushy one. The worst case is Rigby – he's lost a lot of blood, and Pickney doesn't reckon he'll make it.' He turned his eyes to Caine's hand again: the dressing was already soaked with blood. 'It's a wonder we didn't have more casualties, though,' he said.

Caine was thinking about Rigby and Jackson, whom he suspected had both been hit by fire from the Schmeisser MG30 mounted on the Jerry armoured car. Here were two more things to chastise himself with. How could he have missed that armoured wagon? Why would the Germans hide it when they obviously weren't expecting an attack?

That thought raised another question. 'Todd,' he said, 'I want you and Harry Copeland to take a detail of four men each and clear all the buildings that aren't yet on fire. God knows what else they might have been concealing.'

'Right,' Sweeney said, with a perceptible lack of enthusiasm.

Caine found Wallace and Trubman leaning on the Dingo's hatch sharing a cigarette and conversing amicably. He was mildly surprised: Wallace didn't normally talk to the rotund signaller, and now they looked the best of friends. 'I heard the Vickers stop,' he said to Wallace. 'Thought you'd copped it.'

A big smile split Wallace's moon-sized face. 'My mate Taffy here saved my life,' he said. Caine gave the tubby Welshman the thumbs-up, and Trubman turned pink and averted his gaze. That reminded Caine of how the Free Frenchman, Cavazzi, had saved him from being skewered on a Jerry bayonet. He looked around, wanting to thank him, but Wallace said he'd gone off with Sweeney's clearing party.

Caine told Wallace to bring the Very pistol out of the armoured car. He jacked in a red flare and fired it off with a pop. The flare would bring in the lorries and alert the cut-off sentries that the action was over. 'We need to get moving,' he said. 'This whole place is giving off smoke signals, and we don't want to get clocked by a shufti-wallah.' He asked Trubman if he'd tuned into the emergency frequency. The signaller looked worried. 'I can't get comms, Sergeant,' he apologized. 'I've tried both No. 11s. See, it's the mountains – this is signals dead ground.'

Caine nodded. 'Have another bash in a few minutes,' he said. 'Keep trying.' His eyes swept the square for Sheikh Adud and his daughter. He saw them conversing with a group of Arabs who were shepherding flocks of goats and sheep, leading a caravan of tired donkeys laden with household goods – pots, waterskins, sacks of grain, string cages of chickens. Caine realized that the Senussi didn't need to be told to evacuate the place – they were doing what he imagined they always did when trouble threatened – running for the hills. He beckoned Naiman and told him to bring Adud and Layla over, setting out wooden petrol cases for them to sit on.

He offered them water, gave them cigarettes and took from his haversack a photograph and a letter in Arabic. The photo showed the Senussi leader, Grand Senussi Sayid Idriss, now exiled in Egypt, and the letter was a request from him to all Senussi to assist his British allies. These items were standard issue to all Allied units operating in Cyrenaica. Caine gave them to Sheikh Adud, who examined the photo and read the letter with interest. He passed them to Layla.

Caine pulled off his black beret and scratched his head. 'Where will your people go now? he enquired.

Naiman asked the question in Arabic, and listened carefully to the reply.

'The sheikh says they'll go up into the Green Mountains,' Naiman translated, 'and stay with relatives till they get on their feet.'

'Why were the Germans doing this to them?' Caine asked. 'What had they done?'

Sheikh Adud had just opened his mouth to answer when there was a crisp detonation from a nearby street, followed by a salvo of gunshots. '*Grenade!*' Caine gasped, grabbing his Tommy-gun. 'Fred, Maurice, come with me.'

17

All the way there, Caine had a good idea what he'd find. When he, Wallace and Pickney arrived in the adjacent street, they saw Todd Sweeney with three other commandos, squatting over the twitching body of Gian-Carlo Cavazzi. Caine saw at once that he was in a critical condition. His intestines had spilled out and his chest and face were badly charred. He noticed a dead Jerry a few yards away, spreadeagled under an open first-floor window. 'We were about to clear that house,' Sweeney said, his voice flat, 'when the window opens, and this Jerry drops a potato-masher grenade right on top of Janka. Those things usually have an eight-second delay, but it must have been on a short fuse or something, because it went off as soon as it hit him. Whacked his guts right out. We shot the Hun, and the boys searched the house – there wasn't anyone else in there.'

Caine knelt by the Corsican, who was writhing, moaning and wheezing. 'Do me in, for Christ's sake,' he croaked, his breath coming in a rattle. 'I can't stand it, shoot me, *please*, finish me off.'

Caine and Sweeney exchanged glances. Pickney dipped into his chest and began prepping a morphia shot, holding the syringe up to the light and flicking it with his forefinger. When he leaned over Cavazzi, though, the Corsican knocked away the syringe, gasping. 'Not that. I'm a soldier. Shoot me, you cowards, *cazzati* English *stronsi*.' He launched into a stream of Corsican dialect. Caine scoped around him, and feeling exposed, sent two men off to cover the street, in case they'd missed any other survivors. He motioned to the rest of the group to move out of the wounded man's ear-shot. 'He's in a bad way,' he said to Pickney. 'Can't you do anything for him, Maurice?'

The ex-merchant seaman swallowed hard. 'I'm sorry, skipper,' he said. 'Even if we had the services of a field hospital it wouldn't help him. Trouble is, abdominal wounds are excruciating. He's had it, and he's going to die in agony – maybe today, maybe tomorrow, but he's had it all right.'

'We have to put him out of his misery,' Sweeney said. 'You couldn't let even a dog die like that.'

Caine felt suddenly sick. 'What about an overdose of morphia?' he asked the orderly.

Pickney shook his head. 'I know it's done,' he said, 'but I can't do it, Sarn't. It's against my oath, and anyway, you saw how he reacted. I know it sounds like I'm trying to get off the hook, but Janka's an ex-Legionnaire and he wants to die like a soldier.'

'A man ought to be able to go the way he wants to go,' Sweeney said.

Caine stared at the ex-MP. 'All right, Todd,' he said. 'Are you ready to do it?'

Sweeney flushed, his eyes reddening. 'Me? Why the heck should I do it? You're the one who got us into this. The whole thing was your idea. This had nothing to do with the mission we volunteered for. You wanted to play the big-timer, saving a wog village instead of sticking to our mission. You could of got the whole lot of us killed by not noticing there was an enemy AFV around. We've got four good men down and a lot of walking wounded – including yourself. We'll be lucky if the Boche aren't already on the way here in force. No, this is your doing, Caine. If anyone ought to shoot Janka, it's you.'

Caine was taken aback by the unexpected onslaught. The worst of it was that almost everything Sweeney had said was true. In attacking the enemy, he'd taken an enormous gamble with other people's lives, without even being sure his intelligence was sound. The basis of every military op was good planning and sound intelligence, and he'd failed on both counts. What if there had been camouflaged pickets out? What if the Jerries had managed to signal their base? What if there had been more than one AFV? It was only a moment's chance – good shooting by Copeland and Murray – that had prevented the battle from going the enemy's way.

Caine heard Wallace's thundering voice: it seemed to come from far off. 'Wait a minute, Todd,' he was saying. 'The skipper gave everyone the chance of refusing this job. Why didn't you say what you thought at the time?'

Sweeney pursed thin lips and made a face. 'No one could refuse,' he said. 'Not without feeling they were letting the side down. All right, it's too late to argue about that, but we need to do something about Janka *now*, and the patrol commander is the only one who can do it.'

Caine cast a glance at the other faces, but no one met his eye. He felt suddenly alone. When he looked at Wallace, the big man reacted as if it were an accusation. 'I'm sorry, skipper,' he said. 'Fighting the Jerries is one thing, but I never reckoned on having to shoot a mate. Todd's right about that. You're the boss, and this is down to you.'

Caine recalled that Cavazzi was married, and that his wife had escaped to London with him when he'd fled occupied France. For a split second he imagined himself ringing her door-bell after the war, explaining that he'd shot her husband dead. He recalled again how Cavazzi had saved his life in the melee, and knew he owed the man an honourable death. He took a deep breath, drew his Colt with his good hand and checked the magazine. He had five rounds left – the last one he'd fired had killed the Feldwebel. He shoved the mag back in and rose to his feet. He realized that he didn't even know the best way to go about this. 'Where do I shoot him?' he asked. 'How can I be certain he'll die?'

'Put the barrel in his mouth,' Pickney said. 'Fire upwards into the brain.'

Caine shuffled over to Cavazzi, who was still writhing madly, swearing to himself. He knelt down, feeling the prick of tears in his eyes. He didn't know the Corsican well, but he knew that he'd fought like a tiger, and that a brave man shouldn't have to die like this. As he was bending over, Cavazzi opened his eyes wide and focused on the pistol. '*Do it*,' he said urgently.

Caine took another deep breath. His hands trembling, he grasped the Corsican's nostrils with his injured fingers, wincing in pain. As Cavazzi opened his mouth, he pushed the Colt's barrel inside, squeezed the trigger. Nothing happened. To his undying embarrassment, Caine realized that he hadn't cocked the weapon. '*Stupid bastard!*' Cavazzi whispered. '*Cazzato, stupido.*'

Tears running down his cheeks now, he withdrew the Colt and cocked it with his bad hand. He saw the strained faces of his comrades staring at him. He grasped the Corsican's nostrils for the second time, shoved the barrel into his mouth. 'Thanks for saving my life, mate,' he intoned. 'If there's a Valhalla, that's where you deserve to be.' He closed his eyes and pulled the trigger once. He felt the recoil and a lash of blood, and opened his eyes to see that Cavazzi's skull had developed a giant exit wound discharging bits of bone and bloody pulp. He stood up, staggered over to the nearest wall, put his hand against it for support, and was violently sick.

When his senses came back into focus, Sweeney and Wallace were standing in front of him. 'It was a brave thing to do,' Sweeney stammered. 'I couldn't have . . .'

'Never mind that now,' Caine snapped. 'It's done. I want you to make sure that soldier gets a proper burial – and that's an order. Fred – find Copeland and tell him to RV in the square with his detail. Time's up.'

Caine got back to the square just as his four lorries were pulling in, and he saw that the cut-off squad had also arrived. He looked around for the sheikh and his daughter, and found them with Naiman, supervising the burial of the dead Senussi in the mosque yard. Todd Sweeney and Mick Oldfield arrived carrying Cavazzi's body between them, and he told them to bury it alongside the Arabs. Then he walked over to the Dingo and found Trubman there. 'Did you get anything on the emergency net?' he enquired.

'Sorry, Sarn't. Not a dickeybird. We need to move to higher ground, see.'

Caine took out two Player's Navy Cut and gave one to the signaller. Trubman's eyes searched his face. 'What happened?' he asked gently.

Caine lit the cigarette with hands that had almost stopped shaking, and took a long swig from his water-bottle. 'There was a German still alive,' he said wearily. 'He's dead now, but he bagged Lance Corporal Cavazzi before they got him.'

He realized suddenly that he hadn't mentioned anything about shooting his comrade in the mouth. He was rescued by Adud and his daughter, who came over with Naiman. 'He's asking what to do about the German dead,' the interpreter said.

Caine shrugged. On the spur of the moment, he decided not to do anything about the corpses – their murder of civilians disbarred them from an honorable burial. He knew it would be pointless to ask if there were any enemy wounded. As if in confirmation, the tall, tattooed Senussi woman he'd had a tussle with earlier came up and handed him a scrap of paper. He stuck the fag in his mouth, opened the note one-handed, and found that it was an official document, typed in German. He passed it to Naiman, who glanced at it, questioned the woman briefly. 'She found it on the body of the officer,' he told Caine. 'The one you shot.'

'What is it?'

Naiman perused it again, but before he could answer, a voice yelled, 'Hey, skipper.' Caine looked up to see Copeland jogging up, with Wallace and the rest of his detail behind him. His blue eyes were sparkling and his Adam's apple was working overtime. 'Look at this,' he said breathlessly. 'We found it in a house down the street.' He held out a slim, flat, round box, painted gold.

Caine took it. 'What *is* this?' he asked. He opened the catch and caught feminine fragrance. Inside were tiny compartments containing different shades of eye-shadow, face powder and a powder-puff. On the back of the lid was a mirror. Caine grinned despite his sombre mood. 'Just what I needed,' he said.

Cope looked irritated. 'That's a European woman's make-up compact,' he said sharply. 'Arab women don't use that stuff. It's new – and we found these.' He held up a pair of khaki drill trousers, tailored to fit a woman's shape. Inside the band was the familiar British forces 'arrowhead' label.

'*Runefish*?' Caine said, doubtfully.

'I dunno,' Cope said, 'but a European woman was in this village very recently – a woman who wears British khaki drill trousers. How many of those are kicking around Cyrenaica?'

Caine passed the objects to Sheikh Adud and his daughter. 'Do you know anything about these?' he asked. The sheikh examined them, then launched into a long explanation. 'There *was* a *nasraniyya* – a European woman – here until this morning,' Naiman translated. 'She was the one who caused all the trouble.'

Caine looked puzzled. 'What does that mean?' he asked.

'He was about to tell you all this when that grenade interrupted,' Naiman said. 'The Germans came here looking for her. She arrived day before yesterday in a jeep. There was a man with her – a European. They wanted to stay here, and the Arabs couldn't refuse – for them it's a disgrace to turn away guests. He says they never mentioned why they were here, but he guessed they were hiding from the Jerries. He was right. A Jerry column arrived this morning and searched the place. They found the foreigners, shot the man and took the woman off with their convoy. They left this platoon to punish the village for harbouring them.'

Cope and Caine exchanged glances. 'How did the Germans know they were here?' Cope asked.

Sheikh Adud couldn't answer that. Neither could he tell them the names of the woman or the man, or which country they came from.

'If this was *Runefish*, who was the man?' Copeland asked suddenly. '*Runefish* was alone, wasn't she?'

'Maybe the pilot survived,' Wallace suggested.

Caine considered it. The Royal Navy spotter tagging along with *Runefish's* Bombay had seen the aircraft go down, but it wasn't impossible that the pilot had made it. If so, though, where had they acquired the jeep?

'It's not really important now,' Caine said. 'The point is that, whoever was with her, the poor sod's dead.' He turned back to Naiman. 'Please ask the sheikh where his body is. It might tell us something.'

Naiman quizzed the old man, but Caine knew from his expression that there was no joy, even before Naiman said, 'The Jerries threw it into one of the burning houses.'

Caine considered it for a moment. 'Could you ask what the woman looked like, how was she dressed – and what language did she and the man speak?'

Naiman quizzed the sheikh again. 'She was blond,' he said, 'and pretty. She was young – maybe the age of his daughter. She was dressed military style – in khaki. The man spoke some Arabic, but she didn't – she spoke to the Arabs in Italian.'

'*Runefish* speaks fluent Italian,' Caine said, suppressing his excitement. 'Did the sheikh notice whether she was left- or right-handed?'

The old man said he thought she was left-handed.

'That clinches it,' Wallace said. 'Blond, spoke Italian and left-handed, wearing military rig. Ten bob to a pinch of shit it's her, skipper.'

Copeland's blue eyes glittered. Caine smiled.

'Before we start celebrating, Sergeant,' Naiman cut in soberly, 'I think you should consider this.' He held up the paper the Arab woman had just given Caine. 'This is a movement order for a company of the Brandenburg Special Duties Regiment.'

The others stared at him. 'You mean the jokers we've been fighting were *Brandenburgers*?' Wallace said wonderingly. 'I *thought* they was a tough crew.'

Naiman nodded and turned to Caine. 'Sergeant,' he said, 'didn't you say at the briefing that a company of Brandenburgers had been deployed to hunt down *Runefish*?'

'Nope. I said there was intelligence that a company had been deployed in our target area,' Caine corrected him. 'The idea that it might be searching for *Runefish* was just speculation.'

'Yes, well, whatever the case, it occurs to me that there isn't much to party about, then. If the lady who was here is *Runefish*, the Brandenburgers have just pipped us at the post.'

There was a hiatus as everyone ruminated over this. It was Caine who broke the silence. 'Corporal Naiman,' he said, 'can you ask the sheikh how long ago the rest of the column went off?'

Naiman was about to translate when the sheikh said, 'No, I understand. How long since *Tedesci* went with girl . . . you want to know, yes?'

'Yes.'

'Was one hour after sunrise.' He turned and extended both arms, pointing them due north. 'They go that way – Benghazi.'

'One hour after sunrise is around 0800 hours,' Caine said, glancing at his watch. 'Dammit – that's three hours ago. We'll never catch them now.'

The sheikh shook his head. 'No, no, no,' he repeated. 'You catch. Yes – you get there *before Tedesci*.'

'How is that possible?' Caine asked.

Adud pointed to his nose with a slender, gnarled finger. Obviously feeling that he'd exhausted his English, though, he spoke to Naiman in Arabic. 'The sheikh knows a short-cut,' Naiman translated. 'The road the Boche take avoids the Green Mountain, but the sheikh's way cuts through it. They call it the Hag's Cleft. He says it's an old route known only to the Senussi. The Arabs do it on foot or by donkey – it's hard in places, and it might be dangerous for motor-vehicles. He says if we're willing to risk it, he's ready to show us. He'll guide us personally as a mark of gratitude to Allah for what we did here.'

'The Hag's Cleft,' Caine repeated. He stared at Naiman. 'How far ahead of the enemy will this put us?' he enquired.

Naiman repeated the question to Adud. 'You get there *long* before *Tedesci*,' the old man said energetically. 'Long enough you hide and wait – *boom*.' He grinned and drew a hand across his throat. 'You kill them. You take woman. You kill them all.'

18

It was three o'clock in the morning when Sim-Sim unlocked the door of her flat in Zamalek, exhausted from the Benzedrine hangover, from the endless coasters of cheap champagne she'd consumed, from the physical exertion of her act, and worst, from the strain of having to keep smiling and to maintain a constant flow of inane banter with the clients. She sometimes brought johnnies back to her flat, but not today: today she wanted nothing more than to collapse on her cot and sleep for a week.

The flat was dark and full of shadows, but she didn't switch on the light in the sitting room. Instead, she went straight to the bathroom to empty her bladder, and to remove her make-up. As she wiped it off with cotton wool, she studied herself in the mirror, wondering how long her good looks would last in this twilight profession, and whether, with a name like Levi, she would survive at all when the Boche took over – as many predicted they soon would.

She detested being 'Sim-Sim', but in a sense it was a fitting name for a trade in which it paid to appear more stupid than you were. The whole 'Sim-Sim, a Lebanese Christian from Beirut' routine was part of the act – in fact, she was Rachel Levi, a Palestinian Jew from Safed, near the Sea of Galilee.

She let down her gorgeous black hair, changed into her dressing gown and walked through to the sitting room. She was groping to switch on a standard lamp when a rough hand grabbed her wrist, twisted her arm sharply behind her: another massive hand clamped her mouth. 'If you scream I'll kill you,' a voice croaked.

Her assailant dragged her to a straight-backed dining chair, pushed her down into it, and tied her hands to its back. She felt the cold, sharp prick of a knifepoint against her throat. 'I'm going to switch on the light,' the voice said. 'If you make any noise, believe me, you're dead.'

Electric light exploded in her face and she blinked frantically, bringing into focus a strapping man in a black suit. He looked at first like one of the Egyptian playboys she'd frequently entertained in the club – cleanshaven, dark suit, dark glasses, greasy dark hair, shiny patent-leather shoes. He spoke Arabic with an unmistakable Cairo accent. Rachel's eyes fell on the slim stiletto in his right hand. She'd known clients who carried weapons for self-defence, but this struck her as being the weapon of an assassin. 'Who are you?' she stammered. 'What do you want?' It had to be sex, she thought – it was always sex. He was one of those crazies – the bane of her profession – for whom simple submission wasn't enough. She shuddered at the thought of what 'those crazies' had been known to do.

'Come on, my dear Sim-Sim,' the man said, his voice almost unctuous. 'Your memory can't be that bad. We met only two days ago – it's not very flattering that you've forgotten me already. Let me give you a clue.' He switched to perfect, accentless English. '*You are a nice, respectable British officer, but there's at least one person out there who has good reason to want Betty dead.*'

Rachel's mouth fell open in shock. 'You?' she gasped. 'Captain Sandy Peterson?'

'Good, very good, but not exactly. You see, Captain Sandy Peterson is a figment of my imagination.'

Rachel twisted her face up at him incredulously. 'Who *are* you?' she asked weakly.

'Who am I? I am the person who wants information about your friend Betty. You weren't very kind to me the other day, so I have returned. It was an easy matter to follow you here. Now I want to know all those things that you refused to tell me the first time around, and you are going to tell me, or I shall disfigure you so badly the only thing you will be good for is doing sex acts with donkeys for money.'

Her eyes fixed on him, wide with horror. Even when he had been dressed as an officer she'd felt that there was something familiar about him. Now she was certain of his identity. This was the man who had brutally raped and murdered Lady Mary Goddard at Madame Badia's – the man whom Betty had discovered in the ladies' room, the man she herself had seen Lady Goddard attacking verbally in the bar, only minutes before her death. What other reason could he have for asking questions about Betty? He was obviously afraid that she might be able to identify him. What really frightened Rachel was the thought that he might recall her own presence in the club that night, and consider her a threat too.

'Go to hell,' Rachel said.

Eisner took a flying leap over to the chair, and in a flash of movement pinched the lobe of her right ear between finger and thumb and sliced it off with his knife. Blood spurted from the clean cut. Rachel tried to scream, but once again he stifled her with a big hand over the mouth. He scrabbled at the neck of her dressing gown and ripped it off her shoulders, exposing her ripe breasts. 'No,' he whispered in her bloody ear. 'You are the one who's going to hell, my dear. It would truly give me pleasure to carve up this beautiful face of yours – I would enjoy that.' He held up the piece of ear he'd just cut off. 'This you won't miss much, but your nose, your lips . . .' He let the knifeblade linger on a perfect nipple. 'Or one or both of these . . .' He felt excited at the thought.

Rachel shuddered. Blood from her injured ear was dripping on her shoulder, running down one breast. She cried silently, the tears running down her cheeks. 'What do you want to know?' she sobbed.

'I want to know about Betty.'

Rachel screwed up her face again. She was aware now what her fate would be if she didn't do what he wanted. In her trade, she'd learned to read men, and she had seen it in the man's eyes, heard it in his voice. It wasn't just talk. This was a man who really did enjoy hurting women. She didn't want to betray her friend, but she reasoned that Betty was safe. She was too far away for this man to be able to hurt her.

Eisner wrenched the dressing gown again, slitting it with the knife all the way down the back, so that it fell in pieces, leaving her body naked. He grinned with evident enjoyment, stroking her belly with the flat blade. Suddenly he pinched her nose hard, jerking her head back, touching her nostrils with the knife. 'Once it's gone, you won't grow it back,' he growled.

'All right,' Rachel squeaked. 'Let me go. I'll tell you.'

He released her nose and she hunched forward, winded. 'Her name is Betty Nolan,' she panted. 'She's British. She was an actress before the war – she was too good for a cabaret girl . . . She had a wonderful memory. She was popular, got on well with the clients. Like I told you before, she never dated them . . . never took them home.'

Eisner let the knifepoint touch the nape of the girl's now-bloody neck. Rachel trembled, cringing at the pain from her severed ear-lobe, which was still pulsing blood.

'Why not?' Eisner asked, his voice silky. 'She doesn't like men?'

Rachel tried to clear her head. 'No . . . it wasn't that,' she whispered. 'It was . . . she had a boyfriend in England . . . Peter. They were going to be married . . . only Peter was killed by the Nazis . . .'

'Killed in action?'

'No – she said he was a secret agent in France. He was betrayed. The Nazis tortured and murdered him. Betty said she couldn't go with anyone else until she'd . . . laid him to rest in her mind.'

Eisner nodded, thinking that the jigsaw pieces were beginning to fit.

'How long ago did Betty leave Madame Badia's?' he demanded.

'It was . . . about . . . six months ago. She was never the same – never felt the same – after that night . . . the night I told you about.'

'And what did she say about that night – about the man she saw in the ladies' room?'

Rachel shivered again. She dreaded approaching this dangerous ground. 'She didn't say anything,' she stammered. 'She was questioned . . . but she couldn't give any information . . . not enough to identify him. A lot of people saw him in the club – we were all . . .' She stopped suddenly, realizing she'd made a slip.

'Go on,' Eisner said coaxingly. 'You were going to say, "We were all there, and we all saw him," weren't you? So you were in the floor show that night.'

The barman had told him that she'd been there the longest. He should have remembered her face, he told himself, but part of him knew why he hadn't. It was the same reason that had prevented him from recalling where he'd seen Betty when he'd first glimpsed her in the staff-car – the need to deny to himself that he'd been in the club that night, that he'd had anything to do with the murder of Lady Mary Goddard. There was a battle going on inside him, a war between the professional spy and the man who enjoyed having a beautiful woman like Sim-Sim tied naked to a chair, and at his mercy.

'Why do you want to know about that?' Rachel sobbed, cutting short his musings.

'I don't,' he snapped. 'What did Betty do after she left Madame Badia's?'

'I don't know. I never saw her again . . .'

Eisner pushed the knife gently against one of her breasts. 'Don't!' she squealed. 'It hurts.'

'Of course it hurts. It's supposed to hurt. Now, what did she do after she left?'

'All right. Stop, I'll tell you what I know.'

He withdrew the knife, leaving a small, V-shaped incision on the breast, from which came a trickle of blood.

Rachel felt her head gyrating and had to take deep breaths to prevent herself from passing out. 'I didn't see her again after that,' she said, her voice almost a whisper. 'I heard she joined the army – the British Army.'

Eisner surveyed her face, and knew she wasn't lying. 'The army?' he said. 'You're sure it was the army?'

'Yes, I'm sure.'

'Did she join as an officer or a private?'

'It must have been a private . . . a . . . a clerk or telephonist or something.'

'Where does Betty live now?'

'I don't know . . . really . . . She used to have a flat on the Gezira, in al-Hegida Street.'

'Number?'

'Twenty-Two . . . but I don't know if she still uses it.'

Eisner paused. He doubted that Sim-Sim had much more to tell him. Actually, in a few words, she'd told him plenty. There was something strange going on, and he could almost smell deception.

'Why are you asking these questions?' Rachel said. 'What are you going to do to Betty?'

'Nothing – necessarily,' he said, smiling. 'Your question should be, what am I going to do to you?'

'Let me go,' she said. 'I've told you everything I know.'

'Now I'd like to do that but, unfortunately, I can't.'

Rachel stared at the grinning mask of a face, focused on the stiletto in his hand. A quiver ran down her spine. The knife. Betty *had* said something about the man who'd murdered Lady Mary – that he was using a knife with a long, narrow blade. A knife like this one. That made it certain. This was the man who'd sold secrets to the Germans, who'd raped and killed Mary Goddard in cold blood.

'It *was* you,' she said, her voice dead now. 'You're the one Betty saw. Whatever you do to me, one thing is certain: *you're going straight to damnation.*'

Eisner didn't seem to lose his cool, but there was a green tinge to his face that revealed a terrifying inner battle. How pathetic he was, he thought. Trying to deny it to himself. Trying to pretend to himself that he was a cold, logical operator when in reality he was what he'd always been – a sadistic punisher of women, and there was nothing – *nothing* – he could do about it. A tidal wave of fury burst in his head, overwhelming him. With a sudden movement he cut through Rachel's ropes, snatched her long, beautiful hair and dragged her, shrieking, towards the bedroom.

19

They glimpsed the Hag's Cleft not long before sunset – from afar a barely perceptible slit in the wall of the Green Mountains, a warren of heat-weathered hills, rubblestone slopes, cave-riddled valleys and steep-sided canyons that rose to sixteen hundred feet and filled the whole bulge of Cyrenaica. The pre-Saharan slopes of the jebel were covered in goat-grass and camel-thorn, but the further north you penetrated, the deeper you pushed into dense thickets of maquis scrub and cool forests of cypress, cork-oak, pine and juniper, that seemed a million miles from the sterile emptiness of the desert.

Caine halted the column at the foot of the cleft, and he and his crew jumped out to survey it. Wallace was grinning all over his broad face. 'You can see why they call it the Hag's Cleft, can't you?' he said.

Caine nodded. It was clearly the mouth of a steep, narrow wadi, cutting deep into the heart of the mountain, but at close quarters its eroded edges gave it the unmistakable shape and texture of giant, raddled female genitalia.

Copeland didn't join in the joke. 'We'll never get the wagons through there,' he said.

Caine ignored him and lit a cigarette, holding it in his bandaged hand. He was satisfied that they'd made good time, despite the fact that they'd had to run for cover twice when Axis planes reamed over the horizon. He had no doubt the pilots would spot the burning Senussi village and drop altitude to scope it out, but they wouldn't see much. Before his column had pulled out, he'd had a change of heart over the German dead and had ordered his men to collect their rifles, Schmeissers and spare ammo and throw the corpses into the blazing buildings. They hadn't been able to do anything about the vehicle wrecks, but he guessed that the place would be screened by thick smoke for a while yet – and it would soon be sunset. Axis patrols would certainly have been alerted, but they wouldn't know what they were looking for. The damage could just as easily have been done by an RAF bombing raid.

Sheikh Adud came over to the White with Layla and Naiman. The old man crouched down by Caine, sketching lines in dust with a gnarled finger. 'It is steep and narrow,' he confirmed, 'but only in one place *very* steep. That place is Shallal – like a . . . a waterfall. In that place sometimes Arabs have to drag donkeys up by rope.'

Caine gulped. He didn't like the sound of 'waterfall'. If even donkeys could only get up with difficulty, how would the 3-tonners fare, or the Marmon Herrington? He considered taking only the armoured vehicles but rejected it. The lorries had all the kit on board – weapons, rations, spare ammo. He would need everything he'd got to take on the Brandenburg convoy. He thought ruefully of the column his men had avoided that first morning. A couple of those six-wheeled Bredas would have been ideal for this.

'It looks mighty narrow to me,' Copeland said, 'and it'll get narrower as we go up. If we get stuck in there, that'll be the end of *Runefish*.'

Caine was thinking about what his rash attack on the village had already cost them – two good men, Cavazzi and Rigby, lying in unmarked graves by the mosque. Of the two seriously wounded, Jackson was still laid up in one of the trucks. O'Brian, his throat thickly bandaged, was already on his feet. Then Caine remembered that the assault on the village had also produced something positive: without those clues to the whereabouts of *Runefish*, they'd have been high and dry.

He flicked away his cigarette butt and glanced at Copeland. 'It's a gamble,' he said, 'but on the other hand, it has advantages. The Boche will be on our trail by now. Even if they manage to track us here, they'll never follow us through, not unless they have an Arab guide. No one's going to spot us in the cleft, not even from the air.'

Cope hadn't lost his dubious look. 'How do you know we can trust the old man?' he asked. 'He might be setting us up. If we get bumped at the other end, it'll be a massacre.'

'Harry,' Caine said, shaking his head almost pityingly. 'The old fellow just saw his daughter escape death by the skin of her teeth, not to mention a bunch of cousins strung up like dogs. Whose side is he likely to be on?'

'Who can tell how these Arabs think?'

Caine yawned and realized he was dog-tired. If they were going to get through this they'd need half a ton of Bennies. The men had been up all the previous night and had fought a sharp action. To expect them to keep going through another night and fight a second action at the end of it was asking a heck of a lot from anyone, even special-service troops.

'I don't see that we have a choice,' he told Copeland. 'If the Hun get *Runefish* to Benghazi, we'll never get her out. She'll be on a submarine to Deutschland before you can say "Adolf Hitler".' He looked the corporal in the eye. 'We'll go for it, Harry. Don't underestimate the sheikh – he seems pretty switched on to me.'

Cope nodded, impressed once more with Caine's

determination. 'Let's do it then,' he said, smirking suddenly. 'Only I hope it doesn't rain.'

At first the going inside the cleft was better than Caine had expected. The wadi bed was smooth water-graded gravel and the sides wide enough apart for two wagons to pass each other. The column moved at walking pace, and Caine tramped ahead with Sheikh Adud, Layla and interpreter Naiman. Most of the men debussed from the vehicles and walked along with them, clearing stones or tangles of vegetation out of the way as they walked.

The sun dipped, casting zebra-stripes of light and shade across the gravel floor. The wadi sides grew higher and higher until they were soaring hundreds of feet above, giving Caine the feeling that they were walking along the bottom of a deep dyke, like the ones sunk across his native Fens. Sometimes he found himself staring upwards at places where the patina had fallen away in vast flakes, or where the rock seemed to have liquefied and oozed down the sides to solidify in purple blotches. As the wadi closed in around them, though, he began to feel claustrophobic. He was aware that it would soon be so narrow that the vehicles would have no chance of turning round.

Darkness descended like a dead weight, and the wagons rumbled forward with their headlights off, filling the gorge with grumbling echoes and petrol fumes. The men fell silent, stalking on in the darkness like phantoms. The floor became increasingly steep: jagged boulders scraped against the lorries' sumps. In places the lads had to build ramps and guide the vehicles up them one by one.

Around midnight, when they'd been climbing for a good five hours without a break, Caine thought he heard the sound of water. He tapped Sheikh Adud on the shoulder. 'What's that?' he asked.

The old man's face was a dark hollow above a sprout of beard, made almost luminous by the aquamarine moonlight. 'That is Shallal,' Adud said. 'Place of waterfall ... but no problem. Not much water now.'

Caine called a halt. He drew his torch and went forward with Copeland, Adud and Naiman. They hadn't covered more than ten yards when what looked like a sheer cliff reared suddenly out of the wadi bed. 'Christ,' Caine gasped. He was about to reel angrily on the sheikh, when Cope stopped him. 'It's an illusion, Tom,' he said. 'It's not as steep as it looks.'

They began to stumble up the rise, over stones and jagged boulders. Adud pointed out a narrow channel to one side where they could just make out a slim ribbon of water, silver in the moonlight. A climb of about fifteen minutes left Caine breathless but not disheartened. 'You were right, mate,' he told Cope. 'I reckon the gradient's about one in three – steep, but not *that* steep.'

They rested for a few minutes, swigging water, then Caine sent Copeland with Adud and Naiman to recce the way ahead. When they'd disappeared into the opalescent moonlight, he scrambled back down into the wadi and gave the lads an hour to rest and eat. He took the opportunity to pay a visit to Jackson, who was lying bandaged on a stretcher in the back of *Gracie*, with Pickney in attendance. The ex-Rifleman seemed alert and chirpy.

'Was it the Schmeisser MG30?' Caine asked.

'Don't know where it came from,' Jackson grunted. 'I just felt this white-hot pain, like I'd been kicked in the chest by a bloody great mule.'

'He was lucky,' Pickney said. 'It's a cushy wound – no vital organs hit. I've tried a new treatment – plugged both the entry and exit wounds with an ointment of crushed sulphenamide tablets, mixed with petroleum jelly and cotton wool. I'm also giving him sulphenamide tablets by mouth.'

Jackson grinned weakly. 'I'll be up and about by tomorrow, skipper,' he said. 'You'll see.'

'Make sure you are,' Caine said, his voice mock-stern. 'We need you.'

After Pickney had examined and re-dressed his own wound, Caine returned to the White, where Wallace was cooking bully stew in a dixie. By the time Copeland and the others arrived back, they were already digging into it.

'It's about the same gradient all the way up,' Cope reported, slipping his mess tins out of his belt-kit. 'The slope extends about two hundred feet, and there's a plateau on top, where the watercourse goes off to one side. On the other side there's what looks like a natural ledge, with the mountain wall on the right and a sheer drop on the left. Hard to say how deep the drop is.'

'Don't really matter, does it?' Wallace chuckled, slopping stew into Cope's mess tin. 'If a wagon goes over we ain't likely to get it back whether it's ten foot or a hundred, are we?'

Copeland attacked the stew ravenously with a spoon, while Caine searched his face in the greengage moonlight. 'The *width* is the crucial factor, Harry.'

'As the bishop said to the actress,' Wallace cut in.

Chuckling, Cope put his mess tin down and held out his mug for tea. Wallace poured him half a pint of fluid, then added Carnation milk. The corporal sipped at it with small noises of appreciation. He wiped his lips. 'I reckon it's just wide enough to take our widest wagon,' he said, 'but there isn't much margin, and I can't swear what it's like further on. Adud told me it doesn't get any narrower, and what he's

172

told us has held up so far.' He sipped more tea. 'Only one thing, though. I wouldn't want to take on that ledge in the dark. I mean, one slip and you're over.'

Caine scraped out his mess tins with sand. 'It's just gone 0100 hours,' he said. 'I reckon it will take us till first light to get up the next two hundred feet.' Another thought struck him. 'Is there enough room up there to leaguer all the wagons?'

Copeland considered it. 'It'll be tight,' he said, 'but it'll do.' He put his mug down and lit a Player's Navy Cut. 'You thought how we're going to do this?' he enquired.

Caine fitted his mess tins into each other and replaced them in his pouches.

'Yep,' he said. 'I'm sending the Dingo up first – she's got four-wheel drive so it shouldn't be any problem for her. She can tow *Gracie*, and the water-bowser. On top, we'll use the winch to haul up the rest of the wagons. Anything up there we can secure her on?'

Cope blew out smoke, nodding. 'Some free-standing boulders.'

'We ain't got a two-hundred-foot cable, skipper,' Wallace butted in.

'There's an extension,' Caine said. 'I remember ticking it off on the list.'

'OK,' Cope said, 'but who's going to drive the Dingo?'

'You are. Just as soon as you've finished that.'

Within ten minutes the men had been briefed, and the drivers were in place.

Caine divided the co-drivers and crews into two parties. One group would go ahead, clearing the larger stones and boulders out of the way. The other would push the wagons, haul on toggle ropes or place chocks under the back wheels if there were any sign of slippage.

Caine watched Wallace ease the White scout-car out of the way so that the Dingo and *Gracie* could pass – there was just enough room. While Wingnut Turner yoked the six-ton truck securely to the Dingo with a tow-rope, Caine hopped on to the running board of the lorry's cab, where Todd Sweeney sat behind the wheel. 'Just take it steady,' he said. 'Don't overdo the throttle.'

Sweeney shot him an irritated glance. 'I know, I know,' he snapped. He punched the starter and the engine roared. The clearing party was already climbing the slope, hidden by the darkness. Caine checked that the team with chocks and toggle ropes was in place at the rear. Cope was ready in the Dingo, with the engine gurning. 'All right,' he bawled. 'Hit it.'

The Dingo crawled forward and the tow-rope tightened steadily. At the wheel of *Gracie*, Sweeney let out the clutch a fraction of a second too late, and there was a twang as the rope snapped. Caine and Wallace leapt out of the way.

'You tosser,' Wallace yelled at Sweeney.

Caine marched up to the truck and opened the cab door. 'Stand down, Corporal Sweeney,' he said.

Sweeney looked flustered. 'Are you saying I don't know how to drive a lorry?' he demanded angrily.

'No, Corporal, I'm not saying anything. I'm ordering you to stand down. I want you to take charge of the clearing party.'

Sweeney shot him a vitriolic glance. He was a muscular man, squat and powerful, but he knew better than to aggravate Caine when he was in a determined mood. Muttering, he opened the door and dropped out. Caine took his place. Wallace jumped on the cab's running board. 'She's yoked up, skipper,' he said.

Caine nodded. Minutes later they tried again. As the

rope tightened, Caine eased the clutch out. *Gracie* moved steadily forward. The Dingo began to crawl up the gradient, and Caine kept his foot on the accelerator, his eyes riveted on the tow-rope, reading its tension. He felt the big lorry's wheels shudder and her coil-springs wobble as she rolled over loose stones. He smiled to himself, remembering that one of those coil-springs was an inflated inner tube. They were about half-way up the slope, and doing well, when *Gracie's* engine suddenly lost power. Caine stabbed the accelerator frantically, but a fraction of a second later she spluttered and died. The lorry stopped abruptly: the tow-rope snapped, whiplashing his bonnet. A few yards above, Copeland braked the Dingo.

Caine could feel *Gracie's* wheels grinding, slipping back under the drag of the heavy water-bowser. He ramped on the handbrake, but she slipped back even faster. 'Hold her, lads,' he yelled through the open side window. The team behind the truck threw in the wooden chocks. The clearing party ran back down the slope to help, and as Todd Sweeney passed, Caine saw or imagined he saw a gloating look on the ex-Redcap's face. Even with the chocks in, and the whole team straining, *Gracie* continued to creep backwards with a sickening crunch of stones. Wallace ran forward with the men carrying toggle-ropes. They looped the ropes around the winch-bar, and Caine saw Wallace's face in the moonlight, rutted with strain as his great muscles heaved. Gracie's backwards momentum was checked momentarily, and for an instant it seemed to Caine that Wallace's prodigious strength alone was holding the truck. Then she lurched backwards again, shuddering dangerously.

Caine was debating whether to abandon her when he remembered that Robin Jackson was lying helplessly in the back. He was about to call out to Wallace, when his eye fell on the petrol gauge. The tank was empty: Sweeney had forgotten to top it up. That was why the engine had cut.

Gracie was rolling back even faster now, and Caine saw that Wallace and the others were being dragged forwards on their toggle ropes. Cursing himself for not having checked the fuel earlier, Caine switched over to the reserve tank and pressed the starter. The engine coughed. He could feel *Gracie's* wheels shivering, going out of control. 'Get out, skipper,' Wallace yelled. Caine thought of Jackson: if he jumped, it would mean abandoning the wounded man to his fate. He hit the starter a second time. Again nothing happened. The truck was slithering back faster and faster. Caine took a deep breath and hit the starter a third time. The engine exploded into action.

Caine put her straight into first gear and let the clutch out. *Gracie* jerked forward with her six wheels spinning, but didn't stall. Then she got traction and Caine hit the clutch and brake: she stopped abruptly. The men behind the lorry cheered.

Holding her in first gear, Caine saw Wallace's broad face leering at him through the left-side window. 'We're not going to be able to splice the tow-rope, Tom,' he said.

Caine made an instant decision. 'I'm going to play the winch cable out,' he said. 'Take the hook and yoke it to the Dingo. Then go up there with Harry, and attach it to a secure rock. Give me the word and I'll winch her up.'

Wallace gave him the thumbs-up. Still balancing the truck in first, Caine began to unwind the winch-cable, as Wallace took the hook and ran with it to the Dingo. A moment later the little scout-car was crunching up the slope taking the cable with her.

It worked better than Caine could have imagined. He kept playing out the cable until it was fully extended. Wallace was back within ten minutes, saying that the end was secured to a rock on the summit. Caine started to wind the cable in, giving the vehicle a little throttle. *Gracie* juddered but started to grind steadily upwards. The winch whined, the engine grumbled. The commandos behind the wagon clapped and whistled.

With the winch reeling in the cable steadily it took only ten minutes to cover the hundred feet to level ground. Once the lorry and trailer were safely on the ledge, Caine had the lads unyoke the bowser, detach the winch-cable. After checking that there was enough room, he turned her round and sited her facing the slope. He applied the brakes and jumped out of the cab, to find Cope and Wallace waiting for him. 'What happened, Tom?' Copeland asked. 'How come she stalled?'

Caine wiped sweat off his brow, took in the rock wall rising steeply above them. 'You won't believe it,' he said. 'Petrol ran out.'

'I'll kill that tosser,' Wallace roared.

Just as Cope had said, there were large boulders up here that had been separated from the rock face by erosion. The three of them worked to secure *Gracie* to them with side cables, then Wallace attached the winch-cable extension. While the big man worked the winch, Caine and Copeland took turns to run down the slope to yoke the cable to the other vehicles. It was hard, slow, painstaking work, but one by one *Marlene*, *Vera* and *Judy* and the two armoured vehicles creaked up the slope. By the time the last wagon, the Daimler, reached the summit, the men were dropping with fatigue.

Dawn was already firing up in the east, a vast band of gold and pink spreading across the sky, revealing a labyrinth of mountainpeaks and deep wadis stretching as far as the eye could see. Caine ordered an hour's rest for breakfast. As he, Cope and Wallace leaned against the bonnet of the White, smoking cigarettes, Cope said, 'You deserve a medal for that, skipper. Nobody's done anything like this since Hannibal crossed the Alps with his elephants.'

Caine was so done in he could barely manage to force a smile. 'Don't count your chickens, Harry,' he said. 'We haven't got down yet.'

20

In the same limpid morning light, five hundred miles away to the east, Captain Julian Avery emerged from a staff car at the block where Sim-Sim's flat was situated. He found the flat easily enough – it was cordoned off with tape and crawling with Field Security personnel. Avery, still clad in his service dress and Sam Browne, was pooped. He'd come straight from an all-night conference at GHQ, chaired by Auchinleck, to discuss the implications of Rommel's imminent attack on Tobruk.

He found the Defence Security Officer, Major John Stocker, in the sitting room, drinking coffee with his sergeant, and a corporal. Avery didn't miss the bloodstains on the furniture and the Persian carpet. He saluted, then whipped off his service cap, smoothed his pale moustache and wayward blond hair. 'You look all in,' Stocker told him. 'Have some coffee.'

Avery took the coffee gratefully. He sipped it, winced at its bitter strength, but enjoyed it all the same. 'What news from Tobruk?' Stocker asked.

'It doesn't look good, sir,' Avery said. 'Rommel encircled the town yesterday. The word from GHQ is that he'll be through the perimeter this morning, and will probably move in for the kill tomorrow.'

'It had to come,' Stocker sighed. 'Will Klopper hold out?'

'To speak frankly, sir, I think he'll fold on the first wave of Stukas. Holding it was only viable while the Gazala Line was in place. Now that's gone . . .' Avery gulped savagely at the bitter coffee and surveyed the DSO with interest.

Stocker was what Avery called the 'boffin' type – a stout little officer with a domed forehead and thick-framed glasses who wore the badge of the Intelligence Corps on his service cap. All Avery knew about him was that he'd been a professor at Cairo University before the war and had virtually no military training yet was reckoned mustard as a spy-catcher, and had scored some outstanding successes.

'So,' Avery said, giving his mug back to the corporal, 'you said it was urgent.'

Stocker took him by the arm and moved him away from the others, lowering his voice. 'This flat was rented by a young woman known as Sim-Sim,' he said. 'She was what I believe is referred to as a "cabaret girl", at Madame Badia's nightclub. The term implies both entertainer and prostitute.'

Avery chortled. 'I'm familiar with the term,' he said.

'The name "Sim-Sim" was, of course, assumed. In fact, she was a Palestinian Jew named Rachel Levi. She was raped and murdered here in the flat in the early hours of the morning. Her body was found by the civilian police after a tip-off by neighbours, who'd heard screams. The police noticed something familiar in the perpetrator's modus operandi. It was identical to that of the murder of Lady Mary Goddard, the diplomat's wife, last July.'

'I remember that case. It was all over the newspapers.'

'Yes. Levi's body was found in the room through here.' He ushered Avery through an open door into a small bedroom, where two Field Security men in smart khaki drills were taking forensic samples and dusting for fingerprints. The body had been removed, but Avery's glance was drawn to the double bed, the sheets and blankets of which were caked in dried blood. 'Levi's body was on the bed,' Stocker told him. 'She had been raped in the anus and her throat had been cut from behind, probably *while* she was being raped. This was precisely the manner of the homicide of Lady Goddard in the ladies' room of Madame Badia's. Now, you may remember that the perpetrator in the Goddard case was never found, even though he was witnessed in the act of committing the crime by a woman called Betty Nolan.' He dropped his voice to almost a whisper. 'I believe this Miss Nolan is of some interest to you?'

Avery bristled. His tired mind interpreted the word 'interest' as implying a personal involvement. Certainly, if circumstances had been different, he'd have liked to have become involved with Betty, but her heart had always been elsewhere. Then he realized that Stocker couldn't possibly be implying anything personal. The fact that the DSO had called him indicated only that he was aware of a professional connection. This, in itself, was unexpected enough.

'Are you indoctrinated, sir?' he whispered.

'Into *Runefish*? To a certain level. Only in as much as it affects the counter-intelligence scene.'

Avery suppressed his surprise. 'This is connected with the counter-intelligence scene?'

'Intimately. The man who murdered Mary Goddard was an Axis agent. He was using her infatuation with him to obtain secrets from her husband and passing them to the Germans. Now, having seen both bodies, I'd stake my reputation that Levi was murdered by the same man.'

Avery looked puzzled. 'I can see the rationale for the Goddard murder – she would've been able to identify him – but why snuff a cabaret girl?'

Stocker produced a ready-filled pipe from his pocket, tamped the tobacco down with his thumb and began to light it with a match. In a moment, he was enveloped in clouds of smoke. 'Rachel Levi was present the night

Goddard was murdered,' he said, puffing energetically. 'Of course, so were dozens of others, but Levi was an associate of Nolan's and might possibly have learned something from her – a detail that didn't come out or wasn't noticed when Nolan was questioned. My first conclusion, therefore, was that this might be a case of the perpetrator eliminating witnesses. Then I asked myself why he should do so after he had gone undetected for a year. In fact, if he was simply concerned with witnesses, a murder like this would have been counter-productive.'

Avery nodded. 'So what was your second conclusion?'

Stocker let the pipe lodge in the corner of his mouth, while he whipped off his glasses and began to clean them with a scrap of felt. 'Two nights ago,' he said, 'a man arrived at Madame Badia's with a recent photo of your Betty Nolan. Did you know about that?'

Avery looked slightly annoyed. 'No,' he said. 'I wasn't told.'

'Funny,' Stocker said, replacing his glasses. 'The brief should have reached you by now. Actually, I was tipped off by one of my men, who is working undercover at the club. He reported that this man was dressed as a British Army captain. He wanted information about Nolan, and my man directed him to Levi. A fateful move, as it turned out, but my chap wasn't to know that. He thought, quite rightly, that by quizzing Levi later he could find out what the man was after.'

'So who was the officer?' Avery asked.

'He signed his name in the guest book as a Captain Sandy Peterson, General List. I've checked, and there is no such officer on the General List, or any other list. I believe that this "Peterson" was the killer of both Goddard and Levi.'

Avery was fascinated. 'All right, but if he was Goddard's killer, wasn't it a big risk returning to the club? He must have had some very compelling reason.'

Stocker's eyes were blue, Avery noticed, and very bright behind the lenses. 'Exactly,' he said. 'Hence the British officer's disguise – a clever touch. Yes, you are perfectly right, Captain. Whatever brought him to the club two nights ago, it was urgent. I believe it was connected with Operation *Runefish*.'

Avery stared at him, as the connection suddenly became clear. 'You mean he's rumbled *Runefish*?' he said.

Stocker didn't answer, but beckoned Avery with a finger. They moved back out of the bedroom into the sitting room, which was now empty. Stocker pointed to the bloodstains on the carpet and on an upright chair and drew Avery's attention to a loop of rope attached to the chair, with ends that had clearly been cut through. 'The thing about our man,' Stocker said, 'is that he's not only a spy but also a sexual sadist. He interrogates Levi while she's tied to this chair. The bloodstains indicate torture – incidentally, Levi's body had been cut in various places, including a breast. A piece of her left ear was missing – it wasn't found, so we assume he took it as a souvenir.'

'Good grief.'

'Yes. So he interrogates her about Nolan, extracting the information he failed to get out of her at the club two nights ago. We have to presume she told him all she knew, which was nothing about *Runefish* but would probably include the fact that Nolan was recruited into the army – that, as you know, was her cover story.'

Avery smiled. He ought to know, because he had invented the cover story himself. Stocker continued. 'Once he's got the information he wants, he drags her to the bedroom and does his thing on her – cuts her throat in the act of raping her, just as he did with Goddard. He's clever enough to know that his MO will be identified, so we must assume that his urge to simultaneous rape and murder is too strong for him to resist.'

Avery frowned, trying to assess the threat to Operation *Runefish*. It was, he realized, serious.

'Now, here's some relevant intelligence you will probably know about,' Stocker went on. 'On the night *Runefish* departed, our "Y" Service intercepted an unlicensed transmission from the central Cairo district. It went out almost simultaneously with her departure. We decoded the transmission, which contained the intelligence that a female naval officer, codenamed *Runefish*, was transporting top-secret documents from GHQ Middle East to London. These documents were for the eyes of the Prime Minister, and the courier had been issued with a cyanide pill, presumably to commit suicide if subjected to interrogation. The salient point about that transmission is that it came from an Abwehr agent known as *Stürmer* who is operating undercover in Cairo, and whom Field Security have been trying to identify for more than a year. You knew about this transmission?'

Avery shifted slightly. 'As a matter of fact, I did, sir,' he said. 'That intelligence was derived from a 'leak' my division deliberately disseminated to known Abwehr assets.' He paused for a moment and flashed a glance at Stocker. 'Are you saying that *Stürmer* and the Levi-Goddard killer are one and the same?'

Stocker's bright eyes were on him again. 'Let's call it a hunch,' he said. He paused and swallowed hard. 'The night that transmission went out, one of my agents – Cpl Salim Tanta – was murdered. He was last seen tailing a car that was spotted behaving suspiciously at the Helwan checkpoint.

What was left of his body was found in the remains of his burned-out Vauxhall, in a derelict back-street in Maadi.'

'Christ. You mean the person he was shadowing was the same one who sent the transmission? The Levi-Goddard killer – Peterson – *Stürmer*?'

'I admit it's speculation, but I think there's a strong possibility.'

Avery thought about it. There was, he saw, a logical flaw in Stocker's thesis.

'The transmission suggests that the sender didn't know that *Runefish* was Nolan,' he said, 'but the fact that the killer – "Peterson" – came looking for Nolan at the club suggests that he *did* know. How else would he have made the connection? And he had a photo of her, you said? Doesn't that indicate that the killer and *Stürmer* are two different men?'

Stocker removed his pipe from his mouth and sighed. 'There are other possibilities. Say, for example, this man sends his initial report and only later realizes from the photo that *Runefish* is Nolan. Or that he knows it all along, but holds back the information because Nolan is also a witness of his murder of Goddard.' Stocker sighed again. 'Not being privy to the exact nature of the operation, I can't say any more. You're in a better position to judge than I am. I'd strongly suggest, though, that whether we're dealing with one person or two, the *Runefish* mission is in imminent danger of being compromised.'

Caine crouched in the cover of an arbutus tree, watching as *Gracie* began her slow descent of the spur from a panhandle three hundred feet above the wadi bed. She was the last of the wagons to come down. The tightness of the spur – only finger-lengths of clearance on both sides – made the operation almost as dicey as the ascent at Shallal in the early hours of that morning. Though the other six vehicles had all made it down nose-first under their own steam, there had been a flap when *Marlene* had suffered a crack in her differential cover-plate. Caine didn't anticipate any such problem with *Gracie*. Her driver, Bob O'Brian, had engaged six-wheel drive, and despite her massive load of fuel, and the fact that she was towing the water-bowser, Caine felt confident that she would make it without a hitch.

In the limpid light, the truck and bowser looked bigger than they really were. Caine couldn't make out O'Brian's face in the shadows of the cab, but he could clearly see the pumpkin head and tanned, muscular back of Todd Sweeney, poised on the slope ten feet below the lorry, directing the driver with hand signals. Sweeney, clad only in boots, socks, shorts and stocking-cap, with his Tommy-gun slung over his shoulder, seemed impervious to the heat, which was coming down like ladles of scalding grease.

The hint of salty moisture in the air reminded Caine that the sea wasn't far off, and the thought troubled him. If the Med was that close, so was Benghazi. According to

Sheikh Adud, now curled up under a tree in seemingly untroubled sleep, the track they'd bypassed lay only a short distance down the wadi, and they still had ample time to bump the Brandenburger column. Considering they'd been going at slug-speed for the past twelve hours, that sounded incredible, but Caine had no reason to doubt the word of the Senussi sheikh, who had proved correct in almost everything else.

He stood up yawning, and wiped waxy sweat off his forehead with his silk tankie scarf. It had been a long night and an even longer morning. All the way along the side of the Jebel from Shallal he'd felt naked and vulnerable. It had only needed one Axis shufti-wallah to pole up, and the whole unit would have been steak tartare.

It had seemed for ever before the ledge had played out into the panhandle, with the narrow spur falling sharply into the wadi bed, dappled by thickets of ilex, arbutus and cork oaks. The three 3 tonners and the Daimler were now leaguered under the trees, well concealed from the air, while Caine had sent the Dingo on ahead to recce an ambush site and to locate the enemy column. He would feel much happier when this last vehicle was down.

He took a last glance at *Gracie*, satisfied that she was on track, and that Sweeney and O'Brian, between them, could manage to get her down, and turned his back on the truck. He wandered back to the leaguer, where the wagon crews were stripping machine-guns, chugging petrol, mending punctures, replacing spark-plugs and fan-belts. Wingnut Turner called him over to inspect the repair job he'd just completed on *Marlene's* crushed cover-plate. 'Hammered it back into shape and bolted it on, skipper,' he said. 'It won't give us any more trouble.'

'Outstanding job, mate,' Caine told him. 'Especially in

these conditions.' He meant it – it was work that even his perfectionist father would have been proud of.

He heard roars of laughter from a knot of men in the shade of an ilex tree, Wallace's great thorn-bush of a head conspicuous amongst them. Striding over to investigate, he was met by a sight that struck him as shockingly obscene. Medical Orderly Pickney was straddling the body of Private Ross MacDonald, attempting to shove a grease-gun up his arse. MacDonald, a grizzled, bearded vet of the Black Watch, was stretched out on his belly with his hands braced round the tree-trunk and his rifle next to him. He was buck naked apart from his socks and boots. It dawned on Caine rather belatedly that this was a medical operation. MacDonald had been complaining of painful constipation for the past two days, and lacking equipment for an enema, Pickney had improvised with a grease-gun from one of the wagons, attached to a tube of soapy water. Though Caine didn't know it, what was causing the ruckus was the fact that the grease-gun's nozzle was square, not round, and though Pickney had wrapped it with a cloth smeared in petroleum jelly, the operation was proving unexpectedly difficult.

'You're *enjoying* this, Pickney,' Mac roared. 'For God's sake go easy with that thing.'

'Stop belly-aching, MacDonald. You *asked* for it, re-member?'

'Hey, Mac,' Wallace bellowed. 'You highlanders are all sheep-shaggers, ain't you? Well, now you know what it's like to be the sheep.'

Caine joined in the general explosion of glee, but Mac-Donald turned his face aside to glare at Wallace. 'Eat shit, you big baboon,' he yelled.

Caine was about to tell them to give Mac some privacy when he clocked Todd Sweeney weaving into the cover of the trees, his Tommy-gun dangling from a naked, mutton-chop shoulder. He was surprised to see the corporal back so soon. 'Is *Gracie* down?' he enquired.

Sweeney shook his football-sized head. 'Nah. O'Brian's competent, so I left him to it.'

Caine was about to ask more, when there was a *crack – crack – crack* of rifle fire from beyond the trees – three or four crisp gunshots sounding impossibly loud against the valley's tranquil backdrop. Caine braced his Tommy-gun and whirled round to see that the men had dropped everything and were fanning out into the scrub. Sweeney was inching cautiously towards the edge of cover. As Caine followed, he found that Copeland and Wallace had taken up positions on either side of him. Caine crouched down next to Sweeney, in time to hear the ex-MP whisper, '*Oh shit.*'

Following his gaze up the spur, Caine saw *Gracie*, about a hundred feet up the slope, with both her front wheels hanging over the precipice. This time, Caine could see the head and bandaged neck of O'Brian in the driver's seat, slumped across the steering-wheel. The glass in front of him had been shattered by gunshots. 'O'Brian's hit,' Copeland whispered. 'She's out of control . . .'

For a moment, Caine thought the weight of the water-bowser would hold her, but an instant later both her left-side rear tyres were over the rim. The four-wheeled bowser arched out in a jack-knife: its wheels reeled out into empty space. Caine let out a moan, his eyes riveted on the bowser as it tipped sideways, pulling the truck with it. 'She's going,' Cope gasped.

Wallace's chiselled jaw dropped: his eyes bulged. '*Jackson*,' he hissed. 'Jackson's in there.' He took a pace forward: Caine jerked him back. All four of them gaped helplessly, as, with exquisite slowness, *Gracie* tumbled sideways into the abyss.

They hurled themselves flat just as lorry and bowser kerauned into the wadi bed a hundred and fifty yards away, detonating instantly with a lung-crushing *vrrrrooooom* of high explosive. The air folded, the ground pitched, sand and gravel slingshotted, loose grenades trumped like firecrackers. Caine saw the spindling starflash of the wagon's convulsion – the frame turning fluid, snaking out of shape, un-riveting into a million black slivers – engine fragments, scorched flesh, spatters of boiling rubber, spurts of liquefied glass – all blowing outwards, riding a tidal wave of roiling red lava and black smoke. A lobe of gas and flame ballooned across the wadi, expanding until it buckled like a windless parachute, whip-cracking back in a dark hail of dust, pebbles, shrapnel shards. Gouts of foul smoke plumed up from the valley floor.

'Jesus wept,' Copeland mouthed.

They struggled to their feet, lungs and throats scorched from the blast, faces lucent with shock. Caine sensed movement behind him, saw commandos careening through the thickets with fire extinguishers, waved them back. 'There's a sniper out there,' he yelled.

It would have been hopeless, anyway. The Marmon Herrington was a gutted-out skeleton in a nimbus of licking flames, and there was a mat of crackling debris strewn over hundreds of feet – gobs of shredded rubber, slugs of white-hot metal, rissole-like knobs of matter giving off the stink of charred meat. There was no sign of a body – not even a whole limb. 'Not enough to fill an egg cup,' Wallace grunted, his voice quavering. His eyes were poisonous black peridots. Mauve blotches bloomed on his cheeks. 'Poor buggers,' he croaked. 'Didn't even know what hit 'em.' He reeled, his castle-like body hanging over Copeland. 'I told you about them Hawkins grenades, didn't I?' he bellowed.

'The crush igniters must of gone up and set off the petrol – that's why the blowout was so big. I *told* you. I warned you about them.' He looked as if he was itching to belt somcone – most probably Cope – but Caine thumped his arm. 'Don't be a turd, Fred,' he said. 'It wasn't the Hawkins grenades. Once she went over, there was no stopping the fuel going up.'

He wheeled round on the other men, now hunkered in the trees with weapons trained. 'Anybody clock muzzle flash?'

No one answered. Wallace was still glowering at Copeland and was about to say something else when Ross MacDonald padded out of the shadows behind them, head and body held in a low slouch. He was carrying his rifle in both hands, cocked and ready: he had managed to slip on a pair of shorts. 'I saw smoke, skipper,' he said. 'When I was on my belly. I saw it through a gap in the trees. Look left down the wadi, about four, mebbe five hundred yards.'

Caine craned his neck to look down the wadi, but the angle was too acute and the foliage too thick for a good view: in any case the air was now opaque with smoke from *Gracie's* burning wreck. He came up into a crouch and tried to peer around the trees, while MacDonald inched forward to indicate the target. Mac had taken one step beyond cover for a better look when gunshots zipped and whizzed: the back of his head globed-out like blown glass, ruptured, blistered, shredded apart in raw red ribbons. The force of the strike lamped him off his feet, cartwheeled his body ten feet through the sand, thumped it down in a nearly headless bloody parcel. Caine teetered, swayed back. '*Take cover,*' he screamed.

Commandos ate dirt, swallowed dust, dry-swam sand, as another rasp of fire crinkled air, spiffled leaves, scuttered off stones, chugged up sand-smoke. Caine clocked flashes in the scrub five hundred paces east down the wadi. Raising himself on his elbows, he tweaked the rear sight on his Tommy-gun, knowing even as he did so that the target was out of his range. 'One o'clock,' he yelped. 'Five hundred yards. Enemy in scrub. Fire.'

Nobody fired, and Caine clicked that none of the men had a clear view of the target. Wallace was lying with his Colt pointing down the wadi, and Caine could see the frustration written on his cave-man features. In his hurry to find out what was happening, he'd left his Bren on its bipod brace twenty feet away, and his Colt was good for close-quarter battle only. Copeland crawled closer to Caine, peering through his telescopic sight. 'Incoming's stopped, skipper,' he grunted. 'Whoever bumped us, it's a small squad – maybe a two-man sniping team. Now they've done the business I reckon they're crawling out through the scrub.'

'Whoever it is, they're good,' Caine said. He considered ordering the Lewis gunners to blitz the whole segment, or to have the two-inch mortars set up, but thought better of it – it would just mean more wasted ammunition. He could hear the Daimler's engine strobing, and a moment later she edged out of a thicket with Murray's head popping from the top hatch. 'Get that wagon up the wadi after them, Flash,' Caine shouted. As Murray gave him a thumbs-up, he turned back to Cope. 'Go with him, Harry. Stay in cover behind the AFV unless you see the shooters making a break for it. If they climb the escarpment, Murray won't be able to follow. Take Wallace and . . . where's that Arab? Take him with you as tracker. I want those bastards found. I don't want any sod warning the Brandenburgers we're here.'

Caine yelled for Adud, and a moment later the old man moved cautiously into view, his Mannlicher rifle in his hands, his eyes bird-bright. Behind him came his daughter, Layla, and Naiman. Layla was still wearing her black robe, but Caine noticed that she had tied back her glossy dark hair with a leather thong, and now wore a belt at her waist, into which a pistol was stuffed – he recognized the dead Feldwebel's Mauser. 'Go with Cope,' Caine said, gesturing. 'Follow the armoured car. No, not her, just you, Sheikh.'

Adud gabbled something in Arabic, and Naiman said. 'He reckons his daughter's a better tracker than he is.'

Caine hesitated. It went against the grain to expose a girl to danger, but he'd seen the fury of the Bedouin women at Umm 'Aijil, and knew she'd go whether he agreed or not. 'Whatever,' he swore irritably. 'I don't give a toss who goes, just get down there, pronto, or the buggers will be well out of it.'

Copeland paused to let the Daimler draw alongside, with Murray still peering over the hatch. 'Go steady,' Caine told him. 'Cover the group behind you.'

'Right you are, skipper.'

'And get your nut inside, Flash. These blokes just made a head shot at five hundred yards.'

The AFV rumbled off, her four balloon-tyres grooving sand, her turret grinding, swivelling left and right. Copeland followed the vehicle at a slow trot, with Wallace, Naiman and the two Senussi close behind him. Caine eased himself up and saw Todd Sweeney hauling Mac's corpse into the cover of the trees, leaving crimson tramlines in the sand. 'Must have been a dum-dum,' Sweeney muttered.

'Stay here,' Caine said.

He called a couple of the men over to bury the Scotsman's body, remembering guiltily how, only minutes ago, he'd joined the others in poking fun at him. O'Brian, Jackson, MacDonald: all good men. It was too many for one day, and it wasn't over yet. Sour fury and frustration beavered at his chest as he watched them carry away Mac's mutilated body. He wanted to lash out at the nearest target, to tear and rip someone to pieces, to hear them scream. He would rather have taken a hit himself than have MacDonald go down. It was his responsibility to bring his men home safely, a duty he'd already failed in dismally, thanks to his own folly, his own bad judgement. His unit was now down to seventeen men – almost a quarter of its strength gone. The loss of so many good mates weighed on him like a millstone, and he was furious with himself for accepting such a mission, furious with St Aubin for risking these men's lives on a wing and a prayer.

Caine remembered that Sweeney was still waiting and turned on him with fire in his eyes. 'I told you to guide O'Brian down,' he roared. 'Why did you ditch him?'

Sweeney bristled, stuck out his chin. 'He was doing fine until that sniper opened up. Even if I'd been there I couldn't have done much, or are you trying to pin his death on me now?'

'I want to know why you disobeyed orders.'

'I used commando initiative. O'Brian didn't need me, so I decided to let him go it alone. It could just as well have been me hit as him. How was I to know there'd be a contact the minute I left?'

Caine felt rage sour-mashing his stomach, fought to keep it down. 'It didn't occur to you that O'Brian was a wounded man and might need some help?'

'Now wait a minute,' Sweeney gasped. 'If he was wounded that bad, why did you let him take the wheel? I was designated driver on that rattletrap, not O'Brian. I could have brought her down myself, but you dismissed me last night, in front of all the men. I've got ten years' experience on you, and yet you stood me down, and gave my job to a wounded driver.'

Caine bit his lip as it dawned on him that Sweeney's action had been a deliberate gesture of contempt. He'd put lives at risk through his own resentment. Caine sucked in breath, tasted hot dust and bile. 'I stood you down because you're an arrogant bastard, Sweeney. So you've been in the army ten years longer than me? So what? Pity you didn't learn a few things while you were about it. Like how to be a decent soldier. None of us is an expert at everything, not me, not you, nobody. Your trouble is that you think you know it all, even when you know nothing.'

Sweeney's punch-ball face contorted with rage, his simian arms swinging listlessly, fists clenched as if he wanted to beat Caine to death. 'That's just it, isn't it, Caine? You think I've never got my knees brown before this stunt. Let me tell you, I was with the minefield pathfinder squad in the MPs. We used to lay out routes through the minefields with red and green lamps, after your Sappers had cleared them. One wrong step and you could kiss your arse goodbye. We lost half the squad with limbs blown away.'

Caine shook his head, tried to damp down his fury. 'When will you get it into that fat bloody head that this isn't about you and your ego? Nobody's ever questioned your courage. I don't give a rat's arse what mob you were with, it doesn't qualify you to ignore orders . . .'

'You're lecturing me on *orders*. That *really* takes the biscuit. The Sapper subaltern who lost his commission because he refused an order to clear a minefield. The sergeant who was almost court-martialled for risking his mates' lives to bring in some wounded men he'd been ordered to abandon. I know all about you, Caine, and now you're telling *me* . . .'

'You don't know a damn' thing about me, Sweeney, and

I don't give a tinker's cuss what you think you know. I'm patrol commander on this jaunt, and if you ever fall short in your job again, I shall personally make sure that you never serve with another special-service unit . . .'

Caine's pronouncement was nipped in the bud by the slap of a gunshot from further up the wadi. He turned away sharply, groping in his haversack for binoculars. He brought them out and scanned the area. There was no movement, but he continued to scan for the next few minutes, until he saw the Daimler emerge into view in a bolus of dust. The search party was huddled behind the AFV, and he counted off Adud, Layla, Cope, Naiman and Wallace, dragging along with them two prisoners. Even from this distance, he could tell that they weren't Ities or Jerries. '*A-rabs*,' Sweeney announced with wonder in his voice. 'They've bagged a couple of Senussi.'

They were Bedouin boys named Saalim and Sa'id, aged no more than fourteen or fifteen, clad in sand-hued shifts and baggy trousers, their hair in shoulder-length rat's tails, smeared with what smelled like animal fat. They might have been twins, except that while Saalim sported a thin fluff of whisker on his chin, Sa'id's face was as smooth as a billiard ball. They looked sullen, contemptuous and completely unafraid, and possessed an aura of dignity that was not diminished by their rags, nor by the fact that their hands were bound.

Copeland shoved them roughly into a sitting position and showed Caine the rifles and cartridge belts he'd taken from them. 'This one took a pot-shot at me,' he said, pointing at Saalim. 'Missed me by a hair. Good job he was running away at the time, or I'd have been dogmeat. See the cartridges? Homemade dum-dums, the lot of them.'

Caine slipped a cartridge out of one of the belts and

examined it – a flat-topped round whose soft head was scored deeply with a cross-cut. On impact it would tumble through the vital organs, mash them up, cause sympathetic fractures, create cavities – that was why MacDonald's exit wound had been so huge. Caine remembered Lt Rowland Green, killed by a dum-dum on the Gazala Line. It hadn't been much more than a week ago, but it might have happened in another life. The boys' rifles were antiques: Martini-Henri breech-loaders of the type issued to British troops fifty years earlier. Caine couldn't believe that these rag-arsed kids had kept such old weapons in such good nick, nor that they were capable of making the deadly long-range shots that had taken out his men.

'You sure it was them?' he demanded.

'It was them all right,' Cope said. 'They admitted it. They told Moshe they thought we were Jerries: said they heard from some Senussi who fled from that village yesterday that the Huns were executing Arabs. They thought we were coming to do them in. It was a mistake.'

'Oh, a *mistake*,' crowed Wallace, who until now had been glowering silently at the boys. 'That's just dandy then, *innit*? Come on, skipper, let's get this over with, or we'll miss *Runefish*.' He squared his giant shoulders towards the boys and drew his fanny in a fluid movement.

'Hold it, Fred,' Caine said, turning to Naiman. 'Corporal, can you ask the sheikh what Senussi custom is in a case like this?'

Naiman exchanged words with the old man, then turned back to Caine, his face impassive. 'He says that the custom is clear. It's an eye for an eye, even if the death was an accident.'

'Hah,' Wallace said.

'That's not all, though,' Naiman went on, looking hard

at the big gunner. 'He *also* said that these boys are his relatives. Their father is ... I don't know ... his second cousin or something. He says that they're just shepherds, protecting their flocks and families. He asks for clemency.'

Wallace drew himself up and sheathed his fanny. He pulled out his Colt .45 pistol and cocked the working-parts with a snap. 'Tell you what,' he said slowly, 'I'll give 'em clemency. Same clemency they give Mac and Bubbles and Jacko. I'll shoot 'em in the head.'

He took a pace towards them, but Adud intercepted him. With the Gunner's long-shanked form towering over him, the old sheikh looked small and brittle, yet his gravel-hewn face was as hard as cut stone.

'Leave it out, Fred,' Copeland said, assuming his familiar expression of professorial disdain. 'Is it *just* possible there might be things you haven't considered?'

Wallace flared at him. 'Don't give me none of your school-ma'am bullshit, Harry. The old boy hisself said it's an eye for an eye. It don't matter who they *thought* we was, they offed three of our mates, and they're going to get what's coming to 'em.'

'I didn't say they don't *deserve* it,' Copeland said. 'I feel the same as you about our mates, but like I said, there are other factors. Whether it was a mistake or not, how do you think the rest of the Senussi are going to feel if you do these lads in? We're in their territory, five hundred miles behind enemy lines. It wouldn't be a great idea to turn them against us now.'

'I'm damned if I come here to worry about a bunch of towel-heads ...' Wallace snarled. He bumped Adud aside like a skittle, only to find that Naiman had taken his place.

The interpreter put a firm hand on Wallace's hairy, tattooed gun arm. 'You don't get it, you great dollop,' he said.

Wallace stared at the hand as if it were something dirty, then slapped it away. 'Who the hell d'you think *you* are?' he demanded.

Naiman didn't blink. 'Last time I looked,' he said, 'I was Lance Corporal Moshe Naiman. In an ordinary unit, you would address me as *Corporal*, but since we're the commandos, we can let that ride. The point is that this eye-for-an-eye business works both ways. Whether they did it on purpose or not doesn't matter to the Senussi. If you bump off the sheikh's relatives, he'll be forced to declare a vendetta against us, and that will extend to the whole family – scores, maybe hundreds of tribesmen. It's their custom, and it's like a death sentence. None of us will get out of Cyrenaica alive.'

Wallace scowled, appealing to Caine. 'Are we going to let this clap-trap stop us?' he demanded. 'It should be tit for tat, like the old boy said.'

Caine thought it over quickly, knowing they hadn't got time for niceties. The easiest solution would have been just to let Wallace have his way, and be done with it. He understood exactly how the big man felt, because it was how *he* felt. In the end, Wallace wanted desperately to kill someone. It wasn't that he was a mental case or a born murderer, it was just that when you lost your mates it was the most obvious way to relieve the tension.

Copeland's attitude was cold-cocked, practical. The rights and wrongs of the case didn't matter to Cope: all that mattered was getting the commandos out of this situation intact. Caine had sympathies with both arguments, but he wasn't profoundly moved by either. 'I don't know these kids from Adam,' he said, 'and I'll never know whose side they're really on. Maybe with all the coming and going, they don't know themselves. To me, the only point is that they're kids. They can't be above fourteen years old. I don't care what they did, or what their motives were, there aren't going to be any children executed while I'm in command. If we do them in, we're no better than those Krauts who hanged women and children at the village yesterday. No doubt they thought they had their justifications.'

Wallace opened his mouth to argue, but Caine locked eyes with him, raised his chin, squared his tank-like torso, clenched his fists. 'Put it away, Fred,' he said. 'Or are you going to shoot me too?'

Wallace looked outraged. He made a gargling sound, as if he were trying to summon up an argument. Finally, with an expression of utter revulsion, he holstered his pistol, turned and stumped away.

Adud gestured to the boys to stand up and drew out a small pocket knife to cut their ropes. 'No,' Caine said, holding up his hand and darting a look at Naiman. 'They'll have to stay under restraint until after the engagement, so we can be sure they don't warn anyone we're here.' He turned to Copeland. 'Tie them to a couple of trees,' he said, 'but don't hurt them, and make sure they're comfortable.' He unslung his Tommy-gun and cocked the top handle with a crash. 'That's it for this morning's session, ladies,' he barked. 'Put what's left of *Gracie's* fire out and cover the fragments, then move to your wagons. We've got a date with the Brandenburg Special Duties Regiment.'

By the time Eisner had arrived at his quay in north Zamalek, the euphoria he'd felt on quitting Sim-Sim's flat had evaporated. The twenty minutes it had taken him to get home would normally have been enough to render the events of the night distant – the actions of a perpetrator only remotely related to himself. This time, though, the girl's words kept drifting back to him like a far-off bugle call: *One thing is certain: you're going straight to damnation.* He couldn't seem to get that thrilling contralto off his mind.

The bitch had bled like a stuck sow, and his clothes were spattered with gore. As he parked his car down a side-street, removing his black wig and the rubber pads he used to distort his features, he found that his hands were shaking. He donned a mackintosh, stuffed his knife and .38 pistol into its pockets and slouched the two hundred yards to his houseboat, teetering like a drunk.

As he crossed the gangplank, he noticed the wine-coloured vein of fire running along the seam of the Muqattam plateau to the east: the air was cool, but already he could feel latent heat promising another sweltering Cairo day. On the sundeck he paused to listen for any sounds that might be out of place, sampling the air for unfamiliar odours. He smelt only the bouquet of jasmine from a nearby garden, heard only the bass honk of bullfrogs, the falsetto rasp of cicadas in the sycamores along the riverbank, the almost indecent suck and squelch of the Nile around the boat's hull. He glanced across the lapping water at the houseboat moored a hundred yards away. No lights were showing, which meant that his friend, Major Beeston, was still in bed. That his neighbour happened to be an officer of GHQ's Inter-Services Liaison Department – a cover name for MI6 – had been one of the main reasons he'd rented this boat. No one would suspect a man living under the nose of a senior British Intelligence officer of being a spy.

He descended the steps, unlocked the cabin door. As he opened it, he made sure that nothing had disturbed the hairpin he always left underneath. It was still in place, and he closed and bolted the door, satisfied that no one had been inside since he'd been away.

He walked through the padded passage to the main cabin. The state room was palatial – luxuriously furnished with deep carpets, Kashmir sheepskins, woven drapes showing voluptuous women from the Arabian Nights, soft divans with brocaded silk cushions, intricately carved Arab tables, a large radiogram, a telephone, a refrigerator, a fully stocked bar.

Eisner went straight through to his bedroom, stripped off his blood-smeared garments and threw them on the bare boards. Standing naked in the bathroom, he cleaned the blood off his knife and hid it behind the cistern, together with his memento: the carefully wrapped piece of Sim-Sim's ear. He doused himself with buckets of cold river water, and feeling much better, put on a bathrobe, wadded his discarded clothes in newspaper and hurled them through a window into the Nile.

He considered pouring himself a stiff Scotch but instead decided on coffee. For Eisner, brewing coffee was a soothing ritual – it wasn't the usual ersatz malt muck, nor the new-fangled Nescafé, but real mocha bought on the black market. When it was ready, he took the cafetière through to the main cabin, set it on a low table and sat down on the divan, relaxing on the wonderfully lush cushions. After he'd drunk two cups of coffee and smoked a cigarette, he felt ready to broach the wireless cubicle concealed along the passage.

The suitcase transmitter was open on the desk, and it only remained for him to connect the battery, the Morse key and the antenna. When that was done, he sat down at the desk with his codebook and encryption pad. He put on the headphones, picked up a pencil, paused, then slapped it down again. He realized that he didn't know what to write.

At Sim-Sim's he'd been convinced that he'd unearthed a high-level decoy plan – a scheme that had the British Deception Service stamped all over it. Now he was nagged by doubt. Sim-Sim's curse – *One thing is certain: you're going straight to damnation* – had at first seemed a shot in the dark. Now, he found himself wondering if it might be the key to a secret agenda. Had the girl known something she'd kept hidden from him – something that he hadn't quizzed her about in his zeal to get the goods on Betty? What did he really know about this *Runefish* operation, anyway? He'd been handed a schedule that mentioned a cyanide pill, and Natalie had talked about a G(R) – Special Operations Executive – officer named Julian Avery, whom she claimed had referred to Winston Churchill. He'd seen a female naval officer in full uniform riding in a GHQ staff car that had ambled along as if its occupant *wanted* to be shadowed. By an amazing coincidence, the woman in the car had turned out to be about the only person in the world who might be able to identify him as a rapist and murderer. Could that really be random chance?

The Field Security bloodhounds had been after him for

months, ever since the Goddard incident. What if this entire plan was their gambit to flush him out? What if he'd been fed the supposed *Runefish* schedule deliberately?

As for Betty Nolan, he hadn't actually seen her get on an aircraft at Helwan. He couldn't be sure that she'd gone anywhere: for all he knew, she might be in Cairo still. The more he pondered it, the more it seemed to him that this flaunting of a beautiful blonde in full naval regalia, in a conspicuous staff car, wasn't British style. The British made a fetish of understatement and discretion: why send someone who was going to stand out like a nun in a nudist colony, unless you wanted her to be noticed? Could Betty Nolan be the bait in a noose that was slowly tightening around his neck?

Eisner switched off the transmitter. Having had no feedback from Rohde, his controller, on the initial *Runefish* report, it was impossible to say whether any action had been taken, or even if the information was significant. Rohde had once accused him of 'maintaining a millionaire lifestyle at the expense of the Wehrmacht' in return for 'worthless intelligence'. It had been embarrassing, and he did not relish the idea of its happening again.

Rohde was one of the few men who scared Eisner. He had a disturbingly high-pitched voice that didn't fit his robust physique, and a feminine broadness of the pelvis that gave his postures a look that in anyone else might have been camp but in Rohde was grotesque and alarming. He had the revoltingly long fingers of a violinist – so spidery that, behind his back, his colleagues called him the 'Black Widow'. Eisner had heard rumours about Rohde's actions in Poland and with the Jews in Russia that made his own private activities look like kindergarten romps. The main difference between Eisner and Rohde, though, was that his boss was a family man with a good Nazi wife and four children who had been fanatically devoted to Hitler and to the party since its pre-war street-fighting days. Eisner, who regarded Egypt as his home, wasn't exactly a patriot – at least not in the fanatical sense that Rohde was. Rohde was astute enough to know that Eisner was in it for the adventure, and for what he could get out of it. It wasn't that Eisner didn't want Hitler to win, only that he'd rather it didn't happen just now, when his life was going so well.

He sat down on the divan and closed his eyes, focusing all his attention on the problem. Within ten minutes he had come up with three possible courses of action. The first, to interrogate Natalie, would be simple enough, but he quickly struck it from the list. The French cabaret girl might possibly be working for Field Security, but he strongly doubted it. If anything, she'd be their unwitting tool. The second course would be much more tricky: snatch and interrogate the officer from whom Natalie claimed to have stolen the *Runefish* schedule, the G(R) captain, Julian Avery. The third course was to investigate Nolan's flat on the Gezira, to find out if it was still being used, and if so, by whom.

The flat job would have to be done at once, before Field Security found the dead Sim-Sim and started thinking about what she might have told him. He knew that he was drained mentally and physically, and that he couldn't go out again without sleep. He decided to delegate the job to his assistant, Pieter Shaffer. Shaffer was expendable, and in any case this was a job he could manage perfectly well.

He lifted the telephone receiver, dialled 18343 and heard a voice say 'Zamalek Cotton Exporters'.

'Pieter?' he enquired. 'It's Leonard. Are we secure?'

'Yes.'

'Make a note of this address: Flat 1, 22 al-Hadiqa Street,

the Gezira. I want you to go and find out who's living there, if anyone.'

'Got it. Is this a surveillance job?'

'No, there's no time for a long stake-out. Go right up to the door, ring the bell. Say you're working for the Red Cross and that you have a package for a Betty Nolan. *Betty Nolan*, got that? Treat whoever answers to your most winning smile.'

'What if no one answers?'

'There'll be a concierge. Ask for information.'

'What if the place is already under surveillance?'

Eisner glanced at his watch. It was now 0729 hours, almost ninety minutes since he'd left Sim-Sim's. The odds were that no one had discovered her body yet. On the other hand, if this was a set-up with himself as the target, Nolan's flat might be staked out as a matter of course. If so, then it would be Shaffer who would cop for it, not him. That would be inconvenient, but not fatal: Shaffer could lead them to his houseboat, but he didn't know anything about major projects, or about Eisner's 'extracurricular' activities. He didn't know the whereabouts of Eisner's reserve transmitter or his other safe house. He didn't even know Eisner's real name. It was worth the risk, he thought.

'If I believed that was a possibility, I wouldn't ask you,' he lied.

He heard Shaffer take a deep breath. 'All right,' he said. 'When do you want me to go?'

'Now. The longer you delay, the more chance of compromise.'

'I'm on it.'

Eisner put the phone down, popped four Phenobarbital tablets, and threw himself on the divan. Within minutes he was asleep.

Betty Nolan was chasing him through a labyrinth of dark alleys lined with open-fronted butcher's shops, where his boss, Heinrich Rohde, and other ghosts in tattered Waffen SS uniforms were cutting the throats of lambs hanging from meat-hooks. There were pools of blood on the floor, and blood smeared the walls. Betty was pointing a crooked finger at him, and whichever way he ran he couldn't escape her burning red eyes. It was like that poster of Lord Kitchener he'd seen on a trip to England – *Your country needs you* – only instead, Nolan was whispering, '*One thing is certain: you're going straight to damnation.*' For a second, Nolan's face was replaced by Sim-Sim's, veiled in her magnificent black hair, then the same hair was framing the face of his equally beautiful mother, Eva – the mother he'd hated, the mother who'd betrayed him by marrying the Egyptian, Idriss, the mother he'd silenced for good. Eisner surfaced from the dark river of sleep, gasping for air, and realized that someone was banging on the passage door.

He rolled off the divan, snatched the .38-calibre Smith & Wesson from under a cushion, and tied up his bathrobe. Speckles of light fell across the state room from the venetian blinds. He stalked down the passage, peeped through the spyhole in the door, and saw Shaffer – a tall, sandy-haired man with classic, square-chinned looks wearing a crumpled off-white tropical suit. He was slapping a rolled-up news-paper against his open palm in a rhythmic tattoo – sets of three long slaps and two short ones – a signal that he hadn't been compromised.

Eisner let him in and closed the door. Shaffer's clear blue eyes fell on the .38 in his hand. 'I was battering on the door for ages,' he said, showing a perfect set of pearl-white teeth. 'You must be getting past it, old man.'

Eisner forced a grin. 'Long surveillance job last night,' he said. 'Absolute murder.' He was in no mood for Shaffer's irrepressibly jolly manner, but it had to be tolerated. A South African by nationality, Shaffer belonged to a German immigrant family in Pietermaritzberg who had almost lost their culture, and who preferred to speak English rather than German. His German was flawed, and he knew no more Arabic than he knew Chinese, but he could pass convincingly as a South African cotton broker with British sympathies.

Eisner told him to make more coffee, and went to dress. When he returned, Shaffer was perched on the divan with a cafetière of fresh coffee and his newspaper spread out on the low table. 'Did you see this stop press?' he said excitedly. 'The Luftwaffe launched a massive attack on Tobruk just before dawn this morning, 20 June, bombing the mine-fields. Rommel's probably inside the perimeter already.' He turned a page. 'The BBC scored a wonderful home goal last night. They declared in a broadcast that Tobruk isn't important, and that it doesn't matter a damn if Rommel takes it. That'll really set the cat among the pigeons – imagine the slap in the face to the thousands of soldiers who've died defending it.'

Eisner sat down next to him and poured himself coffee. 'It's up to your lot now, isn't it?' he said. '2nd South African Division. General Klopper.'

Shaffer's blue eyes glinted in a bar of light. 'Klopper will fight to the last bullet. If Rommel *is* inside Tobruk today, you'll see some real fighting.'

'Sometimes I wonder whose side you're really on, Pieter,' Eisner chuckled. 'Whether you're convinced, or just practising your cover. Or maybe you don't know yourself.'

Shaffer put on a hurt look. 'My good man, how dare you? My heart is with the Afrikaners at Tobruk, and ever will be.'

'In that case you've had it. Klopper will hoist the white flag the moment the first panzer enters the town – if he hasn't already.'

'So what will Rommel do then? Will he march on Alex and Cairo?'

'He'll be here in a week. Haven't you noticed that our Jewish, Turkish and Greek friends have done a bunk already?'

He offered Shaffer a cigarette from a box, took one himself and lit both with his gold Ronson lighter. Shaffer sat back and blew out a jet of smoke, watching it swirl in a lightshaft. 'So why do I sense that you're not exactly over the moon at the prospect?' he enquired.

'That's easy,' Eisner said, making a sweeping gesture around the state room with his cigarette. 'I've grown accustomed to certain standards. Cairo's the most exciting city in the world. When Rommel gets here, we'll both be out of a job.'

There was a moment's silence while the two men puffed. 'So, did you do it?' Eisner asked.

'I did, but I wish you would tell me what this is about.'

'All in good time. Now, what happened?'

Shaffer let out another long stream of smoke. 'It turned out to be a first-floor flat,' he said. 'You go through a hallway and up the stairs. There's a concierge – an old Berberine, black as your hat. I left the car hidden in another street, and did a turn up and down, looking out for watchers – you know, surreptitious movements at windows, that kind of thing . . .'

'Spare me the counter-surveillance lecture. I trained you, remember? Get on with it.'

'All right. well, it's quite a busy street near al-Gala'a bridge – newly built flats. Lot of pedestrians, a few cars going past.

I don't see anyone eyeballing me, so I finally approach the address – art-deco block, five storeys. The concierge is a bit obstructive, but nothing five piastres won't settle. He says there's a girl there – been there years. He can't tell me her name because it's against the rules, and he can't say if she's in right now. "What does she do for a living?" I ask. The old boy winks. "Nightclub dancer," he says. Anyway, I ring the bell. Nothing happens. I wait a few minutes, and ring again. Nothing. I decide to give it one more go – otherwise it's going to look a bit fishy to the Berberine. I ring a third time. Nothing again. I'm just about to give it up when I hear footsteps. The door opens, and there she is, this girl.'

Eisner stared at him intently. 'What was she like?'

'Beautiful – tall, legs to drive you wild. Nice figure, green eyes, shortish blond hair. Young, maybe twenty-three, twenty-four. Regal bearing – fit – might be an athlete. Anyway, she's giving me the once-over with these big green eyes, very haughty, saying, "Can I help you?" and I flash her the lady-killer smile. I can see it works, because a second later she's melting, and the old eyes are twinkling, as if to say, "Now, there's a handsome man."'

'Pieter, get on with it.'

Shaffer smirked. 'If you've got it, flaunt it, I always say . . . anyhow, I tell her that I work for the Red Cross and I have a package back at the office for a Miss Betty Nolan. Does she live here?'

Eisner bent forward, making no attempt to conceal his excitement. 'What did she say?'

Shaffer noticed the change in his manner and sat back, as if drawing out the moment deliberately. He paused, then went on. 'She said, "I'm Betty Nolan, but who'd want to send me a Red Cross parcel?" "I don't know, miss," I say, "but now I know you're here, I'll send it along." She smiles again, and for a minute I think she's going to invite me in. But then she says, "Thank you, that's very kind of you. Goodbye." A second later the door's closed.'

Eisner let out a low whistle. He brought out his wallet, extracted from it the photo of *Runefish* and slapped it on the table in front of Shaffer. 'Study it closely,' he said. 'Is this her?'

Shaffer picked up the snapshot and held it up in a beam of light. There was a short hiatus while he examined it. Then he laid the snap back on the table and surveyed Eisner with crystal-blue eyes. 'I'd lay a thousand guineas on it,' he said. 'That's the woman I saw.'

23

The Dingo was parked in a pool of shade under a wind-twisted pine where the wadi met the track, her camouflage making her invisible from more than a few yards. As the convoy approached, George Padstowe peeked over the hatch, a pipe stuck in his mouth. He was an ex-Marine, so completely bald that his head looked like a smooth brown boulder. He clambered out through the lower hatch, while Taffy Trubman's fish-shaped head poked up over the top. Caine told Copeland to stop and jumped down to meet Padstowe.

'They're on the way, skipper,' the bald man said breathlessly. 'I reckon we've got half an hour at most. There's a top-hole ambush site just on that bend.' He pointed his pipe down the track to where it vanished around the foot of a forested escarpment. On the right-hand side lay an undulating gorse-covered plain, stretching away like a horsehair carpet. The smell of the sea was stronger here, but any view of the Mediterranean was blocked by a succession of low ridges covered in acacia bush and hummock-grass. Caine saw that the escarpment would give the ambushers a clear advantage: the maquis scrub was thick and high enough to conceal men and vehicles, and the steep ground would give them a commanding view. The only drawback he could see was an irrigation trench on the other side of the road, which would provide the enemy with cover when they debussed. From the high ground, though, even that would be susceptible to enfilade fire. 'There's a slope on the other side of the bend,' Padstowe went on. 'That means the wagons will have to change down just as they're approaching.'

'Perfect killing zone,' Caine said. 'How many vehicles in the convoy, what's the composition, and how far apart?'

Padstowe ran a hand over his bald skull, stuck his pipe back in his mouth nervously, then took it out again. 'Can't rightly say, skipper,' he said apologetically. 'I reckon there's no more than five, but they were kicking up quite a dust-cloud, and we couldn't get near enough to be certain. The road crosses an open plain past the slope, and we were going in for a close recce when an Itie kite rolls over, drops altitude and starts circling. Had to freeze.'

'We saw her,' said Caine. 'A C42 biplane. You weren't spotted?'

'No, but by the time she'd cleared off, I reckoned it was too late for a shufti. It's hard to be sure, but I estimate the wagons are doing about thirty, so I thought we'd better backtrack and report.'

'You did right,' Caine said, sounding happier than he felt. He knew that Padstowe had done his best, but the variables worried him. For an ideal vehicle ambush, he needed to know the number and composition of the wagons, the number of men, their firepower, and if possible even their orders on being attacked. He had already had Naiman quiz Adud and his daughter about the convoy's composition, but the events at their village the previous day had been too traumatic for them to recall precise details. Layla thought there might have been an armoured car, but wasn't sure.

Caine hustled the commandos over into the shade for a quick O-Group, getting Padstowe to draw a rough plan with a twig in the sand. It would be a classic ambush – a fire-group in the centre, cut-off groups and an AFV at each side. 'Our information is sketchy,' he told them. 'So it's going to be a hit-or-miss affair. You'll hear the wagons change down as they come up the slope. Hang fire till it looks like there's nothing else coming, then give them all you've got.'

'Hold on, skipper,' Copeland cut in urgently. 'This is not going to work.'

The commandos gawked at him. Caine glanced irritably at his watch. 'We haven't got time to debate it, Harry,' he said. 'They'll be here in twenty minutes.'

Cope was wearing his best school-ma'am expression. 'Skipper, we don't know where *Runefish* is being carried. If we blitz the column like you said, she'll be killed.'

Caine's heart flipped a beat. In the excitement he'd forgotten that they were there to snatch *Runefish*, not to wipe out an enemy convoy. He opened his mouth to answer, but Wallace cut in over him. 'So what?' he said sullenly. 'I thought that was the big idea.'

There were murmurs of surprise from the group, and Caine wondered why he hadn't told them before that *Runefish* might have to be taken out. Probably, he thought, because he'd never fully accepted the order himself. 'All right,' he said. 'For those who aren't clear on this, our orders are to snatch *Runefish*. We are only to execute her if it looks like there's no other choice, and Cope's right – that doesn't include cutting her down because she happens to be among the enemy.'

There was more murmuring, and Caine realized that even now he was skirting the truth. The execution order was intended to prevent Maddaleine Rose from giving secrets to the enemy, and for all he knew she might have talked already. Whatever the case, he had no intention of going in with all guns blattering before she'd been given the benefit of the doubt. He was about to speak when Wallace hissed, '*Listen.*' Caine cocked his ears: he could just make out the grumble of motors from far off. There was a second's apprehensive silence as everyone listened closely, straining to pick up the sound, as if they might be able to read some special meaning into it.

'All right, Harry,' Caine said. 'What's your plan? Make it fast, or they'll catch us with our pants down.'

Copeland scratched his bottle-brush blond hair. 'Bluff,' he said. 'We need to halt the convoy before we open fire. I suggest we use one of the 3-tonners and make out she's broken down. There's so much captured Allied transport around, they'll assume it's spoils of war. Set up the ambush groups and AFVs, just as you said, only no shooting till we locate *Runefish*. Me and you will stick our heads under the lorry's bonnet. Fred will hide in the cab, ready to brace the Lewis on top. Give Moshe one of the Schmeissers we liberated yesterday, and let him flag down the first wagon. When she halts, he'll talk to the driver in German. While he's doing that we'll locate *Runefish* and snatch her.'

Wallace chortled. 'You think those Brandenburgers are just going to hand her over? You're out of your tree, mate.'

'I didn't say they were going to hand her over. Why, you got a better idea?'

Wallace looked stumped, and Caine didn't wait for him to reply. 'My hunch is that they'll keep an important prisoner like that where they can see her,' he said. 'In an open wagon or a cab. If I'm right, we'll sight her in the first minute or so. If not we'll have to search the soft-skins under covering fire.'

There was a snort from Todd Sweeney. 'That's going to be *really* easy, isn't it? I mean, they're just going to wait while we do a search. As soon as they click what we're after, they'll hold her hostage. In any case, if we've got men farting about in the killing zone, it's going to hamper our fire.'

Caine ignored Sweeney's sarcasm. 'It's not a perfect plan,' he admitted, 'but we do have an ambush site straight out of the manual – a blind bend with a gradient, a steep rise on one side, and an open area on the other . . .'

Caine considered who to put in charge of the fire-group. Sweeney was senior corporal after Cope, but Caine no longer trusted him entirely. On the other hand, the ex-copper had always been dependable in combat, and if Caine gave him a key role it might stump his continuous second-guessing, which, he thought, arose from a sense of inadequacy. He made a quick decision. 'Corporal Sweeney, you'll take charge of the ambush party. Harry, we'll use *Marlene* for the decoy. The White and the 3-tonners will remain here in the wadi with pickets and the Senussi, and this will be our emergency RV. Fall-back RV will be where *Gracie* piled in.'

The growl of engines came again, sounding much nearer this time. Caine caught sight of Moshe Naiman's hawkish features. 'Are you up for this?' he asked.

Naiman nodded. 'I can do it. It's a good plan, and I think it might work.'

'Good man. All right, let's get to it.'

Within ten minutes the ambush parties and armoured vehicles were concealed in the maquis – a tangled growth of six or seven different species of thorny shrub, rarely more than shoulder-height, growing in a tightly knit jungle on the escarpment. The maquis was hard to penetrate, but it was cut through by enough goat tracks at least to get access to the higher slopes. From there it was a matter of crawling, clawing, fighting their way into the brush: none of them got away without multiple cuts and scratches. Sweeney sited the Bren-gun groups in a rough line, at ten-yard intervals, about a hundred and fifty feet up. From here, the gunners had a field of fire for about a quarter of a mile along the road as far as the bend on their left, and the wadi mouth on their right. The Daimler was scrimmed half-way up the slope on the side nearest the bend, with the Dingo taking flank position on the opposite side, nearest the wadi. The terrain on the other side of the road, beyond the irrigation ditch, was a fractured landscape of bowl-shaped buttes, low ridges, gullies and hillocks – an endless upsurge of corrugations as far as the eye could see.

Marlene was parked on the left side of the track, about a hundred yards along from the ambush party. While Wallace curled up in her cab, Caine and Copeland leaned over the engine, clad only in khaki drill shorts and boots – they had stashed their weapons in the shade of the truck's chassis, together with sword bayonets and haversacks packed with grenades and spare magazines. Naiman, wearing shorts, shirt and an Afrika Korps peaked cap someone had rustled up, waited tensely by the roadside thirty yards away, the Schmeisser slung muzzle-forward from his shoulder. As they listened to the snarl of motors coming closer, Copeland shot a glance at the young interpreter, wondering if he could pull off the ruse. He was the only man in the squad who spoke German, but with his olive skin and hooked nose, he didn't look much like an Afrika Korps soldier. 'I used to think those Palestinian Jews weren't much cop,' he said softly, 'but Moshe's got bottle.'

'Never underestimate *anyone* in this job,' Caine whispered. 'One thing's for sure – however bad it gets, you won't see Moshe with his hands up, shouting "*Kamerad*". If the Jerries found out he was a Jew, they'd chop his balls off.' He was interrupted by the crank of vehicles changing gear, of engines labouring. 'Here we go,' he said. He dipped his head under the bonnet just as a German lorry teetered round the bend, followed closely by another.

Naiman raised his hand, assuming a suppliant expression as he strode towards the approaching wagon. Her cab had two occupants – a bare-chested, tousled-haired driver with a fluffy beard and a slimmer, dark-haired soldier in khaki drills whom Naiman guessed was an officer. He quickly scanned the rest of the convoy as it emerged – another 3-tonner, an open staff car, then a third lorry. He noticed with a pang of apprehension that all the lorries had Schmeisser MG30 machine guns mounted on their hatches. The good news was that the guns weren't manned, meaning that the enemy wasn't expecting an attack. He didn't have time to take in further details, because the leading truck was creaking to a halt. He walked casually up to the driver's side, feeling the Germans' eyes on him, and before the driver could move, had reached up and opened the door. 'Morning, friends,' he said, in German. 'We've got a problem. Can you help?'

The Brandenburgers considered him dubiously, and Naiman had a second to register the driver's bull-like chest covered in golden down and football-sized biceps. In that instant he knew they weren't buying it. He snapped the Schmeisser's muzzle towards them: before he could fire the huge driver dropped on him with a blood-curdling bellow. Sixteen stone of flexing muscle hit Naiman like a steam-hammer, knocking him flat. He wriggled frantically, feeling the big soldier's weight suffocating him, smelling his sweat, aware of his large hands tearing the sub-machine gun from his grip. Gunshots kicked up dust by his head: he flinched, realizing that the officer, leaning out of the cab, was trying to shoot at him without hitting the driver.

Naiman's fingers found the trigger: his weapon burped. The driver howled as blood palpitated from his thigh. The officer nose-dived from the cab with a hole in his chest, crunching into the ground a foot away. The driver went limp. Naiman felt wetness soaking his legs and belly. He freed himself from the heavy corpse, his hands on the sub-machine gun slick with blood. He heard a motor grind and squirmed away from the bodies, clocking the tyres of the staff car crunching gravel. There was a hawk-faced officer standing in the car, pointing a pistol at him, and next to him, her face creased with fear, sat a pretty young woman with green eyes and short blond hair.

A pistol shot took off a piece of Naiman's right ear as he came up blipping bursts, shearing the flesh off the officer's chest. Tatters of khaki and streamers of blood whiplashed the girl's face and hair. The car braked, the girl arched forward, bumped her head on the dashboard. Naiman saw the driver groping for a weapon, pumped steel twice, heard his slugs strike flesh. Smoke drifted, the driver slumped, the girl squealed, head in hands.

Naiman didn't see the Jerry spotters popping out of hatches, bracing MG30 machine guns. He was blind to Brandenburgers debussing, deaf to the bellowed orders, to the stutter of small-arms, the tracer chomping air. Only the blond woman existed. He made the car in two bounds, wrenched open the door, daubing blood on the handle, snatched the screaming girl, jerked her out. He threw her over his shoulder, sprinted, hurdled the irrigation ditch on the open side of the road, raced for the cover of a low ridge. Two Jerries bounded after him: Copeland popped them both in quick succession from a hundred paces.

Todd Sweeney watched Naiman's action from the escarpment. Dozens of bare-chested Germans in shorts, boots and battle-rig were swarming from the backs of the soft-skin trucks, humping weapons towards the trench. He saw enemy spotters bracing their guns on the cabs, heard the explosive punka-punka-punka of MG30 machine-gun fire, saw tracer patterns curving in on his position. The Brandenburger gunners were shooting blind up the escarpment, rounds clittering in the foliage, shaving bark, dingling stones. Most shots went wide, but Sweeney knew they'd hit someone sooner or later, if only by chance. He hung on until Naiman had carried the girl outside the killing zone, then ordered '*Fire.*' Three Brens blowtorched flame: ball and tracer racked air, hacked dirt, raddled canvas, punched gaps among the milling Jerries on the track. .303 rounds blistered their bodies, gnashed limbs, sent men bucking, skipping and capering like cake-walkers. From his right, Sweeney heard the snare-drum pump of Padstowe's Vickers starting up.

Down on the track, Caine and Cope skirmished forward along the track while Wallace laid down covering fire from behind, with the Lewis gun on *Marlene's* hatch. Copeland saw a shock-haired, black-bearded machine-gunner on the forward Jerry truck pivoting the MG30 towards him. He hunkered down, aimed through his scope, shot the gunner in the solar plexus. The German went squinch-eyed as if belted with a sledgehammer. He flew backwards off the cab, fell almost on top of Caine.

Caine side-stepped the fallen corpse. His Tommy-gun was back-slung and he had a Mills grenade in each hand. Copeland saw him bite out split-pins one after the other, saw him lob the dark pineapples through the truck's open window. Caine dropped and rolled away. A massive Brandenburger with a wrestler's physique and shaggy hair leapt down on him, sword-bayonet glittering. Cope fired without his sights, cleaving the Jerry's chin, sending him riffling back, hands pawing air. Two more Germans, coming up to support their mate, ran into the grenade blast – a funnel-shaped side-swipe of shrapnel and black smoke stabbing out of the lorry's cab like a giant penny-poke, taking the door with it. The wagon lufted a foot in the air and crashed back on her wheels, her bodywork shredded: poison fumes billowed, chrome-yellow flame hooshed, steel chips tickered, glass shards flew.

Cope advanced through the smoke, saw Caine hefting his Tommy-gun with its pregnant mag, boosting rounds from the hip at the gunner on the second lorry. He missed. Cope saw the MG30 barrel tilt at Caine in slow motion, saw the grin of triumph on the Brandenburger's face. He heard a brace of mortar bombs crake down on the cab, saw them whip apart in spines of steel and fire-opal blaze. The lorry fireballed, the machine gun ruptured, the gunner soared off on wings of fire like a great black burning bird.

A hundred and fifty yards up the scarp, hidden in the maquis, Wingnut Turner, manning a Bren, saw the truck disintegrate. He pulled iron on an empty chamber, cursed to himself. He told his No. 2, Victor Bramwell, Coldstream Guards, to switch magazines, and while Bram was clicking the fresh mag into place, Turner observed the rear lorry of the convoy attempting to reverse back round the bend, out of the killing zone. He cocked the weapon, toggled it left, sighted up on the Jerry driver, put a double tap through the cab. The German's skull imploded like a punctured balloon.

Two Brandenburgers, crouching at the roadside, glimpsed Turner's muzzle-flash. They zeroed in: their Gewehr rifles walloped. 7.92mm rounds riffed foliage: a slug hit Vic Bramwell in the throat, whizzed out of his ear in a spliff of blood and bone mash, yawed off Turner's helmet, splattered him with grunge. Bramwell sagged. Turner swore. He saw the Jerry shooters leg it behind the truck and double-tapped again and again, ribbing their bare backs with .303 ball. He saw them dry-swimming, twitching in the road. He saw another clutch of mortar bombs cruise parabolas, skew down on the rear truck, strike with a single *baruuumph*. As she blew, ammunition boxes on her back detonated: hot tracer cartridges went off like pinwheels in orange and blue.

Turner heard a motor gunning, stared in shock as a German AFV chirred into view from behind the bend. 'Where's the Boys?' he gasped. 'Hit that bloody wagon.'

Gunner's Mate Gus Graveman plumped down next to Turner with the heavy 5.5 mm Boys anti-tank rifle. Graveman, the richly bearded former Royal Navy commando who reminded Caine of the Player's Navy Cut sailor, cocked the mechanism. Turner splayed the bipod legs. Graveman zoned in the sights, beaded up on the AFV between body and turret, pulled iron. The Boys twitched, clumped, spunked gas: the round fried air. Graveman followed it through, clocked no damage to the Jerry wagon. 'Bloody crappy piece of junk,' he swore, ratcheting in another big shell. He fired again, but Turner knew it was useless: the AFV's armour was just too thick. The two watched helplessly as the great ironclad trawled up the verge straight towards *Marlene*, where Wallace was working the Lewis gun.

Caine and Copeland had run into dense fire from Jerries holed up in the irrigation ditch, and were proned-out on the road shooting back at them. The AFV passed behind them, past the halted convoy, through the tunnel of smoke: they both saw her emerge on their right at the same moment, her 40mm cannon groping towards *Marlene* like the feeler of a giant snail. Caine made frantic hand signals to Wallace, a hundred yards back along the road, yodelling, '*Fred, get off there. Now.*' He didn't have a chance to see if Wallace made it, because just then the cannon kerblunked: the sky folded, the earth heaved.

Caine felt a rip-roaring swell of air, a deadening of ear-drums, a hot poultice on the chest. He dekkoed sharp right, clocked *Marlene* brassing up in sunburst sears of flame, squirming black smoke, ripples of shrapnel like black silt. He heard another crump, heard a shell scrape air, saw the Jerry armoured car's gun-turret lopped off like the cap on a soft-boiled egg. There was a numbing concussion as the wagon tipped over on her side, and a thrashing human torch dropped out of her mangled turret. A slice of jagged armour plate buzzed over them, hit the desert fifty yards away.

Up the escarpment, Sweeney had seen *Marlene* go up, and had observed the bulb of smoke from the Daimler on his left as Flash Murray took out the German armoured car. Through roiling smoke he could just see Caine and Copeland lying on the track, still hammering shots into the irrigation ditch, where he thought almost all the surviving Jerries were holed up. Sweeney directed the Bren-gunners to drop fire into the ditch. Down to his right, he saw the figure of a gigantic soldier in scorched khaki shorts jogging towards Caine's position, clutching a sawn-off shotgun. He couldn't suppress a wry smile. 'The big dollop made it then,' he murmured.

Ten yards to Sweeney's left, Turner dropped fire into the trench until the smoke from the burning wagons was too dense to see anything. He sensed that the Brandenburgers down there were all dead or too badly wounded to move. He stopped shooting, noting that the other gunners had also ceased fire. A second later the engine of the Dingo burst into life. Although Turner couldn't see her, he guessed that Padstowe was taking the car down the scarp, rat-tat-tatting .303 ball as he moved.

Caine heard the Dingo's engine hum, heard her Vickers rattle then abruptly stop. He tottered to his feet, sniggered stupidly from concussion. His eardrums were numb, his head lurching: he coughed, choking on cordite fumes. He took in the five vehicles burning on the track, and realized that it had gone strangely quiet. There was no shooting from up on the escarpment, probably because the smoke was now too dense for the gunners to see their targets. The Jerries in the ditch had ceased fire too – they were either dead or too badly injured to fight.

He stared groggily around and noticed something odd. To his extreme left, two hundred yards away towards the bend, a group of dark Jerry figures was forming up steadily in ranks on the road. He blinked and shook his head, thinking for a moment that he was dreaming. The Germans fixed bayonets with rigid drill movements, as if on parade: he heard the slap of rifle stocks, heard an order bellowed out, saw the ranks of soldiers advance. It suddenly came to him that this wasn't a dream: that these were all that were left of the Brandenburger platoon. Every man who'd survived the shoot-out had crawled down the irrigation ditch and mustered at the far end for a counter-attack. Their problem, Caine realized, was that they were out of ammo: the brave buggers were coming on armed with only cold steel. They had no way of shooting back at their ambushers on the heights, so they were homing in on Caine – the only enemy soldier they could see.

He was brain-numb, concussed from the shock of the ordnance: the thought of taking cover never crossed his mind. He tried to tot up how many rounds he had left; he came to the conclusion that he was out. He drew his bayonet and clapped it on the special lug he'd made for his Tommy-gun. At that moment, Harry Copeland dragged himself up, equally shell-shocked, licking dry lips, aching for water. He saw what Caine was doing, snorted with laughter, fumbled for his own bayonet. 'What happened to the bloody Dingo?' he demanded.

As if in answer, three sharp detonations echoed off the dense smoke, followed by bursts of Vickers fire. 'Under attack,' Caine growled.

He clocked movement to his right, and recognized Fred Wallace easing out of the smoke-shrouds with a stunned look on his Neolithic face. He was carrying nothing but his sawn-off twelve-bore. His fanny was slung from his belt, his shorts were ripped and bloody, and his body was black with powder burns. '*Gunner Wallace*,' Caine drawled. '*Get over here.*'

The giant swayed drunkenly over to Caine and Copeland. 'Lost me bleedin' Bren, didn't I?' he growled, clicking back the shotgun's hammers one-handed and drawing out his fanny. He held up the commando knife. 'Good job we got these back, *innit*?'

The three of them burst into gales of madcap glee. 'What are we doing, then?' Cope enquired, still hooting.

'Taking out that lot,' Caine snickered, nodding towards the silently padding enemy. The spectral crew was still moving in on them, now only a hundred paces away. 'They must be out of rounds.'

Copeland noticed them for the first time, looked mildly surprised. 'What a coincidence,' he tittered, 'I've got one round left.' He worked the bolt on his SMLE, forced his last bullet into the chamber. The three commandos squared up shoulder to shoulder, facing the oncoming Germans, Caine in the centre, Wallace on the left, Cope on the right. 'Bet I cop for more than both of you put together,' Wallace chortled.

There was a second's silence: the two groups – the small one and the larger one – eyed each other. Caine heard another snapped order: the Jerries launched into a ferocious charge, screamed Brandenburger war cries. As the leading man emerged from the smoke-roils into clear sight, Cope shot him plumb through the temple. Caine saw the entry wound, saw flesh and brains jettison from the back-skull, saw the body fly, somersault, clump the deck. The oncoming horde vaulted over it: the three commandos braced forwards to engage them.

The groups met with a shattering clash of steel on steel. Wallace was bayonet-charged by a squat gorilla with rippling buff pectorals and grinning pearl teeth, as wild-bearded as a berserker. The big gunner squeezed both triggers of the Purdey: the weapon tromboned, guffed gas; twin charges of buckshot pepper-potted skin, scalped hair, flayed the Jerry's limbs to mincemeat. The gorilla went down in a raw lump, his grin a rictus, and was replaced by a cat-eyed Jerry with cropped blond hair, jabbing a bayonet. Wallace shed the shotgun, parried the thrust with his fanny's knuckle-duster hilt. He grabbed the soldier's rifle, jolted it out of his grip: he swung it one-handed, chinned the Squarehead, parted flesh, scrunched jawbone. The Jerry dropped on his knees keening, spewing blood, teeth and vomit. Wallace brained him again and again, until his head was stoven in, and the rifle stock broke off.

The big man trail-eyed Caine twisting steel out of a Hun's gullet in a spout of gore. He threw the rifle aside and sprang forward, snagging another Brandenburger in the guts with his fanny. As he ripped the dagger out, a python-thick arm viced his neck from behind – a Boche was swinging on his back, heaving him off balance, mashing down on his skull with a pistol stock. Wallace roared, tilted his vast shoulders, skip-danced to fling him off. Another Hun dipped at him with a twenty-two-inch steel blade. Distracted by the Kraut on his back, the big man saw it coming too late. He lumbered sideways to deflect the thrust: the point grooved his chest and embedded itself in the thick muscle of his shoulder. Before the bayonet-man could follow through, Wallace had lashed out with his fanny's hilt, pulped his assailant's nose. He bashed him aside with such force that the bayonet twanged and snapped off, leaving an inch of steel in Wallace's flesh. Bellowing like a wounded elephant, the giant dervish-whirled, thrust back-handed at his rider. He squidged a nostril, gouged an eyeball, felt snot, gore, eye fluid soaking his neck. The Brandenburger squealed and let go of him. As he fell, Harry Copeland rammed almost two feet of claw-sharp iron in through one cheek and out another, pulped tongue, minced palate, mangled teeth.

Wallace banked around like a great galleon turning, his eyes poison slits, his ruby skin tight, his blackened face hardly human. Copeland clocked the fanny upended in his huge fist, saw his mate's eyes narrow, ducked as he lofted it, harpooning the Jerry Cope hadn't seen, about to pig-stick him from behind. The fanny thunked finger-deep into chest muscle and spare rib. The Jerry clomped back, arms sawing: Copeland rammed his bayonet into soft belly-meat. The Brandenburger slumped, took Cope's blade with him, bent it hoop-shaped. Cope gave up trying to withdraw it. He clicked the catch, released the bayonet, jerked his rifle free, yanked out Wallace's fanny. He chucked the bloody dagger back to the giant.

Wallace caught the knife without looking, his gaze fixed on something else behind Cope. He advanced, honking, nose-blowing snot, his shoulder gouting blood, his eyes shooting sparkler-fire. Cope lurched round and saw Tom Caine in the midst of five Brandenburgers, who were cutting, stabbing and slashing at him like devils. Copeland clocked a Hun bayonet as it plunged into Caine's side, saw blood pulsate, saw the other Boches cluster about Caine like vultures, going in for the coup de grâce.

Wallace slammed into them like a whirlwind, ramped out with blade and knuckle-duster, snapped jaws like twigs, popped out eyeballs, crushed cheekbones, splatted noses, sawed through necks like roasted hams. Cope leapt to join him, rifle butt arching, smashing, cleaving bone, grinding flesh. Cope and Wallace stood back to back, parrying, thrusting, cutting, driving back Jerries. Huns howled soundlessly, ditched weapons, pitched over fingernailing wounds, retching, vomiting. Two of them rolled back on their feet, grabbed their weapons, went in for a second assault. They walked into a sudden spurt of .303 ball from the advancing Dingo that sent them skittling backwards.

Wallace tugged Caine up, saw blood spurging from his side. He clocked a No. 36 grenade in his blood-soaked palm, saw a split-pin in the other, guessed Caine had been planning to plant the Mills as a booby-trap under his own body. Now it became his parting gift to the last of the Brandenburgers. Caine's eyes fell on two Jerries monkey-running back to the irrigation ditch, and he tossed the pineapple after them, yelling. *'Hey, you've forgotten something.'* Caine, Cope and Wallace lamped flat as the grenade detonated: the blast barbecued air, flipped over the retreating enemy like straws.

The Dingo had been delayed by a pair of Jerries who'd crept up the ditch in the opposite direction and attacked her with grenades. Now, as she cruised out of the smog, Wallace scrambled up to see Padstowe tilting his guns at an acute angle, pumping lead into any Jerries still moving. Taffy Trubman peeked over the hatch and added a few rifle shots to the mix for good measure. Padstowe stopped shooting: silence came like an ebb-tide after the ear-shattering blare of the Vickers. Wallace saw the ex-Marine pull up his smoking guns, wipe gun-black off his face and bald pate. His eyes showed up like white slits in a dark mask. He licked blackened lips. 'Now that's what I call a good dusting,' he said.

The spell of silence was fractured by the cries of Sweeney's group moving at last from their positions on the escarpment. No one, not even Cope, had foreseen how long it would take them to descend tactically through the dense maquis. Caine felt the heat of the nearest conflagration on his face, boosted himself to his feet. Wallace was already leaning on Cope, trying to extract the bayonet point from his own shoulder with gore-smeared fingers the size of liverwurst sausages. Caine clutched at the wound in his side – it was pumping blood, and he groped in his shorts for a dressing. He would have murdered for a drink.

Todd Sweeney wove around the Dingo, his helmet tilted over one eye, his Tommy-gun at the ready. After him came Wingnut Turner, his Bren slung crosswise, still smoking. Sweeney scanned the ambush site, took in the five burning wagons, the staff car, the toppled AFV, the smouldering cadavers. He stared at the blood-drenched figures of Caine, Wallace and Cope – barely able to stand up, in the centre of a circle of mangled dead, like the survivors of some brutal gladiator's carnival. His eyes lingered on the smoking remains of *Marlene*, and a momentary expression of hilarity crossed his face. 'So the bluff worked then?' he said.

Wallace yowled like a maimed animal as he wrenched the fragment of steel from his wound. He gripped Cope's shoulder with one hand, holding the point up like a trophy with the other, his breath coming in bursts like a steamtrain. He stared at Copeland as if he'd never seen him before. 'We scuppered them, didn't we, mate?' he panted.

Cope stared round-eyed at the savagely mutilated bodies lying about them, as if he'd just woken from a dream.

Wallace opened his mouth to add something, coughed instead, keeled sideways, crashed like a felled tree among the enemy corpses.

Most of the ambush group had now descended and was assembled around the halted Dingo. They had brought with them the bodies of Vic Bramwell, and a second man KIA, Mick Oldfield, who'd been hit when the Jerries raked the brush from below: they laid them reverently on the hot ground. Maurice Pickney pushed through the squad, carrying his medical chest. Cope crouched beside Wallace. Pickney set the chest down. 'He'll be all right,' Caine groaned, holding the open dressing to his side. 'Hide like armour plating, that bloke. Let's grab the girl and get out.'

'Oh yes, the girl,' Sweeney said. 'Where is she?'

Caine scanned the ground and pointed to a low bank, not twenty paces away. Sweeney swivelled towards it, but Caine held up his hand shakily. 'No,' he said. 'I'll do it.'

He beckoned to Copeland and together they limped towards the bank. Peering over it, they found Moshe Naiman, nursing a wound in the ear, perched in blood-soaked sand with a blond-haired, green-eyed young woman clad in a khaki drill shirt and trousers. The girl had a cut on the forehead, and both of them were covered in blood from head to foot. They were laughing uncontrollably. When Naiman caught sight of his two mates, he stopped laughing and pointed his Schmeisser in their direction, his eyeballs huge and white against the dark gore on his face. Recognizing them, he dropped the weapon. Caine stared at the woman. 'Are you *Runefish*?' he enquired.

The blonde looked suddenly bewildered. 'I'm not a fish,' she said.

Naiman snorted. 'This isn't *Runefish*, skipper. Not unless they're recruiting Wrens from the Italians now, that is.'

24

Twenty minutes of bone-shaking brought them back to the cork and arbutus groves where *Gracie* had piled in – although there was almost no sign of the 6-tonner's crash now. As Cope pulled up in deep shade, Caine instructed him to get the wagons leaguered. 'Tell the lads not to put down roots,' he moaned through gritted teeth, spitting dust and sand. 'I want the Lewis guns manned, and pickets with Brens on all arcs. The boys can get a brew and some scoff. A few minutes to get ship-shape and we're off.'

Caine's wound felt like fire. He leaned heavily on the door of the White and watched with a sinking feeling as Todd Sweeney strode over to him with the familiar simian roll, his helmet still askew on his beach-ball head. 'So, where to, skipper?' he enquired, a gloating smile on his face.

'I'll let you know,' Caine said, drawing a ragged breath. He expected Sweeney to push off, but instead he stood his ground. 'So it was all for nothing,' the ex-MP went on. 'Attacking the village, the grind across the Jebel, bumping the column – the casualties, the lost wagons – all wasted. Instead of *Runefish*, we picked up some enemy civilian bint.'

Caine realized that the palm branch he'd offered Sweeney hadn't worked. He glowered. 'Isn't there something you ought to be doing, Corporal? If so, I suggest you clear off and do it, before I look for that grease-gun Pickney used this morning and stick it right up your arse.'

Sweeney walked away, still sneering. Caine bit his lip as he watched him go, reflecting that, even if his observations were negative, they were once again true. All their costly efforts had been squandered on a snipe hunt, and right now he had no idea where they were going. Thanks to the loss of *Judy* and *Marlene*, they didn't even have enough petrol to make the RV with the Long Range Desert Group. He was furious with himself: instead of locating *Runefish's* downed aircraft and making a systematic search around it in ever-increasing circles as they should have done, he'd got drawn into contacts with the enemy, the very thing he should have avoided. He'd followed hunches and red herrings, and all it had brought them was casualties, lost wagons, lost time, fruitless effort. He considered returning to the coordinates St Aubin had given him, but at once he dismissed the idea. After hitting the village, the whole area would be buzzing. It would soon be buzzing here, too. No, the only bet for now was to retire further into the mountains: he had no idea what the next step should be.

He forced himself to limp over to where the Daimler and Dingo were parked together in a broad pool of shade. Flash Murray and Shirley Temple were scouring the Daimler's barrel with a ramrod while Trubman fiddled with the wireless and Padstowe, his face still soot-black, chugged petrol into the Dingo's tank from a flimsy, through a funnel. Caine gave Murray the thumbs-up. 'Mean shooting, Flash,' he said. 'That Jerry AFV could have done for us. That's twice Hun armour has turned up when we didn't bargain for it.'

'That was my fault, skipper,' Padstowe cut in, screwing shut the cap of the petrol tank. 'I cocked up the recce, didn't I?' Caine heard the embarrassment in his voice and remembered how Sweeney had blamed him and Cope for missing the AFV at the Senussi village. 'It happens,' he said. 'You couldn't have got any closer.'

He noticed that Trubman had removed his headphones,

and enquired if he'd picked up anything on the emergency net. 'I've been trying since we left the ambush site, skipper,' Trubman said. 'I'm still getting nothing.'

'Keep at it,' Caine said. 'It's our only hope now.'

He was about to turn away when Trubman added, 'I was listening in to Rome Radio on the Phillips short-wave.' Caine glanced back at him sharply, and the Welshman reddened again. 'There's no security risk, skipper,' he said quickly. 'The Phillips is receiver-only. We use it for getting the Greenwich time signal.'

'That's all right, Taffy,' Caine said. 'I'm familiar with it.'

'Well, I thought you'd like to know: at 0520 hours this morning, 20 June 1942, the Panzer Group penetrated Tobruk's perimeter. Waves of Stukas cleared the minefields. Last report, at 1400 hours, puts Rommel himself at King's Cross, overlooking Tobruk town. They predict he'll be inside by last light.'

Caine swallowed hard and shook his head. Before he could speak, Padstowe cut in. 'Rome Radio? That's just Axis propaganda.'

Caine shrugged, staggering slightly. Murray leaned the ramrod against the Daimler's turret, wiping his hands on a greasy rag. His emerald eyes took in Caine's ghostly face and the blood-soaked dressing. 'You sure you're all right, skipper?' he asked. 'You ought to get that looked at.'

Caine nodded. He pottered back to the White and plumped down heavily on a petrol case, still holding the dressing to his wound. It felt as if he'd been branded with a red-hot iron. He wanted morphia but didn't have a syrette: Pickney was busy probing Wallace's shoulder with forceps and Caine didn't want to distract him. The giant was stretched out under a tree – the same tree under which MacDonald had endured the grease-gun operation. Caine found it hard to credit that MacDonald was dead, and that they'd been laughing and joking here only two hours before. He suddenly remembered that Vic Bramwell and Mick Oldfield were dead too: five men taken out in one day, eight men KIA all told: Hanley snuffed by friendly fire, Rigby, and Cavazzi lost at the Senussi village, O'Brian, Jackson and MacDonald, killed in error by Arab kids, and Oldfield and Bramwell shot in the ambush. Apart from himself and his two close mates, there were only a dozen men left standing: the Daimler crew, Murray and Temple, orderly Pickney, signaller Trubman, interpreter Naiman, RAOC-man Turner, ex-MP Sweeney, former Marine Padstowe, Bluejacket Graveman, Gunner Dave Floggett, Barry Shackleton, the ex-farrier from the Scots Greys, and Albert Raker, the ex-navvie from the Pioneer Corps. Caine felt momentarily weighed down, not only by the losses, but also by a terrible despair, a feeling that there was no hope, even for those who had made it this far.

Copeland was sitting on the White's running-board inspecting his SMLE sniper's rifle. His carefully zeroed-in telescopic sights had been off-centred during the bayonet fighting, but he was relieved to see that there was no damage he couldn't fix. Cope's straw-coloured hair was so stiff with gore and dust that it looked as if it had been deep-moulded in place, and he wore dressings on his neck and left arm, like trophies. 'You all right, Harry?' Caine asked, straining to get the words out. Cope nodded. 'Do me a favour when you're finished. Go with Adud and cut those Senussi boys free. You can give them their weapons back, but no ammo. I don't want to find out that I was wrong about them.'

'Got it, skipper.'

Naiman had cleaned himself up and now wore a padded white dressing on his mutilated left ear: with a matching one on the right, he'd have looked like a hook-nosed rabbit, Caine thought. He had also sorted out the Italian girl, who now displayed a white blob of bandage on her temple. Caine waved them over. With the blood and dirt gone, he saw that the woman had a long, slender face under the crop of golden hair, with jade-green eyes, high cheekbones, a small nose slightly turned down at the end and full lips that gave her a hint of sulkiness. She was long-necked, tall and willowy, her khaki drills hand-tailored to bring out her small, pointed breasts and the elegant curves of her figure. She wasn't classically beautiful, but there was a sensuality about her that was unmistakable, Caine thought.

'You don't look like an Italian,' he blurted. 'You look more like a German.'

Her face twisted, her jade eyes wild with fury. 'Don't dare call me German,' she snarled. 'I hate those *Tedesci* pigs . . .' She spat venomously into the sand through bared teeth. 'They killed my brother, Carlo. They shot him in the head. I hope you English finish them all.'

There was an awkward silence while Caine weighed her up. She sounded genuine enough: her voice had a low, mannish quality and her accent was distinctly Italian. He flushed out a fresh pack of cigarettes from his haversack and tossed it to her. She caught it deftly with her left hand and opened it with long fingers. Her nails, filthy and broken, had obviously once been well manicured. She took out three cigarettes, handed one to Naiman and stuck another in Caine's mouth. As she leaned over, Caine had the impression that he was in the presence of a big, sleek cat. She put one between her own sulky lips and Naiman lit all three of them with a match. The woman was quiet for a moment, inhaling smoke. Caine told Naiman to bring petrol cases, and they both sat down. She blew out a long trail of smoke, and her eyes met Caine's. 'You were at the village, no?' she asked. 'I saw the headman and a girl here. You bring Carlo's body?'

Caine let smoke trail through his nostrils, thinking that tobacco had never tasted so good. 'Carlo was the man with you at the village? Your brother?'

'Of course. You bring him with you, or you bury him there?'

Caine shook his head. 'The Germans burned his body before we got there.'

'Pigs.'

A thought occurred to him. 'What happened to your jeep?' he asked.

'What?'

'The sheikh said you arrived in a jeep.'

'Oh. The *Tedesci* took it, but it break down, so they dump it.'

Copeland arrived with Sheikh Adud and Layla. 'We let the boys go, skipper,' he said. 'They were none too chuffed about their ammo, but I think they were pleased enough to get away.'

The Italian girl stood up, embracing Adud and Layla like long-lost friends, kissing them on both cheeks. Adud looked slightly taken aback. When she sat down again, Caine saw that her eyes were filled with tears. 'I think this is yours,' Copeland said, handing her the compact he'd found at the village.

She took it, giving him a wan smile. 'Thank you,' she said, flipping open the lid and studying her face in the mirror. 'As you see, I am very much in need of it.'

'Look,' Caine said. 'We don't have a lot of time. I want to know who you are, and why those Germans took you . . .'

He was interrupted by Pickney, who had shifted his medical chest over and was crouching down to examine his wound. Wallace loomed over him, his shoulder now heavily bandaged. He eased himself on to a petrol case and swigged water from his bottle.

'Sorry, skipper,' Pickney said, 'but that wound needs stitches right away. You want morphia?'

Caine had changed his mind. His side was still stinging badly, but he realized that he ought to keep his senses clear. 'No, I'm all right,' he said.

'Go on with your conversation, then. Just pretend I'm not here.'

'That's going to be *dead* easy, isn't it?'

He gave his full attention to the girl, who had put her compact away and was now watching fascinated as the orderly started to clean Caine's injury with iodine. Caine coughed, and she switched her eyes reluctantly to his face. 'All right,' she said. 'My name is Angela, Angela Brunetto. I'm from Trento, in the Alps, near the Swiss border. My husband is a communist. He was a soldier in the Italian army, but he didn't like it, so he ran away. There is a big band of – how do you call those who run away from the army?'

'Deserters?'

'Yes. There is a big band of deserters living in the Jebel. Deserters, communists, and many colonists who lost their farms because of the war. My brother, Carlo, is a colonist – he lose his farm after the Italian troops go, and the people are attack by Senussi. My husband, Michele, is *capo* of all deserters and colonists in the Jebel.'

'Ouch,' Caine yelled, making Angela start. 'Steady on, Maurice. That hurt.'

The orderly grinned apologetically. 'It looks cushy, skipper. No internal damage.'

'Good, but just go easy.'

'Either I give you a shot, or you'll have to grin and bear it.'

Caine made a face and turned back to Angela, whose gaze had been drawn again to Pickney, now stitching up the wound with catgut. 'What were you doing in that village?' Caine asked tersely.

Once again she dragged her eyes away from the orderly's work. 'Hiding from the *Tedesci*,' she said. 'Carlo and me go to Sirte to buy fish – it is far, but Benghazi is not safe for us. An aircraft follow us on the way back, and we go the opposite way – into the desert – so as not to lead them to our camp. We think we were safe, but the pigs find us there. They shoot Carlo, and me they take.'

'Why did they kidnap you? I mean why not kill you too?'

She shrugged eloquently, and Caine couldn't help noticing how supple her slim shoulders were. 'At first I believe they want to make me talk,' she said. 'To find our camp. I am scared. These soldiers are not ordinary soldiers – not DAK, you know? I say to myself perhaps they come to hunt Italian deserters, but then why they keep talking to me in English, as if they believe I am English? Then I understand. They think I am someone else.' She gazed at Caine, her eyes glowing with a feline intensity. 'Perhaps they think I am the girl you are looking for?'

Caine stiffened. 'I never said we were looking for a girl.'

'You attack them to save me?' Angela gave an un-ladylike snort. 'I am flattered, but I don't think so. You, too, think I am someone else. That is why you ask me if I am a fish. It is, how do you say . . . *codice* . . . code, no?'

Caine locked eyes with Copeland, then with Naiman, who burst out, 'I never said anything, skipper. I did ask if she was *Runefish*, but then you asked her too. She's not stupid.'

'No, I am not stupid,' Angela said, showing teeth that

were sharp and remarkably white. 'I thank you for saving me, even if it is a mistake. Now, why you don't take me back to my camp? Is not far and is well hidden. You will be safe there from aircraft. You can rest, and maybe Michele is help you find this *fish* woman. We have many contacts with Senussi all over the area – all the news reach us. In any case, Michele will be very grateful to you for bringing me.'

Caine flinched. 'Maurice, for Jesus' sake. Feels like you're carving the pork.'

'Nearly done, skipper.'

'I'm sorry about your brother,' he said, panting slightly, 'but you belong to a nation we're at war with. You're a hostile. I don't know if I even ought to trust you, let alone take you home.'

Angela tilted her face to one side and fluttered her eyelids. Caine wondered whether the action was instinctive or a deliberate attempt to charm him. Whatever the case, he *was* charmed. 'Me, hostile?' she purred. 'I am civilian, not army. Anyway, we are all against Mussolini.'

Caine examined her face, and guessed that, behind the defensive manner, she was scared and lonely. Like Maddaleine Rose, she was on her own in the desert, and today could hardly have figured as a high-point in her life. She'd seen her brother shot down in cold blood, had been abducted by Brandenburgers, had witnessed men being killed horribly within inches of her, and was now in the hands of British troops. He felt sorry for her, and despite himself, he wanted to help. As a soldier, he didn't like the idea of deserters, but then, if they were a thorn in the Axis side, they could only be regarded as potential allies.

Taking his silence for coldness, Angela cast around as if searching for inspiration. 'You are hurt,' she said at last. 'You have men wounded. We have excellent medical supplies . . .

we have everything there, more than the army ... drugs, food, wine, whisky.' She paused, and her eyes suddenly lit up. 'What about *benzina*? We have *benzina* – thousands of litres. Michele will give you all you need.'

Caine sat up too quickly, gasping as pain shot through him. 'Hold still, skipper,' Pickney said irritably. 'Else you'll break the stitches.'

Caine ignored him. '*Benzina* – you mean petrol?' he asked.

'Of course, petrol.'

'Where did you get it?' Copeland cut in, leaning forward suspiciously. 'Where did your people get all that stuff?'

Angela shrugged, showing her sharp white teeth. 'We steal it, of course. We take what we find. There is a lot of *stuff* in the desert now, no? *Benzina* dumps, water dumps, supply convoys. We don't care who it belongs to – it is all the same to us.'

'So that's why you wear British khakis,' Copeland said, 'and British officer's boots.'

She giggled, taking this as a compliment. 'British khakis look heavy,' she said, 'but they are cool. Italian khakis are for *bella figura* only. We Italians make beautiful boots, but your English boots, they are more comfortable.'

'So glad you approve,' Cope said drily.

'Ouch!' Caine spat suddenly. 'Didn't you say you were done, Maurice?'

'That's it, Tom. It's all over. You'll need sulphenamide pills for infection. I've cleaned it out best I can, but for all we know that Jerry might have dipped his blade in piss.'

Caine took the pills but didn't swallow them. When he turned to Angela again, he found that her smile had faded. 'We have warm springs,' she said lamely. 'You can all have a bath.'

To her surprise, Caine's face lit up. ' A bath,' he exclaimed.

'I won't deny that some extra petrol would come in handy. But a bath? Now how could anyone refuse that?'

After Naiman had taken Angela and the two Senussi away for scoff and a brew, Cope moved his petrol case nearer to Caine, who saw at once that he was furious. 'You weren't serious about taking that woman home?' he said.

'I was deadly serious,' replied Caine.

'It's complete madness, skipper. You must still be shell-shocked. I couldn't say anything in front of her, but you've been taken in by a piece of skirt batting her eyelids at you. I know you've got a thing about damsels in distress, but . . .'

'What *thing*? I haven't got any . . .'

'You have, Tom. It's always the "women and children first" with you, isn't it? Look at what happened yesterday at the Senussi village.' He caught Wallace's eye. 'Tell him, Fred.'

Wallace, who had been busy boiling tea on a Primus stove, filled three mugs with hot brew from the kettle. He stabbed a tin of Carnation with a clasp-knife, then dripped generous lashings of the syrupy condensed milk into the mugs. He dipped a spoon into a bag of sugar, shaking his bushy head. 'You do come on a bit strong over the ladies and children sometimes, Tom,' he said awkwardly, spooning sugar. 'What about them wogs this morning?'

'That's got nothing to do with it,' Caine snapped. He took the mug Wallace handed him, crammed the sulphenamide pills into his mouth, swallowed a mouthful of tea, sighed with pleasure. 'God, I needed this.'

'Tom,' Cope said. 'You ever heard of the Sirens?'

'I've heard of air-raid sirens,' Wallace cut in, chuckling.

Cope sent him an exasperated glance. 'The Sirens were beautiful women whose singing used to lure sailors to death on the rocks. This area – Cyrenaica – it's named after them.'

'The last thing I need,' Caine grunted, 'is a bloody history lesson.'

'All right,' Cope said. 'This girl reminds me of the Sirens. For all we know, she might be drawing us into a trap.'

Caine snorted, spilt gobs of milky tea. 'Look, I didn't say I trusted her. We *do* need a place to lay up, though, and if that girl is being straight about her deserters and colonists, the fact that they're holding out there means that their base must be pretty secure. We also need fuel, and this is one easy way to get it. All right, we *could* bump a convoy for petrol, but can we afford another action just now? We've already got eight men down – more than a third of the unit. Fred's wounded, I'm wounded. The boys are knackered. If we take any more hits we'll never pull the mission off.'

'*Pull the* . . .' Copeland choked, spluttered, showered himself with tea. He coughed, put his mug down, wiped milky tea off his chin with his hand. 'Skipper,' he said, 'you can't be considering going on with Op *Runefish*, surely? The mission's shot. We lost our chance of snatching *Runefish* the minute we started following those Brandenburgers. I admit I was convinced, but I made a mistake. What we've got to do now is stay alive long enough to get back behind the Wire.'

Caine surveyed Copeland's face, shaking his head. 'I agreed to take on a mission,' he said. 'Whatever bullshit they've fed me, however many red herrings we've followed, that mission is still on. While I'm alive, anyway, one thing is for certain: We're not going back without *Runefish* – or at least without making sure she's dead.'

Cope sighed, seeing that the battle was already lost. 'So what are we going to do, then? We're stuck in the middle of nowhere, without enough fuel to get back to Egypt, with God knows how many Huns on our trail, nothing on the emergency net, and no way of knowing or even of finding out where *Runefish* is – if she even exists at all, that is.'

Caine was fully aware that the chances of finding *Runefish* were now limited, but he would be damned if he was going to run home with his tail between his legs without even a struggle. 'You're wrong, Harry,' he said. '*Runefish* is still out there somewhere, and going with Angela is our best chance. All right, she might be a "Siren", but there are times in your life, mate, when you've got to make a leap of faith, when you can't just rely on two and two making four. My nose tells me she's above board. That doesn't prove anything, I'll grant you. Maybe her husband will be grateful enough to give us petrol and information, or maybe he'll sell us to the Nazis, or maybe they'll start shooting the moment we show up. Whatever happens, the bottom line is that we're trained special-service troops, and whatever comes up, we'll deal with it.'

25

The deserters' base lay in a vast crater at the heart of the Green Mountain, the hub of a complex of wadis that meandered out in every direction. By the time Caine's column reached the narrow defile that led into the basin, darkness had long since fallen. Angela advised Caine to halt the wagons at the entrance while she went ahead to warn her people of their approach.

She was back within twenty minutes, declaring that her husband and his band were ready to welcome them with open arms. Copeland remained wary of a trap, though, and Caine ordered the wagons through the gap with hatches up and all guns manned. He quickly saw that these precautions had been unnecessary. As soon as he alighted from the scout car, a galaxy of lights sprang up in the darkness – dozens of candles and oil lamps blinked and flickered in the hands of scores of people. The crowd was assembled on a great flat slab of rock, extending like a giant foot from the base of a dark cave that opened in what looked like a sheer cliff. The lights streamed towards him like a current of stardust, in a flurry of voices and the barking of dogs. A moment later Caine was mobbed, a horde of excited men, women and children cheered, clapped, jabbered at him in Italian, clamoured to shake his hand. After the bloodbath on the road that morning, it felt like a hero's return.

Caine heard a voice rasping orders, and the crowd peeled back to let through a short, broad-chested, swash-buckling man with a goatee beard and a shoulder-length mane of wild hair. He was clad in a sheepskin coat, Afrika Korps jodhpurs, high cavalry boots. The newcomer marched up to Caine, threw his arms round him and kissed him on both cheeks. 'I am Michele Brunetto,' he announced. 'My wife told me everything. Thank you for bringing her back. You are welcome here – our place is yours.'

Trubman, Naiman, Pickney, Graveman and Cpl Barry Shackleton, the ex-Scots Greys farrier, volunteered to stay with the leaguer. Caine left them with orders to man the Vickers on the Dingo in two-hour stags, and gave Trubman instructions to renew his efforts on the emergency net. Adud called him aside and explained through Naiman that he and his daughter wouldn't be joining them. Some of the Italian ex-colons here weren't well disposed towards his folk – their homesteads had been sacked by bands of marauding Arabs after the Itie army had gone, and they blamed the Senussi.

Here in the camp, which they called the *Citadello*, Angela and Michele were evidently king and queen. They led Caine and his men up on to the slab, and into the cave-opening. As he entered, Caine caught his breath. It was like the distorted mirror-image of some huge Gothic cathedral, lit with dozens of lamps in niches, its huge vaulted ceiling supported by grotesquely twisted stalagmites as thick as the trunks of oak trees. There was room for a squadron of tanks to leaguer in there.

The rock pillars enclosed recesses that Caine saw were furnished with old carpets, sheepskins and cushions and hung with threadbare drapes and tapestries. In the open area between rock pillars there stood ranks of trestle tables and benches that must have seated scores, and the cave wall was lined with other tables laden with brandy casks and wine bottles in straw envelopes. Caine noticed another cave opening off the larger one, that seemed to be festooned with hanging legs of ham, sausages, and Parmesan cheeses as big as truck-wheels: it was stacked with jars of tomato pulp, glass magnums of olive oil, ten-pound tins of jam and coffee, square chests of tea. There were cartons upon cartons of captured compo rations. Caine surveyed the bounty and shot Michele an incredulous glance. 'You do all right for yourselves here, don't you?' he said.

The Italian shrugged, unbelting his sheepskin, giving Caine a glimpse of the pistol he wore in a button-down holster at his waist. The eyes that met Caine's were shifty, and the face, more lined in the light of the cave than Caine had noticed outside, gave an impression of slyness. 'This is nothing,' Michele said, making an expansive gesture towards the stores of food and drink. 'We have chickens, pigs, even some cows for milk – many of our people were colon farmers before the war, and they bring their animals with them here. We buy fish and lobsters from the Arabs on the coast, and we have more tinned food than we can eat.'

Copeland frowned. 'British or Axis?' he enquired.

Michele opened both hands wide. 'We trade for some. Some we take. It doesn't matter from which side we take, because property is theft and all are class enemies.' He caught Cope's expression and went on hastily. 'Not you, of course.' He turned, seized Angela tenderly in his arms and gave her a long, breathless kiss on the lips that ended only when she pushed him away, snickering. 'You bring back my treasure,' he said, touching the bandage on her forehead. 'She is hurt, but it is nothing. I thought she was dead.' He released her with apparent reluctance and clapped Caine on the shoulder. 'You are blood brothers for ever, and my life is yours.' He gestured at his chest with his right hand, his thumb pressed against four fingers. 'Me, I am like your

English Robin Hood. I take from rich capitalist pigs, and I give to the poor.' He chuckled, showing gold teeth. 'The poor, that is me and you, no?'

He stared at Angela again, his face drained of joviality. 'We will miss Carlo,' he said. 'He was a good man. Tonight, we hold feast to his memory, to celebrate your safe return, and to honour our guests. We eat roast suckling pig, we drink wine, we have music and dancing, and we forget the war.'

Noticing that this news wasn't greeted with unalloyed rapture by Caine and Cope, Michele lifted both of his hands in a gesture of openness. 'My friends,' he said. 'I know you are soldiers, but you are safe here with us. Angela says you need *benzina*. It is yours. You can take whatever you need. Come, I show you.'

He took an electric torch from a stone shelf, and leaving Angela to take charge of the other commandos, led Caine and Copeland back out into the night. They paused for a moment on the slab, drinking in moonlight and starlight, trying to get a handle on the place. It was hard to make out the full extent of it in the moonlight, but Caine got the impression that they were in a huge amphitheatre enclosed by steep rock walls as much as a couple of miles in diameter. On one side, a massive stone buttress obtruded into the enclosed area – an unbelievably monstrous, fairy-tale tower, half a mile long and rising sheer out of the stone slab, hundreds of feet high. This 'tower' was riddled with dozens of natural caves, but the one they'd just seen appeared to be the largest. The area in front of the buttress, where the wagons were leaguered, was a flattish plain of rocky out-crops, grass tussocks and acacia groves stretching as far as the narrow defile where they'd entered the place – according to Michele, the only way in or out. Immediately to their left, where the buttress wall turned sharply north, there lay acres of Mediterranean woodland – juniper, ilex, cork-oak, arbutus, myrtle and Aleppo pine – rolling away to the towering rock walls on the eastern side, their dark mass only just visible in the wan light. Caine understood why they called this place the *Citadello* – the Citadel: if ever there was a natural fortress, this was it. With that single entrance it would be almost impossible to take by storm, and even if it were bombed, these caves would make ideal shelters. Although they couldn't see them from here, Michele explained that the defile was watched around the clock by pickets with machine guns hidden high on the cliffside. 'No one sneak up on us here,' he commented.

'How did you discover this place?' Caine enquired, as the chief ushered them down crude stone steps into the woods.

'Some colons buy it off Senussi before the war. The Bedouins, they use it for cattle, sheep, goats. The animals graze here, shelter in caves during the rains. Is a good place, no? Very hard to find, very hard to see from the air because of the trees. We do not live in caves, of course – too hot. No, we have tents in the trees, but the caves are there if we get bombed. It never happened, of course, because even at night aircraft see only small lights and think it is Senussi camp.'

'But surely they must know you're here,' Caine said. 'I mean, they'd only need a Senussi tracker to find the place.'

Michele shrugged. 'Maybe, maybe not. Is too much trouble for them to fight us as well as you English, no? For now, they leave us alone. Later, who knows? Here . . .' He shone the torch forward and Caine saw among the trees a thirty-foot ziggurat covered in tarpaulins. Michele whipped one of the covers back, revealing hundreds of stacked petrol cases. Caine whistled. Copeland stared at the British War Office arrowhead on the boxes. 'These look familiar,' he said. 'Shell's finest, I see.'

Michele screwed up his face. 'British tins are so bad – one fifth is lost in wastage. Odd, because usually British stuff is practical, no? German *jerrycans* are better – no leaks. We have German and Italian too . . .' He shone the torch around and Caine realized that this was only one of several similar mountains of bounty hidden under the trees. 'This is all petrol?' he asked.

Michele shook his head. 'Petrol, weapons, ammunition, military clothing, medical stuff, more tinned rations.'

'How did you get it here?'

Michele dropped the tarpaulin and ushered them further on through the woods, to where more than twenty vehicles were drawn up in line under camouflaged awnings. In the torchlight Caine saw jeeps, light cars, Bedford, Ford, Mercedes, Breda and Fiat lorries – even motorcycles – all in tip-top condition. Michele pointed with his torch to what looked like an Eighth Army command caravan. 'That is mine,' he said proudly. 'That is where I live when I am not in *Citadello*.' He took a deep breath and turned to face Caine and Copeland. 'So,' he said, 'how much *benzina* you want?'

Cope had already worked out the figures. 'Three hundred gallons ought to do it,' he said.

Michele considered it. 'It is a small price to pay for my Angela,' he said. 'I send my men to load it later. OK?"

'That's very generous of you,' Caine said, grinning. 'Even if it is our own petrol you're giving back to us.'

Michele laughed, tossing back his long hair in a curiously narcissistic gesture. 'You are welcome,' he said, bowing slightly. 'It was generous of you to rescue Angela also, even if it was not her you were looking for.'

'*Ouch*,' Caine said, chuckling. 'Perhaps that's something else you could help us with?'

'The girl?' Michele asked. 'The one you are seeking? My wife told me about her.'

Caine was serious now. 'She's a British officer. Her aircraft was shot down south of the Green Mountains a few days ago, and she parachuted out. Have you heard anything?'

Michele scratched his goatee. 'I might have heard about a plane coming down three days ago,' he said vaguely. 'I did not pay much attention. It happens all the time here, no? Planes go down, people parachute out.'

'Not a lot of women, though.'

Michele was watching them slyly. 'What is the importance of this woman? She is Auchinleck's *ragazza*, perhaps?'

'Something like that,' Caine said, staring at him intently. 'Could you find out?'

Michele shrugged. 'I will send out my people to make enquiries. It will take time, though. It is night.'

'Thanks. I'd appreciate that.'

'You are welcome. Now, my wife say she promise you a bath. I must show you our hot springs.'

He led them through the forest, along the wall of the slab. As they approached they heard the sound of raucous English voices: they emerged from the bush to find themselves in a shallow depression filled with a vast rock-pool of inky water: most of their mates – Wallace, Murray, Sweeney, Turner, and the others – were already bathing up to their chests – splashing, horse-playing, cracking jokes like children at the seaside. Caine was pleased to note, though, that they'd been wary enough to leave two men on stag to look after the weapons. 'Come on in, skipper,' Wallace yelled when he saw Caine. 'The water's beautiful.' Caine remembered his wound, but it hadn't bothered Wallace, and the prospect of a bath was too tempting. He and Cope were soon luxuriating in the lukewarm water beside the others.

Caine heard more excited voices and was astonished to see a crowd of leggy young Italian girls coming out of the bush. The first thing that occurred to him was that they intended to join the commandos in the water. Then he saw that they were carrying fresh clean towels, bundles of brand-new British khaki drills of all sizes and bottles containing what turned out to be a homemade mixture of oil, honey and eau de cologne. They laid out their gifts, chattering and bantering with the commandos, coyly resisting attempts to entice them into the pool. The girls were dressed in clinging khaki trousers or cut-off shorts and tailored army blouses, and with their dark masses of hair, perky breasts and squeaky soprano voices, they were almost painfully alluring, Caine thought. In a moment, though, they had vanished back into the shadows: Caine followed the music of their elvish voices until it disappeared.

Washed, rubbed, clad in a clean uniform and with his dressing refreshed, he felt an entirely new person. The men relaxed, the ugly skirmish of the morning all but forgotten. When they were ready, Caine moved them back to the leaguer in a squad and had them store their main weapons and ammunition in a makeshift 'armoury' in the back of the White scout-car. Every man was to carry his Colt pistol, loaded and made safe, and a spare clip of rounds: under no circumstances was any man to allow a civilian to handle his weapon. Above all, he told them, they were commandos, and whatever happened they must remain alert.

As they climbed back up the steps to the slab, Caine saw that the *festa* was already in full swing: several fat suckling pigs were being roasted on spits over charcoal fires, and the air was full of charcoal smoke and the delicious smell of roasting pork. It was warm inside the cave and the lights were dimmer. Romantic Italian music played on a gramophone, and men and women were locked together on the dancefloor, smooching to the slow melody. Others were standing in groups or lounging in the recesses on the rich carpets and cushions, drinking wine, chattering gaily. It seemed less a wake for Angela's dead brother than a spontaneous celebration: Caine had the feeling that these people were ready to leap at any excuse for a knees-up.

The women had dolled themselves up for the occasion as best they could, some in hugging, low-cut dresses, mostly faded and old-fashioned, but no less eye-catching for all that. Many had arranged their hair in opulent coiffures, had applied lipstick that was evidently homemade, and had darkened their eyes with kohl, which Caine guessed they obtained from the Senussi. Most were evidently the jealously guarded wives of the menfolk, but there were more than enough spare women to go around, and almost all of them were beautiful or, at the very least, nubile. Caine didn't know whether this was an illusion, exaggerated by the fact that he and his mates had lived for years almost without feminine contact, or whether the Italians – or *these* Italians – were simply a people whose women were especially attractive. Or was it just the way they dressed, the way they made up, the way they moved and held themselves? He couldn't work it out, but one thing was certain: he and his men had just dropped like castaways into an exotic and sensuous dimension that was very far from the harshness of war.

Michele arrived, beaming, a ten-inch-long Cuban cigar stuck in his mouth. He was carrying two five-litre flagons of red wine in straw envelopes, one in each fist. He thrust the flagons at Caine and Copeland and waved them towards a table spread with ragged but dazzling white linen, covered in dozens more wine flagons and terracotta goblets. '*Drink*,' he roared. 'Tonight we have Chianti – the very best.'

When all the commandos had poured themselves generous goblets-ful, Michele raised his own cup high, throwing his head back so that his lion's mane of black hair swung like a cloak. 'To Carlo's memory,' he bawled. 'To your fallen comrades, and to liberty, fraternity and peace. *Salute*.'

He drained his cup in one draught, and the commandos followed suit, rolling with incredulous laughter, hardly believing their luck in finding such a cornucopia of excellence tucked away here in the wilderness. 'By God,' Caine said, putting his goblet down. 'That is *good*.' Michele disappeared and came back a moment later hefting a cardboard carton, doled out tins of fifty Player's Navy Cut cigarettes to each man. There were murmurs of delight from the commandos. Michele handed a tin of cigarettes to Caine, then pointed at the cigar in his teeth. 'You have a light?' he asked. Caine fished out his Zippo lighter, and Michele chortled when he noticed that it was wrapped in a condom. 'Unused, I hope,' he said. 'You know they are illegal in my country?'

'Cigarette lighters?'

Michele guffawed. 'Condoms.'

'Condoms can save your life,' Caine said, chuckling. He snapped the lighter open, lit the cigar. Michele took a long toke, blew a weft of smoke, let out a long sigh of pleasure. He peered at the Zippo. 'Very nice,' he said. 'American. You give me as present?'

Caine shook his head. 'I'd like to, but I can't. It was given to me by my Sapper troop, the day I was field-commissioned lieutenant.'

Michele puffed out a chain of smoke blobs, like a model steamtrain, and raised an eyebrow. 'But you are no more a lieutenant? Why?'

Caine shook his head, lighting a cigarette one-handed. 'It's a long story.'

'Is good, my friend,' Michele said, nodding approvingly. 'Is very good you reject the ruling class, the elite who manipulate the rest of us like slaves.' He leaned over to Caine conspiratorially. 'You should stay here with us,' he whispered. 'I say *cazzo* to the war. I say *cazzo* to Mussolini and his thugs. You know how the Blackshirts got power? They were a band of bullies paid by factory owners to beat up communists. The capitalists were terrified there would be a communist revolution in Italy, like in Russia, and they would lose everything. *Ecco qua* – our beautiful country is ruled by thugs and murderers.' He took another long pull on his cigar. 'You should join us, Thomas. We need good men like you, and' – he winked an eyelid, nodding towards the dancefloor – 'there are many beautiful girls here. Beautiful and free . . . you know what I mean?'

The wine flagons were going their rounds with frantic speed, and Caine noticed that the commandos had entered into the spirit of the party like men reprieved from a death sentence. 'I remember when I was out with the Long Range Desert Group . . .' Caine heard Wallace's voice boom.

'You were never with the LRDG, you big blob,' Cope's voice cut in.

'That's all you know, clever dick. When I was in Sphinx Battery in '41 I was attached to them for a mission behind the Wire. Bofors Gunner. They used to portee a forty-mil Bofors on the back of a Ford wagon, and we'd fire from the wheels. No shields in them days – gunners went down like flies. That's why they needed volunteers. Well, on this jaunt we wiped out an Itie supply convoy . . .' He stopped and stared around guiltily, but none of the locals seemed to have noticed. 'Or maybe they was Jerries,' he said hurriedly. 'Anyway, we copped about a dozen casks of Cognac – I don't mean little barrels, I mean great big things, bigger'n oil drums. We dumped most of 'em on the Australian Division HQ. They was planning an offensive for the next day, but the Ozzies got so stinko on Cognac that night they had to postpone the attack.'

Wallace roared with laughter at his own story, and the commandos laughed with him. The explosion of mirth was cut short by general 'oohs' and 'aahs' that greeted the arrival of the roast suckling pig on huge platters. 'This is our speciality,' Michele said. 'Served with roast potatoes and pickled vegetables. It is delicious – so tender. Try it.'

The highlight of the feast, though, wasn't the suckling pig, but the fresh lobsters boiled in garlic. 'We get these from Senussi fishermen on the coast,' Michele informed them. 'This year has been a very good year for lobsters. The ones here are smaller, but more succulent, than those in Italy.' He showed them how to break open the claws to get at the white meat inside. 'Now,' he said, 'you must be careful how much lobster you eat.' He lowered his voice theatrically, and made obscene thrusting movements with his pelvis. 'Too much and you make love all night long.'

Few of the commandos had ever tasted lobster before, but they ignored Michele's warning and attacked the succulent meat with relish. Between courses they quaffed endless goblets of wine, recounted war stories, told jokes, rolled with laughter, chatted animatedly with the locals, danced with the girls.

The only man who seemed out of sorts was Copeland. Caine saw him hovering morosely in a recess, walked over to him and offered him a Player's Navy Cut. 'What's up with you?' he demanded, lighting the cigarette with his Zippo.

'I keep thinking I'm dreaming this,' Cope said, inhaling deeply. 'Maybe I was killed in that skirmish this morning and I'm in the afterlife.' He stared at Caine, his lean, heron-like profile outlined perfectly in the lamplight. 'What are we doing here, skipper?'

'Drinking good wine, eating good scoff,' Caine said, 'and hoping for news about *Runefish*. Enjoy it, Harry. By this time tomorrow we might *really* be dead.'

Just then, Angela separated herself from the crowd and glided towards them. Wearing a tight red dress that showed off her lithe brown arms and legs, her lean hips and her pointed breasts, she moved with the pneumatic grace of a model, a walk so enticingly provocative that both of them stared. She kissed Caine on both cheeks, then turned to Copeland. 'Do you want to dance with me?' she asked, parting sulky lips.

If Cope was surprised he didn't show it. 'I don't think your husband would like it,' he said.

Angela laughed, displaying her sharp white teeth. Her jade-green eyes, heavily made up with kohl, were incandescent in the lamplight. 'My husband is pleased to see me,' she said, 'but there are other girls he is also pleased to see.' She nodded towards the dancers on the floor, and for the first time Copeland noticed that Michele was dancing with a pretty, long-legged, snub-nosed girl of about seventeen with a bird's nest of curly hair, wearing an almost indecently short dress. The two were wrapped around each other like snakes.

Cope glanced back at Angela, embarrassed.

'You don't like me very much, do you?' she said. 'Or perhaps you are shy?'

'It's not that,' Cope said. 'It's just that when I look at you, I think of Sirens.'

Angela let out a delicious peal of girlish glee. 'Sirens. *Sirene?*' She leaned very close to him. 'Watch out, or I tie you to the mast,' she purred.

Caine was distracted by Wallace's big hand on his shoulder, and the next time he looked, he was amazed to see Copeland and Angela in a slow-clinch on the dancefloor. A little later they had disappeared. He couldn't suppress a pang of envy: there was a seductive quality about Angela that had drawn him from the moment they'd first talked, a feeling he'd tried to suppress – especially as he knew she was a married woman. While he'd shown her every kindness, though, Cope had never spoken a civil word to her, and had hinted darkly about 'Sirens'. It didn't seem fair, but there must be some lesson about the female sex here that had eluded him, he thought. Cope had treated her with disdain, and yet she'd homed in on him like a bloodhound, right under her husband's nose. He had no doubt they were already in her tent, writhing between freshly laundered sheets.

Caine didn't waste much time thinking about Cope and Angela, though: there were, as Michele had suggested, plenty more fish in the sea. Time trickled past, wine flowed, the lights grew dimmer, the music grew sweeter and more intoxicating. The smoky air was charged with sensuality. Occasionally there were indignantly raised voices from the shadows and the sound of faces being slapped, but elsewhere men and women paired off: the excited banter dropped to a low hum, to ecstatic gasps and pants of bliss from dark alcoves.

Caine danced with a girl called Lina, a dreamy-eyed beauty with a long cascade of brown curls whose velvet dress seemed constantly in danger of slipping off her shapely figure. Her face was as brown and plump as a peach, but her high cheekbones gave her a pagan look – almost Mongolian. She'd once been married to an Italian settler, she said – he had been murdered by the Senussi after the British had pulled out of Benghazi. 'A lot of bad things happened then,' she told him. 'Houses looted and burned, girls raped, people murdered. Those Arabs can be very bad.'

As they floated round the floor, he saw Lina's eyes become slits, her slightly parted lips succulent and inviting. When he kissed her she responded with a searing blaze of passion, almost frightening in its intensity. It was like kissing Nobel's No. 808, Caine thought. He ran his hands gently down the arch of her back and along her perfectly rounded hips: her body quivered and she raked her small hand through his hair, tugging his head closer. Caine closed his eyes and gave himself up to the feeling, carried away on a tidal wave of desire. For a moment the whole world seemed to go out of focus, and Caine felt as if he'd been drawn into another dimension, a parallel universe far away from death and war. When their lips broke, he felt as if he'd known her for ever. Her brilliant dark eyes glittered, mesmeric in the lamplight. 'Why don't you stay here with us,' she whispered in his ear. 'We need strong men like you.'

Caine felt bewitched and bewildered. He hadn't been prepared for anything like this. The world beyond this dreamers' cave seemed to have no meaning any more – the war, the enemy, the commandos, Tobruk, Egypt: it all seemed like the remote and ridiculous petty posturing of silly small creatures on some anthill somewhere.

He kissed Lina again, and it was as if he were being tugged down inexorably into a timeless garden of delight. The music from the gramophone, the blousy drawl of saxophones, a girl's thrilling, husky voice singing incomprehensible words that sounded as cloyingly sweet and heavy as syrup, seemed to express all the beauty, agony and sadness of his whole life.

He opened his eyes and saw Wallace, looking more serene and peaceful than he'd ever seen him, swaying with a girl whose straight dark tresses fell almost to her waist, whose voluptuous breasts seemed to pop out of her badly fitting dress. She had her arms round his neck and her head laid comfortably on his enormous chest. Most of the commandos seemed to have acquired partners – some, like Copeland, had already vanished into the night. He watched George Padstowe, Flash Murray, Shirley Temple, all smooching with pretty girls on the dancefloor, wearing the expressions of men entranced. 'Hey, skipper,' Padstowe said to him in a low voice as he waltzed past with a lissome-looking woman clinging to him. 'This is a better way of spending the war than fighting the Huns, eh? Makes you wonder why we killed all those Jerries this morning. What's it all for, anyway?'

Caine thought about the Brandenburgers they'd slaughtered over the past two days: young, brave men like his own comrades, who would have had the rest of their lives in front of them, men with wives, maybe children, with sisters and mothers who would mourn them for ever. He realized suddenly that he had no personal grievance against the Brandenburgers he'd shot and blown up and slashed to pieces only hours earlier. Allies and Axis – in the end they were all numbers on a list, expendable tools with precious and unique lives that were being consumed in the fire of a faceless dragon called war. He suddenly understood what motivated Michele – why it didn't trouble him which side he looted, why he talked about the 'class enemy'. Everything made sense, and he was astonished to find that there were tears in his eyes. Lina kissed him again, nuzzling close. 'Would you like to come to my tent?' she whispered.

Caine looked into her huge eyes, hypnotized by their heady beam. 'You don't really have to go tomorrow,' she said, fluttering dark eyelids. 'The war doesn't need you.' Caine felt electric with desire. He closed his eyes, and in his mind he saw a door opening – a door into a world with no more fighting, a world with him and perhaps this girl, a small white-walled farm on a hill, with animals and crops in the fields. He only had to say 'yes', to turn his back on the blood and slaughter, lay down his big Tommy-gun and start a new life in the broad, sunlit uplands. He was about to whisper that he'd go with her and stay with her for eternity when there came a tap on his arm. It was as if someone was trying to wake him from a deep, pleasant sleep, and he resisted, ignored it, hoped it would go away. The tap came again, more urgently this time, and a familiar voice said, 'Skipper, I've got something.'

Caine opened his eyes and found himself staring into the unlovely bifocals of Taffy Trubman, his face twitching with excitement. Trubman was still dressed in his leather jerkin and scuzzy overalls, wearing battle-order webbing and carrying his Lee-Enfield. With his carp's head and dense lenses, his snowman figure, he seemed a bizarre messenger from the outside world – a world that Caine felt he had left far behind in the pleasures of the night. 'Let it wait, Taffy,' he groaned. 'Can't you see I'm busy here?'

Trubman didn't move. 'This is important, skipper,' he said.

Caine turned back to Lina, but Trubman poked his arm again, this time with more force. 'This young lady is very pretty,' he said, 'but is she more important than *Runefish*?'

It was the name that made the difference. Caine disentangled himself from Lina's arms and stepped reluctantly away. He glanced at his watch and gasped. It was almost 0500 hours. He couldn't believe it: in the cave, time had stood still. It would soon be dawn – they had partied away the whole night.

'Christ,' he said. He looked back at the girl, touched her affectionately on the cheek. 'I'm sorry,' he said. 'I would have loved it, but it just wasn't fated. I have to go.'

She burst into tears, but instead of comforting her, Caine forced himself to turn away. As he did so, though, some sort of spell was broken. He was back in the cold grey wasteland of war. Trubman hustled him out of the cave and on to the slab. Outside, the night air was sobering. Caine shivered, but was glad of the cold, refreshing draught . 'What is it, Taffy?' he asked.

'The emergency net, skipper. I've been picking up a message with *Runefish's* signature for the past fifteen minutes. I didn't try to answer, like you said. It's coming from a biscuit-tin transmitter, and the signal strength indicates that it's not far away.'

Caine sighed and followed Trubman down to the leaguer, where Naiman, Pickney and the two other soldiers were wide awake, smoking cigarettes, drinking tea. It was a whole different little world down here, so close to where he'd come from, but as distant as the moon. Caine retrieved his Thompson from the makeshift armoury in the White, cleared it, eased springs, clicked on a mag. These small actions brought him crashing back to reality. He followed the rotund Welshman to the Dingo, whose engine was running to keep the wireless batteries charged, and saw that Trubman had erected a complex Windom antenna – a wire strung like a washing line between two poles, connected to the No. 11 set by a small device known as a balun interface.

The two of them crawled into the scout-car's belly

through the lower hatch. The Welshman plonked himself in the driver's seat and had Caine sit in the passenger's place. He handed him the headphones and adjusted the volume dial on the set. Caine heard it at once – the blip-blip-blip of Morse signals – the staccato rattle of dots and dashes like strange alien chatter from a far-away planet, combinations and patterns repeated over and over. 'You sure it's her?' he asked.

Trubman scratched his double chin with delicate fingers. 'It's her all right. It's the correct call-sign and the signature's very clear, see.'

'But even if it is, couldn't she be sending under duress?'

'Not likely, skipper. There's a security code that would be left out by anyone who didn't know the procedure, see. In this loop, the security code is extant.'

Caine realized he had never heard Trubman talk like this before. His face glowed with the same enthusiasm Caine felt when he talked about engines – with a passion for the mysteries of his trade. Maintaining wireless silence must have been a real penance for him, Caine thought.

He put the headphones down. 'Can you triangulate the signal?'

Trubman hesitated, pulling a wry face. 'You know, skipper, it's not that easy getting a fix with sky-wave, because of the skip distance. These No. 11s are delicate, and they've already taken a pounding. It'll require an adjustable aerial, so I'll have to take down the Windom dipoles and erect the nine-foot poles instead. I'll need some help to manoeuvre the AFV while I track the signal: in fact, it'd be better with two sets and two aerials, so I'll need Lance Sergeant Murray or Temple to handle the Daimler, see, because I can't calibrate both sets at once, and we need to angle the vehicles until we can lock on to the signal.'

Caine listened to the breathless torrent of objections, bemused. 'So in other words, you can't do it?' he enquired.

'Oh no, Sergeant,' said Trubman, looking shocked. 'I'm a signalman first class. It might take a while, but I can do it all right.'

Caine chuckled with relief. 'Good,' he said. 'Get on it right away.' He slipped out of the hatch, and Trubman followed. 'By the way, skipper, the news from Rome Radio is that Rommel is poised to enter Tobruk at first light today – that's any moment now.'

'What day is it?' Caine enquired. 'I've sort of lost count.'

'21 June 1942,' Trubman said.

Caine grunted and waved Moshe Naiman and Maurice Pickney over. 'Come on,' he said. 'We'll go and round up the boys.'

'From what I saw,' Trubman tittered, 'that's going to take some doing.'

While he tramped off with the spare lads to dismantle the Windom antenna, Caine led the medical orderly and the interpreter towards the cave.

Trubman's warning proved correct. No sooner had Caine and Naiman reached the slab than they heard raised voices in the thickets near by – two men and a woman shrieking at each other. Caine looked at the others, lifting up his eyes. Here it was, the classic triangle: the inevitable consequence of the abandoned promiscuity of the night. The trouble was that one of the voices was Harry Copeland's.

It was Michele and Angela who were really at loggerheads, though, poised outside what Caine took to be their tent, their teeth bared like fighting dogs', letting rip at each other with long streams of abuse. Cope was standing a few paces out of the line of fire, trying to calm them down, looking embarrassed. He was dressed only in his shorts, and Angela wore a skimpy nightdress that concealed nothing. When Michele saw Caine, he pointed at him. 'This is how you repay our hospitality?' he bawled. 'I turn my back and this *stronso*' – he jabbed a finger at Cope – 'is fucking my wife?'

'What about you?' Angela screamed, her face contorted with fury. 'I suppose you weren't fucking that little trollop Antonella – my poor Carlo's girlfriend – a girl young enough to be your daughter. You say, *I missed you. I missed you, darling,* and the same night I get back and Carlo just dead, you are making love with his girlfriend in front of everyone, even *me.* This is why you don't come looking for me, eh? Too busy fucking little Antonella? You are happy the *Tedesci* kill poor Carlo, eh, so you can fuck his girlfriend? You would be happy if the *Tedesci* kill me like Carlo, too, no? So you can go on fucking every trollop in the camp.'

Michele stared at her through snake-like eyes, the expression on his face vicious. 'That is a lie,' he shouted. 'What about you dropping your knickers for the first soldier who comes along? You aren't a whore, no?'

'That's it,' Angela screeched, hurling herself at Michele, scrabbling at his face with broken fingernails. Michele held her off for a second, sniggering, then belted her in the face, knocking her down. He was about to kick her when Caine cocked his Colt .45. Michele heard the click, and looked up to see that the pistol was trained at his head from not more than a yard away. 'I don't like to interfere in domestic issues,' Caine said carefully, 'but I'm damned if I'm going to see ladies knocked down.'

Michele halted in his tracks, his face a mask of blind fury. 'You get out,' he bellowed. 'And you take that' – he gestured at Copeland – 'that cocksucker with you.'

'We're going,' Caine said. 'There was just the little matter of petrol?'

'*Hah. Hah.* You are funny man,' Michele said. He spat contemptuously towards Cope. 'You think I give you petrol after that bastard fucked my wife? He's had his reward, and you've had yours.'

Caine didn't lower the pistol. 'What happened to "Blood brothers for ever,"' he said slowly. 'What about "My life is yours"? What about "Property is theft"? Where I come from, a promise is a promise. Either you give me the fuel, or I will make sure the RAF have the coordinates of this place and include it on their next bombing run. My government doesn't take kindly to people stealing material supplied by hard-working tax-payers. Capitalist pigs, you see.'

Everyone stared at Caine in amazement. 'You wouldn't . . . ?' Angela gasped, picking herself up. 'There are women here . . . children.'

Caine nodded grimly. 'Try me,' he said. He cocked an eye at Michele. 'Well?'

The Italian tossed his long hair arrogantly. 'All right, but *you*' – he jabbed a long finger at Copeland – 'stay away from her.'

Caine sent Naiman and Pickney to the leaguer with Michele, to collect one of the 3-tonners for the petrol. As soon as her husband was out of sight, Angela threw her arms round Copeland and kissed him. 'Don't listen to that son-of-a-bitch Michele,' she said. 'It was so good with you. Better than that two-faced motherfucker.' She spat on the ground where Michele had been standing. 'Better a thousand times.'

Copeland returned the kiss then broke away gently, facing Caine. 'Give us a minute, skipper,' he said.

Caine waited for him at the entrance to the cave, where he saw that the party had already broken up. Copeland appeared, fully dressed and looking slightly bemused. Caine winked at him. 'What happened to the Sirens, then?'

'Don't start,' Cope snapped, holding up a warning hand. 'She's a . . . she's a very special person.'

'I've no doubt she is. In case you're interested, though, Trubman picked up *Runefish* on the emergency net. We're in business.'

Cope grunted, glancing wistfully back into the forest where he'd left Angela. For all his concern, Caine thought, he might have told him that the moon was green cheese. 'Get a grip, mate,' he snapped. 'Let's get the men assembled and get going.'

It took almost an hour to collect the commandos. A few of them were lying in the recesses of the cave in all stages of undress, mostly in the arms of young women. Caine told them the good news about *Runefish*, but like Copeland they didn't seem impressed. 'Bugger *Runefish*,' Todd Sweeney cursed, extracting himself from the embrace of a plump and attractive widow of about thirty-five. 'I'm enjoying it here.'

'What's the rush, skipper?' Padstowe demanded blearily, as Caine yanked a blanket off him and his paramour. 'Let's stay a few more days.'

The hardest cases were those who had left the party and were scattered throughout the tents in the forest. Caine and Copeland had to force an entry and jerk some of them out of bed physically, hurling them on the floor and dousing them with cold water. When they tried this with Wallace, though, the giant reared up like a colossus, flattened Copeland with a bare-handed slap. 'Take your hands off me,' he bellowed. 'I'm staying here. You can keep your stinking *Runefish*.' He put his log-sized arms protectively around the girl Caine had seen him dancing with that night, and she buried her head in his chest. 'I've been looking for a woman like Giovanna my whole life,' Wallace growled. 'I'm not leaving her now. Stuff the mission. You can do it without me.' His eyes narrowed warily as Copeland moved towards him again, and he let go of the weeping girl. 'So help me, Harry, I'll lamp you.'

While his back was turned, Caine stepped behind him niftily, jammed the barrel of the Colt hard into his ear. The giant felt the chill of cold steel against his flesh: he raised his steam-shovel hands in surrender, rumbling with laughter. 'You're going to shoot me? *Me?* Cope and me saved your life yesterday. You forgotten so quick?'

'Nope,' Caine said. 'In fact I'm returning the favour. It's just that you haven't realized it yet.' He turned to Copeland. 'You got parachute cord?' he asked.

'Right here, skipper,' said Cope, drawing a hank of olive-green cord from his webbing.

'Tie him up.'

'What?' Wallace trumpeted.

'This is for your own good, Fred,' Caine said.

Cope fastened the big man's hands to a torrent of verbal abuse, and Caine frog-marched him down to the leaguer at gunpoint. There, he and Copeland secured him in the back of *Judy*, handcuffing him to the frame. As they emerged, Naiman swept past from the fuel dump at the wheel of the 3-tonner *Vera*. He halted the truck and gave Caine the thumbs-up from the open window. 'Got it, skipper,' he called. 'All three hundred gallons, as ordered.'

'Did Michele give you any trouble?'

'No trouble. Just slunk off muttering about cocksuckers.'

'Good. Let's get this circus on the road.'

All the roll was now accounted for, and the commandos had settled down to man their guns and steering wheels with varying degrees of reluctance. A crowd of civilians – most of them scantily dressed girls – had gathered around the wagons. Some of them were crying, and Caine hoped fervently they wouldn't try to stop the column leaving: there was no way he was going to open fire on a cordon of nubile young women blocking the track. Dawn was creeping across the softly curving peaks of the Green Mountains, painting purple shadows in the crevices, giving the massif the look of a harem of giant, voluptuous female bodies in repose. The sky was marbled in cobalt and ethereal gas-blue, the open hillsides smeared with pink candyfloss light. Caine pushed through the crowd and found Trubman in the Dingo, tinkering with the No. 11 set. 'How's it going?' he enquired.

'It's not been easy, skipper,' he sighed. 'See, it was a sod getting those nine-foot poles set up, and like I said, these sets have been given so much humpty, it's a wonder they work at all.'

'So you didn't get it?'

Trubman sat back in the seat and pushed his black beret off his forehead. 'Well,' he said doubtfully, 'I've got something, but it's not very accurate. I've only managed to narrow it down to an area of about twelve square feet.'

'Twelve square *feet*?' Caine repeated, wondering if he'd heard right. 'That presents *big* problems, then.'

Trubman smiled crookedly, handing Caine a map. 'I've marked the spot with an x. The signal is coming from a point in a big wadi, about twenty miles from here. I've also marked out a route. I reckon it'll take us no more than an hour to get there.'

'Taffy,' Caine said, beaming all over his face, 'you've just saved the mission. You're worth your weight in gold.'

The plump cheeks pinked out. 'Only one thing, skipper,' Trubman said. '*Runefish* has been transmitting non-stop for nearly two hours. If I've been able to locate her position, the Axis will almost certainly have done the same. We have to get there quickly, yes, but let's move in with our eyes open, because there's at least a fifty-fifty chance the Hun will have got there first.'

26

Sixty-three minutes later, Caine, Copeland and Wallace lay scrimmed up in dense maquis scrub on a steep hillside overlooking a sandy dry-wash. Below their position, to the right, the wadi became narrower: to the left it disappeared sharply around a bend. Directly beneath them, across the wadi bed, was the narrow opening of a cave. There was no sign of movement there, but a trickle of smoke from the entrance indicated that it was inhabited. The cave lay within the 'twelve-foot square' area pinpointed by Trubman, and since the emergency signal had been transmitting up to the time the convoy had arrived, ten minutes earlier, Caine was certain that they had located *Runefish* at last.

The morning was stifling hot but overhung with crests of cloud that cast patches of gloomy shade across the hills. The landscape here, nearing the edge of the massif, was ragged and broken – wind-blasted ridges, stunted goat-grass, denuded granite cliffs shattered into a billion segments, thickets of leafless thorn-trees like fractured bones, angular tors rising from hillsides like ancient watch-towers, charred, scoured and dismembered by Greek fire.

Caine and his mates were wearing overalls, boots, helmets covered with scrim nets and full battle-order, their dress camouflaged with grass and dried leaves taken from the surrounding hillside, their faces blackened with burnt cork. Caine doubted that enemy snoopers – if there were any around – would clock them, even if they were to walk directly past. They had crawled slowly into the OP, having secured a fast line of retreat to the wagons leaguered and scrimmed up below, in case a reception committee should be waiting for them.

Now, Copeland focused his telescopic sights on the cave, while Caine scanned the area with his binos, looking out for unwelcome surprises. Wallace was proned-out to Caine's right, lining up the sights of the new Bren he'd drawn from the armoury earlier. It was a replacement for the weapon he'd lost the previous morning when he'd dived from *Marlene* just seconds before she'd been skewered by a shell from the enemy AFV.

Caine had released Wallace from his cuffs a short way out of the deserters' camp, on receiving his promise that he wouldn't try to escape. This small separation in space and time from the site of last night's orgy appeared to have done the trick: 'That bloody lobster's got a lot to answer for,' Wallace had chuntered. While togging up for the current operation, though, Caine thought he'd noticed an intermittent sigh from the giant's direction, and the name *Giovanna* whispered. Wallace wasn't the only one: there'd been the occasional far-away look on Copeland's face, too.

They lay there for another five minutes. Nothing stirred. 'That's it then,' Caine said, preparing to move out of position. '*Runefish*, here we come.'

He was halted by the pressure of Wallace's plate-sized hand on his arm. Below them, a German soldier had just emerged from around the bend in the wadi. He was dressed in a tan bush-shirt, khaki leggings, high-laced boots, scrimmed Kaiser helmet and full battle-gear, and carrying a Gewehr 41 semi-auto rifle. He moved cautiously, hugging the cover of the wadi side. As Copeland followed his progress through his telescopic sights, another soldier appeared, then another. They were spaced about three yards apart, moving with stealth, weaving from rock to rock, from crevice to crevice. They looked as if they knew their business, and Caine would have bet money they were Brandenburgers.

The three Germans took up static positions, crouching down in cover. It was only then that Caine became aware of the deep growl of an engine and the scrape and rattle of iron tracks. As the three of them gaped in surprise, a Mk III Panzer slalomed into view around the wadi bend, a heavy, squat, mottled scarab with a turret like a great iron camel-hump, her 50mm gun raised at an acute angle, her two snubby machine guns wagging from the forward hatches. The commander sat at the turret hatch dressed, like the footsloggers, in brown and khaki but wearing the black side-cap of the DAK Panzer Divisions in place of a helmet. With binos slung round his neck, wireless headphones clamped on his ears, sand-goggles over his eyes and a cigarette drooping from his mouth, he had the immense complacency of a monarch surveying his domain.

Caine felt a frisson of dread as the tank rumbled at a snail's pace along the wadi directly below him, her small and large flywheels rotating, her tracks ratchetting with the discordant musical clatter Caine had once learned to fear, slapping and compressing the sand like a fast succession of flat steel feet. It was a while since he'd seen a Mark III, but he knew from experience what she was capable of. A trio of HE shells from her 50mm cannon would put paid to his entire column once and for all.

If Maddaleine Rose was inside the cave, she would have heard the approach of the tank, and would now know that the enemy had found her. He tried not to imagine the terror she must be feeling at that moment, alone, hundreds of miles behind Axis lines, aware that there was no escape, that she was entirely at the mercy of the Hun. The fact that the

Jerries had assigned a Panzer to her capture showed the importance they must attach to her. He found himself wondering why Rose had started transmitting on the emergency frequency so suddenly, and why she'd kept it up for so long. She must have realized that the Axis would triangulate her signal. It seemed a kind of suicide, and Caine could only imagine that either she'd grown desperate, or that she'd somehow discovered that his rescue mission was close at hand.

He thought of the men Michele had sent out the previous night to find news of her. He'd neglected to ask the deserter-in-chief about them in the fracas that morning – he wasn't even certain that Michele had kept his promise. If they *had* gone out, it was possible that Rose had discovered from them that a British mobile detachment was on her trail. Was that why she'd keyed in the emergency call so abruptly? But then, wouldn't it have been more tactical for her to have returned with them under the cover of darkness? Why risk sending out a signal that was bound to alert the enemy? It occurred to him that she might have been wounded in a contact, injured in the parachute drop. That would explain it: maybe she'd heard news of the commandos' presence but couldn't move. But then why not send Michele's men back with a message instead . . . ?

The tank passed the mouth of the cave, and creaked to a halt a little further up the wadi, her turret pivoting 360 degrees so that the gun was pointing directly down the watercourse. At the same moment an entire platoon of Brandenburgers advanced around the bend on Caine's left, as immaculately drilled as the scouts who'd preceded them, led by a stringy subaltern and a bull-faced sergeant. They spread out in tactical order, responding to the officer's hand signals with well-oiled discipline. They formed a loose cordon round the cave entrance, some training weapons on the cave, others facing outwards, covering all arcs of fire. It was done as precisely as a silent drill movement on the parade ground, Caine thought. The subaltern detailed five men to accompany him. A second later, the group entered the cave.

The single gunshot, muffled by the rock walls, almost made Caine jump. He was painfully aware, though, that any surreptitious movement might alert the tank commander, and result in a 50mm shell whaling into his position. He kept his eyes riveted on the cave entrance. Almost at once he saw the bull-faced sergeant emerge, followed by two men dragging a woman by the arms. She was tall and lean, with the kind of build you might find in a runner or a dancer. Her cheeks were sunburned, and she was more than a little mussed-looking, her khaki drills wrinkled, torn and filthy, her dense crop of short corngold hair in matted tufts. The webbing holster she wore at her waist flapped empty, and Caine noted that it was worn reversed on her right for a cross-body draw – indicating that she was left-handed: he guessed that the shot he'd heard was her attempt to fight off the Hun. Caine daren't lift his binos in case the movement was clocked, but even with his naked eye he could make out the light blue WRNS rings of rank she wore on her shoulder straps. '*Maddy*,' he whispered under his breath.

The party halted outside the cave, and the woman's captors released her arms. Instantly, she let out a deafening screech and burst into a run. She'd made only two paces before the sergeant blocked her way, smashed her in the face with a closed fist. The blow didn't look very hard, but it was hard enough to send her reeling to her knees. Caine felt the blood pounding in his temples: his trigger finger itched. It was the second time he'd seen a woman knocked down by a man that morning, and he felt no better disposed towards it on this occasion than on the first.

He forced himself to watch as the Germans hauled the woman up and lashed her hands behind her back with rope. The other three soldiers came out of the cave, and Caine saw that one of them was carrying a small wireless transmitter in a webbing bag. A second trooper hefted a haversack and various items of personal kit, and a third what appeared to be the charred remains of a leather attaché case and bits of blackened paper. This explained the smoke issuing from the cave earlier: *Runefish* had been destroying her documents. From what he could see, it looked as if she'd pretty much succeeded. The third man showed his prizes to the officer, who examined them briefly, shook his head. He had several of the troopers scour the wooded area around the mouth of the cave, and very soon they returned with a long coil of antenna wire. The officer eyeballed it once, then signalled to the squad to move off.

Maddaleine walked freely now, prodded occasionally from behind by one of the Brandenburgers. She looked remarkably cool considering her position. Her attempt to escape, while futile, had been plucky. Seizing the right moment just after capture, when her captors weren't quite oriented: the loud, distracting noise, the explosive burst of energy – these were text-book escape tactics. *Runefish* had been well trained for the job: she was evidently more than just a spare GHQ pen-pusher, Caine thought.

As the party headed for the bend in the wadi, the rest of the Brandenburgers began to withdraw. The Panzer's motor roared. 'I can take the shot now, skipper,' Copeland whispered, still peering through his scope. 'Once they make the bend, forget it.'

It took Caine a split second to work out that Cope was

talking about execution. With a sinking feeling, he realized that his mate was right: he'd been given the execution order for precisely this situation. Rose had evidently destroyed the documents, but she was still a captive, and the Hun would soon force her to reveal the secrets of *Assegai*, or whatever it was that she was really carrying in her head. He considered going for the snatch – if Cope could take out the Jerries immediately around her, she might be able to make a break for it – after all, they wouldn't want to kill her just yet. Then he eyeballed the Panzer: any attempt to snatch *Runefish* would be doomed from the start.

He found himself casting around for excuses to stop the hit. Wouldn't it be impossible for Cope to take Rose out with that tank down there? Reluctantly, he had to admit that it wouldn't. Copeland was a crack shot: it would only need one round, a head shot, and they could bug out of the OP like greased ball-bearings, down the slope into the leaguer. The Jerry tank-crew would never clock their position that fast. The Mk III was capable of lobbing shells across the escarpment and dropping them on his convoy, but the Jerry gunners didn't know it was there and would be shooting blind. Within seconds of the killing shot, Caine's wagons would be racing back along the wadi they'd come in by. Reluctantly, he had to admit that if Cope took the shot now, they stood every chance of getting away with it. He watched Rose walking gracefully down the wadi and realized that her party was only fifty yards from the bend. In a matter of seconds she'd be out of sight. 'Skipper?' Cope hissed.

Caine heaved a deep breath, closing his eyes. His stomach churned. He felt sick at heart for having to make this life-or-death decision. It had always been on the cards, of course, but he had never really believed it would come to this. Now there was no other choice. He held his breath. 'All right, Harry,' he whispered. 'You can take the shot.'

Copeland lined up his sights. 'What a waste,' he sighed under his breath. 'She's a real stunner.'

Caine took a last peek at Maddy Rose – the woman he and his men had gone through hell to rescue, and whom he would now never meet. It appalled him that his commandos had endured so much – prevailed over almost insurmountable obstacles, fought desperate actions, lost so many good men – just to be cheated by fate at this eleventh hour. He tried to put the blame on his men – their bloody-minded reluctance to tear themselves away from the 'Sirens', for example. If they'd left the deserters' camp an hour earlier they might have made it. Yet the decision to lay up at Michele's camp had been his – a decision that Harry Copeland, for one, had strongly contested. Cope might have ended up in bed with Angela, and might have been reluctant to leave, but he had warned Caine seriously about going there in the first place. Once again, the blame could be laid at the door of no one but himself.

He watched Rose walking to a death that lay only seconds away. As Cope had said, she was a 'stunner'. He felt proud of her dignified demeanour, her refusal to betray the terror she must be feeling. He thought of his mother, lost and alone in her own village, hounded to suicide, unprotected by the son who had arrived too late to save her. How much worse to die here in a foreign land surrounded by enemies, taken out by comrades from the country she had sworn to serve.

The group was approaching the bend now. He guessed that Cope would wait until the last second, when most of the Germans had their backs to the OP and wouldn't clock the muzzle flash. He heard his mate take a deep breath and retain it – the prelude to the strike. He saw Copeland's muscles tense, and thought of his mother's pale, granite face after death. He hadn't been able to save her, but it wasn't too late for Rose. He was here, now, and he could stop it. Whatever his orders, whatever the outcome, he wasn't going to see a brave woman shot down in cold blood. Copeland took the first pressure on the trigger, eased off the safety catch. Caine had just opened his mouth to say, 'Don't fire', when an aero-engine screeched and boomed above them: all three of them ducked.

She was a Storch spotter-plane and she had poled up from behind them and skimmed the escarpment at about three hundred feet. Caine turned his head slightly to get a look at her, and found that he could see her pilot in the cockpit. She buzzed over them, too fast and too high to see them, and dovetailed down towards the wadi bed, where the Panzer was lumbering forward in a cloud of dust. For a moment it looked as if she might crash, but her nose lifted at the last instant, and she climbed steeply, leap-frogging over the opposite slope. Caine's first thought was that the pilot had spotted the leaguer in the valley behind them. As he watched, though, the aircraft looped west towards Benghazi, making no attempt to come in for a second look. Caine let out a breath and squinted down into the dry-wash channel. The Mark III was trundling towards the bend in the wake of the last Brandenburgers. Maddaleine Rose and her captors had gone.

27

Colonel-General Erwin Rommel, General Officer Commanding the Panzer Group Africa, stood at the door of an abandoned Italian roadhouse, his deep grey-blue eyes taking in smoke rising in black pencil lines from the port of Tobruk. The old wound in his leg was giving him trouble again, and that was never a good sign. The wound was almost thirty years old – acquired when, as a young platoon leader of the 124th Infantry Regiment, at Verdun, he'd suddenly found himself confronted with five French riflemen. He'd shot two and had been in the process of charging the rest, armed with only a bayonet, when he'd taken a wound the size of a fist in his right leg. That had landed him with the Iron Cross (Second Class), and three months in hospital. The scar had vanished years ago, but the phantom wound still gave him trouble when he was under stress.

He'd entered Tobruk just before dawn that morning, 21 June, to find himself an observer in a scene from Dante's *Inferno* – bands of ragged, bearded Allied troops, unarmed and aimless, groping like blind men along rubble streets filled with bloody heaps of dead and dying; the blackened hulks of tanks and lorries; the smoking shells of burned-out workshops, plants and warehouses; the ravaged, smouldering hulls of listing Royal Navy vessels in the harbour, sinking to a chorus of shrieks from drowning sailors; filthy, skeletal South Africans covered with desert sores, their faces obscured by shrouds of flies, waving soiled vests on sticks as white flags; almost equally filthy Axis soldiers scuttling like ants around store-dumps, bellowing in glee, carrying off crates of beer and armfuls of boots and brand-new khaki clothing. He had driven four miles along the coast road between walls of flaming vehicles, among tens of thousands of unkempt Allied prisoners who'd stared at him with the stony eyes of cadavers. In the whole of the town there was hardly a single building left upright.

His capture of the so-called 'impregnable fortress' of Tobruk in only twenty-four hours should have been the crowning moment of Rommel's career, yet he felt furious with himself. An hour earlier he'd stalked out of a historic meeting with the defeated fortress-commander, Major General Henry Klopper, beside himself with rage. It had taken the combined efforts of his ADCs, Captain Heinz Schmidt and Lieutenant Alfred Berndt, his intelligence officer, Major Friedrich von Mellenthin, and his devoted batman, Rifleman Alfred Günther, to calm him down.

Klopper had signed the surrender document in front of the assembled Axis staff without a quibble, but instead of treating him with the dignity due to a defeated warrior, Rommel had lost his rag and sworn at him like a fishmonger. His staff had been shocked at this breach of his own protocol – Rommel was renowned for his rigid views on proper military conduct. Even Mellenthin's quip to the South African general, in English, that he had 'come a klopper this time' hadn't broken the tension.

Rommel frowned as he replayed the meeting in his head. What had queered the pitch was Klopper's request for water for his thirty-two thousand prisoners, and for fresh clothing and boots for those whose uniforms had been ruined while dumping their own petrol stocks. '*Water?*' Rommel had bellowed at the astonished South African. 'What am I, a magician? It was your troops who destroyed the water tanks, and wrecked the only sea-water distillation plant available, so as far as I am concerned they can drink their own piss. If their uniforms are ruined, let them go round bollock naked. You should have thought about that before you gave them orders to sabotage vital supplies.'

Rommel had been a soldier most of his life, and knew that, in Klopper's place, he would have given precisely the same orders. What was really gnawing at him was the fact that while his men had captured nearly two thousand vehicles and five thousand tons of food, enemy petrol stocks had only amounted to two thousand tons. Unless he found more petrol soon, and without a secure water source behind him, he might not be able to continue his advance into Egypt. It was crucial to strike now, he thought, while Eighth Army was in total disarray.

It was almost noon and the air was humid and muggy. Rommel was dressed formally in brown bush-jacket, khaki jodhpurs and high cavalry boots, his peaked service cap carrying the sand-goggles he'd looted a year earlier from a British general. He felt envious of Captain Kiel, chief of his Battle Staff, and his men, dressed freely in boots and shorts. He watched them go about their duties in the ruined yard, enjoying the smells of hot oil and canvas, the familiar purposeful bustle that had become his way of life – driver-mechanics repairing punctures and going about the routine servicing of command vehicles, aides setting up awnings and work-stations, men of his personal signals detachment erecting aerials, running out cables, adjusting wireless sets, his bodyguard taking up arcs of fire around the perimeter with the precision of long practice. Back before the Great War – before most of these boys had been born – Rommel had served as both a private and a sergeant in the infantry.

He still preferred the company of his men to that of the top-brass stuffed shirts and the Prussian aristocracy.

He turned and marched into the half-derelict building, grateful for the respite from the mid-day sun. Inside, he found Berndt and Schmidt tacking up maps and arranging camp-chairs around a trestle table for the forthcoming meeting, while Günther brewed coffee on a solid-fuel stove. Rommel had just accepted a cup of coffee when Mellenthin marched in carrying a sheaf of message forms. He held them out to Rommel, who waved them away, focusing his attention on his coffee. 'Just tell me,' he said.

Mellenthin smiled thinly. He was a bean-pole, stiff-moustached Prussian from an old military family who, like Rommel, had once served as a private soldier, though in a cavalry rather than an infantry regiment. As a direct descendant of Frederick the Great of Prussia, he belonged to precisely the group that Rommel disdained, but the GOC couldn't but appreciate his meticulous attention to detail, his ruthless efficiency, and his courage. Only a few days earlier, when his HQ had somehow found itself behind Allied lines, the IO had fought off an enemy attack single-handed with a sub-machine gun.

'We have a confirmation on those captured documents, general,' Mellenthin said. 'One of our agents in Cairo verifies that Eighth Army has been ordered to take up a fall-back position at Mersa Matruh.'

Rommel grunted: this was hardly a surprise. British generals always preferred defensive positions to mobility – it was the same rigidity of thinking that had led to their loss of the Gazala Line. The British were stubborn fighters, but they thought in terms of 'Boxes'. They hadn't yet got the hang of fast-moving mechanical warfare – he'd been told that they even referred to their tanks as 'horses'. They were good at grandiose plans but lacked the individual initiative and the ability to improvise that was the great strength of German troops.

Rommel finished his coffee and put the cup down. 'Ritchie is a dunderhead,' he told Mellenthin. 'He still hasn't learned that any defensive position on the coast, no matter how strong, can always be outflanked via the desert.'

Mellenthin regarded him thoughtfully and stepped over to the theatre-map Berndt had just stuck on the wall. 'That's generally true,' he said, 'but not further east . . . here . . . at Alamein. The open flank there is guarded by the Qattara Depression – all salt marsh and quicksands. If I were Auchinleck and I wanted to make a stand, that's where it would be.'

'There won't be any stand,' Rommel scoffed. 'Eighth Army is finished.'

Mellenthin's brow puckered. 'I've got something here from No. 2 Company of the Brandenburg Regiment,' he said. 'It might be important or it might not. They have picked up a British courier from Allied HQ Egypt. She's being held at Biska, pending interrogation by the Abwehr.'

'*She?*' Rommel interjected, chortling. 'The Auk must be hard up if he's using bints to run his errands now. Who is she?'

'According to the message, she's a Royal Navy staff officer with the equivalent rank of major. Her aircraft crashed south of the Green Mountain three days ago. We had a tip-off from our source *Stürmer*, in Cairo, that her mission might be significant – to Winston Churchill in London, no less. Our "Y" Service people intercepted wireless chatter from her aircraft, and heard her codename – *Runefish* – being used. We were able to track the plane and shoot her down. The woman – *Runefish* – bailed out by parachute, and 2 Company have been looking for her ever since. Incidentally, it seems that a couple of their platoons may have run into enemy raiding units deep behind our lines. It's only conjecture, but it is possible that these units were sent to rescue *Runefish*.'

Rommel glanced at his watch. 'Can this wait?' he asked. '"Smiling Albert" will be here any minute, and you can bet he's got more on his mind than offering me congratulations.'

Mellenthin frowned again. Rommel had been in a curiously fractious mood all day, considering that he'd just achieved one of the more glittering successes of his life. The IO had been astonished at his treatment of Klopper, but he supposed that no matter how brilliant an officer was, a lower-class background would always out in the end. The capture of a female naval officer might be small fry, but there were aspects of this *Runefish* case that looked interesting – if those raiding units *had* been sent to pull her out, it suggested that what she was carrying was highly important.

Mellenthin hated to drop things once the engines of his intellect were engaged. He took a deep breath and tried again. 'Sir, *Runefish* destroyed the documents she was carrying before 2 Company found her, but they did manage to retrieve one line in code. That line has been decrypted by the Abwehr, and it suggests that her mission concerned the condition of the Eighth Army.'

'If she destroyed the documents, she's not much use to us, is she?' Rommel snapped. 'That's what you get when you send Abwehr hounds to do a real soldier's job.'

Mellenthin smiled sardonically, knowing Rommel's mistrust of the Abwehr and its chief, Admiral Canaris. He regarded the Brandenburgers as political troops like the Waffen SS, rather than real soldiers.

'The intelligence isn't necessarily lost, sir,' he said. 'British standard operating procedure is to have the courier memorize the details as a back-up. They will probably have chosen this woman because of her retentive memory. It only requires a skilled interrogator . . .'

'Let me know when you've got something more concrete,' Rommel said. At that moment Lt Berndt came to attention with a click of the heels, rendering a *'Heil Hitler'* salute. 'Field Marshal Kesselring and General Bastico, sir,' he announced.

Wheeling around towards the two staff officers now sweeping in through the main entrance, Rommel and Mellenthin delivered sharp Wehrmacht salutes. Though one of the newcomers was German and the other Italian, they wore almost identical khaki drill uniforms, with full chests of medal-ribbons. Albert Kesselring pumped Rommel's hand. 'Well done, General, well done indeed,' he roared, sporting the familiar toothy grin that had earned him the nickname 'Smiling Albert'. 'A magnificent show. Remarkable. Today, the eyes of all Germany are upon you.'

Rommel took the compliments self-effacingly: as General Officer Commanding the Mediterranean theatre, Kesselring was technically his superior. A Bavarian like Rommel, he'd been a gunner in the Great War, and had only learned to fly an aircraft at the age of forty-eight. A brave pilot who'd been shot down no fewer than five times, and a superb administrator, he was also deep Luftwaffe, and Rommel regarded his knowledge of ground warfare as cursory.

'A thousand congratulations, General,' rumbled Ettore Bastico, a lopsided, bear-like Italian whose good-natured face was framed by a non-regulation beard. 'Today will go down in history as the beginning of the end for the British in North Africa. The start of a new era.'

'Let's hope so.'

'Perhaps it's premature to tell you,' Kesselring said playfully, removing his peaked service cap and drawing a hand across his balding skull, 'but I'm sure you won't object. Our dear Führer has made you a special award: a field marshal's baton. Congratulations again – most well deserved. From tomorrow you won't have to salute me any more.'

Rommel remained poker-faced. 'The Führer is very generous,' he said, 'but with all due respect, I would rather have had an extra division.'

Kesselring and Bastico laughed. It was the sort of remark expected of the 'Desert Fox', Mellenthin thought: one that would be remembered and repeated endlessly in canteens and messes throughout the Panzer Group. Rommel loved to play the bluff soldier, but the faintest reddening of his cheeks showed Mellenthin that he was thrilled. Not that his CO was inordinately vain, either: it was true that he often blamed others for his own mistakes, but it was also true that he had no inflated idea of himself. His vanity was there, but it was altogether of an ordinary, very human kind.

A few minutes later, after Berndt had seated the three generals at the table and handed out cups of coffee, Kesselring leaned forward and said, 'Now, gentlemen. With the fall of Tobruk behind us, the time has come to carry out the next step of the plan we agreed on at Obersalzberg in March – Op *Herkules* – the capture of Malta. The full-moon phase is almost upon us, so the assault must be carried out very soon. Our 1st Parachute Brigade and the Italian Folgore Airborne Division are already in training at Tarquinia and Apulia for the op, under the supervision of Bernhard Ramcke. We also have a sea-landing brigade and seventeen ships assigned to us.'

He paused for breath and saw that Rommel had fixed him with a glassy stare.

'Field Marshal,' he said coolly. 'When we discussed this plan with the Führer at Obersalzberg, you made it clear that the success of *Herkules* would require the deployment of all the Luftwaffe squadrons in this theatre. If that is still the case, may I ask where am I going to get the air support for my advance into Egypt?'

Kesselring scratched his nose. 'Obviously we don't have enough aircraft to support both the attack on Malta *and* an advance into Egypt. Your advance will have to wait until *Herkules* is completed. The Malta op is the more urgent, because as long as Allied air units and submarines are able to operate from Malta, none of our supply columns is safe. As it is, only one out of every four sea convoys to Tripoli is coming through intact . . .' He paused, noticing that Rommel was tapping calloused fingers on the table-top, and that there was a dangerous gleam in his eye. '*Therefore*, General,' Kesselring went on, looking straight at him, 'your forces will proceed to the frontier, where you will await the outcome of the Malta operation. In August, you will be able to advance to the Nile with full air support.'

'*August?*' Rommel repeated, as if he hadn't heard right. 'By that time the Allies will have set up a new front. Eighth Army will have been reinforced by God knows how many fresh divisions and new tanks.' He shook his head gravely. 'No, no, a thousand times no. We have to push across the frontier *now* in a lightning thrust. Eighth Army is shattered: it has fallen to pieces, lost its cohesion. We must overtake what's left of it and crush it before it can escape. To go for Malta instead would be the act of a fool.'

Kesselring now bore little resemblance to the mythical 'Smiling Albert'. 'Be careful, General,' he growled. ''That strategy was agreed on in March, by the Duce, and by the Führer himself. I was there, you were there, and General

Cavallero was there. If there are any fools involved, you are one of them, because I don't remember your making any objection at the time.'

'Things have changed since March. War is fluid. Situations evolve.'

Kesselring took a deep breath and leaned back in his chair. 'General, your troops – both German and Italian – have fought hard, and they are tired. The DAK alone has lost almost four thousand men killed in action over the past weeks. The fact is that you are short of men, short of armour, short of transport, short of supplies. Wouldn't it be more reasonable to rest and refit? You would be in a far stronger position in a month's time.'

'The enemy will be ten times stronger. No, Field Marshal, we must strike now, today. The Eighth Army is on the verge of collapse – the men have been so badly served by their top brass that I wouldn't be surprised to hear of mass desertion, even mutiny. The time is ripe. We must go in now, and we must go in fast.'

'What makes you so certain that Eighth Army is finished?' Bastico asked in a low voice. 'Our intelligence suggests that even after Gazala, the Allies are still capable of mustering more men, more armour, more guns, and more supplies than we are. Do you have any proof to the contrary?'

'My nose tells me so.'

Bastico smirked. 'With all due respect, General, your nose is not always your best advisor. In November last year you rejected our reports that the Allies were preparing an offensive, to such a degree that you were in Rome when they launched it. Even then, you refused to believe it until you saw it with your own eyes. I have great respect for you, General Rommel – you are a master of blitzkrieg and perhaps the only leader we have who truly understands mobile warfare, but this is not just about mobile warfare, it is also about logistics.'

'About pen-pushers, you mean,' Rommel snorted. 'About your fat, indolent supply staffs in Rome who wouldn't know a day's work if it got up and punched them in the face. If those blighters did a decent job now and again, if they put in the same effort my troops in the field put in, then we'd have the supplies you continually promise me at Benghazi and at the forward ports, here in Tobruk, and at Mersa Matruh when we take it, not a thousand miles away in Tripoli.'

'Are you aware,' Bastico cut in sourly, 'that your 8000-ton steamer *Reichenfels* was sunk only this morning by an RAF squadron operating out of Malta? Did you know that, the day before yesterday, the Italian cruiser *Trento* was sunk by the same squadron, and the battleship *Littorio* badly damaged? We can't get supplies to the forward ports, General, because Malta is in our way. While Malta stands, we can't guarantee our supplies, not even at Tripoli. You have won a great victory here at Tobruk, no doubt, but that victory can't be exploited unless the supply system functions smoothly. To push into Egypt without securing the supply base would be a major strategic blunder. I have no choice but to forbid you to advance further than the frontier.'

For a moment, Rommel eyed him incredulously. Then he let out an explosive chuckle. 'You *forbid* me? I'm sorry, General: you may be Governor-General of Tripolitania, but any decisions concerning the Panzer Group are my responsibility, and mine alone. You can't do any more than give me advice, and in this case I consider your advice unacceptable . . .'

'You may not be under my orders,' Bastico said sharply, 'but you *are* under the orders of the Duce, and as far as I recall, it is he who has forbidden any advance until Malta has fallen. Think about it carefully, General. No decision you have ever taken since the foundation of the Afrika Korps will have such far-reaching consequences as this one. If you proceed and are turned back this time, you will effectively have destroyed our chances of retaining influence in Africa.'

Rommel shook his head again, his eyes alight. 'War isn't about paper-pushing,' he said. 'It's about balls – about boldness, force and speed. I won't *be* turned back. My divisions will move like greased lightning: we'll be in Alexandria and Cairo in ten days at the most, maybe a week. The Eighth Army is finished, and nothing can stand in our way. I don't need your damned supply lines. With what I've collected here in Tobruk, and what I can gather on the way, I'll be self-sufficient in supplies –' He stopped himself, remembering that what he had just said was at least partly a lie. He did not have enough fuel to get to Alexandria: he was simply gambling on getting more en route. He smiled truculently as a thought popped into his head. 'In fact,' he said, 'I think I'll have Berndt reserve a table for all three of us at the famous Shepheard's Hotel. What do you say, General Bastico? A nice candle-lit table, dinner for three at Shepheard's, for the evening of – shall we say, 2 July?'

Bastico's plump cheeks glowed, but before he could speak, Kesselring leaned forward. 'That's quite enough of that, General,' he said, his face now pale with fury. 'You insult our allies and you insult me. All the authorities are behind the Malta operation – the Führer, the Duce, the Comando Supremo, the OKH, German Naval Command, even our Italian liaison officer, General von Rintelin. I'm telling you *now*, that you are to proceed no further than the Egyptian border.'

Rommel laughed again. 'You can't give me orders, Field Marshal. The Panzer Army is under *my* command.'

'Maybe,' Kesselring grunted, 'but the Luftwaffe is under *mine*, and from this moment I am withdrawing all air units to Sicily. By all means, carry out your "lightning thrust", and see how far you get without air support. The RAF are very near to their bases, and believe me, they will *not* be holding back.'

Kesselring stood up, sent his chair scuttering. Bastico followed. Rommel got to his feet more slowly, still shaking his head. Mellenthin, who had been standing quietly in the background, suddenly stepped forward. 'Gentlemen, gentlemen,' he said soothingly. 'Please don't leave. There seems to be a misunderstanding here, but I'm sure we can sort it out.'

'Oh?' Kesselring said. 'How?'

'Please, Field Marshal, sit down.'

Kesselring considered him for a moment. He knew Mellenthin came from a good Prussian family, and was aware of his reputation. He shrugged and let himself be cajoled. He sat down again, and the others followed suit.

'Well?' he said.

Mellenthin had remained standing. 'It seems to me gentlemen that the problem all hinges on one thing – that is, the state of the Eighth Army. While General Rommel says that Allied forces are on the run, you claim that they may still outgun us. What we need, I suggest, is sound intelligence – proof, as General Bastico said. If General Rommel can come up with proof that the situation is as he says it is, then surely you wouldn't prevent an advance that would bring almost certain victory in only ten days? It would be far more cost-effective than a full-scale offensive against Malta.'

Kesselring shrugged. 'Does such proof exist?'

'It may do.'

'May isn't good enough.'

'This morning our troops picked up a British courier sent by Auchinleck to report directly to Churchill on the state of the Eighth Army. We don't know the content of that report yet, but we hope to in a couple of hours. Could I suggest, sir, that you make no decision until then?'

There was a pause as Kesselring took a deep breath. 'Very well, Major. I will give you twelve hours. If you produce no convincing proof that your position is correct in that time, then by God, my air squadrons are out of here.'

They stood in silence until the two officers had left the building, then Rommel rounded on his IO. 'You go too far, Major,' he exploded. 'How do you know the girl – what's she called . . . *Runefish* . . . will talk? Even if she does, how can you be certain that what she says will be of use to us?'

'I can't, sir. It was all I could think of on the spur of the moment to stop them walking out. Call it a delaying action.'

Rommel thought it over for a moment. 'I'd prefer it if you would consult me next time you have any such brilliant ideas,' he said. 'As it stands, though, I don't see that we have much to lose. The OKH may be against me, but I'm certain that the Führer's heart is not in the Malta offensive – he lost too many men on Crete. I intend to send Berndt to talk to him in person. That may take time, though. For now, just make sure I have that *Runefish* report the moment it's available. Who's doing the interrogation?'

'Rohde, sir. He's the top Abwehr man in North Africa.'

Rommel stared at him. '*Rohde* – wasn't he one of those scum they deployed to torture women and butcher children illegally behind Russian lines? One of Heydrich's *Einsatzgruppen*?'

Mellenthin nodded wryly. 'He's not exactly the kind of

man you'd want to invite to dinner, sir. He's the sort that enjoys hurting people who can't fight back – especially women and children. I remember seeing him once at the Führer's HQ – the Wehrmacht officers refused to shake hands with him.'

Rommel made a clucking sound. 'Yet here he is working for the Abwehr. I'm astonished that Canaris would give him the time of day, but perhaps I shouldn't be. Like attracts like, after all.'

'Either that,' Mellenthin nodded, 'or Heydrich knows something nasty about Canaris and is blackmailing him to employ his Einsatzkommandos. Heydrich's lot are the dregs – a disgrace to the uniform – but, I'm sorry to say, if anyone's likely to make *Runefish* talk, it's him.'

Rommel nodded sympathetically, torn between his revulsion against filth like Rohde, and his desperate need for the information. 'Poor *Runefish*,' he said at last. 'She won't be fit for much by the time that animal's finished with her.'

28

Concealed high on the rocky hillside, Caine watched Sheikh Adud plodding up the wadi, leading a donkey on whose bony back his daughter, Layla, was mounted. It was a curiously biblical scene, and he was reminded of Christmas in the village where he'd grown up – carols at the village school, nativity plays at the church hall, parties at the vicarage. He felt a pang of nostalgia, knowing that since his mother had died, and his sister had moved away, he had no real reason ever to go back there. In any case, it had ceased to be home the day he'd left, aged sixteen, to join the Royal Engineers. The only home he'd known since then was the army.

He wondered how the sheikh had managed to acquire a donkey in the ninety minutes he'd been in the town. He hoped to goodness he'd done nothing to attract attention. Allowing Adud and Layla to go into an Axis-held centre by themselves had been a leap of faith, and every moment they were away had been harrowing: he'd felt very relieved when he clocked them emerging from the town twenty minutes earlier. He'd tracked their progress carefully with his binoculars from that point, and was as sure as he could be that they hadn't been followed.

The town was marked on Caine's map as Biska, and he guessed it had been an important Italian outpost before the war – the centre of one of Mussolini's model agricultural projects. Trailing the Brandenburg column from the wadi where they'd glimpsed *Runefish* that morning, they'd passed through valleys where the maquis scrub had been cleared, where white colonial homesteads stood on knolls overlooking acres of cultivated red soil. The agricultural experiment had failed. The fields were full of mouldering crops, punctuated by rusted iron ploughs and the bird-infested hulks of tractors. The white homesteads were derelict and deserted, doors hanging on hinges, roofs fallen in, windows smashed, fences broken. There were a few cows mooning in decaying paddocks, and here and there Caine heard the desperate squeaking of pigs. Once, he even fancied he'd glimpsed the face of a little Italian girl, pale and terrified, in the darkness behind a broken window. He knew he'd probably imagined the little girl – most of the families who'd worked these fields were living among Michele's people at the *Citadello*, and it seemed inconceivable that they'd left a child behind. Caine didn't blame them for dumping their crops and animals, but having grown up in a community like this one, where every day was a war against nature – in the case of his native Fens, against the ever-present threat of the sea breaking its banks – it gave him a feeling of melancholy. The Itics were colonists in a foreign land, maybe, but they'd made an attempt here to tame the wilderness, to spread civilization, to show the natives how it was done. You couldn't help but admire them for that.

It had taken them two hours to shadow the Brandenburger convoy to Biska, sometimes moving along wellmarked roads, sometimes heading cross-country. Sheikh Adud and Layla had acted as trackers, following the Panzer tracks and fresh tyre-marks. They'd travelled slowly and cautiously, always remaining well out of sight, far enough behind the enemy so that their dust cloud wouldn't be noticed or their motors heard. Wallace, acting lead-scout beside the two Senussi on the White, had kept his eyes peeled for possible ambushes, and the other spotters behind had scanned the skies continually for aircraft.

Several large dry-washes converged in the hills behind Biska, and it hadn't been difficult to find a narrow branch-wadi ideal for leaguering the convoy. The town itself stood on the edge of an escarpment that swept down into the coastal plain, a grid of streets carved out of the rolling downs amid dense groves of acacias, stone pines and maquis, where a cantonment of flat-roofed, cream-cake colonial oblongs stood on one side of an impossibly wide main street, and a maze of stone-built Arab huts on the other. Surveying the cantonment earlier through his binos, Caine had identified a hospital, a town hall with a block-shaped tower, satellite administration-buildings, a police barracks with wireless aerials sprouting from the roof, a school, and even a sewage plant. The other white buildings, he presumed, were villas once inhabited by Italian officials. The town wasn't exactly flourishing – apart from military patrols and the occasional Arab and his dog, the streets seemed totally deserted.

As far as he could make out through the dense veil of trees, the Brandenburgers' vehicles were leaguered outside the police barracks, together with some wagons he guessed might belong to the colonial carabinieri – Italian paramilitary police. The Mark III Panzer wasn't amongst them, though. A few minutes earlier Caine had had the satisfaction of seeing her loaded on a transporter and ferried towards the road that corkscrewed down into the valley.

Caine watched the sheikh and his daughter until they disappeared round the bend into the branch-wadi, then occupied his time in looking out for any possible enemy reactions, until ex-Marine George Padstowe scrambled up the scarp to relieve him. He left Padstowe with the binos and slithered down to the leaguer to hear the news. In the shade of camouflaged awnings and scrim nets, the boys were brewing tea, scoffing bully-beef stew or just sleeping off last night's hangover, dreaming of nubile Italian girls and a lost oasis of ease they would never find again.

Maurice Pickney ducked under the White's awning and came over to check Caine's wounds. The graze on his left hand was almost healed, but the wound in his side was still giving him problems. Pickney examined it, declared that it wasn't infected and doled out another batch of sulphenamide pills. While the orderly was adjusting Caine's dressing, Wallace appeared with three pint-sized enamel mugs, handed one each to Caine, Copeland and Pickney. 'Get that down yer,' he rumbled. 'Put hair on yer chest, that will.' They took the mugs and Cope sniffed at the dirty brown liquid with a sour look on his face. 'No point asking is there?' he said. 'Smells like a mixture of benzine and piss.'

'Fresh piss, though,' the big gunner winked. 'I just pissed in it meself.'

Caine and Pickney gagged; Wallace chortled. 'It's the Long Range Desert Group special, *innit*. Two parts whisky, two parts rum, six parts lime juice, dash of curry powder, pepper, and Worcester sauce. It's a desert pick-me-up – gets the old circulation going and stops desert sores.'

Caine took a gulp, and the mixture hit his throat like a whiplash. His eyes bulged. 'This is damn' good,' he gasped hoarsely. 'Hits the spot.'

'Got the recipe when I was with the LRDG,' Wallace said, looking pleased. 'It'll sort out last night's hangover all right.'

Cope drank, his big Adam's apple working, and Wallace watched him expectantly. Copeland's face seemed to seize up in mid-gulp. 'It's . . . it's . . . lukewarm,' he said, trying to restrain a retch, not quite succeeding. 'You could . . . have . . . a bath in that.'

Wallace's pinhole eyes shot skyward, his broad, dark-stubbled face assuming an expression of mock solicitude. 'So sorry, O great and wonderful pasha. Only it's about a thousand flipping degrees centigrade out there, and we just don't *happen* to have the icebox with us today.'

He was interrupted by the arrival of Naiman, Adud and Layla, sweeping in under the scrim nets. Wallace pulled up petrol cases for them. Caine saw that Naiman had removed the dressing from his ear: the upper lobe was mangled and shapeless but was scarring properly. 'I've just debriefed them, skipper,' the interpreter said. 'They've done a superb job of scouting.'

'Did they find *Runefish*?'

'Certainly did. She's in the town-hall building, held in a locked room opening off the reception.'

'What, they actually *saw* her in there?'

'No, not quite, but you know Adud has a bunch of relatives in the town? Well, by good luck it turns out that one of them works as a servant at the town hall, and he saw them bring *Runefish* in this morning. She's being guarded by the carabinieri. There are two in the guardroom outside her room, armed with rifles and pistols.'

'All right,' Caine said, smiling broadly at this key information. 'What about the Jerries?'

'They're on patrol outside. The sheikh doesn't know how many are on stag at once, but probably four divided into pairs, with another four on stand-by in the barracks. The two-man patrols circle the whole admin area in opposite directions, a patrol passing the town hall every five minutes or so. There's a doorman at the town hall – a carabinieri who sits on the porch outside. He's armed with a rifle. The door is unlocked while the sentry's there.'

'How many Jerries and how many carabinieri?'

'The Jerries are just the Brandenburg platoon you clocked at the wadi, but the carabinieri are in company strength – about a hundred maybe – the sheikh isn't good on exact numbers.'

'All right. I know it's a long shot, but did they get any idea about what they intend to do with her? How long she's going to be held, for example. Are they going to shift her to another location?'

Naiman looked smug. 'One thing I asked about is whether she's been interrogated yet,' he said. 'The answer is a definite no. Adud's relative told him that this place is a sort of occasional base for the Brandenburgers, and they often bring people here for interrogation – spies, Senussi trouble-makers, that kind of thing. He said he's seen some horrendous stuff. Apparently they're waiting for an officer to arrive from Benghazi this afternoon to interrogate *Runefish*. The bloke's name is Rohde, Major Heinrich Rohde.'

'How the hell do they know that?'

'He's a sort of regular here, apparently. Not Afrika Korps, they said. Intelligence – probably Abwehr. He is *not* a very nice fellow. Adud's relative said he's seen him cripple people with massive electric shocks, hang them up with meat-hooks through their necks – even pour burning petrol on their genitals . . .'

'*Jesus.*' Caine closed his eyes for a moment, wondering what agony his hesitation at the wadi had cost *Runefish*, hoping desperately they could get her out before it came to that.

'Just so long as he doesn't use Wallace's "LRDG special",' Copeland cut in. 'Imagine having *that* stuff poured on your bollocks.'

Caine tittered, peered at the remaining liquid in his cup, set it on the ground. 'Any description of this Rohde?' he enquired.

'A tall, balding fellow,' Naiman said. 'High forehead, clean shaven, crafty eyes like a fox – shifty. Long, thin fingers. The informant told them he's a real pussy-cat. He's never been known to show mercy or give anyone a break – even the local Jerries and Ities are scared of him. Apparently they call him the 'Black Widow'.

Caine nodded. 'All right, what time is this "Black Widow" expected?'

'They weren't sure – late afternoon, maybe four. He always comes by aircraft – usually a Storch – and lands on the airstrip about five miles outside the town.'

Caine glanced at his watch: it was 1230 hours. 'That means we've got three and a half hours to break her out.' He turned to the Senussi and shook hands with them both gratefully. The gamble he'd taken in sending them in alone had paid off. In fact, he was astonished at the detailed intelligence they'd gathered. It was all he could have asked for and more. 'You've done a wonderful job,' he told them. 'Thank you.'

'Is nothing,' Adud croaked. 'The thanks is to God.'

Caine paused. 'By the way, where *did* you get the donkey?'

Adud eyed him uncomprehendingly. Layla took a breath as if about to say something, but then stopped herself. 'Adud nicked it,' Naiman chuckled.

When the laughter had died down, Caine stood up, suddenly businesslike. 'Moshe, call the boys for an immediate O group. We've got to decide how to go about this.'

He briefed the lads on Adud's information, then threw the field open to 'commando initiative'. Wallace wanted an all-out frontal assault like the one they'd done at Umm 'Aijil, but Caine vetoed it. They were facing larger enemy forces this time, and they were down to only a handful of men. 'They've got wireless contact,' he said. 'They'll call up a flight of Stukas from one of the local bases before you can say Benito Mussolini. No, Fred, it's got to be done by bluff and stealth.'

'Yes, and bluff really worked last time, didn't it?' Todd Sweeney said, snorting. 'Ended in a ding-dong scrap and we didn't even get the right person. I can't understand why you didn't bump *Runefish* off back there in that wadi and be done with it, skipper. Then we wouldn't be here, risking our lives. We'd be on our way back to the Wire by now. Squeamish, was it?'

'Yes it was,' Caine rejoindered sharply, 'as squeamish as you were when you proposed putting Cavazzi out of his misery but didn't have the guts to do it yourself.'

Sweeney's mouth clamped tight, and Caine shot him a hard look. Two could play at that game, all right. Yet, as usual, Sweeney had hit the bulls-eye. Caine could have blamed the arrival of the Storch aircraft for his botching the hit, but the truth was that his hesitation had done it. Although Copeland would never come out openly in support of Sweeney, Caine could tell from his dour face that he hadn't forgiven him. 'We muffed our orders, skipper,' Cope had told him earlier. 'One shot and we'd be on our way back now, mission accomplished. Why did you bottle out?'

'It wasn't right, somehow,' Caine had struggled to explain. 'There's something fishy about this whole story. Why did *Runefish* start transmitting so suddenly, and keep it up for more than three hours? She must have known that the enemy would triangulate her position.'

Caine himself wasn't sure whether he was sincere, or just trying to cover up what Sweeney was now rightly calling his

squeamishness over taking out the girl. After all, his questions were easily explained: *Runefish* probably hadn't had
any idea that the commandos were in the vicinity when
she'd started transmitting: she'd just panicked. People didn't
always behave rationally under pressure, and women weren't
the most rational of creatures at the best of times. 'There's
so much that's iffy about this jaunt, skipper,' Copeland had
commented. 'I mean, I never liked the odds of us finding
her, anyway. It wasn't even an outside favourite. It's as if
they just sent us out as a kind of decoy . . . as if our presence
here was enough.'

'I don't follow you, Harry. A decoy for what?'

'I dunno – to take the heat off someone else maybe. It's just
a thought. Anyway, we may as well accept that we missed the
boat. The Jerries are going to get whatever it is she knows out
of her, so why don't we saddle up and head homewards?'

Caine shook his head. 'I'm going after her, Harry, even if
I have to do it alone.'

'I hope you're not expecting gratitude,' Cope said. 'I know
those officer-class bints – they wouldn't spit on you if you
were on fire.'

Now, Copeland sat among the lads, brooding over the
problem of snatching *Runefish* from under Axis noses. 'You
got any ideas?' Caine asked him.

'All right,' Cope said at last. 'If we're doing this by
stealth, in daylight, skipper, we're going to need disguise.
Last time, I assumed we could get away with being taken
for Jerries or Ities in khaki rig, but it didn't work. The only
other alternative is to go in dressed as Arabs – two men
togged up in Adud's Sunday best, carrying spare clothes for
Runefish. We could even take the donkey Adud nicked for
extra authenticity, and hope you don't run into the real
owner.

'We approach the town hall, wait till the patrol's gone by, then gain entry either by bluster or taking out the doorman. Once we're inside, it's a piece of cake. We knock out the guards, dress *Runefish* up in Arab gear, wait till the next patrol's passed, and bunk it. The only real problem is that we're going to need some way of knocking off those guards silently. If any shooting starts, we've had it.'

'Now you're talking,' Wallace boomed, rubbing his hands. 'It's a good job for my dear old fanny.'

'No way,' Swan said. 'Cutting the throats of two or three Itie policemen at the same time, without one of them letting out so much as a screech, is too dicey. We need something that's going to shut them up instantly.'

'Anyway,' Cope chortled, 'no one's going to take *you* for an Arab, you great turnip. Have you ever seen a six-foot-seven Senussi?'

'What about drugs?' suggested Wingnut Turner. 'If we could get Adud's relative to slip something in the guards' food . . . ?'

'Nah, too unpredictable,' Maurice Pickney said. 'One might go down before the others, for instance, and give them time to sound the alarm. We wouldn't be able to time the effect exactly enough to make sure we were there at the right moment.' He thought for a second, then his wrinkled, nanny-like face lit up. 'What about chloroform? I've got some bottles of it in my kit. If we could smash them under the guards' noses it would put them out like a light.'

Caine looked interested. 'Good one, Maurice,' he said thoughtfully, 'but I'm wondering how we can stop our own boys from being knocked out too. We don't have respirators.'

'A wet towel round the mouth and nose might do it,' Pickney said. 'But then there's *Runefish* – you're right, the stuff would probably put her to sleep before she knew what was happening.'

'Wish we had a couple of Welrods,' Wallace grunted.

'A couple of what?' said Caine.

'Welrods. It's a weapon developed by the Special Ops boys – only fires one round but it's completely silent. You just hear a click.'

'I'm afraid our armoury doesn't run to that little item.'

'It's the right idea, though,' Turner said, his windsock ears flapping. 'A weapon with predictable results that we could use even if things don't go as expected.'

'*Abu na'is,*' a female voice said suddenly.

The men wheeled round to see that Adud's daughter had spoken for the first time. '*Abu na'is,*' she repeated, 'is a drug we get from leaves. We shoot it from bow and arrow. It make sleep but not kill.'

Caine stared at Layla in astonishment. Not only had she just spoken comprehensible English, she'd evidently followed the gist of the entire conversation. 'You speak *English?*' he asked incredulously. 'You mean after all this time with us, you speak English? Why didn't you say so before?'

The girl blushed deeply, and her eyelids fluttered. Adud was looking at his daughter with an expression half-way between anger and admiration.

'My father . . .' she stammered. 'You are all . . . men . . .'

'Oh I get it,' Wallace said, nodding his thorn-bush head. 'The old boy didn't want us chatting you up, is that it?'

She blushed again and eyed her father beseechingly, said something apologetic in Arabic. After a moment, the sheikh nodded and his face relaxed.

Layla smiled peachily. 'I study English in Italian mission-ary school when I am small. It is many years. I am forget much, but some I am remember. You excuse me for not talking . . . I . . .'

'Of course we excuse you,' Caine said. 'Now, come on, what is this stuff you mentioned?'

'*Abu na'is*. It come from leaf — a leaf you find here, in wadi. We make medicine. We put medicine on arrow, we shoot. It is not kill, but make sleep like *that* . . .' She snapped her small fingers and let out a chuckle so fresh that some of the men melted visibly.

Adud chimed in with a torrent of Arabic, looking at Naiman. 'The sheikh says that poison is women's work,' he translated. 'So he can't help us make it, but he could make bows and arrows for us. He says that this *abu na'is* works a treat — the victim goes out instantly and stays out for hours.'

There was a pause while Caine weighed it up. 'It *is* the kind of thing we're looking for,' he said, 'but if it doesn't work . . .'

'It work,' Layla cried, clapping her hands in excitement. 'Senussi use it for . . . long, long time . . .'

Caine smiled at her enthusiasm. 'Let's do it, then. Moshe, ask Adud to make two bows and a bunch of arrows. Layla, you go with Moshe here and collect as many of the leaves as you need . . .'

'Just one thing, boss,' Copeland said. 'You haven't said anything about roles.'

'You're right, Harry. Listen in, ladies. As Cope said, this is a two-man job. The assault party's going to be me and one other . . .'

There was a chorus of boos from the men, so loud that Caine had to remind them that they were meant to be tactical. 'That's not on, skipper,' Wallace moaned. 'You're wounded. Let someone else do it.'

Caine's expression hardened. 'There's a big risk of capture

on this one, Fred, and we won't be in uniform. That means we'll be regarded as spies, and you all know what the Boche do to spies. This Black Widow bastard will think Christmas has come early. I'm patrol commander and this is my responsibility. I'd rather not let anyone else in for it, but I can't do it entirely alone.'

'I'll do it, skipper,' Naiman said, his voice like a knife. 'You're going to need someone who speaks Arabic and Italian. I'm the only one qualified.'

The proposal was met by a chorus of objections, and Caine realized that every man in the squad wanted to volunteer. 'We ought to draw straws,' he said.

'No,' Naiman cut in. 'Like I said, it's got to be me. No one else is qualified.'

'He's right, skipper,' said Cope, shaking his head. 'I'd give anything to do it myself, but if you don't have a linguist along, you may as well think of another plan, because it's not going to work.'

Caine blinked guiltily at Naiman. 'Are you sure about this, Moshe?' he asked. 'As I said, the chances of being captured are high. You've got more to lose than any other man here.'

'That's not true,' Naiman objected. 'You already said that the Boche don't like spies. Going into action without uniform means you're no longer covered by the Geneva Convention, so I don't have any more to lose than anyone else.'

Copeland nodded. 'He's got you there, skipper.'

'All right, then,' Caine said slowly. 'I wish I could say you won't regret this.' He looked at Layla. 'Now, madam,' he said. 'It's all down to your hubble-bubble'.

29

Captain Karl Haller, the stringy Brandenburger platoon officer credited with the capture of *Runefish*, drove out to the airstrip personally to meet Major Heinrich Rohde's aircraft. He found the officer waiting for him on the runway, dressed in immaculate bush-jacket, button-down holster, high jack-boots, dress jodhpurs and a service cap bearing the insignia of the Abwehr. Rohde was about the same height as Haller himself, but with a more robust physique. His figure fell short of the ideal only in that his hips were a tad too wide, lending him an oddly incongruous hint of the feminine. He was so cleanshaven that his face seemed as smooth as a baby's, though the hair under his peaked service cap was cornfield-gold and slightly receding. His eyes had something inert about them, Haller thought – if an adding-machine were to sprout eyes, then Rohde's were the kind of eyes it would have had.

Haller was about to jump back behind the staff car's wheel when Rohde said, 'Thank you, Captain, but I make a habit of always being in the driving seat.' It wasn't the sentiment but the voice that surprised Haller – it was curiously high-pitched and nasal – almost a squeak – and the speech was telegraphic, like a series of gasps. Far from being comical, the effect of the squeaky voice and the nervous speech, combined with the quasi-feminine hips and the adding-machine eyes, was sinister. It was Rohde's hands, though, that were his most disquieting feature. The fingers were abnormally long and thin, and made Haller think of a spider's legs. He wondered if this was why he'd heard some of the men refer to Rohde as the 'Black Widow'. Haller had encountered only a few men in his life whom he instinctively feared: Rohde was one of them.

They were driving along the track from the airfield, hugging the edge of the escarpment, and Haller could see the coastal plain spread below him like a hand-woven Persian kilim, stretching as far as the turquoise haze of the sea.

'I understand you had some trouble overpowering the prisoner,' Rohde said, glancing at Haller out of the corner of his eye. The captain couldn't decide whether or not he was being derided.

'She got off a shot at me from a .45 Colt, if that's what you mean, sir,' Haller said. 'Missed though. Slug hit the wall, fragmented, and the bits whizzed round inside: it was amazing no one was hit. Anyway, I soon took the weapon off her.'

'Curious that she should miss a shot at almost point-blank range,' Rohde said.

'She didn't seem to know what she was doing. I felt she was just carrying the weapon as a decoration, never expecting to use it.'

'Really?' Rohde's tone was definitely sarcastic now. 'You think they'd issue a .45-calibre weapon to an untrained woman?' He chuckled. 'It would have been embarrassing for a Brandenburger captain to have been shot by a dame, eh? Funny, though: she'd evidently been trained well enough to operate a wireless – not an accomplishment every staff courier is capable of. You also reported that she made an attempt to escape?'

'That was a farce – only a fool would have tried it with a whacking great tank standing there. She was lucky she didn't get snuffed.'

'Ah yes – the Special Duties troops who needed a Mark III Panzer to arrest a slip of a girl.'

Haller looked daggers at him. If it had been anyone else, he'd have challenged him there and then, and to hell with his superior rank. He could sense, though, that Rohde wasn't a gentleman. This was the type of fellow who'd shoot a comrade in the back without a qualm, then swear it was an accident.

'The tank was there because of the threat of attack,' Haller said, keeping his voice even. 'I don't know if they told you, sir, but two of our platoons have been wiped out by enemy raiding groups in the past two days. One of our units was carrying out reprisals in a Senussi village. The other had left the same village earlier, taking with them a girl whose description was similar to that of *Runefish*, but who obviously wasn't her. It might be coincidence, but it sounds as if this raiding party *could* have been looking for *Runefish*. That's why I requested the Panzer – to cover us when we went in.'

'Why haven't these raiders been located?'

'The Green Mountain is a big place, sir. There's plenty of cover. Anyway, everyone's so taken up with the victory at Tobruk.'

Rohde let out a sceptical grunt. 'Since when did the Allies send a search-and-rescue mission to snatch a downed officer? If they *were* sent after her, it suggests that *Runefish* knows something special. If so, I intend to find out what it is.' He swerved suddenly to avoid an Arab family with a donkey-cart, and the car lurched to within a foot of the edge. He let out a string of curses. '*Filth*,' he spat. 'Subhuman trash.' Haller gripped the seat tightly and gritted his teeth as the car skidded and veered back on to the track. 'I should have just pulped the rats under my wheels,' Rohde squawked. 'It's human manure like those wogs that we're fighting this war to eliminate, Haller. Make no mistake about it, history is shaped by racial struggle – it is the purity of race that decides the fate of nations. We Germans are the pure-blooded descendants of the Aryans, and it is our destiny to dominate and rule the others, as lords of the earth. The sub-humans will be eliminated – the Führer is very clear about this. The dirty Jew traitors first, of course, then the Poles, the Russians, the Slavs. Between you and me, I don't rate the Italians as a master-race. They're useful to us now, maybe, but afterwards . . . You can't understand the British, can you? They could have been almost our equals, but they've thrown their lot in with the Jews and sub-humans. Tainted blood, I suppose.'

'What about the Americans?'

'*Huh*,' Rohde scoffed. 'A bunch of dirty mongrels.'

Haller would have laughed, but Rohde spoke with such hushed conviction that it sounded as if he were reciting a religious text. The captain sensed that to have made fun of it would be tantamount to blasphemy in Rohde's eyes.

'Wouldn't that be rather a big programme, sir?' he enquired, trying to keep his face straight. 'I mean, eliminating all those millions.'

'Nonsense. It's only a matter of ruthless efficiency – of designing the perfect killing machine. When I was with Heydrich on the Polish cleansing operation, we managed to rub out no less than 97 per cent of the Polish ruling class.'

'Really?'

'Yes.' The high-pitched voice sounded excited. 'In Russia with the Einsatzgruppen, we eliminated virtually every single Jew in the operational area: men, women and children – the lot . . .' He stopped abruptly, as if he sensed he'd gone too far. 'Of course, it was entirely necessary. The Russian Jew is the root source of Bolshevism. They had to be utterly degraded and liquidated, you understand.'

'Of course, sir,' Haller nodded. He was relieved to see that they were now entering the town. Rohde was obliged to slow down as the track threaded through the wood-and-stone huts of the Arab quarter. He drove in silence for a moment, then said, 'Can you describe the scene in the cave when you entered?'

Haller tried to recall the details. It had happened only that morning, but it already seemed an age ago. 'Yes . . . let's see . . . there was a wood fire with the remains of some papers and an attaché case on it. The papers had been more or less destroyed, but I did notice something odd. She needn't have lit the fire at all, because the briefcase had its own ingenious little self-destruct mechanism.'

Rohde looked intrigued. 'Maybe it failed,' he suggested.

'Maybe, but my impression was that she didn't really know how it worked. Anyway, one of my boys pulled the docs out of the fire, but there was hardly anything left except a title page with a single line in code. I sent that with my report.'

'Yes, it has been decrypted. Continue.'

'There was a sack spread on the floor with a wireless set on it – what the Tommies call a 'biscuit-tin' transmitter. The whole thing, with the power pack, weighed only about six kilos. We found a wire antenna camouflaged outside the cave. I assumed this was the set she'd been transmitting from, sending out her SOS signal.'

'Ah, the transmission. I spoke with Captain Seeholm, whose 621st Wireless Intercept Company triangulated the signal. It seems that the girl was transmitting non-stop for more than three hours. It takes a good direction-finding unit twenty minutes to dee-eff a signal. Surely she must have known that? You don't find it odd that she should expose herself in that way?'

Haller shrugged. '*Runefish* doesn't strike me as being very bright, sir,' he said. 'One of those upper-class English types who look on everyone else as servants and who muddle through life by having the right connections. I got the impression she's out of her depth.'

Rohde considered this in silence, and Haller saw the town hall looming up in front of them. 'Will you see the prisoner now, sir,' he asked.

'Give me a few moments to organize myself.'

'Then we'd better head for the police barracks.'

Rohde nodded and turned the wheel sharply. Two Arabs who'd been leading a donkey across the street leapt out of the way, shouting in terror. The staff car clipped the donkey's back leg, shattering it instantly. The animal pitched over in the dust and lay there quivering. 'Watch where you're going, *morons*,' Rohde yelled as the car completed her turn and shot towards the police barracks. As she sped away, Haller looked back at the two Senussi, who were now crouching over the injured animal. He noticed with interest that both men were carrying homemade bows and sheaves of arrows. Interesting: you didn't see those old traditional weapons around much any more, he thought.

'Was that him?' Naiman whispered to Caine, as the car swept away.

Caine nodded. 'Major's rank, Abwehr insignia, nasty-looking customer with blank eyes. Who else could it be?'

'We haven't got much time then.'

Caine was wondering what to do about the donkey, and a thought struck him. The town hall was only about a hundred yards distant – a white building of intersecting angles, looking as if it had been made from a giant's set of toy building blocks. Dominated by a flat-roofed tower with tiny windows, it nestled in the shade of some huge, umbrella-like Aleppo-pine trees, its main door opening off the street through a porch under mock pillars. Caine could see a guard seated behind one of them and got a glimpse of a red bandanna. 'We'll drag the donkey over by the door, under the shade of a tree,' he whispered. 'We'll make out we're going to cut its throat, to put it out of its misery. The guard will almost certainly come over to see what we're doing, or to move us along. Then we'll give it to him.'

'Right, but we'd better make sure the current patrol's gone by first.'

They began to drag the mewling donkey towards the town hall. Caine felt sorry for the animal, but consoled himself with the thought that its life was being given in a good cause. They were within thirty yards of the shade when the Brandenburger patrol passed between them and the buildings – two men in khaki shirts, shorts and peaked Afrika Korps caps wearing battle order and carrying Gewehr 41s at the ready. They looked alert, their eyes resting for a moment on the two Arabs. They halted, and to Caine's horror, turned and walked over to them. Caine pulled his hood more firmly over his face, keeping his eyes downcast. With his rosy, freckled, English face he'd be lucky to survive a close scrutiny. Naiman stood up to meet the soldiers – he may not have looked much like a German soldier on the road yesterday, Caine thought, but with his tanned face and hooked nose, he certainly passed muster as a Senussi.

The soldiers halted in front of them, and one – a rangy corporal with a complexion like raw beef – started to speak to Caine in Arabic. His heart thumped – of all the luck, they'd copped for an Arabic-speaking Jerry. He leered stupidly at the soldier, and at that moment Naiman weighed in, gabbling, making gestures towards his mouth and ears. Caine guessed he was explaining to them that his companion was a deaf-mute. Whatever he'd said, it dislodged the soldiers' attention. The German pointed to the donkey, and they exchanged a few words, evidently about the beast's condition. Then the soldier touched the bow slung from Naiman's shoulder, and an intense conversation followed, in which Naiman made emphatic gestures with his hands. Finally, the soldiers turned away and resumed their patrol.

'What was all that about?' Caine enquired in a whisper when they were out of earshot.

'The sod wanted to buy the bow and arrows as souvenirs,' Naiman said.

'Come on then, we've only got five minutes till the next lot appears.'

Seconds later they had dragged the animal into the shade of one of the big trees, only yards from the door. As Naiman drew a knife from under his robes, Caine crouched down, using his body as a screen, and knocked one of Adud's homemade arrows. The arrow had no proper flight or head – its short shaft ended in sharpened wood, hardened in the fire, which had been dipped in Layla's *abu na'is* concoction: she'd been very specific about not touching the arrowhead as they knocked the shafts. Caine had been a dab hand at archery in his youth and they'd had a few practice shots back at the leaguer, but now, faced with the real thing, the whole idea seemed ludicrous, like facing a charging rhino armed with a fountain pen. He felt encumbered in these Arab robes, with his khaki drills underneath, and he felt naked without his custom-built Tommy-gun. He was so used to carrying it that it seemed a third arm was missing.

There was a yell from the doorway, and the guard sprang out into the open – a long-legged Arab in carabinieri uniform, complete with scarlet head-cloth, carrying a bolt-action rifle. He advanced towards them, holding his weapon in one hand, gesturing threateningly with the other, shouting in Arabic. Naiman remained poised with his back to the policeman, shielding Caine from view. Caine waited until the guard was no more than six feet away, gradually pulling back the hide bowstring until it was fully extended. He nodded at Naiman, who leapt out of the way just as he released the bowstring, aiming at the enemy's chest. The string twanged, the arrow whooshed, slapped into the policeman's pectoral just above his heart. It fell out almost at once, and for a moment Caine was certain it hadn't even penetrated the clothing. Then the policeman's eyes went out of focus and he dropped like a stone.

Almost before he'd hit the ground, Caine and Naiman were on him, dragging his body towards the entrance at a run. They were inside the porch, the heavy wooden door arching over them. Caine tried the handle. It was unlocked. He opened the door and they yanked the body inside, closing the door after them.

They were in a small atrium with a short passage leading off to the right, ending in the open doorway to a room from which came the sound of a voice shouting a name in Arabic. 'He's calling for the guard,' Naiman whispered. 'He heard the door open.'

'Let's do it.'

They both strung arrows and rushed down the passage, through the open door, coming on two carabinieri in the act of getting up from their chairs – both had rifles in their hands and pistols at their waists, but neither had a chance to use them. Before they had even registered what was happening, two bowstrings sang, two arrows thwacked. Naiman's shot hit his guard in the neck, Caine's took his in the arm. Both policemen slumped instantly, expressions of utter astonishment dying on their faces. Naiman closed and locked the guardroom door, then began to collect the guards' weapons in case they came round unexpectedly. Caine pulled out the spare Arab clothing he was carrying under his robe. He looked around for the ante-room door Adud's friend had described, and located it immediately: it was locked, but the key was still there. He unlocked the door, stepped into the room beyond.

First Officer Maddaleine Rose was sitting hunched up in a corner, her hands tied behind her back and a gag on her mouth, still dressed in the khaki drills she'd been wearing that morning. She looked filthy, bedraggled and worn out. As Caine stepped into the room her eyes opened wide, and she pushed herself back against the wall, trying to get to her feet, panting with fear. Caine held up a hand. 'It's all right, ma'am,' he said in his most soothing voice. 'You're all right, don't worry. I'm Sergeant Thomas Caine, Middle East Commando, I'm here with a search-and-rescue mission with orders to bring you back safely.' He was over to her in a bound, his knife in his hand. 'Please stay quiet, ma'am,' he said. 'I'm going to cut your bindings.' As he cut through the rope, he felt a rush of euphoric satisfaction. He had dreamed of this moment, and after all the doubts, all the tribulations, he'd made it. He'd liberated *Runefish*.

He ushered her quickly into the room where he'd left Naiman, hardly noticing that she was struggling against him, choking and spluttering as she wrestled with her gag. She staggered against a desk, finally pulled the gag out of her mouth, let out a hacking, stifled cough. 'What in the name of hell do you think you're doing, Sergeant?' she screeched, making no attempt to keep her voice down. Her tone was commanding, stentorian, and it hit Caine like an electric

316

shock. It was the haughty upper-class voice he'd heard so often in the officer's mess but never really grown accustomed to – a voice devoid of human warmth, an artificial voice that seemed unable to address anyone other than in terms of authority. For a split second Cope's words popped in to his head: *I hope you're not expecting gratitude . . . those officer-class bints . . . wouldn't spit on you if you were on fire.*

Rose surveyed the two of them with contempt in her almost supernaturally green eyes. The eyes were poison, Caine thought: her whole face was a deathmask: haughty, merciless, arrogant. 'You pair of cretins,' she snarled. 'You ignorant half-wits. Leave – *now.*'

'Shut up, ma'am, for God's sake,' Naiman whispered. 'The guards will hear. We'll never get you out.'

'*Out*? I'm not going anywhere with you, you bloody fools.'

Naiman shot a terrified glance at Caine: they had considered every possibility but this – that Rose wouldn't want to be liberated. 'She's delirious,' he whispered.

'I am not delirious,' Rose yelled. 'I am in perfect control of all my faculties. You, on the contrary, are a pair of blundering plebs, who have just about messed up everything. For Christ's sake, get out of here now.'

'Grab her,' Caine snapped.

They seized one arm each and began to frog-march her towards the door. Rose shrieked at them, kicking, punching, scratching viciously at their faces. 'For the last time, ma'am,' Caine growled, 'pack it in, and shut up, or so help me, I'll lay you out.'

She spat in his face.

Incensed, Caine drew back his fist and was willing himself to hit her with all the force he could muster when there was a thump on the office door, and excited voices in German.

'They're here,' Naiman said. 'We've shot it, skipper.'

Caine let go of Rose and picked up one of the guards' pistols from the desk where Naiman had laid it – a .38-calibre Beretta. He cocked the mechanism and pointed it at her. 'You're right, we are bloody fools,' he croaked bitterly. 'We risked our lives for this. I wanted to give you a chance, but it seems I made the wrong choice. I have a habit of doing that.'

Rose looked like a cornered beast, her barbed-wire body under the ragged khakis poised for a fight, her sneering full lips curling back from uneven teeth, her eyes burning gashes. He lifted the weapon, and as she turned to face him, he saw a drop of sweat run down the side of her face, scouring a track through dust and grime.

'Eight of my men are already dead because of you, First Officer Rose,' Caine said, his voice breaking slightly, 'and a lot more of them will probably die before we get home. My orders are to bring you back or execute you. Now you've left me no choice.'

Her expression remained as hard as granite, but twin pearls of tears glistened suddenly and almost imperceptibly in the corners of her eyes. It was the first time she'd shown any real emotion. 'I don't care what you *think* you've been ordered to do,' she hissed, her voice lower but no less harsh, 'but it's a mistake. If you pull that trigger, I promise you, Sergeant Caine, you will regret it for the rest of your life.'

'Which, thanks to you, may not be very long.'

He snapped off the safety catch, took the first pressure. Afterwards, he was never quite sure whether he would have squeezed the trigger or not. As it happened he never had the choice, because at that moment the door exploded inwards off its hinges, smashing into him and sending him flying, knocking the weapon out of his hand. He hit the floor winded, and before he could get to his feet German soldiers were swarming around him. A Jerry rabbit-punched his neck, another whacked him in the guts with a rifle butt, a third kicked him in the head as he went down again. Rough hands jerked him up, and he saw that two Brandenburgers had pinioned Rose's arms while another was crushing her breasts in a vice-like grip, making her yelp in pain. Naiman was belly-down on the floor, trying to protect his head, gasping as half a dozen men kicked seven bales out of him, ripping off his Arab robes to reveal the khaki drills underneath. One of the Jerries cut away Caine's own robes with a bayonet, tore them off. The beef-faced corporal who'd spoken to him in the street earlier put a size-twelve boot into his balls: the kick doubled him over, his head reeling, gasping in pain. Another Jerry whacked him in the side with a rifle stock, slamming his bayonet wound. Acid fire erupted, gripping his whole body in a shocking clinch, bringing darkness cascading in scarlet and black.

He was on his knees now, sucking air desperately, fighting to stay conscious. The big corporal snatched his hair and yanked his head up high enough to see a pair of legs in jodhpurs and jack-boots striding through the doorway. 'Now, this is a very interesting situation, isn't it?' a voice said in English – a falsetto voice that seemed to scrape the air like a cannon-shell. The hand on his hair wrenched his head up higher, and Caine found himself looking straight into the arid, adding-machine eyes of Major Heinrich Rohde.

30

There was a near-naked body boneless as a rag doll writhing in a chair in a far-away place, and there was a fool who wouldn't stop screeching and bellowing like a bull in his ear. Caine's eyelids flickered: there was the stench of charred meat in his nostrils, fresh vomit on his chin, and it hit him suddenly that the shrieking fool was himself.

Heinrich Rohde, stripped to shirtsleeves, moved with the ponderous actions of a deep-sea diver. He wasn't exactly smiling: his face was sleek with attention as he applied the red-hot iron once again to Caine's open wound. Pain shot off like a rocket: Caine was rushing down a stream of fire like the clappers of hell, head churning in a carousel that spun off its axis, slingshotting him into wild terra incognita, flipping his mind over in a somersault that made him crash and burn. It was pain as he'd never known it, worse than a bullet, worse than ripping shrapnel, worse than a razor-edge knife. The fool down there whimpered, begging for the pain to stop, spitting, wheezing, drooling vomit. Rohde's scraping voice was in his ear. 'Why were you ordered to execute *Runefish*, Sergeant Caine? What does she know that is so important that you would kill one of your own officers? Tell me now and the pain will stop.'

Rohde lifted the hot iron up to Caine's eyes, flexing his long, spider-like fingers. Caine saw the fingers moving on the rubber handle, caressing it, and the sight nauseated him. He could feel the rod's heat, smell the scorched steel. It was the smell of the forge, he remembered suddenly – burning carbon and burned iron – his father whacking in those impossibly accurate sledgehammer blows, the twelve-year-old Caine playing duet with the smaller hammer, the perfect cadence of the two hammers, like music, the perfect knowledge that not a blow would miss its mark. 'It's hard, Dad,' Caine whispered.

'Of course it's hard, son. It's trust. Perfect trust.'

'What?' Rohde snapped.

'I'll tell you,' Caine wheezed.

'Don't,' another voice whined. 'Don't tell the bastard anything.'

Caine forced his iced-over eyes wide, to see Naiman, trussed up naked but for his shorts, in a chair not five yards away. He felt a surge of fury seeing his mate helpless like this – anger, not against Rohde or the Germans, but against Maddaleine Rose. She had betrayed them, ratted them to the Nazis. If he ever got out of here he'd teach that bitch, with her snooty ten-pound-note voice. *You are a pair of blundering plebs, who have just about messed up everything.'*

'It's all right,' Caine stammered, his voice hollow.

'Don't tell him,' Naiman whispered again.

'What is it?' Rohde squeaked. 'Tell me now.'

'All right, I'll tell you.' Caine took a deep breath and shivered: despite the atrocious pain in his side, he felt that he was still articulate, could still string together a sentence. *'Runefish* is carrying a secret,' he panted. 'British Intelligence . . . discovered something of immense propaganda value. If known to the world, it . . . would turn the tide of the war against the Axis . . .'

'What secret?' Rohde whispered eagerly. ''Tell me.'

Caine drew in a deep breath, formed the words in his head so that he wouldn't stumble over them. 'It used to be common knowledge that Hitler had only one ball,' he gasped, 'but we know now that this is utter nonsense. The truth is that Hitler has *no* balls – no balls at all.'

He burst into a paroxysm of crazy laughter that ended abruptly when Rohde, his lips working with wordless rage, jabbed the hot iron again into his wound.

It took a dousing of cold water to bring him round this time. He came to, cursing *Runefish* to hell, thinking of that deathmask face, of the good men he'd lost because of her. He wanted this pain to be hers – not the physical pain of torture, but the longer-lasting grief over fallen comrades, and the knowledge that they had been led to their deaths for a worthless cause. There were two people who'd never be forgiven for that: one was Maddaleine Rose, and the other was himself.

Caine was aware that he'd broken every rule in the commando book about resistance to interrogation. You were supposed to give your name, rank, number and date of birth, and after that nothing, not even a yes or a no. You answered all questions with 'I'm sorry, I can't answer that question,' but one thing you never did was antagonize your interrogator – that only made the situation worse. Caine knew he'd messed up, but he didn't care: if he was going to die anyway – and no one looking at Rohde could doubt that was the way this would end – he wanted these Nazi scum to know what he thought of them and their shit.

The cold water had brought him back to consciousness with a bang, and for the first time he took stock of his surroundings. He couldn't clearly recall what had happened to him after the Brandenburgers had beaten him up. They weren't in the guardroom in the town hall any longer, but in a windowless place – a vault perhaps – and a glance told him that this was Rohde's regular interrogation centre. There was a table on which lay a set of surgical tools, an iron charcoal-brazier, there were hooks hanging from the ceiling, bloodstains on the walls, and a sinister-looking electrical contraption with wires and electrodes. He realized that Rohde was no longer attending to him, though. The major was now standing over Naiman, whose eyes were focused on the sharp little butcher's cleaver Rohde was holding in his right hand. The Abwehr man snapped an order. A pair of raw-boned Brandenburgers brought up a small wooden table, which they set in front of Naiman's chair.

Rohde wheeled round and faced Caine, still nursing the cleaver. Though Caine fought against it, he could not prevent his eyes from being drawn to the savage little tool. 'You are a fool, Sergeant,' Rohde rasped. 'A pawn to Allied propaganda. Adolf Hitler is a great man, a great leader, and it is an honour to be in his service. He saved the German people from the pits of debility and depression into which we were flung by the November Betrayers, by the Bolsheviks, by the filthy Jews, who sold us out in the Great War . . .'

Caine said nothing this time, and Rohde smiled at him – an alligator smile that sent a chill down his spine. 'You think you can hold out until I kill you, and perhaps you are correct. It does happen. In my experience, though, people will often give information more readily to prevent punishment being meted out to their comrades or loved ones. That is what I intend to do now. I intend to cut off Corporal Hussain's fingers one by one until you tell me what I wish to know.'

Caine wondered for a moment who 'Corporal Hussain' was. Then he remembered – they'd agreed that if captured Naiman would give his name as Hussain Musa, an Indian from Calcutta. To reveal a name that was so obviously Jewish would have been fatal.

'Don't,' Caine panted. 'Torture me if you want, but not him. He was only following orders.'

Rohde ignored his plea. 'When your comrade is mutilated and shrieking in agony,' he said, 'you will remember that it was your doing – no one else will be to blame but yourself.'

Caine watched the German's smug expression, the caressing motion of the daddy-long-legs fingers on the cleaver, and knew suddenly that he was in the presence of a man with an extraordinarily acute insight into others' weaknesses. It was almost as if Rohde had read his thoughts. *I'm patrol commander and this is my responsibility. I'd rather not let anyone else in for it . . .*

Rohde wasn't simply doing his job, though: he *believed* in it, believed that his actions were of real benefit to his country. This was a man who identified himself with Hitler but was completely without feeling for others: a man who would excuse any crime, any inhumanity, on the grounds that it was of service to the state. The machine-like eyes, the high-pitched voice that seemed so out of place on a man so big, the disturbing hint of femininity in the posture, the spidery fingers, the perverted intuition, gave Caine the feeling that he was up against one of the most dangerous men he had ever met.

Rohde croaked another order, and one of the soldiers cut Naiman's bonds. The two of them stretched out his right hand until it lay palm-down on the table. Rohde lifted the cleaver. 'The thumb first, I think,' he said.

'Wait,' Caine gasped.

'What information is *Runefish* carrying? I want the truth.'

Caine considered telling Rohde about *Assegai*: he knew that *Runefish* had destroyed the documents, without which, St Aubin had said, it wouldn't matter if he spilled the beans under interrogation. In fact, his CO had virtually given him the green light to mention *Assegai* under duress, yet something inside him, some stubbornness, just wouldn't give way. 'I can't tell you,' he said. 'They sent us with orders to pull her out or kill her. That's all I know.'

Rohde brought the cleaver down on Naiman's hand with a savage motion, shearing the thumb clean off. Blood squidged from the stump, and Naiman vaulted high out of his chair, his body arching rigidly as if he'd been electrocuted, screaming in agony, letting out a stream of curses in a language Caine didn't recognize. Rohde evidently did recognize it, though, because he froze instantly. He stared at Naiman, his normally blank eyes alive with predatory interest.

'Hebrew?' he whispered. 'You speak Hebrew? Now where would an Indian Muslim learn Hebrew? Unless . . . unless you are not a Muslim. Only a Jew or a scholar would know Hebrew, and you don't strike me as a scholar. I think you are a Jew. The Brandenburgers said you spoke to them in fluent Arabic. I put that down to your religion, but now . . . I see it: you are one of those Palestinian Jews, a refugee from Europe – from Germany, even? Well, well, well – now that *is* a surprise.'

Blood was still spurting from the place where Naiman's thumb had been, and one of the soldiers doused it with a rag. Naiman was sobbing with rage and pain, moaning to himself, clutching at the cloth, his bleach-white face contorted. He lifted his head suddenly, and Caine saw that his dark eyes were on fire. 'Yes, I'm a Jew and I'm proud of it,' he spat. 'I am German by birth, and ashamed to admit it, ashamed that I was brought up among uncivilized pigs like you. I know all about your pogroms and your disgusting camps. You can do what you like to me, you filthy stinking butcher. With all your maiming and murdering you are doing us Jews a favour, because the more hate you build up, the greater the force that will one day destroy you.'

Rohde did no more than raise an eyebrow at this diatribe. 'You know, Corporal . . . Corporal Yid,' he said, 'when I was a schoolboy they used to call me "Blond Moses", because it was rumoured that my family had Jewish blood. It was a dirty lie, of course, and I have spent a great deal of my adult life proving that no German could despise the Yids more than I. Yes, I have had some of the most satisfying experiences of my life among your kind. I was with Heydrich during the invasion of Russia. We had orders to degrade and liquidate every Yid in the operational area – men, women and children. We very nearly succeeded, too. Your dirty Yid cunts were gang-raped in front of their children and husbands before being shot. Your Yid brothers and sisters are now buried in massed graves all over the steppe. Millions of them. That was what one calls very satisfying work. Why? Because it was the Jew traitors who handed our German Fatherland to the Allies, who sold us out for money during the Great War. I am not ashamed of my work in Russia, I'm proud of it, because I know that for every Jew-boy and Jew-girl I degraded and executed, I was taking revenge for my people – rendering a sterling service to my nation and my Führer.'

Caine guessed that, while Rohde was badgering Naiman deliberately, just to see what he would do, he was also speaking the truth. He was proud of his part in the wholesale slaughter of helpless men, women and children. Caine realized that the Nazi wouldn't be admitting such crimes unless he intended to kill them.

Naiman's face was burning with rage. 'You'd better make sure you don't leave a single witness, you scum,' he screamed, 'because when this is over, by God you will answer for your crimes.' He suddenly threw himself out of his chair, pounced on Rohde, hissing like a madman, got his one good hand round the German's throat and spat in his eye. Before he could do any more, the Brandenburgers leapt on him, one of them whacking his head with a rifle butt. Naiman fell to the ground, both his hand and his head pulsing blood.

The major stepped back, scrabbling at the saliva in his eye as if it had been poison, and for the first time, Caine saw him looking disconcerted. He cursed in German and kicked Naiman's inert body in the ribs with his jackboot. 'Very well,' he said, his voice sounding even more nasal. 'I have a special . . . treatment . . . I keep in reserve for cases like this. I will have you taken to the minefield.'

Rohde ordered the Brandenburgers to dress Caine and Naiman in their shirts. When they were ready, he had them marched briskly through the streets, dragged along by a dozen troopers under the command of Captain Haller. Naiman had lost so much blood that he could hardly walk, and even Caine, whose hands were still bound behind his back, found himself staggering from the pain of his wound and gagging with thirst under the hot afternoon sun. They passed a few Arabs on the way, but Caine knew they could expect no help from that quarter. At first the Senussi looked at the two prisoners with interest, but on noticing the 'Black Widow' lowered their eyes and scurried away. Their reaction spoke volumes for Rohde's reputation here, Caine thought.

The minefield lay about half a mile from the town hall, under a rock cliff covered in thorny scrub. It was sealed off by a barbed-wire fence hung with skull-and-crossbones signs, intercepted by a narrow path that led up to the stone rim of a well. Caine was just thinking that it seemed an odd place to lay mines, when Rohde said, 'This isn't one of ours. A legacy from you British when they occupied this area. Ironical, isn't it? They must have installed it to stop us using the well. Evidently they didn't want to poison the water, perhaps thinking that it might be useful to them later. We cleared a path to the well, but left the rest of the mines in place. From what I understand, there is a nasty cocktail of anti-personnel, anti-soft-skins, anti-tank mines here – a little of everything.'

He snapped an order at Haller, who had his men throw Caine down. He hit the earth with a thump, and cursed at the fresh spasms of pain in his side. His shirt was already soaked in blood. The Black Widow stood over him in that disturbing feminine posture, pelvis tilted, all the weight on one leg, like a bathing beauty. Behind him two guards held Naiman, his face still pale, panting from the effort of the walk.

'This is your last chance to talk,' Rohde said. 'I want to know where the rest of your men are hiding, the name and rank of the officer in charge, how many of them there are, what weapons they have and what their orders are. If you fail to give me this information, I shall force Corporal Jew-boy here to tramp around the minefield until he hits a mine. The anti-personnel mines are designed to maim rather than kill, on the theory that a wounded man will always be likely to attract rescue attempts – leaving open the probability of more casualties. Interesting how Machiavellian your people are, eh?, but also how much faith they put in honour. As I say, your friend will be maimed, not killed, and if possible we shall continue to force him to tramp until you talk.'

'Don't tell them anything,' Naiman croaked. One of the Brandenburgers cuffed him: Naiman spat in his face. The soldier swore and clutched the corporal's mutilated hand, squeezing it until Naiman cried out.

'That's enough,' Rohde said.

He strode over to show the soldiers where to open up a section of the barbed-wire fence. Caine watched Rohde mincing back towards him, and a sickening, acid sourness churned his stomach. As an ex-Sapper, he knew better than most what anti-personnel mines could do. Naiman had already been maimed once, and the thought of his blundering around in the minefield until his limbs were blown off was horrific. Death was one thing – this was entirely another. He should never have given in to the interpreter's offer to join him on the snatch – he could have muddled through on his own: in any case, the result would have been the same.

He felt a fresh wave of indignation against Maddaleine Rose: he had the Wren to thank for this situation. She had not only alerted the enemy deliberately, she had also treated him and his mate as if they were dumb beasts whose lives were of no consequence. Whatever her motive, it was unforgivable. Weighed against Naiman's torture, though, were the lives of his men – his friends Copeland and Wallace and all the rest. Neither he nor Naiman had a chance now, but the other commandos did, and he couldn't take that away from them just to save pain to themselves. He buoyed himself up with the knowledge that, whatever Rohde knew about his patrol's actions against the Brandenburgers, he could never be certain that the two of them had been part of that group.

Rohde was standing over him. 'Well?' he said to Caine. 'Where are the rest of your unit?'

'There are no others,' Caine answered in a voice that was deliberately dull. 'The corporal and I came in by parachute. There only ever were two of us.'

Rohde's grin was an obscene leer. 'So, the two of you wiped out a whole Brandenburger platoon at Umm 'Aijil, and another on the road to Benghazi, where you destroyed five vehicles, including an armoured car? What about the 3-tonner Bedford that was destroyed there also? Did you parachute in with that in your haversack, perhaps?'

'I don't know anything about that. It must have been another group.'

'I see, and where exactly did you get that wound in your side, Sergeant? Come to that, where did you get the Arab clothes and those interesting bows and arrows, with the sleeping potion? How did you know that *Runefish* was in the town hall, and how did you know its layout? How did you know she was in Biska in the first place? Who were your collaborators among the Senussi?'

'The wound was an accident – my bayonet came loose when I landed on the drop. The Arab gear and the bows – we brought them with us. We got the other information by hearsay from passers-by, chance encounters – I don't know who the Senussi were. I don't speak Arabic.'

'Where did you leave your weapons?'

'I forget.'

Rohde shook his head. 'This is already getting tedious,' he said. 'For the last time, where are the rest of your men?'

'There are no other men.'

Rohde let out a sigh. 'Throw him into the minefield,' he ordered Haller, speaking English for Caine's benefit. The two soldiers holding Naiman pushed him roughly through the gap in the fence. The corporal staggered, clutching his wounded hand, then stood stock still. One of the Jerries poked his backside with a rifle muzzle, but Naiman didn't budge. Rohde shouted something at the other soldiers, two of whom grabbed Caine and hauled him towards the minefield. For a second he thought Rohde had given up on him and intended to hurl him in there too. Then he realized he was being forced to take a ringside view of the show. Rohde was standing outside the fence a few yards behind Naiman. 'Move,' the major yelled at him. Naiman stared straight ahead. 'All right,' Rohde whispered. 'Stubborn, is it?'

He drew his .38-calibre revolver from its button-down holster, aimed and fired. A single shot cracked: Naiman shrieked as a gaping entry wound appeared in his calf, and his lower leg went crooked, as if the bone were smashed. Caine shuddered, knowing how excruciating the pain must be. Incredibly, Naiman didn't fall over. Instead, he hopped forwards into the minefield, hurled curses in Hebrew, squealed in torment, jitterbugged, gavotted, blebbed gore. The Brandenburgers cackled, yelled brutal remarks at the jerking figure. Caine got the impression they were actually laying bets on how long he'd survive. Rohde fired several more rounds in Naiman's direction, but missed.

Caine felt more sickened than he'd ever felt in his life: the gorge rose in his throat. As a spectacle of sheer brutality, this would be hard to cap. He watched with bated breath, feeling hot salt stinging in the corners of his eyes, praying that his mate would be lucky – that a mine would finish him off in one go. He cast around, seeking any means possible of putting an end to this, even if it meant his own death. One of the Jerries near by was holding his Schmeisser loosely, unslung, and the soldier's attention was totally focused on the sport. If Caine's arms were only free, he could have snatched the sub-machine gun, made a last suicidal effort. He had just started working his wrists, trying desperately to get his hands loose, when there was a heart-stopping *kabuuumfff* from the minefield. Brandenburgers ducked. A blast-wave broke, the air folded, the ground staggered: a parasol of dust and smoke ribbed over the minefield, debris pattered around them.

For a second the air was opaque with smoke. When it cleared, Caine saw Naiman lying in a heap in the sand. He was no more than twenty paces from where he had started, and Caine could see that his foot had been blown clean off. It lay in the sand a good two yards from his body. The corporal was slumped face down on a smoking crater, sobbing and wheezing audibly, swearing, ranting to himself in a mixture of Hebrew, German and English. Caine felt tears running down his face. Nudging his guards back with his massive shoulders, he twisted round and puked into the sand. Forcing his mate into that minefield was the most malicious thing he'd ever witnessed, he thought, and if by a miracle he survived this, he'd make sure that these Nazi pigs paid and paid.

Rohde strolled over to him, looking light-hearted, as if he'd just done a good day's work. 'I think we'll just let him lie there,' he said. 'Die slowly. The vultures will be in around sunset. They don't care if an animal's dead, as long as it can't move. They usually begin by pecking out the eyes.' As if on cue, a large brown Nubian vulture glided in on majestic wings and landed on the crest of the cliff, inspecting the scene superciliously. Rohde laughed.

Caine gritted his teeth. 'I'll see you in hell,' he spat.

At a nod from Rohde, two soldiers seized him from behind, yanking him backwards. His lungs sponged up air as a new oscillation of pain hit him from the wound in his side. Rohde lifted his pistol and held it against Caine's temple. Caine felt the muzzle digging into the skin. 'Go on,' he grunted. 'Do it.'

Rohde let the weapon drop. 'I don't think I'm going to get much more out of you, Sergeant,' he said, 'but no matter. I expect *Runefish* will tell me all I really need to know, and my carabinieri trackers will quickly find out where you came from. Since you insulted my Führer, though, I feel that shooting is too quick for you. Instead, I'm going to have you thrown into the well. How do you like the idea of dying alone in a watery dark hole a hundred feet down, listening to your friend's agonized cries as he bleeds to death or the vultures peck his eyes out, knowing that you can't do anything to help him? You'll die very slowly down there, of hunger and hypothermia – oh, and you'll have some charming visitors too – scorpions and snakes are very fond of wells. The last Senussi we dropped in there thought he was a hard man: wouldn't talk, just like you. He kept going for five days, and in the end he was begging and pleading with us to let him rat on his relatives, offering to let us fuck his own daughter if we'd only pull him out. We told him that we'd arrested his entire village, so we didn't need any names, and that we'd already fucked his daughter, his wife *and* his sister. He wasn't too happy about it . . .' Rohde paused and holstered his pistol. 'Anyway,' he said. 'You will excuse me if I don't wait. I am long overdue for a cosy chat with that little girl. Goodbye, now.'

As Rohde stalked off, Haller had six Brandenburgers seize Caine: they were taking no chances, he thought. As they shoved him towards the cleared pathway, he caught the eye of the young captain. 'You're a soldier,' he shouted. 'How can you allow this?'

Haller evidently understood, because he reddened slightly. 'Orders,' he said in English.

The Brandenburgers half dragged, half carried Caine, struggling and fighting, along the narrow path to the lip of the well. As they bent him over the rim while they cut his bonds, he got a momentary impression of a dank, humid, bottomless shaft. A frail voice inside his head snivelled with blind terror: once inside that pit he would never get out. He felt the rope fall from his wrists, but before he could make any last attempt to lash out, the soldiers had jerked his legs from under him and sent him plummeting head-first into the dark abyss.

3 1

Caine remembered falling, turning slowly like Alice in Wonderland, but he didn't recall hitting the water. The next thing he knew was the smell of burning carbon and scorched iron. There was fire in the forge and his father was whacking in sledgehammer blows while he played duet with the smaller hammer. After a while you didn't have to think about it – it seemed to work by itself, as if some great invisible force were working through the two of you, and the perfect cadence of the two hammers came like music, like the throb of two hearts beating. A single smash from the sledgehammer would have crushed his hand, but he knew that not a blow would miss its mark, and it wasn't hard any longer, because he had perfect trust in his father's skill, and he had trust in his own skill too, and the steel formed into shape under their blows as if by magic. He knew that, if he wished, he could stay here for ever in the warmth of the forge, and his father's presence, but there were things he hadn't finished, things he still had to do. The hammering stopped and he was looking at his father's face: a blunt, heat-weathered face, wise only with the simple wisdom of a man who had spent his entire life working with his hands. 'I have to go, Dad,' he said.

His father shook his head. 'You don't have to. You could stay.'

'No, I want to stay, but there are things I haven't finished. People trusted me, and I can't let them down.'

'Ah well, then you're right. You have to go.'

Caine opened his eyes and found himself lying face up, his head resting against a stone shelf, his body immersed in four feet of water. The first thing that hit him was an overpowering stench – the stink of death. The well towered above him, a vast black chimney with a cap of wan starlight at the apex. He could hear, if only faintly, moans of pain from beyond the well, and knew that it was his mate, Moshe Naiman, bleeding to death with his foot blown off. Caine had no idea how long he'd lain there, but guessed from the starlight above that it must have been at least an hour, perhaps two. He hadn't been injured in the fall – he felt nothing but a dull pulse of pain from his side, where Rohde had used the iron.

Caine's first thoughts were about *Runefish*: he'd sworn to bring her back or execute her, and he hadn't completed that mission. It was probably too late now to stop her talking – Rohde would surely have been interrogating her for the past couple of hours. He couldn't be certain, though. People were often tougher than they looked, and his brief encounter with Rose had given him a glimpse of a character of rigid determination. The problem was that she didn't want to be rescued. No matter – he still had his orders, and before he could carry them out he had to extract himself from his current predicament.

Caine stood up in the water, feeling mud squelch under his feet. The stink of rotting meat made him gag, but it was almost pitch dark in the well and he couldn't make out where the smell was coming from. He gazed up at the dark spiral above him. There was only one way out, and that meant scaling the wall. It looked impossible, but Caine had been trained in climbing cliff faces in the commandos and knew that few surfaces, even man-made ones, were without some kind of hand- and foot-holds. He had always excelled in climbing – his massively strong shoulders and chest and relatively light legs were the ideal physique for it. Still, he'd always climbed with ropes and pitons – he'd never encountered anything as difficult as this.

Caine's bush shirt and shorts were heavy with water, but his shirt felt lopsided, as if heavier on one side. He grappled frantically in the inside pocket on a hunch, and incredibly, miraculously, it was there: his Zippo lighter in its waterproof condom. He took a deep breath to control shaking hands: he flicked open the lid, worked the flints. He smelled lighter fuel, caught his breath as a flame licked up on the wick. He cast around in the globe of light, and almost jumped out of his skin.

He was sharing the water with a dead man. It was the bloated corpse of an Arab, still dressed in his robes – the Senussi, Caine thought, whom Rohde had boasted about. The one who'd lasted five days. It was from the cadaver that the dreadful stench emanated.

Caine retched again, but forced himself to turn the corpse over: the Arab's face was ghostly white in the Zippo's light, the milky eyes staring madly. Then Caine noticed something strange: there was a hole in the Arab's robe at the belly, a glimpse of severed, bloodless grey flesh beneath. This was a serious knife wound. Rohde hadn't mentioned anything about stabbing the prisoner, and with a wound this size he'd never have held out for five days. No, this was a self-inflicted wound, Caine was sure. The Arab had done himself in, probably when Rohde had told him about the fate of his village. He had stabbed himself, which meant he'd had a sharp weapon. The Jerries hadn't searched him properly and hadn't found the knife, just as they hadn't found Caine's lighter. That meant that it must still be there.

Calming himself, Caine put the Zippo away and ducked

under the water, groping along the muddy bed. It was difficult work – twice he had to surface for breath – but the area wasn't very large, and if the knife was there he was bound to find it. On the third dive his fingers closed round something cold and hard. He burst out of the water gripping it with triumph: it was a Senussi dagger, ten inches long, curved at the end – rusty and blunt, but still functional. It might just be his ticket out of the place.

He heaved himself out of the water and stood on the stone shelf, feeling for crevices – as he'd suspected, there were plenty. The stone lining of the well was ancient and the stones were both uneven and without mortar. The wall was full of tiny gaps where he could wedge the knife in firmly and use it to pull himself up. He found such a place at full arm's length, stuck the knife into it, finding a hold for one foot. His sandals were sopping wet, and as he tried to lever himself up, his foot slipped. The knife dislodged itself from its cavity under his weight, and he fell back into the dark water with a splash. Cursing, he tried again. This time he'd managed to scale three or four feet up the wall before he missed his footing and fell smack on top of the floating cadaver beneath him. For a second he lay in the water, ignoring the stinking flesh, wondering if it was worth the pain, the effort. He could just lie here and die; his father, the forge would be waiting.

Naiman's sobs and groans came again, bringing him back to the present. Caine heaved himself out of the water and attacked the wall with new determination. He worked the knife with frenzied effort, balancing on inch-wide footholds, thrusting the blade in, securing each step as he'd been trained to do. Slowly, but with increasing confidence, he made progress – ten feet, fifteen feet, twenty feet. At twenty-five feet he paused, panting, flush against the wall, and glanced up. The moon had come out – a three-quarter moon, directly over the well head, casting gilded light straight down the shaft. He was a quarter of the way up the well, and about five feet above him he sensed another rocky shelf. Beyond that, though, he glimpsed something that excited him much more: the moonlight reflected dully off a pattern of steel – a ladder of iron rings climbing from the shelf right up to the well head. He only had another five feet to go, and he'd made it.

Two more panting, agonizing efforts and he had his hand on the shelf. He was dragging himself on to it when something large and scaly uncoiled out of the shadows directly towards him – he felt the movement, saw the moonlight reflected off silver scales, glimpsed a savage, vicious dragon-head, saw a flicking fork-shaped tongue, heard the terrifying hiss. He was so shocked that he let go of the shelf and plummeted thirty feet down the chimney, crashing into the water like a wrecking-ball.

32

Erwin Rommel sat at the table in the roadhouse marking maps with coloured pencils and sifting through sitreps and intelligence reports. He had recovered his normally buoyant spirits. His old wound was no longer giving him problems. Among the int. reports was one suggesting that further east, at Capuzzo, he would find supplies to equip an entire division – more than enough to reach Alexandria and Cairo. He had no doubt that, once the OKH/OKW in Berlin had granted him permission to cross the frontier, he would take Mersa Matruh easily. He had already dispatched his 90th Light Division down the Via Balbia to seek out the new dumps. Victory was within his grasp. All he needed was intelligence that would convince Kesselring and the High Command that the Eighth Army really was about to disintegrate.

He looked up as Mellenthin strutted in, carrying yet another report. 'It's here,' he said, calmly handing him the paper. 'The *Runefish* report, sir. It arrived from Rohde in Biska just a minute ago.'

Rommel laid the single sheet on the table and pored over it, his eyes devouring the words, reading phrases out loud: '*The Eighth Army has been more fragmented . . . than the Axis knows . . . Our armour has been destroyed . . . Our infantry divisions are wheeling aimlessly . . . We have lost more than 80,000 men . . . Our logistical system is in ruins.*' He paused and shot a glance at Mellenthin, who saw the shadow of a smile on the severe features. 'Listen to this,' he said. '*Eighth Army's morale has*

reached rock bottom. The men have lost confidence in their officers . . .
officers are now openly questioning the . . . High Command. More
than 25,000 men have deserted . . . the Army is a hair's breadth from
mutiny . . . Rommel is likely to push into Egypt immediately . . .
Eighth Army will almost certainly be destroyed . . . the Commander-in-
Chief . . . requests permission to evacuate Egypt forthwith. He wishes
to withdraw to Palestine or . . . up the Nile to Port Sudan.'

When the GOC looked up from the paper, Mellenthin
saw that his face was glowing. 'This is it,' he said, and the
IO could hear the exaltation in his voice. 'Twenty-five
thousand men deserted. The army on the brink of mutiny –
exactly what I predicted.'

'Shall I have it sent to Field Marshal Kesselring immediately, sir?'

Rommel hesitated. 'No,' he said. 'No, he gave us twelve
hours. Let's sit on it just a little longer.' He got up abruptly
and started pacing around the room, deep in thought.
'Kesselring was bluffing,' he said at last. 'He was certain
we wouldn't get any proof. No, what we must do now is
get confirmation from our sources in Cairo as a back-up,
so that when Kesselring prevaricates, we'll be ready for
him. What was the code-name of the agent who primed us
on this?'

'*Stürmer*, sir.'

'Yes. Contact *Stürmer* at once and ask for corroboration.'

'We can only contact him via Rohde, sir. Abwehr security
regulations: Rohde is his controller.'

'Tell Rohde to get on to it immediately,' Rommel said.

'Very good,' said Mellenthin, 'and congratulations, sir.'

'Thank you, Major. We shall be eating dinner in
Shepheard's hotel by this time next week. Nothing can stop
us now.'

*

The sun was already melting in gold and blood-orange through the dust haze in the Western Desert when Johann Eisner broke into Betty Nolan's flat in al-Hadiqa Street. He had been apprehensive about the possibilities of risking it in daylight, but speed was of the essence now. It was typical of Rohde that he would sit on Eisner's reports for days without responding, and then suddenly want an answer in five minutes. Eisner was perfectly aware, too, that Shaffer's visit to the place might have set alarm bells ringing at Field Security HQ, but the Black Widow's request was urgent, and there had been no other option.

Eisner's first reaction to Rohde's message had been incredulity. If the major had *Runefish* in custody five hundred miles away, in Cyrenaica, then who was the girl Shaffer had identified as *Runefish* only that morning, at Nolan's flat? Obviously, she couldn't be in both places at once. Rohde had wanted an immediate confirmation of the identity of the girl he had interrogated, whose name he'd given as First Officer Maddaleine Rose. Was Rose the girl Eisner had photographed in the staff car, in Wren uniform? Was she Betty Nolan? Eisner had requested a couple of hours to make absolutely certain.

He hadn't had time for the usual counter-surveillance measures. Luckily, he had discovered a fire escape at the back of Nolan's building with easy access to a bathroom window on the first floor. Almost as soon as he'd jumped down inside, he'd realized that this flat couldn't be permanently occupied, whatever the concierge had told Shaffer. Though there was a towel on the rack, toilet paper by the WC and a bar of soap on the sink, there was no trace of the small personal items one would have found in any woman's bathroom – perfume, lipstick, make-up powder, bath-salts, toothbrush: it had the look of a stage set.

This conclusion was confirmed as Eisner moved cautiously through the rest of the flat — there were made-up beds in the two bedrooms but no clothes in the closets, minimum furniture in the sitting room but no food in the kitchen — nothing but sugar and tea — no books, no magazines, no letters, no ornaments, no photographs. The only outstanding feature was a telephone on a low table next to the front door. The flat had the impersonality of a hostel or a spy's safe-house. If he'd been hoping for any evidence of Nolan's existence, any clue to her current employment, he clearly wouldn't find it here. The place had been swept as clean as a whistle.

He was nosing methodically through cupboards in the kitchen, when he heard the scuffle of footsteps outside the front entrance. A key turned in the lock. He was at the kitchen entrance in a bound, but by that time the front door was already opening, ruling out a frontal attack. Instead, he lurked in the shadows of the kitchen, and peeping out, saw a tall woman closing the door. She had her back to him, but he took in a nest of shortish blond hair cut in fashionable style, a white blouse, a knee-length black skirt and an elegant calfskin hand-bag slung over her shoulder. Eisner felt for the knife in his waistband and drew it out slowly. To his surprise, instead of proceeding into the room, the woman lifted the telephone receiver, and before he could move, had pressed a button and was speaking into the mouthpiece. She just had time to say, 'Captain Avery, I'm in,' when Eisner was on her, one arm crooked round her neck, his knife at her throat. She dropped the receiver, snapped her head towards the crook of his elbow and wrenched the throttling arm downwards with astonishing force, flipping Eisner off balance. In an instant her head was out of his grasp, and she had dodged round and twisted his arm behind his own back in a perfectly executed ju-jitsu move.

Eisner's mouth fell open as he found himself propelled against the wall, hitting it with a crunch, dropping the knife. He had recovered in a second, wheeling round furiously on the girl. She was going for a .38 Webley pistol concealed under her blouse, and had it half-way out when he snatched her arm, yoiked it back with all his strength and clouted her in the jaw with a shattering blow. The woman grunted and pitched over backwards. As she went down, Eisner slipped his Smith & Wesson from its holster and threw himself on her prone body with all his weight. He lay over her full length, his knees digging into her thighs, jamming the pistol under her jaw. 'Try that again, bitch, and I'll blow your chin off,' he spat. Her body relaxed, her eyelids fluttering, her breath coming hard through her nostrils.

It was a good attempt, Eisner thought. She *did* look like Betty Nolan – same height, same lean, lissom figure, same short blond hair. It wasn't her, though. Eisner had a good memory for faces, and he was certain of that. She might have been the girl in his photo if seen from far off, or even for someone like Shaffer, who'd never seen the genuine article, but the features were subtly different. Eisner forced her head back savagely with the muzzle of his weapon, beside himself with rage. He'd been cleverly cheated – it was a set-up, and he'd walked straight into it. 'Who *are* you?' he spluttered.

The girl's seagreen eyes were remarkably steady, and she didn't whimper or cry out. Her lack of panic infuriated Eisner – he felt like pistol-whipping her face to rid it of the calm expression. 'I'm Betty Nolan,' she gasped. 'I'm just a cabaret girl.'

'Lying cunt. I've seen the real Betty Nolan, and you're

not her. I never met a cabaret girl yet trained in unarmed combat, or who carried a pistol under her blouse. You're Field Security, aren't you?'

'Go fuck yourself.'

There was a sudden squawk from the telephone mouthpiece, and Eisner froze. He swore to himself, realizing he'd made a serious tactical mistake. The person she'd been speaking to – Captain Avery – had heard everything. Stupid. Stupid. Wasn't Avery the one Natalie had told him about – the officer from whom she'd stolen the *Runefish* schedule? Taking advantage of his momentary lapse of attention, the girl pivotted her body, smacked the pistol muzzle aside with her arm, tried to jerk Eisner off her. Blind with rage, he knuckle-smacked her twice in the face with his left hand. Her eyes lost focus, and her body went limp. Eisner jumped off her, grabbed the telephone cable and ripped it feverishly out of the wall. He picked up his knife and looked down at the unconscious girl. She wasn't Betty Nolan, but he had to admit that she was lovely – especially the way she was lying, with her skirt up, revealing shapely, cream-white legs and soft thighs. *Legs to drive you wild*, Shaffer had said. Eisner licked his lips, fingering his knife. This was absurd, he thought. He had no need to kill her, and in any case the Field Security boys would be on their way – maybe they were here already. He'd made enough gaffes for one day without doing something even more stupid. He wasn't going to do it, and nothing could make him. What he had to do now was to get out of there *pronto*. He put the knife away and had taken a step towards the tunnel that led to the bathroom when the girl moaned, her eyes flickering open. He stopped and squinted at her over his shoulder. *Get out of here now*, hissed a voice in his head. The room lurched abruptly as if there'd been an earthquake: the floor

345

shuddered, threw him to his knees. The light dimmed, hard surfaces turned nebulous, the solid world liquified. 'No,' he protested. 'I'm not going to do it.' Then the sun switched off.

When it came on again, Eisner was standing over the girl's body, drenched in sweat. His flies were undone, he was clutching his knife, which he saw was smeared with blood. There was blood on his trousers and shirt, and his hands and wrists were thick with it. The girl was still lying on the bare floor, but she was now belly-down and stark naked. There were gore-spatters like blemishes on her perfectly sculpted ivory back, gore-splodges on the soft white skin of her buttocks. Her ripped and torn clothes lay scattered around her, and there was a rapidly spreading pool of dark blood under her head. A gaping wound like a second mouth stretched all the way across her milk-white throat.

'Oh God,' Eisner moaned. 'Oh God.'

There were footsteps outside the door. He closed his flies, drew out his .38 Smith & Wesson, and backed into the kitchen just as the door flew open. From where he stood in the shadows, he could see two British soldiers – a sergeant in khaki drills with a Tommy-gun at the ready, and an officer in full service dress holding a .45 Colt. The officer had a pale moustache and wayward blond hair and wore parachute wings on his sleeve. This must be Avery, Eisner thought.

The two soldiers saw the dead girl at once. 'God Almighty,' the sergeant hissed.

'*Susan*,' Avery said. '*Susan*.'

As he knelt down to feel her pulse, Eisner launched himself into the room with his Smith & Wesson blazing. He shot the sergeant twice in the stomach, sending him tottering back against the wall. As Avery came up Eisner put a slug through his right bicep. The captain gasped and sank back to his knees, panting, his weapon skittering across the room. In a trice, Eisner was looming over him. He brought the handle of his Smith & Wesson down towards Avery's skull with brutal force, but the G(R) man blocked the blow with his left forearm. He clamped Eisner's gun hand with a vice-like grip, prised apart the fingers, yanked the pistol free. The weapon clattered on the floor, but Avery didn't release Eisner's hand: he bent the index finger back in an expert aikido move, until the bone fractured with the dry snap of a pencil. Eisner yodelled in pain, staggered, tried to pull his hand free. Twisting it sideways, Avery heaved himself up and kicked the German hard in the balls. Eisner stopped shrieking: he doubled up in agony, his eyes bulging. Avery swung his good left arm, chinned him with a powerful roundhouse punch that loosened teeth and sent him sprawling against the wall.

Eisner might never have got up again if, at that moment, the door hadn't suddenly been flung open. The Berberine concierge stood there, glowering in astonishment, a tower-like black-faced figure in a pure white turban and gallabiyya. As Avery turned, distracted by his sudden appearance, Eisner grabbed the G(R) man's discarded Colt .45 with his left hand. He squeezed iron. The pistol lumped, speared flame: a round whamped Avery in the shoulder, cartwheeled him down. The concierge's dark face was a mask of horror. He took a step back, gabbling in Arabic, throwing up his hands. Eisner shot him in the face and groin.

He pulled himself to his feet, spitting blood and tooth-fragments, hissing with the pain from his broken finger and the throb in his balls. Out of the corner of his eye, he saw the sergeant's hand creeping towards his fallen Tommy-gun. He shot him twice more, in the head.

Eisner dropped the Colt and put his left hand against the

wall to steady himself. He was chomping down air, his lungs windpumping so rapidly that his senses started to swim. He whiplashed his head to dissipate the faintness, examined his badly swollen finger, swore in Arabic, then in German. He staggered over to Avery's body: the captain's eyelids were quivering. Cursing him, Eisner toecapped him viciously in the ribs. Then, taking a deep breath, tensing his muscles, he bent over, picked up Avery in a fireman's lift, and heaved him over his shoulder. To his relief, the captain was relatively light. Rumbling with pain, Eisner carried him through the open door, stepping over the Berberine's corpse. He lugged the body downstairs into the atrium, paused to get his breath by the main door. His car was parked only a block away. He knew he was taking a big gamble carrying a wounded officer out into the street like this, but it was dark outside now, and in any case, it would be worth the risk and the agony. Despite his foolish mistakes, fate had put the one person he needed to talk to into his hands. Avery was a prime mover in the *Runefish* operation: once he'd been persuaded to talk, Eisner would at long last know it all.

33

Caine stood up in the water feeling furious. He'd almost made it: but for that creature, he'd be on his way up the iron ladder to the surface by now. He let the fury work through him, using its strength. He still had the knife, but he needed a different, blunter weapon, a crushing weapon rather than a stabbing one. On impulse he began to test the firmness of the stones around him. Within a few minutes he'd found one that was loose, and of the right size. He began to work it looser with the knife. Soon he had it in his hand – a stone the size of a large grapefruit. He stuffed it with some difficulty into the patch-pocket of his shorts, and began once more on the hard climb.

Despite the extra weight of the stone, it was easier this time – the knife-holds and footholds were familiar to him now, and some strange strength possessed him – it was like that point during his work with his father, when some divine force seemed to be working through him, directing his movements without any conscious effort on his part. He passed the place where he'd paused, twenty-five feet up, and moments later he had his hand on the ledge. Using that hand to secure his weight, he stuck the knife in his teeth, jerked out the stone. A second later the snake issued out of its lair, hissing ferociously. With a Herculean effort of his enormous arm, chest and shoulder muscles, Caine raised himself half over the ledge and brought the stone down on the snake's head with all the force he could muster. He felt flesh and bone pulp, and in the same instant, lost his hand-hold and felt himself falling yet again.

Crouching in the water with the pain from his wound searing through him, it took all his willpower to brace himself for another climb. He did it though, working with unswerving tenacity and the knowledge that there was nothing to stop him but his own weakness. Time stopped. He was no longer willing or directing his own movements: his body was working to the authority of some all-powerful, primeval force. Suddenly, unexpectedly, he was hauling himself up on to the ledge at the thirty-foot mark, grasping the first of the iron rings. Naiman's groans were louder from here, and at once he began to climb up the iron ladder towards the sound, almost laughing to himself at the ease and speed with which he covered the last sixty feet after the unbearable exertion of the previous stretch. With a last effort of his aching muscles, he burst out into the moonlight and found himself lying on the stone rim from which they'd dropped him, God only knew how long before.

Caine could see Naiman's body not much more than twenty yards away. The sobs had ceased now, but he could hear wheezing, rattling breaths that told him that his comrade was still alive. He knew that there was nothing he could do to save him, but he wasn't willing to let him continue to lie there in agony – it might take him days to die. Caine had put all thoughts of Maddaleine Rose out of his mind during his epic climb, but now, seeing Naiman's state, he was once again filled with utter loathing for her. If she had just kept her mouth shut they would already be back with the rest of the group, roaring off into the safety of the Green Mountains.

Naiman lay only a short distance away, but he lay inside the minefield, and Caine knew there was no way he could approach his mate in safety without clearing the mines. The idea made him shudder – the most horrific experience of his life had been lifting German mines outside the Tobruk perimeter. This would be worse, because these mines were old and could be unstable. Still, there was nothing for it if he wanted to reach his mate.

He scanned the area carefully – there were no enemy in sight. No one would have been expecting him to get out of that well. He made his way unsteadily to the gap in the fence, hesitated there a moment, then backtracked a few paces to a white-thorn acacia tree he'd spotted. The shrub was in full leaf, and Caine spent a few minutes breaking off the stiff two-inch-long thorns until he'd collected about a dozen of them. He put them in a pocket, returned to the gap and threw himself on the dry ground. Caine knew by experience that trained Sappers could clear a minefield by hand at a rate of a hundred yards an hour. If all went well, it would take him between twelve and twenty minutes to reach his mate. He began to probe the earth in front of him with the knife, keeping it at exactly the correct forty-five-degree angle. His first probes revealed nothing, so he inched forward into the area he'd cleared, then started to probe again. This time the knife struck metal. He crept forward, dug the sandy earth away with his fingers, exposing a dish-shaped anti-tank mine – a No. 2 landmine, a type now superceded but still on issue to the Allies. Very cautiously, he felt the mine's submerged skin for booby-traps or 'daisy-chain' wires – used to connect mines in sequence. He found none, and when the No. 2 was completely exposed, he lifted it out of the pit and set it aside. Then he moved into the space he'd cleared and began the process again. Almost at once he located an 'S'-type anti-personnel mine – a slim iron cylinder from whose head protruded a set of small horns.

If trodden on, the horns ignited a charge that shot the cylinder into the air, where it exploded at about waist-height, scattering ball-bearings and shrapnel. It was deadly to infantry advancing on foot, but a man lying flush with the ground had a good chance of escaping its main blast. The 'S'-type mine could be defused by inserting a nail into the hole from which its safety-pin had been removed. Caine didn't have any nails, but this was where the stiff, hard spikes of the white-thorn acacia came in. Inserting a spike into the hole was unnerving work, requiring total focus. 'In this job,' he remembered his Sapper instructor saying, 'you will exercise two things most: your hands and your nerves. Your hands must be steady as rocks; your nerves as cool as ice.' Caine deliberately put every other thought out of his mind – Naiman's wheezing, his fury against Rose, the danger of being spotted by enemy sentries: he gave the operation his full concentration.

Once the spike was in the hole and the mine secure, he resumed his probing. There were whole stretches – two or three yards at a time – that were free of mines, but occasionally he found two mines in close proximity – the No. 2s were relatively easy to locate but the smaller 'S'-types more difficult. Where the two different kinds were close together, he had to be careful not to set one off while dealing with the other. Caine knew that to rush it would be fatal, and kept reminding himself to work slowly. By the time he reached Naiman, he'd cleared half a dozen mines.

Instead of closing in on his mate at once, though, he probed around him vigilantly. As he'd anticipated, there was an 'S'-type mine within a few inches of his friend's body. He started to clear it but realized that he was working too fast now, and without caution. He checked himself consciously, sat back on his haunches, took deep breaths, willed himself to calm down. He held out his hands and examined them – they were scarred, grazed and pitted: the knuckles of his left hand were mutilated from the gunshot wound he'd taken at Umm 'Aijil. Both hands were trembling badly. He kept them spread out. He went on taking deep breaths until the trembling ceased.

He began work again, slowly and methodically as before. In minutes he'd cleared the anti-personnel mine and inserted a thorn into its pin-hole, disarming it. He crawled nearer to Naiman's body and touched him. The young interpreter was lying face down in sand that was completely saturated in his own blood. His left leg had been ripped apart by the same blast that had severed his foot, leaving a ragged stump. With this, the bullet-wound in his calf, and his amputated thumb, Caine was astonished that he hadn't bled to death already. He wondered if the heat of the explosion had somehow sealed and cauterized the wounds.

Naiman's face was grey in the moonlight, so creased with pain lines and concussion cracks that the nineteen-year-old might have been ninety. His dark-shadowed eyes flickered open, and he recognized Caine. 'Do me in, Sergeant,' he croaked. 'I can't stand it . . . Do me like you did Cavazzi.'

Caine choked back his own tears. 'I'm going to get you out, mate.'

'No. Just kill me . . . please . . . stop the pain.'

Caine cast about him desperately, wondering if there were any other possibilities. Sadly, he realized that there weren't. Naiman was going to die: it would happen even if Caine managed to drag him out of the minefield. The only question was how long he was going to suffer this agony.

'All right,' Caine whispered, biting his lip. He recalled shooting Gian-Carlo Cavazzi at Umm 'Aijil. It had seemed hard at the time, but compared with this it had been a piece of cake. He had no firearm now, nothing but a rusty knife. He considered cutting Naiman's throat, but the idea made him shudder. Using the blunt weapon, he would make a pig's ear of it, only adding to his friend's torture. He knew he couldn't do it. He looked at the 'S'-type mine he'd just cleared, and a thought occurred to him. 'Can you move, mate?' he asked.

Naiman spluttered, drooling saliva, and Caine realized he was trying to laugh. The sound was spine-chilling. 'Can you roll over?'

'I . . . can . . . try.'

Caine dug a shallow depression in the sand next to Naiman, then reached out, lifted up the anti-personnel mine and set it in the hole. He took a deep breath and gently removed the white-thorn pin. 'All right,' he said. 'I've laid an 'S'-type anti-personnel mine next to you, and I've armed it. All you have to do is make a last effort, roll over on top of it with all your weight, and it will go off. You must roll on top of it, you hear, Moshe? If you don't, it'll go off in mid-air and the blast won't touch you. Just give me two minutes to get clear. You got that?'

With huge effort, Naiman extended his maimed hand an inch, touching Caine's leg. Caine put his ear to his mouth. 'Caine,' the youth whispered. 'There's something about this mission . . . something wrong. The way that woman . . . acted. Just be . . . bloody . . . careful.'

'I'm sorry I got you into this mess, Moshe.'

He saw that Naiman was trying to smile. 'It has been an honour . . . to serve . . . with you.'

This time, Caine couldn't stop the tears. 'No, brother,' he said, his voice shaking. 'It's been *my* privilege. I don't care what god you pray to, if there's a hall of heroes somewhere, you'll be up there with the bravest of the brave. I'll see to it that you get the highest decoration for this, mate. I'll see that your parents are so proud . . .'

'No,' Naiman hissed, drooling blood and spit. 'Both . . . both dead. The Nazis . . . killed them . . . in 1939.' He gripped Caine's arm with unexpected strength, and when he spoke again, it was with a last-ditch surge of lucidity. 'Caine . . . swear . . . swear the Nazi scum won't win. Swear you'll kill them . . . kill them all. Let me hear you swear.'

'I'll do my best, mate.'

'No . . . *say* it. Swear.'

Caine suckered breath. 'All right, Moshe,' he whispered, trying to keep his voice from breaking. 'I swear by all the gods of war, by the most sacred bond of the commando brotherhood, that these Nazi scumbags won't win. I swear that I won't stop fighting until every last man jack of them gets what's coming to him, or I'll die doing it. I swear . . .'

Naiman's eyes were closed: the faintest glimmer of a smile played round his mouth. 'Goodbye, brother,' Caine said.

He didn't bother crawling back through the minefield, but ran as fast as he could along the path he'd cleared, tears streaming down his face. He had passed through the gap in the fence, and was already racing for the streets of Biska, when he heard the mine go off.

34

Half an hour earlier, Johann Eisner had left his car in the usual place, ditched his facial disguise and made for his houseboat. His broken finger was still cucumber-sized, but at least the morphia he'd shot up had reduced the pain to a dull throb. He was anxious to get to his wireless transmitter, but was too old a dog in the security game to neglect the customary precautions. Somebody would certainly have found the dead girl and the sergeant by now – not to mention the Berberine concierge – and the hunt would be on. Of his associates, only Shaffer knew about the houseboat, and Shaffer was certain he hadn't been followed from the Nolan flat earlier in the day. There was no reason why the boat shouldn't be secure.

Eisner's interrogation of Avery hadn't been as successful as he'd hoped. At his safe-house on Roda Island, the G(R) officer had revealed that Betty Nolan was indeed posing as Maddaleine Rose, but on the content of *Runefish's* message had refused obstinately to say anything at all. Eisner, frustrated, infuriated by the pain of his broken finger, and aware that he'd promised Rohde an answer within two hours, had grown increasingly abusive – and careless. With the two gunshot wounds Avery had received, Eisner hadn't believed him capable of standing up, let alone making a break for it. The man's effrontery was unbelievable. While his back was turned, the G(R) officer had somehow managed to get free of his bonds. He'd almost made it to the villa's gate, when Eisner had shot him five times in the back, like a dog.

It irritated him that he hadn't been able to discover the text of the message, but he consoled himself with the knowledge that he at least had a definitive answer to Rohde's query: First Officer Maddaleine Rose was an impostor.

He slowed down as he reached the end of the street where he'd left his car. He stopped. The houseboat was there, as peaceful as ever in the light of the three-quarter moon. Nothing looked out of place, but Eisner couldn't rid himself of the feeling that something was badly wrong. He smelled the jasmine, heard the familiar honk of the bullfrogs, the lap of the water. What was missing? The crickets. There was no sound of cicadas in the sycamores, which suggested to him that someone – a group of people, in fact – had invaded their territory. He knew suddenly, and with stone-cold certainty, that a whole squad of men was lying there in the darkness among the sycamores, waiting.

A voice yelled. 'Hey. You there. Stop.' Two men in battle-dress uniform were running towards him out of the shadows. Eisner pulled out his Smith & Wesson and fired six times in their direction. He fired left-handed, not expecting to hit anything, but to keep their heads down long enough for him to leg it. He fled back the way he had come, made his car in two minutes flat. His escape route had been planned out long before. Minutes later he crossed Tahrir Bridge into downtown Cairo, heading by a tortuous back-street route to the place where his reserve transmitter was concealed.

Major John Stocker jogged back to his wireless van, parked further down the quay, where a field telephone link had been set up. He opened the back door and found Pieter Shaffer staring at him expectantly, still wearing handcuffs. Next to him was his MP guard, and behind them a wireless operator, hunched over a No. 19 set. A driver lounged in the cab with a cigarette in his mouth. 'He got away,' Stocker announced, his blue eyes flashing furiously behind his thick lenses.

'Well, don't look at me,' Shaffer said. 'There's no way I could have warned him, was there? I mean, I've been in your custody for the past three hours.'

Stocker ignored him and addressed the W/T operator. 'Put out an alert to all MP patrols and civil-police roadblocks,' he said. 'He's driving a white Cadillac.' He turned to Shaffer. 'What's the registration number?'

Shaffer told him, and Stocker repeated it to the operator.

'They won't get him, though,' Shaffer said, shaking his head. 'Eisner knows this city better than my Redcap friend here knows his tart's fanny. He was brought up here – he's got a map of the bloody place in his head.'

Field Security had picked up Shaffer at his Gezira Cotton Exports Company office late that afternoon and transported him straight to the Central Detention & Interrogation Camp. It hadn't required much pressure to make him talk. He'd confessed that his heart had never really been in intelligence work. He was a loyal South African, he'd claimed, but the Nazis had exerted pressure on his family by arresting relatives still in Germany. When Stocker revealed that Eisner was the brutal sex-murderer of at least three young women, he'd been horror-struck and sickened, and only too anxious to give him up. The first gems he'd given up were the location of the houseboat, and the wireless transmitter in a hidden cubicle on board. Stocker had deployed a section to stake out the boat immediately. Though Eisner had already left when the Field Security boys got there, Stocker guessed it would only be a matter of time before he returned.

After finding Sim-Sim's body that morning, Stocker and

Avery had worked frantically to close the net on the man Stocker now knew as Johann Eisner. Avery's first action had been to send G(R) agent Susan Arquette to occupy Betty Nolan's deserted flat, in case their quarry showed his face there. Avery had long ago groomed Susan as a *Runefish* lookalike who might be useful if anyone needed convincing that Betty Nolan was still in Cairo. The flat had been carefully swept clean of any clues before the mission, and the concierge bribed and briefed. They had agreed to stake out the place, but the Field Security surveillance party had arrived too late to observe the first caller that morning. Susan had been able to identify him as a South African, though, and a fast scan of the files had brought up the names of several suspect South African nationals. From their mug-shots, Susan had picked out Pieter Shaffer, director of the Gezira Cotton Exports Company.

As Stocker seated himself in the van beside the operator, the wireless beeped. The signaller listened carefully to his headphones and tapped out a reply. 'That message was relayed from Sergeant Miller's section, sir,' he told Stocker. 'They've found the safe-house – an isolated villa in its own grounds on Roda Island, as we were informed. Captain Avery's body was found in the grounds. I'm sorry, sir – but he's dead. Miller reports that he had multiple bullet wounds in the back, and others in the shoulder and arm. He was probably shot while trying to escape, but his body also showed signs of severe torture.'

Stocker slammed the wireless table with a small, horny fist, let out a string of curses. 'Dammit,' he barked. 'Now we have to assume Eisner knows the lot.'

It was Shaffer who'd given them the address of Eisner's safe-house on Roda. Eisner wasn't even aware that Shaffer knew about it: he'd shadowed Eisner there once, out of pure curiosity. If they'd only managed to get to Shaffer an hour earlier, then Avery's death might have been prevented.

Shaffer had been trained in wireless procedure, but it had always been Eisner who'd sent the messages. All Shaffer knew was that the encrypted texts went to an Abwehr controller whose real name was Heinrich Rohde. Eisner's codename was *Stürmer*.

'I suggest you think again about the location of his reserve transmitter,' Stocker told Shaffer. 'That's where he'll be heading, and if he gets there before we do, the game's up. The more you help us, the better it will be for you.'

Shaffer made a face. 'You're asking too much,' he said.

'Stop bellyaching and *think*,' Stocker urged him. 'Did he make any references to places he visited often – places that might seem an unlikely venue for a man of his sort?'

'Give me a cigarette,' Shaffer said. 'It might help me concentrate.'

Stocker frowned and asked the guard if he smoked. The MP flipped out a Senior Service and stuffed it in the prisoner's mouth with obvious resentment. Stocker lit it for him. Shaffer took a long drag and removed the cigarette with his cuffed hands. Stocker watched him impatiently. 'There is one place he talked about a couple of times,' Shaffer said at last. 'St Joseph's Church in Emad ad-Din Street.'

'A church?'

'Yes, I think it's a Roman Catholic church. It surprised me a bit at the time, because Eisner told me he'd been brought up a Muslim. His family are still in Cairo – he never told me his Islamic name, though.'

Stocker thought it over, then picked up the field telephone. 'This is urgent,' he told the base-operator. 'Please find out ASAP the name of priest or priests incumbent at the St Joseph's Roman Catholic church in Emad ad-Din Street. I'm particularly interested in foreign nationals and, if possible, their known affinities.'

He put the phone down and looked at Shaffer. 'I know this is a tough one,' he said, 'but can you remember any specific dates when Eisner might have visited the church?'

Shaffer snickered. He dropped his cigarette butt on the floor, crushed it out with a shoe and stared back into Stocker's bright, intelligent eyes, which were magnified by his lenses. 'You're really hunting the snark,' he said.

'*Think*,' Stocker insisted again, sticking his pipe in his mouth and chewing the stem.

The phone buzzed. Stocker grabbed the receiver, listened for a moment, said 'Thank you,' and put it down. 'There's a French priest at St Joseph's,' he told Shaffer. 'Father Pascal. He's thought to be a Vichy supporter. Did Eisner ever mention him?'

'Nope.'

'Have you remembered any dates?'

Shaffer coughed. 'I'm sticking my neck out,' he said, 'but I'd plump for June 15 and June 19.'

Stocker picked up the phone again. 'First,' he snapped into it, 'I want two sections dispatched at once to St Joseph's church, Shari' Emad ad-Din. One is to throw a discreet cordon round the place and watch out for our man. And I mean discreet – they are to keep completely out of sight. The other squad is to arrest the French priest, Father Pascal, and search the entire premises for a possible wireless trans-mitter. Second, I want to know at once if we recorded any unregistered transmissions from the downtown area on June 15 and 19.'

He returned the receiver to its bracket, and a moment later it buzzed again. He listened briefly, then replaced it.

'There were transmissions on June 15 and 18,' he said. 'Could it have been June 18?'

'I suppose so – I told you I wasn't certain.'

Stocker turned and bawled to the driver in front. 'St Joseph's Church, Shari' Emad ad-Din, and make it snappy.' When he turned to Shaffer again, the South African saw a gleam of victory behind the thick spectacles. 'Now,' he said, 'it's just a matter of who gets there first.'

35

Eisner felt safer after he'd ditched the Caddy in one of the alleys behind Emad ad-Din. The car stuck out like a sore thumb, and although he'd managed to dodge roadblocks so far, he felt sure that if they'd tumbled to the houseboat, they would certainly have his registration number. How they'd found his boat was a mystery that he preferred not to brood over at present. The key thing was to pass on the crucial intelligence he'd acquired.

St Joseph's stood tucked away in a niche at the end of Shari' Emad ad-Din, a narrow conduit of open-fronted shops lit from within by carbide lamps – a row of small stages upon each of which its own little drama was being enacted: a butcher chopping hanks of meat on a block, watched by a woman clad entirely in black, her face masked in a burqa like the head of a falcon; a barber lathering the chin of a reclining man, still smoking a cigarette, with thick cream; two youths sharpening knives on grinding-stones in showers of sparks.

Eisner, clad in his black suit, fez and dark glasses, wearing a pair of oversized leather driving-gloves to disguise his injured finger, let himself merge into the crowd, a ghost among disconnected faces, fellahin in kuffiyas, Berberines in white turbans, women veiled with hejabs. At the end of the street men were sitting around braziers on little stools smoking hubble-bubbles, drinking coffee, listening to the wail and grind of Arab music from a wireless. Despite the news that Rommel had taken Tobruk, there was little evidence of panic here. Eisner felt at home walking through the squares of light cast by the shop lamps on the pavement, but still he played the counter-surveillance game – pausing to peer into a shop here, lurking in a doorway there, backtracking as if to examine something he'd missed. There was no sign that he was being followed.

The church was a nest of curves and angles dominated by a rounded tower like the bastion of a medieval castle. The heavy door was reached down a short portico lined with potted shrubs. Eisner stopped before entering and glanced at his watch. It was almost nine o'clock. Mass was recited at seven thirty sharp, and would be over by now. The church would be empty of celebrants, and Father Pascal would be in the vestry, putting away the wine, having a private swig, or doing whatever it was that priests did after mass. He pushed open the door, took in the scent of incense, lit candles, empty pews, deserted altar and pulpit. Everything was quiet: not an object out of place.

He opened the door of the vestry and found Father Pascal sitting motionless behind a desk, his furrowed face and shock of steel-grey hair highlighted by the flickering flame of a tallow candle. The room was large and full of shadows: there were no windows, but a second door lay in a narrow archway beyond the priest's desk.

Father Pascal rose when Eisner entered, standing very straight in his soutane, his shadowed eyes like dark caves. 'I wouldn't have expected you so late,' he said in French.

'The war waits for no man, Father,' Eisner answered. 'I've got special intelligence to pass on.'

The priest's hawkish eyes fell on Eisner's hands clad in their leather gloves, and he cocked a curious eyebrow. 'Are you injured?' he asked.

Eisner shrugged impatiently. 'Just a little accident. Can I have the set please?'

The old man nodded, and as he moved towards the cupboards to his right, Eisner turned and locked the main door. He made a move towards the second door, but the Father stopped him. 'It's all right,' he said.

The priest opened a cupboard, brought out the suitcase that held the transmitter and laid it gently on his desk. Eisner unfastened it and began to set up the antenna. When that was done, he hooked up the batteries, connected the headphones and Morse key, and sat down with the code-book and encryption pad in front of him. As the priest looked on, he pencilled out his message painfully, using his left hand. He laid the pencil down, checked the cipher, then donned the headphones, removed his left glove, and sat with his fingers poised on the key.

Totally focused on the task in hand, his hearing muffled by the headphones, he didn't notice the door behind him open. Neither did he see the dark figures slipping silently through it, until a sudden movement caught his eye. His reaction was instantaneous. He kicked his chair backwards and went for his Smith & Wesson. At that moment a black-jack whacked into his shoulder, paralysing his whole arm. Eisner yelped and dropped his weapon, sensing the cold muzzle of a Tommy-gun against his neck. 'Move, go on,' a voice goaded him. 'I'd love to blow your bloody block off.' Eisner froze, feeling an icy ghost-finger scrape his spine. The electric light was switched on suddenly, making him blink: he saw that the vestry was full of khaki-clad British soldiers, armed to the teeth.

Arms rammed him against the wall, and his right glove was pulled off, exposing his bloated, broken index finger.

365

'Hello, what have we here?' the same voice said. 'Looks like Captain Avery gave you something to remember him by.'

A hand grabbed the broken finger and snapped it backwards: a shock of pain electrified Eisner's muscles, an agony so intense that he jumped a foot in the air, howling like a belaboured dog.

'Oops, sorry,' the voice said.

They were no gentler in slapping steel cuffs on his wrists, though, and Eisner pig-squealed as they manhandled him. Probing hands ran up and down his body, found the concealed knife, removed it. Almost sobbing now, Eisner was wrenched around again to find himself staring into the spectacles of a short, dumpy man with a domed forehead and sparkling blue eyes. The man, who wore major's crowns on his shoulder straps, was fingering his knife. 'Vicious,' he commented in a soft voice. 'I presume this is the weapon you used to murder Lady Goddard, Rachel Levi and Susan Arquette. Dear me, two ladies in one day. Wasn't that a bit greedy, even by your standards?'

'I don't know what you're talking about,' Eisner stuttered. 'Those murders were nothing to do with me.'

'Bloody liar.' It was the voice of the soldier who'd held the Tommy-gun to his neck and twisted his finger: Eisner glanced sideways to see a burly sergeant major in bush-jacket and peaked service cap, still holding his sub-machine gun. 'You are a human louse, matey,' the man said. 'You raped those women and slit their throats. You shot Sergeant Maffey, you murdered Corporal Salim Tanta and burned his body, and you tortured and killed Captain Avery. If I blew your balls off right now it'd be too good for you, you piece of dog-shit.'

'You may yet have the chance, Sarn't Major,' the bespectacled man said. 'It all depends on Mr Eisner here.'

For the first time, Eisner looked shocked. 'How do you know my name?' he demanded.

The major smiled wistfully. 'The same way I knew about your houseboat, your car, your safe-house on Roda. You see, your friend Mr Shaffer was a loyal South African after all, or at least enough of one to give you up.'

Eisner stifled a gasp, rocked to the core by the knowledge that Shaffer had ratted on him – and more. Shaffer wasn't supposed to know his real name, or the location of his safe-house. That meant that he'd been doing some private snooping of his own. It suggested that he might have been planning to rat for some time. He cursed Rohde's short-sightedness. Hadn't he always warned him that a man working under duress could never be completely trusted? It was typical of Rohde to believe that in fear lay absolute security.

'More crucially for us,' the major went on, 'Mr Shaffer knows your signals procedure – call signs, security codes, that sort of thing.'

'So what?' Eisner said.

'So we will know if you attempt to botch up the message you are about to send on our behalf. The message will read, 'Identity of *Runefish* confirmed: First Officer Maddaleine Rose, Women's Royal Naval Service, staff officer at Allied GHQ Middle East Forces, Cairo. Authenticity of material carried corroborated.'

'No,' Eisner said.

The eyes behind the thick lenses were unflinching. 'On your knees,' said the major quietly. Before Eisner could move, the two soldiers holding him forced him into a kneeling position. Slowly, very deliberately, the officer laid the knife on the desk, drew the Colt .45 automatic he was carrying at his waist, and held it to Eisner's temple. 'I don't consider myself a violent man, Mr Eisner,' he said. 'In peacetime I was a professor at Cairo University, but I share the sentiments of the sergeant major, as, I dare say, does every man in this room – even your ecclesiastical friend, who was also ready to turn you in when he found out the true nature of the monster he'd been nurturing. It is one thing to fight for your country, Eisner – even to spy for it. It is quite another to rape defenceless young women, and to kill them in cold blood.'

'Defenceless?' Eisner gasped, as if facing rank injustice. 'That bint in the flat almost did for me.'

The sharp eyes blazed behind the dense lenses, and Eisner sensed suddenly that the major was holding volcanic fury in close check. The deadly passion behind those lenses terrified him. Major Stocker was not an imposing figure, but there was a chilling quality about the intense eyes, the pedantic diction, the schoolmasterish manner. Stocker pressed the muzzle of the Colt so hard against Eisner's head that it was forced back. 'I knew Susan Arquette,' he said softly. 'She was a very fine young woman. If I were a less civilized man, Mr Eisner, I should be sorely tempted to pick up your wicked little stiletto, sever your penis at the root, insert it in your throat, and let you asphyxiate on it. You are not a man, you are a cowardly, craven animal. However, as I do not propose to sink to your level of bestiality, I shall content myself with putting a bullet through your skull instead. Indeed, I hope very much you do *not* cooperate, as it would give me unspeakable pleasure to send you to the hell where you belong.'

'You're bluffing. I'm too valuable for that.'

'How valuable is a filthy rapist and murderer? You are not a soldier, Mr Eisner, and you deserve to die like a dog. If you refuse to send the message, I will kill you now. I shall simply have Mr Shaffer send it instead.'

Eisner ran his tongue along dry lips. He had no doubt that Stocker would carry out his threat: this was wartime, and Field Security could probably get away with anything, even murder. If he played along with them, though, he'd survive, and he'd almost certainly be able to escape later. It would mean sending Rommel a false message, but then, if Rommel captured Cairo, he'd be redundant anyway. What did he have to lose by going along with the British for now?

He dry-swallowed, and stared at Stocker. 'All right,' he said. 'I'll do it.'

'Good, but one word of warning. We cracked your code some time ago and, as I have said, we know your security signatures. One wrong digit and, believe me, you won't leave this room alive.'

36

Moving more slowly now, Caine hugged the shadows in the streets of Biska, aware that he no longer had his Arab disguise but hoping that anyone spotting him by chance would take him for a German soldier. His wound was agonizing, and he was seething with anger about Naiman's death – he had half a mind to leave Rose to the mercies of the Black Widow. As it stood, he was faced with the task of infiltrating the town-hall area, and armed only with a rusty knife, extracting her from the hands of an entire Brandenburger platoon and a company of colonial carabinieri. His only advantage was the fact that they would not be expecting him. How much easier it would be, he thought, just to make his way back to the leaguer, declare the mission aborted and head back home. That was what Rose deserved. The sudden appearance of the town-hall building in front of him came almost as a surprise, and he realized that an unconscious urge had brought him here. It was as if, deep down, some remote part of him not under rational control knew that he could no more leave Rose than he could have abandoned Naiman to a long-drawn-out death.

As he paused under a tree opposite, he became aware that a small party was making its way across the street. Three Brandenburgers, armed with Gewehr 41 semi-automatic rifles and bayonets, were shoving ahead of them a gagged and bound prisoner. Caine realized with a shock that the prisoner was Maddaleine Rose.

The squad wasn't moving tactically – in fact, the troopers

were laughing and joking, subjecting Rose to lewd gestures, whose meaning neither she nor Caine could mistake. The gestures told Caine that she was no longer of use to Rohde: she'd evidently blabbed under interrogation. From what he could see, she looked relatively unharmed, which suggested that she'd caved in easily. Caine didn't want to judge her on that – she was a woman, after all – but he still couldn't get over the fact that she'd betrayed him and Naiman to the Jerries. He'd never be able to forgive her for Naiman's death.

The moonlight was still strong, but by keeping to the darkest places, crouching in the trees, squatting under walls, Caine was able to follow the group unobserved. The Brandenburgers were obviously so focused on what they intended to do to Rose that they'd thrown all caution to the wind. He didn't know if Rohde had warned them that there might be an enemy raiding unit in the area, or whether the Black Widow had swallowed his story that there had only ever been the two of them. He wondered how he was going to take on three fully armed Jerries with no more than his rusty old blade. He would have to dispose of them swiftly and noiselessly, without allowing them to get off a shot that would alert the rest of the garrison. He put the thought out of his mind, sure that an opportunity would arise, aware that surprise was by far his most powerful tool.

The party had covered about half a mile when it halted beyond the outskirts of the town, in what Caine saw was an Islamic graveyard: oval plots bordered by rings of stones, interspersed with thorn bushes. Wasting no time, the Jerries immediately tripped Rose over, hurling her on her stomach. While she lay there panting, inert and helpless, they put their bayonets and Gewehr 41s down and began to unclip their webbing. Recognizing that he had only seconds, Caine closed the distance between them rapidly, ducking behind a thorn bush not two yards away from where they had downed their semi-automatics.

The Brandenburgers were standing over Rose now, unbuttoning their flies, sniggering together like adolescent schoolboys, debating who would go first. Rose lay face-down in the dust. She neither moved nor uttered the slightest sound, as if she were totally resigned to what was happening. Or perhaps she was so dazed after her interrogation that she wasn't even aware of it. Two of the soldiers squatted by her and started pulling down her trousers. Caine saw his chance. He took a quick silent breath, stepped forward, scooped up a discarded Gewehr 41 in one hand and a bayonet in the other, and without even breaking step, swung the rifle like a club. He brought it crashing down on the head of the standing soldier with all the momentum of his body, all the force of his massive torso, all the speed of his unusually fast reflexes. The pent-up rage of Rose's betrayal, Rohde's torture, his ordeal in the well, Naiman's horrific death, found expression in that blow. Caine felt the skull cleave, crack, cave in, felt the rifle-stock snap off.

The soldier went rigid, poleaxed. As he toppled, Caine hurled the bayonet left-handed at one of the crouching men. It was a throw whose accuracy he could never have hoped for in a less adrenalin-pumped condition: the blade took the man in the neck, the point passing through it and emerging the other side in a spume of blood. The Brandenburger's eyes popped out with astonishment. He swayed, gurgling, spitting gore. The third Jerry wasn't even fully on his feet when Caine attacked him with the mutilated stump of the rifle. The soldier was a red-haired man, bigger and broader even than himself, but there was merciless fury in Caine's onslaught. Before the redhead had time to defend himself, Caine had bashed his pate three times with the blunt stock, twisted the rifle and thrust the muzzle into his mouth: it mashed teeth, pulped his tongue, ruptured his larynx, came to rest half-way down his gullet. The Brandenburger sagged, seething, gagging, croaking on air: Caine put all his weight behind the weapon, thrusting it in deeper until the soldier's windpipe burst. Kicking the fallen man aside, Caine wheeled round, his knife at the ready. Neither of the other two soldiers had risen: the first was clearly dead, the second was moaning and wheezing in the process of bleeding to death.

Caine decided not to take any chances. He picked up a second sword-bayonet, tested its sharpness against his thumb, crouched down by the wheezing soldier. He grabbed the Jerry's blood-stiff hair, jerked his head back, cut his throat from ear to ear. He felt ragged tissue part, saw the severed gullet and windpipe twitch, saw blood gush. The wheezing stopped. He moved to the Jerry he'd poleaxed, knelt down, did the same. The third Hun was already so disfigured that Caine had to force himself to make the cut. He crouched, jerked the rifle out of the Jerry's mouth, sawed through what was left of his neck. He was half-way through when he became aware of eyes watching him. He glanced sideways, saw Rose lying two feet away, saw her bruised face shocked, saw her gagged mouth working silently, saw deep-green eyes riveted on him, wide with horror. He turned away, finished the job, left the bayonet stuck in the Jerry's gullet. He stood up, panted, lurched, reeled, fought back vomit. He helped himself to another Gewehr 41, slung it over his shoulder, palmed water-bottles from the dead men's webbing, turned his attention to Rose.

He hauled her to her feet by her own bindings. She turned to face him, her eyes bulging, just as they had a few hours earlier when he'd approached her in the locked room. She mumbled something frantic under her gag, evidently expecting him to remove it. Caine ignored her. 'Just shut up and do as you're told,' he growled. He pulled up her trousers, buttoned the waist roughly. Then he seized her by one arm and began to hustle her, still bound, in the direction of the leaguer.

37

At sunset on 21 June, Rommel had moved out of the roadhouse, pitching his camp in a little oasis of dense scrub on the plain, where he could enjoy the cool of the moonlit desert night. When von Mellenthin arrived there hot-foot from the signals detachment, he found the general sitting under an awning with a captured British brigadier, his ADC, Captain Heinz Schmidt, and Panzer Group interpreter, Lt Manfred Hoffman, of the German Navy. The four officers were lounging at their ease in camp-chairs around a low table, quaffing mugs of warm beer looted from British stocks in Tobruk. 'You will find the first days of captivity the worst, General,' Rommel was advising the prisoner, 'but you won't be mistreated. My men respect brave soldiers.'

Mellenthin couldn't suppress a chuckle. There was nothing the GOC liked better than hob-nobbing with captured enemy personnel, sometimes rebuking them paternally for tactical mistakes, as if discussing a friendly football match. Rommel could be as ruthless and calculating as the next general, but despite thirty years of combat experience, he'd never lost his sense of war as a sport: always grim, sometimes foolish, often tragic, but an essentially honorable sport nevertheless. For the general, hatred of or even rude behaviour towards the enemy was normally unthinkable – which was why Mellenthin had found his treatment of Klopper that morning so shocking.

The intelligence officer saluted, and waited politely for the GOC to conclude his conversation. '. . . all the more deplorable,' Rommel was continuing, 'to see, as I have seen, photographs of wounded Italian soldiers dismembered by the enemy after capture. This is the work of beasts, not men.'

He paused while the interpreter did his job. The brigadier, a craggy-faced man with bushy eyebrows who looked a shade too warm in full battle-dress, grew animated. 'No British soldiers would have done that,' he protested. 'I am certain it was the work of Abyssinian auxiliaries.'

'Perhaps,' Rommel commented after Hoffman had translated. 'If so, I find it regrettable that you Britishers should employ such savages in a war against white men.'

He stood up to show that the conversation was at an end, shook hands vigorously with the POW. 'I hope your captivity will not last long, General,' he told him. 'Surely there is room in the world for both of our nations without fighting?'

'Indeed, General – those are my sentiments entirely.'

As soon as the others were out of earshot, Rommel gestured Mellenthin to a chair. 'Well?' he enquired.

The IO's smile was triumphant. 'Field Marshal von Kesselring acknowledges his receipt of the *Runefish* report,' he said, 'and accepts the confirmation of its authenticity from our asset *Stürmer*, in Cairo. He has agreed not to withdraw his air units, pending approval from OKH/OKW in Berlin.'

'Good,' Rommel said. His laugh-wrinkles were suddenly prominent, and it seemed to Mellenthin that he was struggling to suppress the urge to jump up and do a jig. 'What about the Italians?'

'Generals Bastico, Cavallero and Barbasetti have all registered disapproval of your intended actions. So has von Rintelin in Rome, but none of them in strong terms. I think they can be relied on to toe the line.'

Rommel beamed, his blue-grey eyes twinkled, laugh-lines corrugated his face from the corner of his eyes to the edge of his cheekbones. 'Signal them that, as from first light tomorrow, I intend to go straight through the Delta, across the Nile, the Suez Canal and the Sinai Desert. I shall not pause until I have reached the Persian Gulf. You may reiterate my invitation, to all of them, to dine with me at Shepheard's Hotel in a week's time.'

'Excuse me, sir,' Mellenthin said, 'but may I advise you that it would be prudent to wait for official permission before sending such a message?'

Rommel feigned surprise. 'No, Major, you may not advise me. Those old women have delayed me long enough already. I lost valuable days over the Gaullist French at Bir Hacheim, and I have no intention of stalling any longer. At dawn my Battle Staff moves to Bardia, and 15th Panzer and the Ariete Divisions will move up to the frontier. By then we should have news from 90th Light on the supply dumps they've been probing for.'

'Very good, sir,' Mellenthin said. He was about to get up when Rommel continued. 'I want you to signal Rohde in Biska,' he said. 'Tell him he's done a good job, but inform him that I want that woman – *Runefish* – sent up to the front on the first available aircraft. I want to talk to her personally.'

A slightly bemused look crossed the IO's face. 'But, General,' he protested, 'you said yourself that there wouldn't be much left of her when that swine had done his business. We both know he doesn't wear velvet gloves.'

Rommel's expression turned severe, and Mellenthin guessed that he was experiencing a pang of guilt. This Maddaleine Rose might be just a woman, but she was also an enemy officer captured in uniform. She was entitled to the rights of any prisoner-of-war. Rommel deplored cruelty to male prisoners, let alone females, but he'd been too avid for the information she carried to remind Rohde of this earlier. Now he was regretting it, the IO thought.

'Whatever state she's in,' he snapped. 'I want her sent here. I do *not* want her dumped in a shallow grave in the Green Mountains. You tell that . . . that piece of horse turd . . . that, grateful as I am for the intelligence he supplied, I am holding him personally responsible for her safety. If *Runefish* doesn't arrive at my HQ in the next twenty-four hours, I shall want to know the reason why.'

The three Brandenburger corpses lay in the graveyard at Biska, blanched and glassy-eyed, in ellipses of burgundy-coloured sand rich with their own blood. A clutch of giant Nubian vultures was hovering around the perimeter, and the troops chased them away with stones. When Captain Karl Haller had finished examining the dead soldiers, he stood up and flashed Rohde a grim look. 'You'd think they'd been hit by a pack of savages, sir,' he said. 'One had his skull stoven in, another was asphyxiated by a rifle muzzle being shoved down his gullet, and the third got his own bayonet right through the neck. All three of them have had their throats slit. None was shot, and by the state of their weapons not one of them got a round off, either.'

'Too intent on having a romp with the prisoner,' Rohde said drily. 'So this is the standard one can expect from "Special Duties" troops . . . ?' He stared at the captain with burning eyes. 'You lost me my prisoner, Haller – a prisoner that General Rommel has asked specifically to see.'

Haller felt his gorge rising. 'Sir,' he said. 'You told me that the prisoner was of no further use. You announced in front of my men that they could do whatever they wanted with her.'

Rohde's eyes narrowed hazardously. 'That's a lie –' he started, but before he could finish he was interrupted by the arrival of the police tracker – a short, spare Senussi in khakis and a red headcloth. Haller listened to his report and told him in Italian to stand by. 'He's sure that this was the work of one man,' he told Rohde. He pointed to a nearby bush. 'Whoever it was followed the party from the town paused behind that bush and attacked them with their own weapons.'

'One man?' Rohde snarled. 'Who?'

'There's only one person it could have been,' Haller said, feeling a lump in his throat. 'The sergeant we threw in the well.'

Rohde looked as if he were about to explode. 'Caine? Are you telling me you let him *escape*?'

'I followed your orders to the letter, sir,' Haller objected. 'In any case, he was wounded and disoriented from interrogation. I wouldn't have put money on his even surviving the fall, let alone getting out of a well with sheer sides, a hundred feet deep.' He paused and scanned the three cadavers again as if to make certain that he hadn't been mistaken. 'By God, that joker's tough,' he said. 'Must be a one-man killing machine.'

'He must have had outside help, you mean,' Rohde snapped, his nostrils flaring. 'I'll tell you what I am going to do, Haller. I am going to assemble the entire Senussi population of this town, men and women. I'm going to have them shot, one by one, until I find out who helped him.' He put his face so near to Haller's that the officer could smell his stale breath. 'As for you, Captain, if you don't get me that cocksucker's balls on a plate, and the *Runefish* woman back unharmed before noon tomorrow, your next posting will be the Russian Front.'

38

Sunrise came upon Caine's small convoy as the wagons crested the head of the last escarpment on the southern side of the Green Mountain. Leaning on the White's observation hatch next to Wallace, Caine caught his breath. The sun lay on the rim of the world, bigger than he'd ever seen it – half a golden galleon upturned along the horizon. New light sketched lines across the landscape, slicing up the night's monolithic solidity into corries, canyons and gorges, in the foothills beneath him. Beyond that tame little garden, though, the wild Sahara was unstitching itself from the cloak of night, an endless, rolling, amber ocean of space, stretching onwards to the ends of the earth. It might be easier to hide in the mountains, but Caine could never rid himself of a sense of claustrophobia there. In the desert, though, he felt as safe and free as a bird breasting a flawless sky. He had, he told himself, at least accomplished his mission, even if not quite in the way he'd envisaged it. The rendez-vous with the LRDG escort – the Muqtal plateau – lay no more than two days' drive away. Now, that place glowed as brightly in his imagination as the promised land.

The convoy had been moving almost non-stop for seven hours, grating and rattling along precipitous tracks, sweeping down the floors of deep wadis, juddering over the tops of plunging screes. Caine had spent almost the entire journey at the hatch, smoking cigarettes, foiling with inarticulate grunts Wallace's attempts to grill him. For most of that time Maddaleine Rose had been curled up on the hard floor beneath them, still bound and gagged. 'If you don't give her water soon, skipper, she'll croak,' Wallace had observed at ever-decreasing intervals, the note of anxiety in his voice growing steadily more shrill. 'Why don't you untie her? At least take the gag off and let her breathe. I don't remember you sayin' our orders was to bring her back trussed up like a pound of brisket.'

Finally, tired of pussy-footing, the big gunner had knitted his shaggy eyebrows and glowered at his patrol commander. 'Why the hell are you tormenting her, Tom? What's up with you?'

'Naiman's dead, that's what's up,' Caine had growled at him. 'It's her fault. She ratted on us to the Hun.'

'Jesus, what *happened* in there?'

'I don't want to talk about it, all right?'

The only mishap on the descent was a set of burnt-out gear-bands on *Vera*. Caine told Wingnut Turner to leave the repair job until they halted in cover – dismantling the transmission box would be a long job, and he didn't want to be caught in the open by any shufti-wallahs the enemy might put on their tail at first light.

As they came down into the labyrinth of dry water-courses in the valley, the sun rotated slowly in a basket of dark sludge, firing off streamers of light like spear-points, searing through the last filaments of night-mist, detonating in small explosions of heat. Rubber tyres scrunched on the hard shingle of a wadi bed – a gravel beach coiling beneath a sheer cliff on one side and along a great plain of wind-graded serir on the other – a plain scattered with free-standing pedestals, narrow at the base and wide at the apex, giving the impression of battalions of petrified Black Gods on parade. Further on, the cliff had in places been eaten away by what might have been giant termites, into grottoes and overhangs, some of them large enough to conceal a vehicle. Caine thought it was the best cover they could expect to find in the circumstances: he had Copeland give the three-honk signal to halt and scrim up.

While Cope manoeuvered the White under an outcropping, Caine hopped out and went off to relieve his bursting bladder. He returned to find Fred Wallace carrying the limp but still conscious form of Maddaleine Rose into the shade of an immense smooth-skinned boulder. She looked as fragile as a china doll in his huge arms, and Caine was reminded instantly of the way Wallace had handled the orphan gazelle on the march out.

Caine gripped his Tommy-gun furiously and strode up to the big gunner. 'Who ordered you to do that?' he demanded. 'Who told you to take her out of the wagon?'

Caine glanced round for Copeland and found the corporal lolling against the car's bonnet, hands folded non-committally across his chest, a lit cigarette in his mouth. When Caine had hustled Rose into the leaguer the previous night, almost speechless with exhaustion, his mates had clamoured around him shooting questions, slapping him on the back. To their consternation, though, Caine's only statement had been that Naiman had bought it. He'd confounded them further by issuing terse orders that no one was to talk to Rose, or remove her restraints.

Now, ignoring Caine, Wallace laid Rose gently on soft ground with her back against the stone, where she sat motionless, her aquamarine eyes blinking, rivetted on Caine. Her breath came through her gag in quick, ragged pants. Wallace raised himself to his full height, his thorn-bush mop of black hair bristling. He stared Caine down. 'No good your lookin' at Harry, skipper,' he boomed. 'It's down to me, and if it's insubordination, tough shit. I couldn't stand to see her suffer no more. This ain't no way to treat a lady, and you know it – if you was yourself you wouldn't treat a *dog* like that. It ain't two days since you excused a pair of skuzzy A-rabs who'd just popped off three of our boys on the grounds they was only babes and give me down the road for wantin' to snuff them. Now, are you going to cut her loose or am I?'

Caine inserted himself between the big man and the sitting woman, and faced Wallace down. 'Don't touch her,' he snapped. 'I told you, she can't be trusted.'

Wallace ran a boxing-glove-sized hand through dense black chin-stubble that was quickly becoming a full beard. 'Skipper,' he said, his granite brow furrowed. 'You took a lot of humpty back there, didn't you?'

'It wasn't exactly a night out on the town, if that's what you mean,' Caine chuntered. 'We were doing fine until your new pal *Runefish* here deliberately made a racket that turned out the guard. We were bagged and worked over pretty well by that Black Widow scum. I escaped, but Moshe didn't make it. I want Rose kept under restraint until I know what's going on.'

Wallace's black eyes were belladonna pinpricks. 'What's *up* with you, mate? You just ain't seeing straight.' He sent an appealing glance at Copeland, who shrugged and blew smoke. 'I'm not getting into this, Fred,' he said. Caine remembered abruptly how Cope had laid into him for botching the snipe outside the cave the previous morning. If he'd had his way, this problem wouldn't have arisen: Rose would already be dead.

'All right then,' the big man grunted, whipping out his fanny. 'I'll do it myself.' Caine faced him, bracing his broad shoulders. 'You want to know what happened?' he yelled, his voice border-line hysterical. 'I'll tell you what happened,

Fred. First, that Nazi creep applies a red-hot iron to my bayonet wound here. Then, when I won't talk, he chops off Moshe's bloody thumb with a cleaver. When he finds out Moshe's a Jew, it's like he's just won the lottery – makes him tromp around a minefield until his foot gets blown off. Oh, and did I mention that he also shot him in the leg at point-blank range? Moshe might have taken days to die if I hadn't got to him first – I had to crawl through the minefield to get to him, though, and since I didn't have any proper weapons, I had to make him roll over on an anti-personnel mine. That was after I'd climbed out of the hundred-foot well they dropped me into. I should never have taken Moshe with me, of course, but he'd still be alive if Miss Butter-Wouldn't-Melt here hadn't scuppered us.'

'*Jesus*,' Wallace whispered. He pondered Caine's words for a moment, and Caine could almost read his thoughts reflected in his broad, open face. 'It's bad about Moshe,' the gunner said slowly, with unfamiliar gentleness. 'Really bad. But he ain't the first one we lost, Tom. How long you going to go on blaming yourself and the lass here for something neither of you could do anything about? Ain't you the one as said you lose mates in war?'

Caine felt agitated, confused, almost on the verge of collapse. As Wallace pressed forward, though, he raised a hand to push him back. 'Don't try anything, Fred,' he warned.

'Get out of my way, skipper.'

Caine balled a fist, but the action was slow and without conviction. At the first sign of movement, Wallace slapped him open-handed across the jaw with a giant, calloused hand, swatting him aside with the same economy of effort he'd used to flatten Copeland at the deserter's camp the previous morning. The blow wasn't as hard as it might have been, but it was enough to make Caine's head spin. By the time he'd recovered himself, the gunner had already removed Rose's gag and was crouching behind her, cutting through her bindings with his fanny. Rose snuffled, and tears fell down her grimy cheeks. Her ocean-soul eyes never left Caine for a second.

'Let's have a look,' Wallace growled, kneeling in front of her. She presented her small, delicate hands obediently, and Caine saw that her wrists had been chafed raw by the tight cords. The wounds looked ugly. Wallace stroked her small fingers with his enormous ones, making mother-hen clucking sounds. 'That's nasty,' he purred, as if he were reassuring a child. 'Very nasty. I'm going to call our orderly – I'm sure he's got dope for it.' He yanked a full water-bottle out of his webbing, uncorked it and handed it to her. She took it, but was trembling so badly that Wallace took it back and held it to her mouth. 'Just wet your lips, ma'am,' he murmered. 'That's right. Easy does it. Then maybe a little sip. If you drink too much at once it'll make you bad.'

Rose sipped, coughed, then sipped again, finally managing to take the water-bottle herself. As she swallowed, Wallace sat back on his rhino-like haunches and looked round for Copeland. 'You'd better call Pickney, Harry,' he said. 'Those wrists could go septic.'

Caine said nothing, and Cope went off without a word. Wallace turned back to Rose. 'You hurt anywhere else, ma'am?'

She nodded, coughed, handed the bottle back to him, then pulled up her trouser-cuffs, showing ankles that were a purple mass of bruises and burns. 'They clamped electrodes there,' she said, her voice soft and without rancour. 'There and here.' She gestured to her armpits. 'They used electric shocks.'

Wallace stared accusingly at Caine. 'She suffered all that, and you left her tied up without water for seven hours, rattling about in that wagon like a dried pea in a tin-can? You practisin' for a new career with the Gestapo or what?'

Wallace's words stabbed Caine like daggers. The slap in the face, followed by the sight of Rose's injuries, and her mention of electric-shock torture, had brought him back to earth with a jolt. He felt hard tears well up in his eyes as the enormity of his cruelty dawned on him. He'd been so obsessed with the horror of Naiman's mutilation and death that he'd never even considered the possibility that she might have been dreadfully tortured too. Wallace was right: he'd forced this young, helpless girl to go through a quite unnecessary torment, bouncing about in the back of the AFV over rough terrain with open wounds, without offering her water, food, medical treatment, or even a word of comfort.

Caine broke out in a cold sweat. His body began to tremble so much that he had to steady himself against a rock. Wallace had hit the nail on the head. This was Gestapo treatment – unadulterated cruelty that he wouldn't even have doled out to an Axis POW, let alone an injured female compatriot. He couldn't believe he'd behaved so pitilessly – it was against everything he'd ever stood for or believed in. Something must have gone wrong inside him, he thought. The long-drawn-out agony of the march-in, the slaughter, the blood, the pain of his own torture, the ordeal in the well, of clearing the minefield, of setting up Naiman's suicide, and his berserk butchery of the three Jerries, had tipped him over the edge into some kind of demonic dark underworld of the soul.

So she'd spat in his face, sworn at him, called him a few names – so what? Just when he should have been offering her support, he'd treated her as viciously as that psycho Rohde – worse, because at least in Rohde's case there had been a logical reason for it. Caine had no reason except vindictiveness – the pain he'd inflicted on her was completely gratuitous. His head ached. The blood drained from his face. His breathing came in short gasps. He felt as if he'd just woken up from a bad dream. He couldn't explain why he'd behaved like this – it was as if he'd been possessed by an evil spirit for the past eight hours – as if some black shuck that had always lurked inside him had suddenly broken free. Now, he wanted to run away and hide, to flee until he fell off the edge of the world, to conceal himself, to go anywhere to get out of her sight. 'I'm sorry, ma'am,' he stammered. 'I . . .'

'Sergeant Caine,' Rose said quietly, focusing her luminous green eyes on him again. 'You don't need to apologize.' Her voice was faint but firm and steady. 'You don't know me, and you had every right to be cautious. It must have been a real shock when I reacted like that at the town hall, and then the terrible loss of your comrade. I lost a close friend once in similar horrible circumstances, and I know how savage it can make you. It might be poor comfort, but I want to say how grateful I am. I know you've risked your life over and over for me, and I'll never forget that.'

Caine could hardly believe his ears. He'd been expecting a haughty tirade of officer-class invective – the kind of arch abuse she'd poured on Naiman and himself at Biska. He felt so revolted with himself that he would have welcomed it, accepted it as his due. Her statement disarmed him totally. It wasn't only what she'd said that astonished him but the way she'd said it. Her voice was quite devoid of the knife-blade arrogance he'd heard in Biska town hall. Even her accent was different. This voice was so warm and intimate, in fact, that it might have belonged to someone else.

Copeland reappeared under the overhang. 'Maurice'll be here in a sec,' he said. Caine nodded and turned back to Rose, who was still staring at him, her face full of sympathy. 'I am so, so sorry about your friend,' she said. More tears etched clean grooves across the filthy cheeks. 'Believe me, if it could have been any different . . . if I could have done anything to stop it . . . I would have done.' Her tearful eyes searched his face for understanding, and it hit him like a second bang on the head that she held herself responsible for Naiman's death. 'The way I spoke to you back there,' she whispered, '. . . I was taken by surprise. When you pointed that pistol at me, I didn't know what to do. You see, I'm just a courier, and I never expected my aircraft to be shot down. They tried to prepare me for the worst, but of course you never really think it's going to happen to you. I was lucky – I was able to bale out when the plane got hit, but my poor pilot – Flight Sergeant Orton – he never had a chance. I'm certain he went down with the crate. Anyway, they mentioned the possibility of a search-and-rescue team in my briefing, in the event that the worst happened, but I never took it seriously. Even if the idea of a rescue mission was at the back of my mind, I wouldn't have expected you to get there so soon – not to get there at all, really.'

Caine stared back vacantly, and it was Copeland who spoke for him.

'I don't quite follow you, ma'am,' he said, moving closer to the group. 'If you didn't expect us, why did you transmit your emergency call for more than three hours yesterday? If you hadn't done that you wouldn't have been bagged –'

'I suppose I just panicked,' she cut in quickly. 'As I said, I'm new to all this.'

Caine felt sick and confused. He no longer seemed to have a clear idea why he'd been sent up the Blue. Wires had got crossed: there had been some kind of massive cock-up somewhere, but he was too tired to work it out. 'I'm sorry, ma'am,' he stammered again. 'I . . . back there in the town . . . I'd almost made my mind up to dump you . . .'

Rose's long eyelashes quivered, and she closed her eyes for a moment. He guessed she was picturing his ferocious butchery of the three Brandenburgers: he remembered how her eyes had bugged out with horror when she'd seen him sawing through the big Jerry's neck. She was a staff courier, not a combat vet: even though her life had been at stake, it must have been deeply traumatic for her to witness such feral savagery. However genuinely grateful she was, she must think him no better than a beast.

When Rose opened her eyes they were stonily calm. 'You *should* have dumped me, Sergeant,' she said. 'It would have made things so much simpler. You could have saved yourself and your men. Now, I'm not sure if any of us will escape . . . I didn't expect to be rescued, you see, and it wasn't necessary. I'm expendable. I volunteered for this job knowing that . . . if something went wrong . . . I wasn't likely to get out alive. What happens to me doesn't matter. All we can hope is that –'

She was interrupted by the arrival of Pickney, who slammed his medical box down without ceremony. 'I'm sorry to break this up, skipper,' he said, 'but how about letting me do my stuff?'

39

Caine was pleased to have an excuse to leave. After the way he'd treated Rose, he felt he wouldn't ever again be able to look her in the eye. He had to admit, though, that he was totally confused – especially by her last remarks. Since her bindings had come off, he'd found no trace at all of the woman he thought he'd glimpsed in the guardroom at Biska. The sea-green eyes, the boyish cap of golden hair, the full lips: they were all there, but it was as if they'd been reassembled in a different way. There wasn't the slightest trace of that impassive death-mask that had sent shivers down his spine. On the contrary, she was sweet – shy, self-effacing, dreamy-eyed, compliant – quite without the despotic manner she'd seemed to possess when he'd first encountered her. She had a wistful, waif-like, almost elfin touch that under normal circumstances, he thought, would have driven a lot of men crazy – would have driven *him* crazy.

She was just a courier, she'd said: she hadn't expected to be shot down. Yet she'd endured horrors, loneliness, torture and privations that few people ever encountered, even in the war, almost without a whimper. She'd thanked him humbly for rescuing her, then told him he should have dumped her in Biska. The statement had hit him like a slap in the face. He remembered the way she'd lain passively in the dirt as the Jerries prepared to rape and murder her, as if totally resigned to it – almost as if she felt she *deserved* it.

That there were unexplained holes in her story – the

three-hour SOS transmission, for instance – no longer troubled Caine deeply. He reminded himself that while she was an officer of field rank, he was no more than a grunt NCO. Her mission was top secret, and there could well be security aspects – signals protocols, for example – that were beyond his 'need to know'. It really didn't matter now. What amazed him was how rapidly everything had changed. He'd started up by hating Rose for betraying him and Naiman to the Jerries, had sworn that he'd never, ever forgive her for Naiman's death. Yet he'd ended up by admiring her and despising himself. He'd begun by regarding her as the devil incarnate, and ended up by feeling attracted to her. It was confusing: it was almost more than he could take.

He stepped out into the broad sunlit swathe of the wadi, glad to have the hot sun on his face. He marched towards the rock shelter harbouring *Judy*, where Copeland had stashed the spare sets of khakis Michele's mob had given them. He wanted to replace his filthy, blood-stained kit – he reminded himself to pick up a couple of sets for Rose while he was about it. The sun was higher now, and the early morning dust-clouds had dispersed, leaving only a tight white fireball in a pure methylene sky. Further up the wadi the cliff walls shattered into jagged crags, braised and abraded into surreal shapes – a coiled serpent, a gallery of jellyfish, a giant, bloated infant with a stump for a head. Across the wadi he could make out the ranks of top-heavy pedestals – *yardangs* was the geological name. Now the shadows had diminished they looked more like a forest of giant toadstools than petrified Black Gods, but still their presence lent the landscape an eerie sense of otherworldliness, as if his unit had leaguered up on Mars.

Judy's crew was brewing tea under the rock overhang when Caine came in. There were only three of them left now – Bombardier Dick Flogget, a trim, pugnacious five-foot-five ex-Gunner from Newcastle, the heavily bearded former Royal Navy commando, Gus Graveman, and Caine's old nemesis, the truculent, barrel-chested ex-Redcap Cpl 'Todd' Sweeney. Caine greeted them, and declining tea, swung on to the lorry's tailboard using the scaling rope, and started poking about among the stores. When he swung down ten minutes later with three fresh suits under his arm, he was accosted by Sweeney, stripped down to shorts and chapplies, Tommy-gun slung from his side-of-mutton shoulder. He was swigging milky tea from a pint mug. 'Got the right one this time, then, Sarn't?' the ex-MP sneered. 'Or aren't you certain? Is that why you're keeping her tied up?'

For a moment, Caine seriously considered rearranging Sweeney's beach-ball face for him: it was an action long overdue. He thought better of it though. 'Not any more,' he said. 'That was just a temporary precaution until I could make a positive ID.'

'I see. Listen, skipper, I spotted gazelle tracks in the wadi – lots of them. I fancy going off to bag a couple. Some fresh meat would be just what the MO ordered.'

Caine tapped the stock of Sweeney's Tommy-gun. 'You won't bag many with this,' he said. 'Gazelle move like the clappers. In any case, the answer's no. Stay with the wagons until further notice.'

Sweeney cocked his brow. 'Did you know we've been short of rations since *Marlene* and *Gracie* went up?'

'Of course I knew,' Caine lied, making a mental note to speak to Copeland about it – as the mission's official 'Q', Cope should have kept him informed. 'The answer's still the same, Todd. No one's to leave the leaguer without my orders.'

'If you say so, Sarn't,' Sweeney said sourly, 'but I think you're being unduly cautious.'

Wingnut Turner called Caine over to the 3-tonner *Vera's* niche, where he was grappling with stubborn screws on the truck's transmission box. The bonnet was up, and a smell like scorched chocolate lay over her engine. *Vera's* crew was also down to three, Caine noted: Turner, Pte Albert Raker, the thirty-two-year-old ex-Pioneer Corps man with biceps and calves like steel springs and a charge-sheet eleven pages long, and Cpl Barry Shackleton, the ex-Scots Greys farrier, who was one of the few men in the British Army legally entitled to wear a beard and who consequently shaved every day. While Shackleton and Raker cooked stew, Turner showed him the gearbox. Caine knew that the RAOC man was perfectly capable of tackling the problem on his own, but he welcomed the work. It was good to have a mechanical task to divert him from his brooding over Naiman's death and the nagging of his conscience over Rose: it was good to be able to work with his hands. 'The only problem,' Turner commented as the last screw popped out, 'is that the gearbox fluid's finished. Don't know what the hell I'm going to put in there.'

Caine scratched his stubble. 'Just whack in some cooking oil or a couple of pounds of margarine,' he said. 'We had the same problem with a 3-tonner's gear-bands on one of my first journeys up the Blue. The fitter I was with bought a sack of bananas off a Senussi and packed the transmission box with the skins. There we were in the middle of nowhere, stripping off banana skins and cramming bananas into our mouths, so as to get the old rattletrap moving before the Boche arrived. Worked like a dream, too – got back to base without a hitch. Mind you – I haven't been able to *look* at a banana since.'

Leaving Turner to hunt down something that would pass as grease, he visited the Daimler, where he found Flash Murray leaning over the AFV's open inspection-hood while Temple gunned the engine. The short Ulsterman lifted his head as Caine approached. 'Hear that, skipper?' he enquired. Caine listened to the motor's rumbling, and thought he knew what the Armoured Corps man meant. *'Pinking,'* Murray declared. 'It's the fuel them Ities gave us. It's either dirty or watered down. I suppose we should have expected it from those bloody crooks.'

'I didn't hear you make any objections when you were smooching with that pretty Itie girl, though,' Caine said, chuckling.

Murray, a married man, blushed. 'Should be all right,' he said, ignoring Caine's observation. 'We'll mix it with the other – dilute the bad stuff.'

'No need,' said Caine. 'Have you got any chamois-leathers in your kit? If you can find some, pour the petrol through – use them as filters. It's a pain in the arse, and it takes for ever, but it'll get rid of all the gunge.'

Murray's face lit up at this piece of information. 'Thanks, skipper,' he said. 'Amazing what you Sappers come up with.' About to turn away, Caine caught the lance sergeant gazing at his fresh bush-shirt and looked down to see that the brand-new cloth was already soaked in blood. 'You better get that looked at again,' Murray said. 'What happened in that village, anyway?'

Caine shook his head. 'You don't want to know,' he said.

Maurice Pickney had long since finished treating Rose, and was now at the Dingo's position. Caine found him there under the outcrop crouching over George Padstowe, who was lying spreadeagled on a blanket, half comatose. To Caine's surprise Rose was there with him, kneeling by the bald ex-marine's head, timing his heart-rate with a finger on his carotid artery. She seemed perfectly fit and at ease despite her injuries, her rough treatment and the trauma of the past twenty-four hours. Caine was impressed. 'What's the problem?' he asked.

'Heatstroke,' Pickney announced. 'Blighter spent too long in the sun yesterday – insisted on staying on the ridge in case he spotted you coming back. Thought you might need help.'

'Can you do anything for him, Maurice?'

Pickney screwed up his granny-wrinkled face. 'Normally I'd use chilled water or ice, but we're a bit short on those right now.'

'Have you thought of methylated spirits?' Rose suggested. 'It would cause a chill by evaporation.'

Pickney's face crinkled again as he considered it. 'Not a bad idea, ma'am,' he said. 'I should have thought of that. We've got plenty of white spirit for the cookers. If we swabbed his whole body down with it, it might just do the trick. Have you had medical training, too?'

Rose wiggled her slim shoulders. 'Just the basics,' she said. 'By the way, we can drop this *ma'am* business. My name is Maddy.'

Pickney looked embarrassed. 'You're a commissioned officer, ma'am,' he said. 'We're all just grunts.'

Rose smiled, displaying her charmingly overlapping front teeth. 'I want to be a grunt, too. Call me Maddy, please. That goes for everyone.'

'Right you are, ma'am . . . I mean, *Maddy.*'

Though Rose still wore the same dust-caked, blood-stained khakis, she had evidently cleaned up her face. When she stood up, Caine noticed for the first time how much she differed from Angela Brunetto. Both girls had precisely the same shade of blond hair, but while Angela's had been cut in fashionable Judy Garland style, Maddy's was short-cropped and provocatively boyish. While Angela was tall, slim and angular, Maddy's figure, though still sleek, was fuller and a touch more robust, with the wiry strength of a dancer. While the Italian girl's expression had held a hint of hardness, her mouth moody, her manner challenging, Rose's full lips, misty ocean-soul eyes and long eyelashes gave her a sleepy, dreamy quality that was disturbingly feminine. Far from being the martinet he'd originally taken her for, she seemed all soft edges: modest, sympathetic, anxious not to appear special or exalted, and only too ready to please.

The white-spirit trick worked, and when Padstowe started visibly reviving, Caine stuck his head through the lower hatch on the Dingo to find Trubman at the wireless op's post. 'Anything?' he enquired.

The Welshman shook his carp-like head. 'Latest report from Rome Radio is that Rommel's forces are moving towards the border. That was at first light today, 22 June. Looks as though he's poised for the invasion of Egypt.'

Rose's face was suddenly transformed, as if an invisible hand had passed over it, laugh-lines flashing like a neon network from the corners of her eyes to her chin, sultry lips drawing back in ecstatic glee over gleaming white teeth. For a split second her whole countenance glowed. '*Yes*,' she whispered.

Caine gasped. 'What's that about?' he asked.

'What do you mean,' she enquired.

Her face was back to normal now, as if it had never been any different, and Caine thought he must have imagined it or misheard what she said.

Rose and Caine walked back to the White together. Caine would rather have avoided being alone with her, but to have forced it would have appeared doubly offensive. He handed her the changes of kit, and for the first few minutes there was an awkward silence. Then Caine asked shyly how she was feeling. She showed him the bandages on her wrists and ankles. 'I'm fine,' she beamed.

'It must have been bad,' he commented uncertainly. 'I mean . . . the electric shocks.'

Her face clouded. 'I don't really want to remember, Sergeant . . .'

'Tom . . .'

'Tom . . .' She glanced at him. 'No worse than being dropped in a well, I suppose. Of course, I didn't hold out too long. I spilled the lot.'

'No one can blame you for that. Everyone breaks in the end.' He paused. 'Look,' he said, 'the way I treated you was unforgivable. I deserve to be hung, drawn and quartered for it.'

'Maybe,' she agreed, 'but then so do I, for getting you bagged. I can't believe that I actually spat in your face. But if we're both going to spend the rest of our lives saying sorry, we'll never get anywhere. At least you didn't shoot me.'

'I was a hair's breadth away from it.'

She gave him a long look of appraisal, her eyelashes fluttering. 'I don't think so, Tom,' she said, her voice soft. 'You're not a woman-killer. I saw that in your eyes a second before you were knocked down by that door.'

'You seem very sure of yourself.'

Maddy stopped and turned towards him, her face grave. 'I once saw a man cut a woman's throat in the act of raping her, in a nightclub in Cairo. You remember the Lady Goddard case?'

'Yes, I read about it. You witnessed that?'

'It was the most horrible thing I've ever seen. I entered the ladies' room just as he was finishing it, and he turned and stared at me. In that instant I knew I was looking into the eyes of a man who got real pleasure out of hurting women, who wasn't even human – not at that moment, I mean. He was possessed by something . . . he would have murdered me too, except that he heard someone coming. Taking out those three Germans was different – you had no choice. I'm not pretending it was a pretty sight. It revolted me, if you want to know the truth. But I never doubted that it had to be that way. If you'd shot them it would have alerted the garrison. You had to take them on hand to hand, and once they were down, you had to make sure they *stayed* down, otherwise we wouldn't even have made it back to your leaguer. I never had the feeling you were doing it for pleasure. Call it a woman's intuition, if you like, but I'm certain that whatever orders you've been given, you would never have shot me down in cold blood. Not in a million years.'

Caine didn't know how to respond to this: on the one hand it seemed like a compliment, on the other an accusation of weakness. He cradled his big Thompson protectively, gazing up and down the wadi: the rock-shelters and over-hangs interrupted the smooth flow of the rock wall like cavities in teeth. He was pleased to see that the men had done their scrimming-up professionally. None of the wagons was visible, even from this distance. A slight breeze was blowing up from the desert, riffling the loose white sand on the surface of the wadi bed. He turned his eyes back to Rose. 'You may be right,' he said, 'but if that's the case, why did the brass choose me for the mission?'

'I can think of at least one good reason,' Rose said, a half-smile on her face. 'They didn't *want* me executed. If I judged the situation that critical, anyway, I didn't need an assassin's bullet.' She opened her mouth and pointed to a large, ugly back tooth. 'See that?' she said. 'It's a Bakelite insert, held in place by gutta percha. Contains one hundred per cent potassium cyanide. I only have to bite through it, and it's curtains in sixty seconds.'

Caine winced and examined the false tooth with concern. 'Is that thing safe? What if you were knocked over and bit through it by accident?'

'It survived a parachute jump. Anyway, I might still need it.'

They continued walking until they came to the White's overhang, where Copeland and Wallace, now clad only in shorts and chapplies, were crouching over a spirit-stove, surrounded by compo tins. 'Here, let me do that,' Rose insisted.

She went behind the vehicle, changed into her new set of khakis and emerged rolling her sleeves up and looking business-like. The shorts and drill trousers were too big for her, but somehow their looseness only served to emphasize the lean femininity of her curves. She knelt down and started sorting through the compo. Soon she was making a stew of tinned bacon, soya-bean sausages and tinned potatoes. When it was on the go, she took some flour and tinned margarine and started making pastry, rolling it out on a discarded map-board, with an empty beer-bottle as a rolling pin. While she was working, Pickney turned up again to doctor Caine's wound, and shortly they were joined by Adud and Layla, who both welcomed Rose regally.

Layla explained that they'd decided to leave: they had some relatives living in the area with whom they intended to seek shelter. They seemed cut up about the news of Naiman's death. 'They always told us Jews were bad people,'

Layla said, 'but they were wrong. Moshe . . . he was a very good boy . . . very brave.'

Caine asked directions to his final RV on the Maqtal plateau, and Adud spent some time talking, sketching in the dust, showing Caine the best way of approaching it. Finally, they got up to go, refusing Caine's offers of cash. 'God knows,' Adud scoffed. 'What we've done cannot begin to pay for the lives of those of our people you've saved,' he said, with Layla's help, 'and in any case, the thanks is to God.'

Layla took Caine's hand, searching his face with her black eyes. 'You saved my life, twice,' she said. 'You are always welcome among our people. Wherever we are, our place is yours. Thank you.'

'The thanks is to God,' Caine said, smiling.

Naiman had once told Caine that while Arab greetings were drawn out, their farewells were short and sweet. This proved to be true. After shaking hands with Caine's group, the two Senussi simply shouted, 'Peace be upon you,' to the others, collected their few belongings and set off up the wadi. When Caine looked for them a few minutes later, they'd already vanished.

'Well,' Maddy said, as she served them stew and hot pastries in their mess tins, 'you really scored a hit with that girl, Tom.'

Caine's cheeks pinked. 'What do you mean?'

'You didn't notice? She only had eyes for you. Maybe men don't notice these things.'

Wallace and Copeland snorted, and Caine attacked his stew vigorously, slightly abashed. 'Now this is *good*,' he murmured, spooning bacon and potatoes. 'I really needed this.'

When the others had gone off to relieve the sentries, Maddy sat down on a poncho, assuming an easy cross-legged posture, and began methodically cleaning the mess tins and cooking pots with sand. Her manner was unpretentious, and Caine marvelled that she'd managed to reach the rank of First Officer without losing the human touch. For the first time he wondered if the compliant character she'd shown him could be an act conjured up for his benefit. He recalled Copeland's comments about 'Sirens', whose sweet singing lured sailors on to the rocks. Was Rose the type of woman who could adjust chameleon-like to her surroundings? Did she perhaps have the ability to be what other people – men – most wanted her to be? Wasn't this, in a sense, what all women did?

On the face of it, she seemed completely open and unreserved, yet Caine sensed that beneath the candid manner she was holding something back – that there was a sadness inside her belied by her warm, cheerful style. He knelt down to help her. 'You said you "spilled the beans" about your message,' he began. She nodded, apparently unembarrassed about it, and Caine felt encouraged to press on.

'Well,' he said, 'I was wondering – since the enemy already know – what the real story is. I mean, I was told some pack of lies about *Assegai* – a new glider-bomb system – but none of us really swallowed that.'

Maddy studied his face, and he suddenly became aware of her proximity – of a flux of energy between them. It flowed both ways and it was almost palpable, yet he knew that neither of them would ever admit it. When he'd first met her in the guard-house of Biska town hall, he'd thought her almost nondescript. Now he felt that he couldn't have been more wrong: she was beautiful. She had the same high cheekbones as Lina – the Italian girl he'd danced with at the deserters' camp – though instead of reminding him of Mongol hordes, Maddy's features somehow evoked images of Vikings, jade-green seas, desolate blizzards and melting white snows. When she smiled, her cheekbones stood out, and tiny, almost invisible lines spread from the corners of her eyes, as far south as the dimple in her chin. Her lips had an expressive, almost compulsive quality – she smiled easily, showing the slightly overlapping front teeth that Caine found entrancing.

'Tom,' she said seriously, 'you deserve to know, but I can't tell you. Better not to know anything until you're out of it.' Her eyes were like freshwater torrents, flooding his. 'I promise you one thing, though. If we get through this – and that's still a big if – I'm going to take you to dinner at Shepheard's Hotel to prove to you that everything is forgiven, and to share the whole story.'

He scratched his nose, grinning self-consciously. 'That's a generous offer,' he said, 'but they don't allow sergeants in Shepheard's.'

Maddy's ironic chuckle went on for longer than Caine thought his remark warranted. 'Really?' she breathed softly. 'Well, there's always a first time for everything . . .'

She was interrupted by three shrill blasts from a sentry's whistle, and when she glanced questioningly at Caine, he was already cocking his Thompson. The skin on his face was taut. 'We've got visitors,' he said.

40

Cammed up with Wallace in a natural sangar half-way up the screeside, Harry Copeland stuck the whistle back inside his top pocket and tried to draw a bead on the pilot of the Messerschmitt 110 that was trawling above the sarir like a mottle-feathered kite. The big twin-engined fighter-bomber was honing in at only two thousand feet, casting a menacing aquiline shadow on the pale desert surface. Wallace changed the elevation of his Bren-gun and tweaked the sights. 'Don't move,' Copeland hissed. 'She's spotting. She doesn't know we're here.'

Cope scanned the line of the cliff through his telescopic sights to make sure all the wagons were invisible, the men in cover. They'd done a good job: nestling in the dark cavities along the base of the scarp wall, their scrim nets covered with sand and brittle vegetation, the vehicles would be impossible to discern from that altitude – even their tracks had been brushed out.

Cope was shifting his gaze back to the looming aircraft when Wallace nudged his arm. 'Who the hell is *that*?' he gasped. Cope eye-scoped the bed of the serir across the wadi: a single, dark figure was moving down there, heading straight for the cliff. Cope squiffed through his sights, recognized a football-headed, barrel-chested man in khaki drills, tabbing along with a sort of rolling simian gait. He was carrying a rifle and something that looked like a furry pack on his back. 'It's Todd Sweeney,' he said. 'He's bagged game.'

Their eyes zeroed in on the solitary form – apart from the steel bird above, the only moving thing in the whole vast landscape. Five minutes back they'd heard the far-away bark of a single gunshot from that direction, but not having clocked anyone, had put it down to an echo or auditory illusion. Sweeney was lolloping on doggedly, thumb-up-bum, chuffed with his bag, entirely oblivious to the enemy aircraft poling up behind him. It was suddenly, horrifically evident to both Cope and Wallace that the 110's pilot couldn't miss him, couldn't help but deduce his destination from his direction of travel. They both froze, knowing it was too late to warn the ex-Redcap without exposing themselves and revealing the leaguer's position.

They looked on helplessly. Only a minute before the aircraft's shadow ghosted him, Sweeney seemed to become aware of her presence. Instead of going to ground, though, he jettisoned his catch and began to run.

'*No. No. No.* Get in cover, you stupid bastard,' Wallace honked to himself. 'Get down. Play possum. Do *something . . .*' As they watched in horror, the big bird shucked sky, cruised low towards the running man, as if trying to scoop him off the desert floor. They saw the German pilot and rear-gunner in the big cockpit, the black and white Luftwaffe cross painted on the fuselage, heard the thundersquall boom of the twin, wing-mounted engines, heard the curiously deadened blatta-blatta-blat of the 7.92mm machine gun in the aircraft's nose. Wallace's eyes boiled as he observed the pattern of dust licked up by the gun like a long ladder in a nylon stocking. He cocked the Bren's mechanism, tromboning the knob forward with a clack. Cope dug his fingers into his bulbous bicep. 'Don't shoot,' he warned. 'There's nothing we can do.'

Wallace swore, his eyes groping the strike pattern as it

converged with the sprinting Sweeney: he saw the man jackknife, vanish momentarily into a spray of dust-spume, fancied he heard a shriek of pain, then saw him lying on the desert floor like a curled-up turd. The big Messerschmitt flitted over the prone body, righted herself, chandelled up gracefully, poled towards them on a wide drift-angle. 'Get down,' Copeland grated. Wallace pressed his face more deeply into the dirt, watching out of the corner of his eye as the aircraft swooped over their position, barnstormed across the top of the escarpment behind them and began to gyre into a long turn. The dragon roar of wave-shifting aero-engines reached Copeland's ears. 'She's spotted the leaguer,' he whispered. 'She's coming in for a bombing run.'

Wallace was no longer watching the 110, though. His hawk eyes were on the horizon, where he'd just spotted something else: four black smudges like a flight of dark geese reaming out of the heat-haze at their ceiling altitude of about ten thousand feet. 'Stukas,' he grunted.

Cope fixed the dive-bombers with needled eyes. As they droned nearer he saw their angled gull-wings, the spatted, fixed undercarriages, the underwing gondolas. They were homing in directly on to the cliff wall where the vehicles were parked, and Copeland suddenly had no doubt whatsoever that the bomber pilots knew the column was here. He and Wallace watched, rivetted, as four dark shadows swished across the desert at 150 mph. About a quarter-mile from the cliff the aircraft suddenly changed vector, angle-pitched, dumped altitude. Their engines dopplered out. With red warning lights flashing on their gull wings, 'Jericho Trumpet' sirens cranking up, emitting bloodcurdling banshee wails, the four Stukas fell like stones into a breathtaking sixty-degree freefall.

Wallace shifted the Bren-muzzle, but again Cope jabbed

his arm. 'Don't try it,' he hissed urgently. 'You'll never hit them on the dive, and even if you did, they're fitted with a device that releases the bombs automatically, then rights the crate. The pilots pass out from G-force. Wait for the pull-out – they're sluggish on the recovery.'

'It'll be too damn' late, then, mate,' Wallace said.

Hugging the rock floor of the overhang with Rose close by, Tom Caine had heard the 110 rumble over the wadi. Now, he was aware of nothing but the squeal of Stuka sirens, the dread-bolt boom of their engines, the bumpa-bumpa-bumpa of 20mm cannon, the ricky-tick of machine guns, then the droning countertenor of fifty-pound bombs, the crumping *barrrroooomm* as they hit the deck outside the overhang. The earth quaked, the air squinched, white-hot grapeshot spiralled, dust and smoke welled into their space like a tidal wave. Caine heard the sirens fade out, engines shift frequency-wave as the dive-bombers lufted, steeple-chased the cliffs. He lifted his head, broke into a fit of coughing, and pulled himself to his feet. Rose dragged herself up, looking stunned but unhurt. It had been a fine feat of combat flying by the Luftwaffe pilots, Caine knew, but the White had been well concealed and they'd been shooting blind. The bombs had exploded in the wadi and, miraculously, none of their cannon-shells had penetrated his overhang.

He rushed to the entrance, peered out across loose scree along the wadi. His heart tripped a double-tap: *Vera* and *Judy* were both on fire. He couldn't see the wagons themselves, but he could see a torrent of flame and black smoke pouring out from the places where they'd been hidden. They'd been positioned too close together under their overhangs, too exposed to enfilade attack, he thought. He guessed that both had been struck by either bomb-shrapnel or 20mm shells that had ignited the explosives and petrol on board.

Caine gawked at unexploded fifty-pound bombs stuck nose-down in the sand with only their fins showing, took in blazing bits of truck fuselage, flimsies still full of petrol, bloated the size of pumpkins from the heat and the expanding gas: he saw sprawled, mashed bodies on the sand, saw commandos milling around with fire extinguishers. He left cover and sprinted towards the burning wreckage, closely followed by Rose; he clocked a heron-legged man running straight towards him down the wadi – Harry Copeland. The three of them almost collided, dived for cover behind a nest of boulders. 'What's the damage?' Caine demanded.

'Never mind that now, skipper,' Cope hallooed. 'Didn't you clock the Messerschmitt 110? She's coming in for another run. Now she'll have a clear target.'

Caine craned his neck to look for Messerschmitt and Stukas. The aircraft were invisible, but he could hear their engines humming behind the escarpment like bluebottles. 'Get out of it,' he screeched, waving to the circling men. 'Get under cover. They're coming back.'

The commandos distanced themselves from the flaming lorries, tumbled behind rocks, crammed themselves into crannies. Crouching among the boulders, Caine saw the 110 reappear out of the sand-mist as she completed her turn, posturing for another run.

'*Judy* and *Vera* are written off,' Cope panted. 'Two men dead – Flogget and Shackleton . . . and one wounded.'

He pointed to what looked like a mud-coloured bundle lying in the sand about a hundred yards distant. 'Todd Sweeney,' he honked. 'He must have gone out to shoot gazelle.'

'That idiot. I ordered him to stay in the leaguer.'

'Yeah, well, when the 110 came over, the bloody prick kept on going, straight towards the leaguer. It must have been as clear as daylight to the pilot where the wagons were concealed, and sure as shit he relayed the position to the Stukas. Sweeney was hit in her strafing run, but he's still alive: I saw movement.'

Rose's mouth twitched. 'We can't just leave him there,' she said. 'He'll be killed.'

Caine and Copeland eyed the fighter-bomber now sailing directly towards them, losing altitude fast. It was a sobering sight. 'There's nothing we can do,' Caine said.

'Bollocks,' Rose yelled, and Caine noticed with alarm that she was poised for a run. He put out his hand to stop her. 'Don't be a fool . . .'

Rose dodged the hand and was off out of cover into open desert, running, weaving, cross-cutting, towards the inert Sweeney. Copeland watched her, dog-eyed. 'She's fucking mad,' he said.

He was speaking to thin air, though, because Caine had already darted out and was bounding after her. Copeland blanched and brought up his SMLE, beading the 110's cockpit through his scope. The plane was still well beyond range.

Out on the serir, Rose had reached Sweeney after a breathless twenty-second sprint, saw a hole the size of a hub-cap in his shoulder, ascertained that he was still breathing and started to drag him back to cover. Hiking up behind her twenty yards away, Caine saw the puffin-nose of the Messerschmitt as she loomed down from a few hundred feet, heard the twin engines scrape, saw the 7.92mm machine gun spliffing white-hot needles of light from the nose-cone, heard the bell clappers of its strikes, saw the deadly beetle-stitch of bullets crinkling up the desert directly towards Maddy. Time froze: the Messerschmitt was out of focus, a nebular blue mass hanging in the air. Then Caine was on Maddy, grappling her slim waist with his strong arms, carry-dragging her five yards sideways. They fell on top of each other in a jumble of limbs just as the crate's liquid shadow strafed them, and in that second a single crack rang out from the base of the cliff.

Following through with his sights a hundred yards away, Copeland saw the red rosebud in the pilot's face, saw him hump over the controls. The big bird ripsawed over and past him, tail-planed low, pancaked into the hillside with a stomach-retching shock-wave, caroomed apart in a balloon of gore-coloured fire. The earth buckled; the air barrel-rolled; a parachute-shaped tongue of smoke whiplashed from the wrecked fuselage, sending stones and gravel cascading down the cliff. The aircraft hung there for a second, then the fuel tanks pitched up flame and split apart, sending shrapnel high in the air, streaming down the cliff like dark rain.

A hundred yards away, Caine and Rose felt the blast. Caine was attempting to pull Rose back into cover while she swore and beat at his chest with her fists. Caine had seen the strike pattern hit Sweeney for the second time, blowing him to bits only a second after he'd dragged Rose out of its path. 'He's dead,' he shouted in her ear.

They got back to Cope's position only just in time to see the four Stukas go into strafing configuration. They watched the gull-wings as they lost height, braced themselves for a second onslaught. Instead of going into a nosedive, though, the aircraft banked abruptly, swept around to the north, zoned off towards the Green Mountains. Caine watched them soaring through the galleries of cloud over the hills with an incredulous look on his face. 'They broke off,' he said.

'They must have been recalled,' said Rose. 'That means they want us – or me, anyway – alive.'

A moment later Fred Wallace's big form came shambling down the scree and along the side of the wadi. He didn't pause to inspect the burning trucks or the dead men, but scrambled directly to Caine's position. 'Skipper,' he wheezed breathlessly, 'there's a dust-cloud on the top of the escarpment, just the way we came. I reckon there's a big Jerry convoy after us.'

Caine nodded. 'That's why they stopped the attack,' he said. 'You were right, Maddy. They want us alive.'

There was no longer any point staying in cover. If they remained where they were they would be encircled by their pursuers. If the Stukas really had been reined in by the ground column, it suggested that another attack was unlikely. They stayed in the wadi only long enough to give Sweeney, Shackleton and Floggett a hasty burial, then mounted their three remaining vehicles, headed off along the base of the mountains towards their final RV.

41

Leaning on the White's hatch with Rose in the co-driver's seat below him, Caine coaxed the tiny column along, navigating with map, compass, and Mk I commando eyeball. He chose to follow narrow goat-tracks that meandered in and out of bald, rocky outcrops, crossed great lava fields of black volcanic clinker, tipped down along the powder-dry beds of wadis, oscillated through wild expanses of tussock-grass and drab camel-thorn. Occasionally they came across places where Senussi tents had stood – oblongs of boulders, broken straw shelters, the discarded bric-a-brac of nomad camps: bent and holed cooking pots, broken hobbles, useless waterskins. They found well-heads where the earth had been trampled by the hooves of goats, sheep and donkeys, but of the Bedouin they saw nothing. Adud had told Caine that many Senussi had moved to the northern side of the mountains to take advantage of the rains that had been abundant there this year.

Just before sunset they bounced across an undulating plain of brown upland reminiscent of the Yorkshire moors, covered in stunted thornscrub, stands of razor-sharp esparto grass, the strange waxy growths of Sodom's Apple bush. The wind was heavy with the scent of wild thyme. To their right, the patchwork quilt dropped away gradually to open desert; to their left it rose towards an escarpment whose face had been hacked and chiselled by natural forces into the gaping maws of rocky ravines.

As the sun slipped behind the sawtoothed edges of the

hills, the column arrived at a junction with a broad dust-track that coiled off to the left. Caine halted the wagons, and scanning in that direction with his binos, saw the last shards of sunlight mirrored back from the whitewashed walls of a human settlement. It was a group of Italian colonial homesteads sited on a low ridge, dominating the country for miles. The buildings reminded him of the abandoned Italian agricultural project they'd passed through near Biska.

Caine told the lads to take a break. The commandos piled stiffly out of the wagons, stretched, relieved themselves, glugged water, lit up cigarettes. They had last eaten twelve hours previously, and Caine knew they were hungry. Almost all the remaining rations had gone up with the 3-tonners, and in the excitement of the last twenty-four hours the 'three-days ration per wagon' rule had been neglected. With the help of Cope, Wallace and Rose, Caine laid out his map on the White's long bonnet. Scouring it by torchlight, his finger came to rest on the fork at which he thought they'd arrived. 'Look,' he said. 'There *is* a colonial scheme marked here.'

He fished a tin of Player's Navy Cut out of his haversack – the same tin Michele Brunetto had given him at the *Citadello* – handed cigarettes to the others, taking one himself. He lit them with his Zippo lighter, then replaced it carefully in its protective condom. 'We haven't seen any Senussi in the area,' he said, pulling on smoke, 'so this may be our only chance of finding food before we reach the RV. I think we should at least give it a shufti.'

Copeland regarded him doubtfully, his blue eyes lambent with shadow. 'The Senussi will have looted it long ago,' he said.

'Yep, I'm sure they will, but at the last place – near Biska

– we saw cattle, and I heard pigs squealing. We might find the same here.'

'The Senussi keep cattle, don't they?' Rose said, pursing her lips. 'Why wouldn't they have snaffled them if they had the chance?'

'They don't keep pigs, though,' Wallace beamed, patting his stomach with a steam-shovel hand as if to emphasize its emptiness. 'Muslims don't eat pork.'

'I don't think we ought to risk it, skipper,' Cope said, letting his cigarette dangle from the side of his mouth. 'The Jerries might find us there, box us in.'

Caine dribbled smoke through his nostrils. 'I don't think they'll follow us at night,' he said. 'In darkness, a big column would be reduced to five miles an hour on those lava paths. I know it's full moonlight, but don't forget we're still over two hundred miles behind Axis lines – more if Rommel is advancing as fast as they say. They'll have shufti-wallahs up at sparrowfart, and they'll be too confident of catching us in daylight to bother tracking us in the dark. They don't know we've got an LRDG squadron coming to collect us tomorrow.'

'I think we ought to have a look, then,' Rose said.

'We'll take the wagons a mile on down the road,' said Caine. 'Then we'll double back and turn off at this junction. We'll brush out our tyre-marks for the first quarter-mile along the dirt track. If there are any Krauts on our tail, that should put them off the scent.'

The settlement was a different configuration from the one they'd passed through near Biska. There, the homesteads had been widely dispersed, but here the farms were huddled together in a single group – about a dozen houses built around a large central mud square. The central area was dominated by a water tank on teetering iron stilts and a broken-down windmill, both liberally peppered with bullet holes. The place was eerie in the lapis-lazuli moonlight. A couple of tractors lay on their sides at the periphery of the square, their motors smashed, corroded parts spread out across the flat earth. Beyond the settlement, towards the hills, hundreds of acres of over-ripe wheat stood bleached and riffling: to the south, the hillside rolled down into a wadi thickly forested with trees.

The households were all of a standard pattern – flat-roofed angular blocks standing in groves of Aleppo pine, eucalyptus and pencil-cedar, each farm with its own small kitchen-garden of olives, figs and almond trees and its own cluster of outbuildings. The white walls looked clean in the moonlight, but closer up it was clear that the whole place had been thoroughly looted and wrecked. Doors hung off their hinges, windows were jagged shards, the small yards were littered with torn clothing, broken utensils, sticks of splintered furniture.

There was no sign of life, but as soon as the column pulled up in the square, Caine smelled pig. 'I'd know that smell anywhere,' he told Wallace. 'We used to keep pigs when I was a lad.'

'That explains a lot,' Wallace chuckled.

Caine ordered the boys to search the entire settlement, starting with the outhouses, and taking Cope, Wallace and Rose with him, set off for the nearest homestead. They were passing in front of the farm's termite-eaten picket-fence, towards the outbuildings, when Wallace growled. 'Shh. Hear that?'

They halted, cocked their ears. Caine heard nothing for a moment, then picked up what Wallace had noticed: a deep panting, coming from the interior of the nearest farm. It was distinctly human, like someone in the grip of a heavy fever. Caine made a silent hand-signal to the others to cover him, and holding his Tommy-gun at the ready, inched towards the gaping black aperture of the homestead's door. The heavy breathing grew louder as he approached. He was within three yards of the door and about to call out when he heard the frantic scuffle of feet on dry stone: something the size of a baby rhinoceros plummeted out of the doorway squealing, charging directly towards him. Caine just had time to take in a bloated body, poisonous pin-prick eyes, a pink snout, long, sharp teeth, when a single shot snapped out from behind. Dodging instinctively, he heard the creature shriek like an enraged infant, saw it pitch over with a round drilled cleanly through its skull. As it slammed to the ground a yard distant, like a heavy, damp sack, he realized that it was an enormous pig.

The others ran up and stood over it, doubled up with laughter. Harry Copeland ejected the case of the round that had just killed the pig and wheeled to cover the doorway on the off chance that the animal had some back-up. When it was evident that nothing else was going to come out, the four of them entered the house and searched it from top to bottom with their torches. They found nothing but the same broken remnants of a simple life they'd seen in the yard, with the addition of pig droppings and a defaced poster of Mussolini on the wall. When they emerged into the night, they found the rest of the boys gathered around the pig's carcase. 'Plenty of meat on him,' Maurice Pickney observed as Caine approached. 'I reckon it'll be a bit tough, though.'

It took four men to hang the pig by rope from an exposed beam in the farm's parlour, where Fred Wallace gutted and butchered it with his fanny. They broke up furniture, smashed doors, lit a fire – in the same room, so that it wouldn't be spotted from a distance. They roasted hunks of meat in the flames on hastily cut wooden spits. Soon, the room was full of the savoury aroma of roast pork, reminding Caine poignantly of the roast suckling pig they'd wolfed down at the *Citadello* two days earlier. It quickly became too smoky to breathe, though, and they moved out to the veranda on the opposite side of the parlour. They squatted to eat the fresh meat, washed down with Chianti from several large carafes that someone had 'liberated' during their sojourn with Michele's deserters. Caine and Rose sat together on the veranda's step, a little apart from the others.

'It *was* a bit tough,' Caine said, laying down his mess tin, 'Still, it was damn' *good.*' Noticing that Rose had also finished eating, he gave her a cigarette and lit it for her. For a moment they looked out through svelte moonlight on the gently falling blue-shadowed hillside. The moon was beginning to wane, giving way to the radiant stars and the long glossy splash of the Milky Way.

Caine paused before lighting his own cigarette. He snapped the Zippo open again and bathed the tip of the fag in fire. He imbibed smoke, clicked the lighter shut and held it up to Rose. 'See this,' he said. 'This saved my life and yours back in Biska. If I hadn't had this when I was in the well, I'd never have found the Senussi's knife. And without the knife I wouldn't have been able to climb the well. And if I hadn't climbed the well, you and I would now be stone dead.' He brought out the Zippo's protective condom, and Rose's eyes fell on it. 'Come to think of it,' he smiled, 'it was this condom that *really* saved our lives, because if I hadn't had the Zippo wrapped in it, it wouldn't have worked. Funny – isn't it? – how your life, future generations, everything, could depend on a rubber johnny?'

Rose giggled, her teeth flashed like polished pearls in the moonlight. Her laughter faded quickly, though, and she turned away. 'Future generations,' she repeated coldly, not looking at him. 'What makes you think there'll be any? Why even bring children into a world where people treat each other like animals? What's the point?'

Caine stopped laughing. 'Is that why you said that what happened to you didn't matter?' he asked. 'Is that why you volunteered for a mission with a cyanide capsule in your teeth? Is that why you tried to save an injured man in full view of an enemy aircraft? I saw how you acted when those Jerries were about to violate you and murder you in cold blood. It was like you just didn't care. Why?'

When Rose turned to look at him again, her features were ice-cold, her eyes like marbles. Caine shivered as he stared into the face of the Maddaleine Rose he'd encountered in the guardroom at Biska: the Rose who'd refused to be rescued, whose resistance had led to his being tortured by the enemy, to Moshe Naiman dying a dreadful death. 'It's none of your business, *Sergeant*,' she said. 'I'm a First Officer of the Royal Navy, and I don't have to answer to the likes of you.'

It was so sudden that Caine felt he'd been rabbit-punched in the scrotum. His head reeled. He took two deep breaths. 'I *see*,' he said slowly. 'I understand now. It's only "Call me Maddy" when it suits you, is it? They told me not to expect gratitude, and I don't expect it. I'm just a stupid piece of shit who carries out his orders, no questions asked. When they tell me I'm being sent to pull out some God's-gift-to-the-earth female officer who's carrying secrets about a Heath Robinson weapon that's supposed to win the war for us, I just say *Yes, sir, three bags full, sir*. I'm too insignificant in the great scale of things to be told what I'm giving my life for. *Just shut up and take it*. Well, First Officer Rose, *ma'am*, like I told you back in Biska, eleven good men *the likes of me*, have died so far to pull *the likes of you* out of this hell, and they didn't know what they were dying for, either. So, I'm ready to salute you, and stand to attention just like the manual says, because I'm a soldier. I don't need the pretence of your friendship to help me do my duty.'

Rose looked away, the corners of her mouth turned down in fury. There was an awkward silence as they smoked their cigarettes, staring at the night sky. It was Rose who broke the stand-off, her voice low and hollow, seeming to come from far away. 'I was engaged once,' she said. 'He was an agent in the Special Operations Executive. They parachuted him into France. He was betrayed by a traitor in his network, and captured. The Gestapo tortured him and murdered him. His name was Peter, and I loved him very much.'

She turned to look at him, her eyes vacant dark caves, each containing a bright pearl of starlight. 'The day Peter died, I died with him,' she said, fighting to keep her voice calm. 'I've thought of little else since then but getting back at the Hun. Revenge, yes, but that wasn't enough. I knew that the only thing that could really balance the scales, the only thing that could redress the wrong, was to go into the dark, to die like Peter. So, yes, Sergeant, you *should* have dumped me at Biska. I didn't need you to rescue me. Those Jerries couldn't have killed me, you see, because I'm already dead.'

Caine bit his lip, distressed by her words, but more confused than ever. Rose had risked her life to courier a secret message to Blighty. That made sense, but it was the only thing that did. When the mission had gone pear-shaped, why had she given up all her secrets? If she wanted revenge and an honourable death, why not just spit in Rohde's face as she'd spat in his, and swallow her damn' cyanide pill? Or did she think suicide by poison too clean and easy a way to go? Was it possible that she'd sacrificed King and country – not to mention Moshe Naiman – just so she could get the Jerries to do her in in as horrific a way as they'd killed her fiancé? If so, Cope was right: she really did belong in the booby-hatch.

Caine glanced over her shoulder to see if any of the others had heard. The commandos were in a jovial huddle at the other end of the veranda, finishing off the wine, intent on each other. They were keeping their conversation low, aware that raised voices could carry in the darkness.

'Listen,' Caine said quietly. 'I don't give a tinker's cuss about your fucking deathwish. All I know is that you aren't going there with *my* patrol. I intend to carry out my orders: I'm taking you back alive, and if I have to restrain you again, I will. The odds are that none of us is going to make it anyway, so I want to know *now* why I was sent on this fool's errand. What was it that you were carrying that was vital enough to justify eleven of my mates getting scragged?'

Rose dropped her cigarette stub and bludgeoned it out furiously with the toe of her boot. 'All right,' she said sourly, giving him a sideways glance. 'You asked for it, so I'll tell you. The dispatches I was carrying had nothing to do with *Assegai*. What they concerned was the state of Eighth Army. After Gazala, the army's morale hit rock bottom: there's been wholesale desertion, even mutiny. At present, we're unable to sustain a concentrated attack by the Axis. My message was from the Commander-in-Chief, Claude Auch-inleck, and was to be delivered personally to Mr Churchill in London. It was a request for permission to evacuate Egypt and withdraw to Palestine, or even the Sudan. If Eighth Army remains in Egypt, it will be crushed.'

Caine's mouth dropped open in disbelief. 'Rommel's already heading for the Egyptian border,' he gasped. 'If your

419

message never reached London, and there's no back-up, that means . . .'

'It means the end of the war in North Africa,' she cut in, her voice flat. 'It means that the Nazis have won.'

42

For long minutes Caine was too shocked to quiz Rose any further about her revelation. What made him speechless was the knowledge that she'd actually *revealed* this vital intelligence to the Hun. That meant that Caine's entire mission – all the blood, all the hardship – had been a pointless waste of energy. Rommel would have known about the *Runefish* dispatch even before they'd left Biska. That almost certainly explained why he'd quit Tobruk and pushed on towards Egypt so rapidly. Thanks to Maddaleine Rose, the Desert Fox was now aware that his forces would meet zero resistance from the Allies. Caine had joked about getting back to find that their new CO was a Jerry. It now occurred to him that if they ever did get back to Egypt, they would find the entire staff of GHQ in jankers, and Mussolini installed as top dog.

If Eighth Army had been ordered to withdraw across the Suez Canal or south into the Sudan, it might be able to regroup and refit for a counterattack. Since *Runefish's* dispatch hadn't reached Churchill, though, and assuming there'd been no back-up, then no such permission would have been forthcoming. Unless Auchinleck had decided to act off his own bat, the remnants of his army would be snared like a bunch of jack-rabbits in the open, skinned, gutted and deep-fried in oil.

'Is it possible,' he asked, a lifetime later, 'that the Auk relied on a single courier to get the message through? Surely there must have been others?'

'I can't answer that,' Rose replied stiffly. 'I only know about myself.'

'Why wasn't it at least confirmed through wireless comms?'

Rose pouted, scraping out her mess tin noisily with a fork. 'Because GHQ has been penetrated by Axis agents. All our signals chatter is being monitored by the Axis "Y" Service: they broke our codes long ago. The C-in-C couldn't risk anything –' She never finished her sentence, because at that moment two things happened. First, a sentry's whistle sounded three crisp blasts from the direction of the wagons, and second, a green Very flare torched back the fabric of the night sky. Caine just had time to leap up and cock his Thompson when scores of wild figures, armed to the teeth, appeared out of the darkness, converging on the house from all sides. 'Drop your weapons,' a voice hissed.

Caine stood poised, balancing his overweight Tommy-gun in his hands, as one of the figures sidled towards him. In the starlight, he recognized the untamed black hair and sheepskin-clad torso of Michele Brunetto, hefting a Beretta .44-magnum revolver in his right hand. Michele's eyes were aflame with pleasure, and there was an oily grin on his lips. 'You may be fast, Thomas,' he said, 'but there are more than one hundred rifles and sub-machineguns aimed at you. Even you cannot move fast enough to get out of that.'

Caine glanced around, clocking the horde of sheepskin- and jerkin-clad bearded bandits who had somehow crept up on them like ghosts in the night. Michele wasn't exaggerating: there were at least a hundred men here, and they were well armed. He remembered the ziggurats of stores, the stockpiles of weapons and ammunition at Michele's camp: he saw in their hands brand-new Schmeissers, Lee-Enfields, Berettas, Thompsons. He stood erect, making no move to drop his weapon. 'What are you doing, Michele?' he asked.

The Italian swept back his long hair with the same narcissistic gesture Caine remembered. His grin grew yet more cunning. 'Simple,' he croaked. 'I am selling you to my friend, Major Heinrich Rohde of the Abwehr, whose men will be here shortly. Lay down your weapons – *now*.'

At the mention of Rohde's name an icy frisson passed down Caine's spine: if Michele had been in contact with the Black Widow, he would have been able to give him vital intelligence about the *Runefish* mission: arms, strength, intentions. He hoped to hell that none of the lads had let slip to any of Michele's band the fact that they were to meet an LRDG patrol the next day. Out of the trail of his eye, he noticed that Fred Wallace, to his right, had drawn himself up to his full, impressive six foot seven and was bristling with fury. His Bren was shoulder slung, muzzle forwards, and Caine guessed that he was a hair's breadth from pulling steel, sweeping Michele and his mob with .303 ball. To Wallace's left stood Turner, Padstowe, Copeland, Trubman, Temple, Raker and Pickney, all with weapons at the ready. The only commando missing was Graveman, the ex-Royal Navy Commando, who'd been on stag at the leaguer on the other side of the house. Caine knew that it must have been he who sounded the whistle: he hadn't heard any gunshots, and hoped that Graveman had simply been overpowered.

Whatever the case, that still left only ten men and a woman against over a hundred well-armed bandits. In a ding-dong scrap at this range, most of his lads would be hit. A few might manage to dive for cover into the parlour, but they couldn't hold out there for long – certainly not after the Jerries arrived. Their best course of action, Caine decided, would be to pretend submission now and tackle the Ities later, when they weren't expecting it – preferably before Rohde turned up. It would be a tall order without weapons, but at least there'd be a chance. Right now they had no more chance than rubber ducks in a shooting gallery.

'Hold it, Fred,' Caine said. 'Don't fire.' He laid his Tommy-gun smartly on the earth in a drill-like 'ground arms' movement. Wallace glared angrily at him and there were groans from the lads, but after a brief hesitation, they followed suit. Michele chuckled triumphantly. 'I want all those little gewgaws you have,' he snapped. 'Those knuckle-duster knives, bayonets, pistols, cheese-wire, grenades – *tutti.*'

When the commandos had divested themselves of everything that resembled a weapon, Michele instructed a handful of his minions to bundle the hardware into the cab of the Dingo. 'They will be ready when the *Tedesci* arrive,' he said. 'We will give them the weapons and vehicles as a tip, no?'

He ordered the commandos to form a line, with their hands on their heads, then sauntered up to them cockily, a ragged little sparrow of a general taking an inspection parade. He halted three feet in front of Rose and gawped greedily at her body. 'So,' he gloated, 'you are the famous *Runefish.* Very nice. Very nice. Is true, you look like my Angela, but you have bigger bum and better boobs. But I do not think Major Rohde wants you for your bum and boobs. I ask myself from the beginning why the British send out a special squad to rescue a girl like you? You must be worth a lot of money, I say to myself. Then, by surprise, last night, I receive a message from Captain Haller of the Brandenburgers. He says you escape from Biska with British commandos. He need my help to get you back, and his boss, Major Heinrich Rohde of the Abwehr, he pay good price, and promise no hunting down deserters.'

Caine snorted. 'What happened to the "Italian Robin

Hood"?' he scoffed. 'What about robbing the rich to help the poor?'

Michele stepped in front of him, squaring up to him. Caine stood half a head taller, and though Michele's shoulders were muscular, Caine's were almost twice as wide. 'Robin Hood is just a story for children, no?' Michele sneered. 'Real life is not a storybook. You have to play both ends – make a little bit here, a little bit there. Major Rohde, he make a good offer – too good to refuse.'

'So, you turned out to be a capitalist, after all,' Caine sniffed. 'How did you find us, anyway?'

Michele snickered smugly. 'Was not so hard. This morning we pick up some friends of yours – the old Senussi and his daughter. She is a beautiful girl, that Layla, no? I threaten to take her virginity – me and all my men together – and the old man squawks like a chicken. He knows which way you go – he track you for us. What you do here at the *bivio* – covering tracks – is clever. It almost put us off, but then we smell smoke from one of the old farms, where no one is living for weeks. We leave our trucks and sneak up in the dark. You are so taken up with your *porchetta* you don't hear us. Only your sentry – the sailor with the beard – hears us, but by then is too late for you.'

'Where is he?' Caine demanded sharply.

'We hit him on head. I don't think he is dead.'

'If you've hurt him . . .'

Michele chuckled and turned his attention back to Rose, moistening his dry lips with a flicking tongue.

'Major Rohde will be here soon,' he said. 'I think there is enough time for us to get to know each other a little better, no?'

Rose ignored him, and he took a step closer, brushing her breasts with the tips of his fingers, running a hand along the curve of her hips. Rose didn't flinch, but stared back at him with narrowed eyes. Caine clenched his fists. 'Don't touch her,' he spat.

Michele raised his eyebrows and chortled. Stepping in front of Caine again, he kicked him hard in the groin with a cavalry-booted foot. Caine doubled over, grunting. The pain in his side-wound flared up, sent spurls of liquid fire through his abdomen. Michele stood over him. 'You don't give orders here,' he crowed. 'I welcome you like brothers, and you pull a gun on me in my own camp. You take my *benzina* without thank-you. Your men fuck my women . . .' He paused as if a thought had just struck him, and looked around, his eyes quickly falling on Copeland in the line near by.

'Ah, and here he is, the great lover of women.' He skipped over to Cope and eyed him appraisingly. Copeland, a foot taller than the Italian, gazed into mid-space with a bored expression, as if he wasn't there. Michele snarled and punched him savagely in the kidneys. As Cope bent forward panting, Michele jammed the muzzle of his revolver into his cheek. 'You, my cocksucker friend, you are *finish*. I see to it that you don't fuck another man's wife, never again.'

He stood up abruptly, cocking his ears: from down in the valley, Caine caught the purr of engines. 'Ah, my transport,' Michele announced. 'Now, we will all move down into the wadi, and wait there for my friend Major Rohde to arrive.' He glared up and down the line of prisoners. 'If any of you tries anything – any . . . how you say . . . *funny business* . . . my men will kill you.' He glanced back at Rose. 'You and me, we will make *funny business* in my caravan, no? Until the Boches arrive.'

It was a short march over rough ground down into the tree-lined drywash, and just as they broke through the trees into the sandy bed, a column of five lorries pulled up in a roar of motors and a flurry of headlamps. Caine recognized the wagons from the leaguer Michele had shown him at the *Citadello*, including the mobile command-caravan the deserter-chief had been so proud to call his home from home.

As the drivers backed the vehicles into the cover of the trees, Michele's men forced the commandos to sit in the sand. Despite the strident orders from their leader, though, few seemed to take much pleasure in what they were doing. Among them there were faces Caine knew – the lined and weathered peasant faces of men he had drunk with, eaten with, laughed with, at the *festa* two days previously. Some smiled in recognition – a few even winked. It was a very different style from the professional truculence of the Jerries who'd put bets on Naiman's life and thrown Caine into the well the previous day. He reminded himself that these Ities weren't real soldiers at all: the majority had either turned their backs on the war, or were simple farmers who'd joined Michele because they had nowhere else to go.

Michele detailed about twenty men to stand guard and strutted in front of the prisoners, baring his teeth, his forehead wreathed in shadow. 'Now,' he said, 'I'll show you what happens when a man touches my wife.' He pointed a finger at Copeland and ordered two of his men to drag him out. Cope knocked them away, got to his feet under his own steam. 'If you're going to shoot me, shoot me,' he growled, his large Adam's apple working. 'I don't need to be manhandled.'

Caine was proud of his friend's poise, but he'd decided already that he wasn't going to stand by and watch another comrade cut down. In Naiman's case there'd been nothing he could do. This time, though, his hands were free, and his mates were with him. He could see from the dark creases on Wallace's granite brow that he wasn't alone. Wallace and Cope might have their differences, but he knew that, whatever the odds, neither would stand by and watch the other murdered in cold blood. He and Wallace exchanged silent glances, and he saw that the others were also preparing themselves, eyeballing the ground around them for sticks and stones – anything that might be used as a weapon.

Michele was arguing venomously with the men he'd detailed to execute Cope. Caine didn't know a word of Italian, but it was obvious from the men's dismissive gestures that they were reluctant to carry out his orders. Michele sent them away and called out others to take their place, but these men, too, answered him derisively. A third group he called out behaved in the same way. It quickly became apparent to Caine that there wasn't a single member of Michele's band who was ready to kill a man against whom they had no personal grudge. In the Angela–Copeland–Michele triangle, Michele was the one who had lost face, and his men knew it: he could only restore his honour by killing his wife's lover himself. The more desperately he attempted to get someone else to do it, the more contempt he was generating among his men. This must finally have dawned on Michele, for with a snarl of rage he drew his pistol and pointed it at Cope's blond head. 'Down on your knees,' he yelled.

Copeland shook his head stoically. 'Nope,' he said. 'You want to kill me, you'll have to do it while I'm standing up.'

Michele looked discomfited and his pistol hand shook. He steadied the weapon and took careful aim, his thumb moving to the safety catch. Caine readied himself to spring, noting that Wallace was about to do the same. The safety catch was off. Caine felt the adrenalin surging through his veins. Michele was only five yards away. He tensed his muscles, was on the verge of jumping, when a voice shouted. '*Stop.*'

For an instant there was silence. Michele looked around curiously. His gaze fell on Maddaleine Rose, now on her feet among the commandos – a shapely, slender figure in her loose khakis, her soft blond hair silvered by the starlight. It was Rose who had spoken – not loudly, but with the same undercurrent of authority that Caine had heard in the guardroom at Biska. Everyone was looking at her now.

'It's me you want, isn't it?,' she asked silkily, her wide, dreamy eyes fixed on Michele. Her features in the darkness were serene and composed, her stance suppliant and delicately provocative: the breeze layering the folds of her uniform closely against the opulent camber of her hips and breasts, gave her the look of a draped odalisque from a romantic painting. 'You can have me,' she said. 'You can do anything you want with me. Anything you like. I won't resist. Just let that man go.'

Michele licked his lips. His face, framed by his long, dark hair, was opaque in the shadow, but Caine noticed the telltale movement as he applied his pistol's safety catch: Rose had already won. She had played her hand perfectly, he thought. By butting in at that moment, by offering herself, she'd allowed Michele to preserve a kind of masculine honour, without having to shoot a man dead in the process. Michele holstered his pistol and smiled truculently at Copeland. 'You are a lucky man,' he grunted. He turned to Rose and nodded towards his caravan. 'Come on,' he said.

Caine's pulse raced. He was glad that she'd intervened to let Cope off the hook, but he was no more prepared to let her sacrifice herself than he had been ready to see Copeland shot down. He was half on his feet when a single gunshot blasted out of the night, as hollow as dry thunder in the confines of the wadi. Caine and his commandos fell flat on their faces: the guards ducked and shifted on their feet trying to work out where the shot had come from. Caine was up, and a heart-beat away from an attempt to snatch Rose, when a willowy female figure in khaki appeared out of the darkness, stopped in front of Michele, jabbed an automatic pistol towards him.

It was Angela Brunetto, and she looked furious: '*Stronso*,' she yelled. 'Bastard piece of *merda*. Worthless dog-turd. These brave men saved my life and you hand them over to the same cats' piss *Tedesci* who murdered Carlo? Is this the way you repay them? You are not a man, you are a cockroach. You bring shame on us all, and now you make it worse by forcing this woman to fuck you? First you fuck every whore and trollop in the camp: you fuck Carlo's girlfriend at his own wake; now you take girls by force. You don't deserve to be chief here, because you are not a man. I am more a man than you. Let these English go, or I will shoot you now. My first bullet will go smack in your balls . . .'

There was a tense silence. Caine was expecting Michele's men to intervene at any moment, but none of them shifted. It seemed that Angela's action had evoked some sympathy – perhaps they too had noticed how Michele had hit on the dead Carlo's girl the day his death had been announced. Maybe they were fed up with his posturing.

Michele made a grab for Angela's pistol. She held on to it tenaciously, clawing at his neck with the nails of her right hand. There was brief tussling match, then the weapon blammed, speared fire, spoofed gas, pumped out a shell-case. Michele howled as a round tore through the top of his left boot and shattered the bones of his foot. He leapt into the air spliffling blood, landed in a heap on the sand, and sat there clutching hysterically at his foot, crying, 'You *bitch*. You shot me, you fucking *bitch*.'

At almost the same instant Caine heard the growl of engines and the creak of brakes from further down the wadi. A second later there came the murmur of German voices and the slamming of wagon doors. 'The *Tedesci*,' Angela whispered, looking around wildly. 'They're here.'

Caine's commandos were already standing up, poised to leg it, but uncertain whether they'd be shot down like dogs by their Italian captors. Caine saw Angela draw herself up and take instant command. 'Get to the vehicles,' she told the deserters. She pointed at the moaning Michele. 'Take that heap of shit with you, and let's get out of here, or they'll have us for dinner.'

If the loyalty of any of the Italians had been wavering, it was forgotten in the urgency of the moment. As the men lifted Michele and jogged towards their wagons, Angela turned to Caine. 'You leave now,' she said. 'I have sent old Adud and his daughter to where you left your vehicles. They wait for you there. Good luck and God go with you.'

She turned to Rose and smiled, and for an instant the two blond women, of almost equal height, hugged each other. The deserters were gunning their engines, and Caine could hear shouts in German drifting out of the darkness from further down the wadi. 'Get going, lads,' he yelled at the commandos. 'Take Miss Rose back to the wagons.' They doubled off in the direction of the homestead with Rose among them, and Caine realized that only one man was missing. When he spun round to thank Angela, he found her wrapped tightly in the arms of Harry Copeland, lost in a deep, passionate kiss that seemed never-ending. 'Come on, mate,' Caine hissed.

Cope broke away, and for a fleeting moment, he and

Angela stared into each other's eyes. 'I'll be back,' Copeland said.

She touched his lips with the tip of a slender finger. 'In another world,' she whispered. 'In another life.'

As she turned to sprint to her wagons, Caine saw tears glistening in the dark pits of her eyes. Then, just as the first Jerry silhouettes emerged from the shadows of the wadi, Caine and Copeland dashed off like greyhounds for the cover of the trees.

43

All night blown grit scoured the convoy like emery-cloth, but at sunup the wind dropped, and the desert packed down before them in ebony plains spandrelled with light, in dried-out playas like crystal eyes, in curried sand-sheets, flurries of fishscale dunes, dark hills like majestic galleons setting sail, in sand-scoured knolls, cliffs grooved and sculpted into spectral shapes. The Green Mountains had long since faded into darkness: the day sparked up so brightly that the sunlight hurt their eyes.

They halted in the middle of a featureless vanilla sand-sheet, three dirt-specks on the pastel emptiness, and as Caine jumped down from the White, he felt as if a weight had been lifted from his shoulders. Not that he believed they had outrun the enemy – he knew it wouldn't be so easy: it was just that huge open spaces like this gave elbow room to the spirit. Adud and Layla, who had guided them through the night, seemed to feel the same. They'd spent much of their lives in the maze of the Green Mountains, yet they became visibly more tranquil here on the open plains.

Copeland lay down on his back and lit a gasper, bleary eyes strafing the desolate sky. He'd driven all night clammed tight as a barnacle, wrestling the steering wheel so hard that desert sores had broken out on the skin of his hands. Caine knew Cope was worried that Angela hadn't escaped the Boche, and was wondering whether he'd ever see her again. When Rose knelt down beside him, bathed and bandaged his sores unasked, Copeland merely smiled.

He was the second casualty she'd tended at that halt. A few minutes earlier, Wallace had been rolling in the sand, whimpering in agony with muscle cramps in the left leg. Rose had crouched by him, spoken to him softly, massaged his tree-trunk limb. When the iron-hard tendons had begun to free up, Maurice Pickney marched over, told the giant that he hadn't been taking enough salt, forced him to glug down a pint of brine. Wallace recovered quickly, shambled off to help Murray, Turner and Padstowe charging the tanks with the last of the petrol. 'The LRDG *better* bloody well be there,' Murray declared. 'This Itie petrol won't get us any further than the RV. It'll be a bloody miracle if it gets us *that* far.'

Caine was concerned. If things were as bad in Egypt as Rose had implied, it was possible that the *Runefish* mission had been ditched. They didn't have enough fuel to get home – not even much past the RV, as Murray had suggested. Without the LRDG they'd have to foot-slog it back to the Wire. He and his men were exhausted: they'd been racing in top gear almost non-stop all week on Benzedrine and adrenalin: they'd narrowly escaped a scragging in several very close encounters with the butcher. Tabbing three hundred miles across sterile desert, on half a cup of pee or something per day, wasn't exactly what the doctor ordered.

Trubman hadn't made wireless contact with HQ in a week, and Caine debated whether it was worth chancing an attempt. He decided against it. The enemy must know roughly where they were, but triangulation would give them an exact fix. Any W/T transmission might bring Stukas tumbling out of the skies like batshit.

Rose made tea on the spirit-stove, and they drank it with lashings of Carnation milk and ship's biscuits – almost the only rations they had left. They were just finishing off the tea when Fred Wallace pointed out a faint grey-brown stain on the north-western horizon. At first Caine thought it might be a sand-storm brewing up, but Wallace shook his mace-like head. 'No,' he said. 'It's them. The Hun.'

They started off again, following Caine's sun-compass readings, adjusted by directions from Adud and Layla, notching three arrow-straight groove-lines across the desert. There were too many stoppages for Caine's liking. The White copped a puncture. Both the White and the Daimler got bogged down in *mishmish*. The AFVs were four-wheel drive, and easier to extract than 3-tonners, but it couldn't be done without a burst of hard labour by the whole squad, shifting at least half a ton of sand. They worked frantically with hands and shovels, aware always of that dark cloud behind them, aware that it was encroaching nearer by the minute.

Three times they saw flights of aircraft – black raptor shapes against the marble-streaked expanse of the sky. They had to freeze or run for cover. The planes made no attempt to strafe or bomb them, though, and Caine decided that either the pilots hadn't seen them, or, as Rose had suggested, that Rohde had given orders to take them alive. Just after mid-day, when the armour-plating on the AFVs was too hot to touch, they came over a rise and saw a vast purple wall truncating the eastern horizon. Caine identified it from the map as the Maqtal plateau, a continuous cliff-wall rising here and there to peaks like knucklebones and canine teeth, lying directly across their line of advance.

Caine halted the convoy, jumped down, scanned the falaise with his binos. He already knew that the rendez-vous point with the LRDG lay along the Maqtal, but his map wasn't detailed enough to show a pass, and from here no sign of a way through was visible. He called Adud and

Layla, and the old man pointed out a twin-tooth peak, just identifiable through the sheen of dust. He explained with Layla's help that there was a gap in the rock just to the right of this double peak – a gorge that ascended gradually to the plateau. 'The wadi is blocked by a steep rise at one end,' Layla translated, 'but my father thinks that with the help of God you can get your cars up. It is not more difficult than the Hag's Cleft at Shallal.' Since they no longer had a winch, Caine wasn't altogether comforted by this revelation. He reminded himself, though, that if the LRDG weren't there, it would hardly matter one way or the other.

He lit a cigarette, folded the map on the hot bonnet of the White, making careful measurements with his pro-tractor. He traced the RV coordinates to a point on top of the plateau that he was certain must lie near the head of the pass. He took a map-bearing on the RV, converted it to magnetic, then had Copeland manoeuvre the White until the sun-compass angle coincided with it. When the bearing was set, they mounted silently and sped off into the swelter-ing heat of the afternoon.

It took two hours to reach the falaise, and checking his watch, Caine realized that they'd shot the RV time by more than an hour and a half. That shouldn't have mattered – he was sure that the LRDG would give them at least until sunset. The cliff towered sheer above them: the edges of the gorge were warped and hammered by erosion into disquieting shapes: Caine saw maimed death's heads and slit-eyed demons embedded in the rock.

As the wagons passed through the shatterstone jaws of the gorge and began to grind up the gently rising wadi bed, Caine's spirits sank even lower. The recognition signal – a blue Very flare – failed to show. The LRDG knew their business, he told himself. If they were here, they'd have set up an OP and would have spotted the convoy hours ago. True, it no longer consisted of the seven vehicles that had set out from Jaghbub a week earlier, but since the Daimler had been flying the Union Jack for the past ninety minutes, there would have been no mistaking it. If they hadn't been seen by now, Caine thought, it meant that there was no one waiting for them at all.

They rounded a sharp bend in the wadi bed and saw the escarpment rising in front of them. It took only another twenty minutes to reach its foot. The plateau lay two hundred feet above, with no way up but a direct ascent of the slope. Though the scarp was scarred and rough, Caine saw to his relief that it was considerably less steep than Shallal's gradient of one in three. It took only a quarter of an hour for the wagons to reach the top, but by then Caine knew for certain that no one was waiting to greet them. From the summit, a breathless panorama panned out east towards the Egyptian frontier – an enchanted land of apricot sand, shimmering quartz and silicon, black volcanic plugs, rubble-stone tors, ironstone plains, whaleback ridges. He eyeball-walked the emptiness in vain for any necklace of mobile black dots that might have been the LRDG.

Leaguering the wagons in a fold in the ground beyond the lip of the scarp, Caine dispatched men in all directions to search for signs of friendly patrols. He sat down and double-checked the coordinates until he was absolutely sure that this was the right place. Then, he and Copeland crawled to the lip of the ridge and surveyed the wadi bed below them.

The wash was about five hundred yards across at its widest point, with sheer cliffs rising straight out of the sandy bed on both sides. The cliffs were ruptured by cracks and crevices where water had cut its way through over countless millennia, and topped by angular peaks the colour of burnished bronze. The wadi bed, scattered with nests of broken boulders and dense little copses of tamarix trees, rose gently towards the base of the slope they were now on, which cut across it at right angles, abruptly truncating it. To the left and right of this ridge, water had sculpted steep paths down the rocks, like vast stone stairways. For a moment Caine wondered if the enemy might outflank them by climbing up these 'stairs', but a few moments' reflection told him that they were too steep and too exposed to make them an easy option.

The slope itself was covered in stunted camel-thorn and hummocks of esparto grass: cheese-grater terrain, sweeping down in long screes, hollows, sandspits, loose, jagged stones, fractured crags. There was a good defensive line about twenty yards from the top where they could pile rocks into sangars and dig shallow shell-scrapes. Caine frowned, knowing that this last job was going to require enormous effort. The surface was already hot enough to fry an egg. He swallowed hard, knowing that there wasn't much time: the menacing brown cloud still lay on the distant horizon.

They withdrew back to the leaguer, where Caine held a dispirited O group in the shadow of the rocks. The men looked hot, worn out and dejected: no one had spotted any sign. All the way across the desert they'd anticipated encountering a well-equipped LRDG squadron – wagons manned by fresh troops, bristling with machine guns, mortars and even a Bofors gun to keep off the aircraft, their boards crammed with food and drink.

It was true that they'd been late for the RV, but there was nothing to suggest that an LRDG patrol had been and gone. Caine's worst fears were confirmed: no one was coming for them. The *Runefish* mission had been dumped.

'We've got a problem, boys,' he informed them. 'The enemy is closing in on us, and we don't have the petrol to outrun them.' He took a deep breath and continued, hacking words out of stone. 'As you can see, the LRDG patrol we expected hasn't turned up. We don't know the situation in Egypt – the last we heard from the wireless, Rommel was massing his forces on the border. Our LRDG patrol may have been bumped on the way, or it may not have been dispatched at all.'

He let this sink in, then said, 'As I see it, gentlemen, we've got three choices. One, we wait for Jerry and surrender. Two, we break up into small parties and trog back to Egypt on foot. Three, we dig in on this ridge and fight it out with the Hun. I'm not going to give any orders. I'll give my opinion, but the choice is up to you.'

There was a moment's silence. The commandos lit cigarettes and weighed up his words. Rose's sea-green eyes searched Caine's face as if some answer might be written there. Adud and Layla sat next to her, quietly smoking.

It was Maurice Pickney who broke the silence. 'If we surrender,' he said, 'they have to offer us our rights as POWs. I hate to be the one to say it, but somebody's got to. We did our best, but we always knew the chances of getting through this were thin. Luck was against us. No one wants to be a prisoner, but it makes more sense to surrender, to take our chance to escape and fight another day, than it does to get scragged for nothing.'

Pickney's declaration was met by boos and raspberries. Caine held up his hand. 'There's nothing wrong with Maurice's opinion,' he said, his sand-scoured eyes on the medical orderly's wizened features. 'If my experience in Biska had been different, Maurice, I might agree. But this lot behind us aren't Afrika Korps, they're Abwehr troops.

They're under the command of Heinrich Rohde who, as far as I can make out, is already a war criminal. He was responsible for the mutilation and death of Moshe Naiman at Biska, and only missed doing me and Miss Rose in by a whisper. Frankly, if we surrender to him I don't hold out much hope, especially for Maddy here.'

The men gaped bug-eyed from Caine to Rose: this was the first time Caine had talked openly to the whole unit about what had happened at Biska. Rose made a rude face at them. 'Leave me out of this, Tom,' she said. 'I'll take my chances.'

Caine touched the dressing on his side: his wound was still painful. 'It's not just for you, it's for me, and all of us. I wouldn't want to go through one of the Black Widow's torture sessions again, and I wouldn't want myself, you, or any man here, to die like Moshe Naiman . . .'

Harry Copeland groaned suddenly, and the others stared at him. Caine guessed he was thinking about Angela – wondering what her fate would be if Rohde had laid his hands on her.

'What about the escape-and-evasion option?' Flash Murray said, covering up Cope's embarassment. 'It's not impossible. When the LRDG got bumped by the Ities near Kufra, one chap walked two hundred miles back across the desert.'

'We'll never make it,' Copeland said, scratching his blond fuzz. 'It's summer. It's bloody hot, and we've got hardly any water, and no rations. We don't even know if we have any lines to walk back to.'

'I'm for making a stand here,' Wallace cut in. 'We've taken on bigger outfits before, and we came up trumps. We can do it again. Let's whack into 'em with everything we've got, pinch their wagons, head for the Wire.'

'It's not going to be that easy, Fred,' Pickney said. 'Last time, we had the element of surprise. We don't have it any more. When the Hun drives up that wadi, he'll be ready for us.'

Caine was deep in thought. 'What this needs,' he declared suddenly, 'is a Sapper's solution.'

'Mines,' Cope nodded.

'That's it,' Caine said. 'We've got about thirty No. 2 landmines and some Hawkins bombs. There's no other way for the Hun to approach us than up that wadi. We'll sow a patch of it with mines – we could even make a grenade daisy-chain to supplement them. Rohde might be ready for us, but he won't be expecting to hit a minefield.'

Cope's dazzling blue eyes lit up abruptly. 'What we need is a decoy to lure them on,' he said, leaning forward. 'How about posting the Dingo at the mouth of the wadi? The Huns clock her, they give chase, she leads them into the minefield. We'll make a path through it that only the Dingo driver can see.'

'We could dig sangars on this slope, and lay the grenade daisy-chain along the lower skirts.' Wingnut Turner joined in. 'The Huns who survive the minefield blast will rush our position uphill. One of us lies hidden, waits till they've gone past and sets off the daisy-chain just as they go into the assault – *boom*, bodies fly, we open up on the rest with Vickers and Brens . . . We'll wipe 'em out just like we did on the Benghazi Road . . .'

'Just a sec,' Taffy Trubman cut in, pressing his thick glasses nervously with a pudgy hand. 'The column we banjoed on the road didn't have air support. This time they do . . .'

Caine shook his head. 'I'm not sure about that, Taffy. I think they might want us alive, or at least want Miss Rose alive. Maybe that's why they called off the bandits this morning. Even if they use aircraft, I don't reckon they'll hit us full whack.'

'The question is,' Pickney said, 'who's going to drive the Dingo?'

Wallace raised a hand the size of a small frying-pan. 'I am,' he said.

Copeland guffawed. 'No you aren't, you great knuckle-head. You've never driven a Dingo in your life. You wouldn't know which gears were forward and which reverse. No, if anyone's going to do it, it's me – I'm an ex-Service Corps driver and . . .'

'No,' Caine said, shaking his head. 'I need your skills as a planner, Harry. And he's right, Fred, you don't have much experience with the Dingo.'

'It ought to be me,' George Padstowe announced mod-estly. 'I think Taffy Trubman and I have clocked up the most hours in the Dingo.'

Caine considered it for a moment. 'All right,' he said. 'You and Wingnut will lay the No. 2 mines, the Hawkinses and the daisy-chain. You'll do the decoy, George. Wingnut, you'll lie in hiding with the daisy-chain igniter.' He glanced at Turner. 'That all right with you?'

The cadaverous RAOC man beamed, remembering how he'd been left out of the action during the fight at Umm 'Aijil. 'Right you are, skipper,' he said. 'The Hawkins bombs won't penetrate thick armour, but they'll blow off tracks or wheels. We'll fit sordo rubbers to the No. 2 mines – that means we'll be able to lay them within two feet of each other without sympathetic detonation.'

'Good,' Caine said. 'We'll have to hope that the Huns don't come in waves, though, because we've only got enough ordnance for one good crack.'

'Just watch those Hawkinses,' Wallace said. 'I never trusted that crush igniter system.'

The giant looked around to see Copeland and Caine both smirking at him. 'What?' he demanded. He paused and glared almost threateningly around at the small company. 'Well, have we decided or not?'

Caine searched the men's faces. They nodded in agreement one by one – Pickney alone remained uncertain. 'Listen,' he said. 'There are only eleven of us . . .'

'Twelve,' Rose cut in sharply.

Pickney screwed up his face. 'All right, I meant eleven *combatants*. How the fuck can eleven shagged-out men take on a large force of Axis troops with armoured vehicles and possibly even air support? It's just not on.'

Wallace preened his cliff-like chest. 'We're commandos, ain't we?' he said.

Copeland chuckled a little disdainfully, and shook his head at Pickney. 'Another chap who doesn't know his history,' he said. 'Ever hear of the battle of Thermopylae, Maurice? Three hundred Spartans used a narrow gorge like this one to hold off a Persian army fifty-thousand strong. This place favours a few defenders, like Thermopylae – it's just a matter of how you use the ground.'

'I've been to school, mate,' Pickney said, looking offended, 'and you're only telling half the story. Three hundred Spartans might have held back the entire Persian army at Thermopylae. The way I remember it, though, it wasn't such a great victory. Every bloody one of them was wiped out.'

44

The O Group was broken up by Caine's reminder that if they didn't get on with it they'd be wiped out sitting on their arses. The commandos leapt into frenetic activity. Turner and Padstowe loaded the Dingo with twenty pan-sized No. 2 mines, fifteen Hawkins bombs, boxes of Mills pineapples and a huge coil of fuse wire. As they eased the AFV down the slope, the rest of the men lined up at the back of the White to collect weaponry and ammo. In addition to his personal weapons, each man was issued a Bren-gun and a thousand rounds of ammunition. Some were given two-inch mortars and bags of bombs: everyone got a haversack of Mills grenades, a bayonet, an entrenching tool and as many bottles of water as could be spared. Pickney doled out the last of the Benzedrine tabs; Caine designated a defensive position for each man in a dog's-leg line across the hillside, then sent them off to construct sangars.

Flash Murray would man the 20mm gun on the Daimler on the extreme right of the line. Caine located a natural depression on the slope there that would serve as a berm, and had Murray manoeuvre the AFV into hull-down position. There was a clear field of fire directly down the gorge. Fred Wallace had removed the twin Vickers from their pintle-mounts on the Dingo and White, and set about mounting them on tripods. The Vickers would be braced by Wallace, Graveman, Copeland and Caine. The White would play no direct part in the battle: Caine decided to hide her in a depression behind the Daimler.

The weapons had been handed out, and the men were digging their scrapes and piling up stones. Caine was about to shut up shop when Rose jabbed his arm. 'What about me?' she demanded, her long eyelashes quivering.

'You're a non-combatant,' Caine told her gruffly. 'I want you to go off with Layla and Adud. Try to reach a Senussi camp, hole up there until you can make contact with British intelligence agents operating undercover in the hills.'

'*A non-combatant*?' Rose repeated, pouting her full lips. She grabbed the Bren-gun Caine had set aside for himself, fell into a prone position, cleared the weapon fast and with perfect precision, snapped on a magazine, ratcheted the first round into the chamber and made safe. Caine's face dropped with surprise. 'You've fired a Bren before?'

Rose laughed up at him. 'I'm a marksman with Bren, .303 Lee-Enfield, Tommy-gun and .45-calibre Colt pistol – oh, and the Gewehr 41 semi-auto and the Beretta SMG as well. I've never missed the target with a single round on any of 'em. Fully small-arms trained.'

'What else did they teach you on that Courier's Course?' Caine enquired. 'You're a trained parachutist, a medical orderly, W/T op, *and* a small-arms expert?'

'I'm also trained in demolitions, subversion, intelligence-gathering, unarmed combat – and mental techniques.' She laid down the Bren's stock, set the weapon's carrying handle at an angle as per strict weapons-drill practice, and stood up, dusting herself off.

Caine watched her warily. 'Mental techniques?' he echoed. 'You mean like mesmerism, that kind of stuff?'

Rose nodded. 'Sort of.'

'Like how you stopped everything back there with Michele, just by saying "*Stop*"? The way you ordered us around in the guardroom at Biska?'

'They call that *the Voice*,' Rose agreed softly. 'Yes, it's a mental weapon. You can project authority by speaking in a certain tone.'

Caine found himself glowering at her. 'In that case, it's a pity you didn't use *the Voice* on that bastard Rohde instead of blabbing your mouth off, flushing the whole Eighth Army down the toilet.'

Rose lost her smile: her head and shoulders drooped. Caine thought he detected the faintest glimmer of tears at the corners of her eyes. 'You haven't got a very high opinion of me, have you, Tom?' she whispered.

'I just don't *get* you,' Caine said, irritated. 'You've got guts, yet you collapsed under interrogation and blew intelligence that might cost us the entire campaign. You're so taken up in your personal tragedy that you don't even seem *bothered* about ours.' He shot her a hard glance. 'I mean, if you wanted to die so badly, instead of spilling your guts, why didn't you just swallow that cyanide pill and get it over with?'

Caine knew before the words were out that it was a vicious thing to have said. Rose's face caved in and she put her arms round him, hugging him. He was so surprised that he forgot to resist. Her mouth was close to his now, her lips parted, showing those two beautifully overlapping front teeth, her eyes tank-slits, almost closed. Caine felt the soft curves of her body fitting perfectly into his, felt her warm breath on his face, experienced an explosion of desire that seemed to crash like a tidal wave across his whole body. He'd always been told that proximity to death made men horny, but this feeling was savage, powerful, like the awakening of some great sleeping dragon in his body. He felt like crushing her to him, tearing off her clothes, making violent love to her right then and there. He shivered, awed at the force of the sensation, wrestling with the craving that threatened to sweep him away. 'It's been really lonely,' Rose whispered. 'You don't know how lonely it's been. These last two days – being with you – it's made a difference. All right, maybe I *am* more than what I said . . . maybe I couldn't tell you the whole truth, but I – '

'Where do you want these Vickers placed, skipper,' Wallace's voice croaked.

Out of the trail of his eye, Caine saw the giant towering over him, hefting a Vickers 'K' on its tripod. A guillotine blade chunked down on his feelings: desire drained away on an ebb-tide. Caine ignored Wallace and broke from Rose's embrace, panting slightly, still gazing into her eyes. 'Look,' he said. 'My mission was to bring you back or execute you. I've failed in the first and I'm past doing the second. Get out of here while you can. If things had been different . . .'

Rose wiped tears out of her eyes and when she spoke her voice had regained its stiffness. 'You know, *Sergeant*, the bottom line is that I outrank you, and you can't order me to go.' She bent down, picked up the Bren with both hands and glared at him, her flashbulb eyes challenging. 'For better or for worse, I'm staying here with you.'

'Hey,' Wallace yelled, a grin like a knife-wound slashing his stony features. 'That sounded like a marriage proposal to me, skipper.' He dumped the big Vickers on its three legs, wiped sweat off his brow with a tattooed forearm. 'Anyhow, seems a waste. We could do with anyone capable of handling a weapon.'

Caine shot his mate an exasperated glance. 'Fred, she may be an officer, but she's also a *woman*. It's against regs for women to fight as combatants in this campaign.'

'Funny,' Wallace honked. 'I ain't seen no Regulations Manual round here, have you? What I seen is a bint – sorry ma'am, an *officer* – who knows her way round a Bren-gun, and only eleven of us against about sixteen divisions of Jerries who'll be here any minute.'

His jovial manner vanished suddenly, and his black-pinned eyes bored into Caine. 'You spent your life treating women like they was precious flowers, Tom, but you can't go on doing that for ever. It's like you think they're a different species or summat. Respect means treating 'em like real grown-up people, too. Anyway, seeing as how she's the same rank as a major, and you're a buckshee sergeant, I don't reckon there's much you can do about it.'

Rose winked at Wallace. Caine looked at the big man in surprise. This was about the most profound dose of home-spun wisdom Wallace had ever come out with, and the simple truth of his mate's words sank in slowly. He felt awkward to have been confronted with such truths in front of Rose, and was tempted to relieve the pressure by throwing up a sharp salute and saying, 'Very good, *ma'am*,' in his most sarcastic tone. Instead he just nodded at her, accepting defeat. 'All right then,' he said. 'Collect your weapons and let's do it.'

Adud and Layla were almost equally reluctant to quit the battle, but Caine insisted that they make their way around the pass and head for the nearest Senussi settlement. If the worst came to the worst, they wouldn't be implicated. Adud argued, but when he saw that Caine wouldn't budge, he beckoned his daughter and they left without ceremony, stalking off silently into the open desert.

Caine busied himself with building his own sangar on the extreme left of the line. There wasn't time to dig a proper shell-scrape – a shallow trench with a wall of solid boulders around it would have to do. Pausing from the work, he saw the Dingo pull up at the base of the scarp – Padstowe and Turner fresh from mine-laying. The two men jumped out, saw him looking down from far above, and gave him the thumbs-up. They set about stringing grenades on instantaneous fuse, burying them across the lower quarter of the escarpment.

Half an hour later, Padstowe brought the Dingo back up the slope, halted it and sashayed down to Caine's position. 'We laid the No. 2 mines and Hawkinses,' he reported, 'in a belt across the wadi bed, about five hundred yards from the base.' He pointed out the place where Turner was holed up with the daisy-chain igniter, in a shallow dip behind a rock-pile at the foot of the slope. 'That's as far as the fuse would take us,' he said. 'Wingnut will stay in cover until most of the Huns have passed by. He'll hit the switch as they come under defensive fire from your position.'

Caine nodded. 'Tell him not to leave it too late,' he said. He cast an anxious glance at the steadily advancing dust-cloud: it appeared much closer now. 'You marked a path through the minefield?'

Padstowe clamped his pipe between his teeth. 'Marked by spent cartridge-cases. I'll know what I'm looking for, but the Hun'll never see it.' He held up a Very pistol. 'I'll give it a green flare as soon as I see they're after me.'

Caine clapped him on the shoulder. They shook hands. 'We'll be covering you all the way, George,' he said. 'Don't worry about ditching the Dingo if you have to. Just make sure you get out alive.'

'*Ditch the Dingo*,' Padstowe said, making a face. 'Good job old Pop Tobey isn't here to hear you say that, skipper. He'd have your guts for cheese-wire.'

He removed the pipe from his mouth. 'Tom,' he said gravely, 'I just want you to know, whatever happens, it's been a privilege –'

'Tell me about it *after* we've got through it.' Caine cut

him short. He stopped himself, realizing that he was being boorish. 'Anyway, George, the privilege is mine.'

Padstowe scrambled back towards the Dingo and a moment later was guiding her down the slope.

Wallace was making the finishing touches to his sangar when he heard two whistle-blasts. Ten yards away, to his left, Caine had gone rigid and was holding up a hand. 'They're coming,' he hissed.

He blew three more blasts on the whistle. Wallace, Copeland and Rose scrambled madly to get into position. Further to their right, Trubman, Temple, Pickney, Raker and Graveman settled into their sangars, toggled sights, cocked weapons, trained muzzles down the wadi. On the far right, in the turret of the Daimler, Murray made final adjustments to his gunsights.

All eyes were on the Dingo now, as she threaded her way across the wadi bed, nosing along like an eyeless dark tick through invisible mines towards the mouth of the gorge. Caine hoped that Padstowe would get there before the Hun, but on second thoughts reflected that it wouldn't matter either way. In fact, if it appeared that they weren't expected, so much the better.

The Dingo cleared the curve in the wadi bed, and suddenly the ridge was very still. Nothing moved. There was silence but for the hum of distant Hun engines – a single tone, like a determined bee, growing louder every second. Caine heard the throb of the Dingo's motor as it faded almost to nothing. There was a brief pause, then a sudden staccato grating of gears and the blub-blub-blub of machine-gun fire, reverberating along the wadi's walls. A Very flare plopped, laddering the gas-blue screen of the sky, coalescing into a streaky green flower. 'That's it,' Caine said. 'They've clocked him.'

Almost at once the Dingo corkscrewed back round the bend, zig-zagging, spraying dust, as Padstowe hugged the path through the minefield. The lub-dub of gunfire came again, louder now, and round the curve swept half a dozen German armoured cars, mostly four-wheelers, but led by a massive Sdkfz 231 six-wheeler, hefting on its turret both an L/55 autocannon, and a Schmeisser MG30 machine gun. The AFVs were racing in two ranks of three abreast, and all but the 231 had scores of German soldiers hanging on to them. Caine gasped at the size of the enemy force: there were more men here than just the Brandenburger platoon at Biska – they'd been reinforced to at least company strength. The front rank of armoured cars was ricky-ticking shrill lines of tracer at the Dingo from mounted MG30s. From where he lay, Caine could see the quiffs of smoke, could hear the pop-pop-popping of automatic weapons.

The Dingo raced nearer and nearer to the foot of the ridge. The 231, with her 8-cylinder engine, was faster, and closed the gap rapidly. Her 20mm gun blazed, a spike of fire blowtubed, a shell skirried air, sawed past the Dingo, hit the deck in a rumbling *roooomfff.* A claw of dust lurched up, gravel blebbed, iron frags blew. At the same moment the other Jerry AFVs stonked into the minefeld: the entire squadron gangrened-out in a fog of dust, peesashing smoke, line-squalling flame. Mines blowgunned, bombs sandspouted, the bed of the ravine heaved up in a belly-aching, head-drumming thunder. AFVs tore apart, scrap iron winged, smoke whorled, wheels blew off, armoured frames shambled and tilted. Germans shrieked, scrabbled, scarfed up fumes, tumbled off burning wagons. Flaming bodies hit the deck, twitched, squirmed, wallowed in gravel, dry-surfed sand. Survivors scuttled for cover, floundered into Hawkins bombs, went up in crimson mousse. Dismembered legs, roasted arms, intestine-rags flew: charred torsos plopped open like waterbags, showered fried tissue, rolled over, spewed flame.

Still Caine's squad held fire, ingested the scene with awe. Caine saw smoke clear, clocked the 231 half on her side with her wheels in meltdown, her turret still intact. He saw her gun pivot, saw the muzzle sunflower, blowpipe flame. He saw the shell bazooka the rear of the still-retreating Dingo, saw the little scout-car's armour-plating buckle, saw her wheels spin off. The Dingo careened, struck a mine, receded into dust-smoke soufflé. A second later Caine clocked Padstowe legging it out of the dust nebula, sprinting towards the cover of rocks, carrying a Colt .45, his body blackened, blood-blistered, slapping at smouldering shorts as he ran.

Caine didn't see what happened to him next. He was focused on the Jerries, who had pulled themselves into some kind of order, and who were advancing to contact off the minefield. He saw smoke wafting, saw the crackling hulls of wrecked vehicles, the archipelagoes of dead and wounded. He saw more motor-vehicles shearing round the bend in the wadi behind the fires – six or seven soft-skinners, pulling up, disgorging yet more troops. He heard the cymbal clap of Murray's 20mm cannon from the hull-down Daimler, sniffed the propellant, heard the two-pound shell craunch, observed a hawk-eye hit on a soft-skin truck almost a thousand yards away. He saw her flashbulb up in yellow and black. He saw Huns slipping like liquid shades through the pea-soup on the defunct minefield, firing as they came. He marvelled at their grit.

He zeroed-in the Vickers, yelled, '*Watch my tracer*', squeezed iron. The Vickers clappered five shots and jammed. Cursing, Caine fell down behind his Bren, tromboned working-parts, curveballed tracer down on the Huns. He heard Brens and Vickers squelching fire from the hidden sangars across the ridge: Copeland, Rose, Wallace, Trubman, Temple, Graveman, Raker and Pickney, all opening up at the same time. A firewind of tracer arched down the ravine, stitching sand, snapping bodies: the German ranks split, dodged, crisscrossed, used fire and movement. Dozens of them made the foot of the ridge, skirmished up the hill, used cover, laid down fire. A burst hit Caine's Vickers, chewed up the barrel, knocked it on top of him, gashed his face. He kicked it away, jerked metal, flugelhorned fire. Another slug whiplashed his shoulder, missed bone, cleavered flesh.

Jerries came uphill in scores, beefy shapes, bare-chested or clad in khakis, wearing coal-scuttle helmets and peaked caps. They advanced behind a forest of supporting machine-gun spritz and mortar shrapnel, kicking up pustules of dust, yoicking up exclamation marks of fire, all the way across the ridge. Caine left his shoulder to bleed, sighted-up Jerries, hauled metal. To his right, Wallace and Cope ditched their Vickers, switched to their Brens: they squeezed triggers, jack-knifed tracer at the Boche. They pumped slugs until their barrels cooked, swapped barrels, pumped again.

Copeland heard his breech-block clack on a void chamber, ripped off the mag, clipped another. A 7.92mm lead-jacket harpooned his hand, shrilled through his palm. Cope screamed, dropped the mag, saw blood soapsudding. He jerked out a field dressing. A round ploughed a furrow through his straw-thatched scalp. He ducked, fixed his hand with the dressing, and thanked thunder it wasn't his shooting hand. He felt warm serum blubbing his face. He touched the bloody groove in his head, gasped at how close it'd come to his skull, wiped the blood away with his neckscarf.

He clocked Brandenburgers hobnailing towards his sangar. He grabbed his SMLE sniper's rifle. He scoped in. He cross-haired a Jerry in a coal-scuttle helmet, shot the helmet off. The Jerry stooped, reached for the helmet. Cope cracker-jacked him through the forehead, saw the head fricassee in roseate shreds.

Rose, sangared up five yards from Copeland, felt Hun rounds squinch air, heard them chirring, squibbing off her makeshift parapet. She saw five Huns ranging her. She drew a bead, pulled iron, traversed the muzzle, hand-wove Jerry chests with a pattern of .303 ball. The group shattered. A Boche went to ground behind a rock, rimfired her from twenty paces. A slug frizzled air, lumped her flesh where the neck met the shoulder, drilled through muscle, grazed bone, whiplashed out the other side. Rose teetered in shock, smelt blood, swore through gritted teeth. She waited for the Hun to pop up again, pom-pommed a tight burst, saw his head splat like a watermelon.

She shuftied Boche regrouping. She groped for a grenade, pinned it, lobbed it overarm. A round ribbed her wrist, fried skin. She snapped her arm back, sopranoed *fuck you*, skulked for cover in the shell-scrape. She heard her grenade ding and burst, spattering fragments: she heard a German scream as the blast hacked off his foot. Rose whimpered, grovelled in gore, felt her head spindling. She fought to keep herself from passing out. She fumbled with field dressings, sucked in air, hyperventilated till the world stopped waltzing. She heard Goth voices, heard boots gallomping: she shimmied into firing pose. She clutched the Bren's pistol grip, chinned the stock, cocked the works, clocked Jerries, pazazzed fire, scythed them down.

Ten yards right, Fred Wallace saw Huns crashing to earth round Rose's sangar, saw a Jerry mortar-team setting up a tube at the base of the ridge. He stopped shooting, braced a two-inch mortar, found the elevation too high, used his elephant-sized legs as a base-plate. He sighted the tube, he slipped a bomb, he tricked metal, he heard the blat, he took the recoil. He heard the bomb hoick air: he pitched another and another and another. He heard the bombs wheeze, saw them strafe the enemy mortar, saw Hun bodies pinwheel in smoke. He saw a phalanx of five Brandenburgers coming at him from ten paces. He tossed the tube aside, braced his Bren, whamped it into the hip, slotted the working-parts. He let rip a spliff of fire, watched Huns thrashing. A handgun round blimped the same shoulder in which he'd been bayoneted. Wallace roared, dropped the Bren, flailed his arms, tottered, windpumped air. He clocked a Squarehead beelining him with a Mauser pistol. He planted size-thirteen boots, drew his sawn-off from its sheath. He heard the Mauser crack, felt the bullet hopscotch his knuckles: he pulled both handles, smoothbored the Jerry.

Further right, Taffy Trubman fumbled a mag-change, felt a ton-weight candlebomb his chest. He sailed back a yard: his glasses flew. He wheezed out snot, spit, blood. He saw gore blubbing, smelt scorched dogmeat. He blinked, wailed, made out fuzzball shapes looming.

Wallace clocked the three Germans closing in on Trubman's sangar from thirty paces. He pulled out a No. 36 pineapple, bit out the pin and tossed it underarm. He crouched, panting, his shoulder foaming gore. He drew his .45 Colt, saw the Jerries wide-eye the bomb and back off. He saw the welt of flame and dirt, heard the grenade cannon-crack, saw Jerries pitchfork. He opened up on the survivors with his pistol, left-handed, watched them go down. He heard Jerry mortar-bombs croak, saw the shells smack the slope. Firehorses reared, gravel spats lufted, shrapnel blew: three of the four sangars turned into smoking wrecks.

Furthest right, the Daimler's gun blowtorched: a shell drubbed, fried oxygen, stonked the enemy mortar five hundred yards away. Inside the turret, Murray wiped sweat and soot, loaded, pumped HE shells like a coolie. He sighted muzzle-flash from a Hun MG30 nest down on the wadi side three hundred yards away. He breeched a shell, swivelled the barrel, pulled the igniter, blitzed the machine-gunners. He saw fire-claws blow, smoke-horses erupt, legs and arms ripped off.

Murray's two-pounder HE shells had cleared most Jerry supporting fire, but the Huns were still charging. Murray switched fire back to the soft-skins a thousand yards away, ramped shells. The gun's muzzle bellowed: HE ordnance whizzed and whined. Three trucks became funeral pyres: the rest withdrew out of range. Murray was so focused on loading and firing he didn't notice that defensive fire on his left had faltered. The three positions hit by Hun mortar fire had created a gap in the line, and the Brandenburgers had broken through. The first Murray knew about it was when a No. 24 stick grenade sailed through the open hatch and landed in his lap. Murray went for the hatch just as the bomb geysered fire. The blast tore out the turret's guts, fractured the cannon's breech, blew off Murray's legs, sent him reaming to the deck, maimed and on fire. Murray rolled in the sand, blubbered, writhed. The Daimler backlashed flame. Half a dozen Jerries moved in from five paces, strafed the screaming lance sergeant with fire. Murray felt the slugs sledgehammer, swallowed smoke, felt his lungs melting, felt his life-force sluicing away. Maurice Pickney popped up from nowhere, a medical bag swinging off his shoulder, his prune-like face a demon-mask. He ripped off .45-calibre round-nose bullets from a Thompson. He hit Jerries. The

Tommy-gun's breech jammed: Pickney dumped it, drew his Colt. A Jerry Schmeissered him. Pickney took rounds, dropped without a sound. The Germans moved past him, past the burning Daimler, found the White hidden behind a ridge. They lobbed No. 24s at her, blew her to shreds.

On the left, Caine had seen Pickney spudsack, had seen the Daimler burning, had seen the White go up. The enemy had broken through the line on the right flank and were fast closing in on the left. Where the fuck was Turner? What had happened to the daisy-chain? The Jerries were getting nearer and nearer: in a few moments the left flank would be overrun and they'd be done for. Caine sucked in fire-gas, breathed in dust: he changed mags furiously, he throbbed fire.

Two hundred feet below him, Turner's position was empty. A few minutes earlier, the RAOC man had seen his mate George Padstowe emerge from cover further down the wadi, with half a dozen Squareheads on his tail. Padstowe had been wounded in the back and right thigh when the Dingo was hit, and had hidden himself in some rocks in the wadi. He'd been spotted and flushed out by Brandenburgers as they advanced. Not knowing what else to do, he'd started limping towards Turner's sangar, thirty yards away. Rounds creased up the surface around him: he dekkoed over his shoulder, saw Brandenburgers skipping out of the sand-dust behind.

Padstowe kept running, wheezing, straining. A bullet chugged his shoulder, snapped him round, frothed up blood. He fell on one knee, brought up his Colt .45, snapshotted rounds. He hit the first Jerry in the chest, the second in the mouth. They went down. Then the rest were on him, bayonets slicking. Padstowe shot a Jerry point-blank, saw mashed tissue where his face had been, saw him with no nose.

A bayonet sliced Padstowe through the solar plexus, missed his heart by a beat. Another jagged his kidney. Padstowe reeled, choked up blood, felt the earth rear up before him in yellow shrouds. He saw his mate Turner, who had just run thirty yards from his sangar, blunderbussing Jerries with a Bren from the hip. Jerries jitterbugged, gurgled gore, fell back, tippled over in the sand. Two Huns worked behind Turner, blasted him with rounds, semi-automatic. Turner felt the hits, lurched backwards, went numb, saw Padstowe fall in a heap. He squeezed metal, steam-shovelled .303 tracer, fire-gutted Jerries, wiped them out. He took in dead Huns, he swayed, he boked blood, he jettisoned the Bren. He crouched by his mate, tried to drag him, gave up the attempt.

Turner saw Germans swarming above him on the slope and realized that they were about to overrun Caine's line. He remembered the daisy-chain. His heart sank. He'd left his post: he'd let down the whole unit: he'd betrayed Caine's trust. He saw more Jerries advancing up the wadi behind him. He crawled back towards his position, trailing gore. Rounds whipped sand in his eyes. He kept on crawling. A slug scourged his buttock: another jugged his thigh. Turner felt the earth reel, saw his sangar through blood-mist, felt life draining. He set his teeth. He *had* to reach the daisy-chain igniter, or the battle would be lost. Bullets spattered around him, but he kept going. He was in the sangar: he was dragging himself to the switch. Blood spurted from his thigh in yard slashes. He summoned his last energy, scrabbled for the mechanism with blood-thick fingers. He took a raking breath: he pressed the igniter.

Two hundred feet up, Caine felt the daisy-chain shockwave. He saw detonations sandspurt all the way across the slope, right in the midst of the advancing hordes. Jerries skittled over: sawn-off bodies spun and flew. There was an instant loss of momentum in the assault. Caine saw two Brandenburgers ten yards away stagger, shell-shocked by the blast. He aimed his Bren, blimped rounds, knocked them down. Bodies and body-parts littered the lower slopes. Everywhere, Germans were turning tail, picking up their wounded, racing back down the scarp. Caine held fire, knowing the daisy-chain had gutted the attack. He switched right, observed a last band of Jerries around the burning Daimler. He picked up his Tommy-gun, shimmied out of his sangar.

Directly below, Turner's position was swamped by retreating Jerries. The dying RAOC man saw Hun faces five yards away, heard the chatter of Gewehr 41s grapeshotting him. He palmed a Mills grenade from the box, pulled the pin, paused, let go the handle. His timing was perfect. Brandenburgers came over his parapet with semi-autos burping: the last thing they saw was a thin man with large ears, his narrow face lit up with a beatific smile.

On the far right of Caine's line, the Jerries who had just whacked Murray and Pickney, heard the daisy-chain shuttlebang like fireworks behind them. They felt the blast, saw their comrades going down, saw their mates retreating. The group leader opened his mouth to order a withdrawal. A .303 dum-dum scrunched his chest, mangled up spare rib, splintered bone, tore muscle, collapsed a lung. The corporal fell, arms gimballing, taking in his comrades doing the turkey-trot, saw a flashwork of bullets nailing them. Three Tommies pitched at them from different angles: one a giant, another a tall, lean soldier with gore-smeared blond hair, the third a tight, muscular man with unusually broad chest and shoulders. Their lips were drawn back in berserker grins: they were covered in blood: they were coming on fearlessly in nebular blurs of fire.

A Jerry coalsacked, his throat torn out by a snub-nosed slug from a Tommy-gun. Another brought up his semi-auto and found himself looking into the nostrils of Wallace's sawn-off. A twin blast of buckshot peeled his face, cratered his scalp, sent him arching five yards through the air. The last three Jerries reeled, crimped together back to back: Caine, Copeland and Wallace crashed into them, Colt .45s crackpotting, fannies carving meat. Wallace brought his blade down with all the force he had left in him on a Hun's chest, stoving in his ribs, piercing his heart. Copeland shot a Jerry in the mouth point-blank, saw his teeth mince, his nose vanish. Caine snatched a Jerry's rifle, stuck his fanny into his carotid. The Jerry sawed air, streaked blood spritzes. Wallace shot him in the head for good measure as he dry-swam the ground.

At last, there was silence. Fred Wallace's tank-like bulk swayed dangerously. Caine put a strong arm round his waist to steady him. Nobody spoke. They studied the charnel house around them – the dead on the escarpment, the retreating Jerries, the burning AFVs, the smouldering wagons down in the wadi bed. It felt as though they'd just walked into hell and back. Caine glanced at his watch: the battle had lasted just half an hour.

45

Caine didn't kid himself that they'd won anything. The Jerries would be back, and there was no way his little band would succeed in fighting them off a second time. He resigned himself to the inevitable, reflecting that his mission would go down in history as the worst ever cock-up behind enemy lines. Seventeen good men killed in action. He didn't feel sorry for himself so much as for them: the steady, brave, loyal troops whom he'd squandered to a chain of inept decisions. He knew there'd only been a fifty-fifty chance of success from the start, but if he'd done things differently, they might have succeeded. After all, despite all the odds, they'd snatched Maddy Rose. It was galling to have come so near, and yet still be so far.

There were only five of them left now – six if you counted Rose. Trubman and Pickney both had chest wounds: neither could stand properly, but both insisted they could still shoot. Graveman and Temple had been taken out by mortar bombs. Temple was bulldogged out in his sangar, steak tartare where his face should have been, half of his brain smeared across the stones. Graveman wasn't a pleasant sight either: his limbs had been scissored off in the blast: he'd bled to death. The weird thing was that his marble-white, bearded features were tranquil in repose, resembling more than ever those of the Players' Navy Cut sailor. Raker had been scattergunned with MG30 rounds in the chest and thighs, and had died from multiple lung-punctures. When Caine peered into Rose's sangar, he found her grinning back at him: the only parts of her body that weren't blood-stippled were her white teeth and her ocean-green eyes. Caine supposed he should have felt resentful that she'd come through when all but four of his boys had got scragged, but somehow he was very glad that she was there.

Not that she, or any of them, was likely to be there much longer. They were alone in the desert, wagons gone, stores and gear barbecued, no water, rations or ammo, except what they carried. The Vickers were all write-offs and there were no bombs for the two-inch mortars. They had a Bren each, a few mags, some grenades, their personal weapons. They had no means of contacting friendly forces, and they were wounded. They didn't have the energy to escape on foot.

The sun was low, a molten slingshot suspended on a sky networked with cream veins. The intense heat of the day had been skimmed off, leaving a dark residue among the rocks, elastic shadows across the gold crust of the wadi bed. Squeezing into the shade of a broken crag, they studied each other's wounds, knowing that they could not survive another assault, knowing that they would not run nor surrender, knowing it was too late for that. Caine nodded towards the top of the ridge. 'I think we should move up there,' he said. 'That's where we'll make our stand.'

Wallace smirked at the word 'stand', but was too weak to make any rejoinder. Neither Rose nor Copeland said anything: Pickney and Trubman needed all their strength just to stay conscious. The others carried them to the top of the ridge, and set them up in a sangar with water, chocolate, Brens and grenades. Then they went back for their weapons and kit, brought them up to the new position, sat down behind rocks and boulders to wait for the final act.

Trubman and Pickney's sangar lay on the left flank, with Caine and Rose ten yards away in the centre, and

Cope and Wallace on the right. Wallace's shoulder had been mushed by the low-velocity round, his shoulder-bone and clavicle fractured: the bullet that had shaved his right hand had knapped his liverwurst fingers down to knuckle-bone. Copeland's left hand was swatched in blood-soaked dressings, and his scalp was a scab of dried gore from the graze. Rose had flesh wounds in the neck and wrist, Caine in the shoulder. They cleaned and patched up each other's injuries with iodine, shell-dressings, butterfly wraps. They glugged water; they snarfed down chocolate and ship's biscuits; they sucked on cigarettes.

Caine couldn't take his eyes off Rose. Despite the mess on her face, despite her wounds, she still had that elfin look he'd first noticed the day Wallace had cut her free. He felt a reprise of guilt at the way he'd treated her. He'd kept her trussed and gagged for seven hours: he'd accused her of blabbing to the Hun, called her a non-combatant. He knew now that no man could have fought better. 'I'm sorry . . .' he started, but Rose put a slender, iodine-stained finger on his lips. 'Don't,' she said softly. 'You did everything you could, Tom. Don't apologize.'

'I didn't do enough. My mission failed.'

Rose took a deep breath, her brilliant eyes soft with emotion, pricked with tears like tiny quartz crystals. She blew out a stream of smoke. 'Your mission didn't fail,' she said. 'It succeeded more than you will ever know.'

Caine, nodded, humouring her, taking her words for soothing consolation. Before he could speak, though, she oared in again. ' I wanted to tell you before, but I couldn't. Now we're finished, and there's no point me holding back.' She stubbed out her cigarette, and when she looked at him again, her expression was vulnerable. Caine couldn't help putting his arms round her. When she'd held him before, he'd felt overwhelmed with desire, but it wasn't like that any longer. Now, he was content just to hold her. He felt her body responding, melting into his hard contours. 'These last few days have changed me,' she whispered. 'I never thought I'd find anyone like you. I wanted to die, to be with Peter. Now I've found you, Tom . . .' She chuckled bitterly. 'Funny, isn't it? You want to end it all, and then the minute it looks like curtains, you find a reason to live, and someone to live for. I just wish . . . I wish things had been different, so that we could have got to know each other . . .'

'Shsh,' Caine said. 'I know all I need to know about you . . .'

When he kissed her it wasn't with the death-defying lust he'd felt before: it was as if time had stopped, as if this was all there ever could be in the universe. The kiss went on and on – the most satisfying, most passionate kiss of his life. When their lips parted, it seemed to Caine that the world really had changed: they were going to die – in an hour, in a day, in a lifetime – but this one eternal, priceless moment had been worth all their blood, toil and sorrow.

Suddenly, Rose let go of him and rocked back. To his surprise, Caine saw tears tracking down her blood-smeared face. 'What is it?' he asked.

'You said you know all you need to know about me . . .'

'I do . . .'

'No you don't. You don't know *anything* about me. You snatched a Wren officer called Maddaleine Rose from the Nazis, but I'm not her. My name is Betty Nolan, and I'm an actress. I was trained as an agent by G(R) – the Cairo Division of the Special Operations Executive. Trained for the *Runefish* mission. Maddy Rose is a character I created . . . me and the planners of the "A" Force Deception Service – it was all dreamed up by them.'

For a moment, Caine thought she was joking. 'You're having me on, aren't you?' he said. Before the words were out, though, the pieces fell into place with an almost audible *clang*: the mysteries, the paradoxes, her unusual skills, her three-hour SOS transmission, her unexplained behaviour. It seemed to him suddenly that it wasn't a surprise, that somehow he'd known it all along.

'The way you behaved at Biska,' he said slowly. 'Turning us in, giving the griff to Rohde . . . that was all part of a decoy, wasn't it? None of the things you've told me up to now was true.'

Betty Nolan smiled crookedly. 'No, it was all lies. I mean, it was true that I was carrying a dispatch reporting that Eighth Army was on the point of collapse, but that message was disinformation. It wasn't intended for Mr Churchill at all, but for Rommel.'

Caine's mouth goldfished: he strove to grasp implications. 'You mean you were dropped behind Axis lines on *purpose* . . .'

'Yep,' she sniffed. 'We made sure that Axis agents in Cairo would find out about *Runefish*, and that the Axis would track my plane and shoot it down. My pilot – Pete Orton – was sick. He only had months to live, and he volunteered for the job knowing he'd be killed. In Cairo, we had to play it dead straight, because GHQ is riddled with moles and informers. But I was never really meant to go to London at all – my objective was always Cyrenaica.

'When I bailed out the Senussi helped me. They showed me a cave in the Green Mountains, looked after me. I was sure one of them would snitch – I didn't make much effort to conceal myself, but it couldn't be obvious, either. When the Huns didn't come for me, I got worried that they weren't going to pick me up. That's why I sent that three-hour long

SOS transmission. It wasn't meant for you. I just had to make sure the Jerries found out I was there, and I knew they'd triangulate my signal.'

Caine sat up straight, stared at her aghast. 'Do you know how close we came to taking you out? We were there, at the cave. We saw you captured. Harry Copeland had you in his cross-hairs. Surely that wasn't meant to happen?'

It was Nolan's turn to look astonished. 'You were well hidden. I'd no idea you were there.'

Caine shook his head, struggling for comprehension. 'I had orders to snatch you or execute you . . .'

Nolan released a chortle, flat and hard, as if cutting off a sob. 'But you *didn't* execute me, Tom. I told you – all right, I don't know this for certain, but I *believe* they chose you because they knew that, when it came down to brass tacks, you would go against orders. You'd refuse to kill a woman in cold blood.'

Caine was confused again. 'Then why the heck did they order me to do it in the first place?'

'Look, Tom,' Nolan said, touching his arm with light fingers. 'Let me start at the beginning.' She took a breath, her tarnished green eyes locked on his. 'The *Runefish* mission was a classic disinformation stunt. It was designed to influence strategy. The morale of the Eighth Army wasn't shattered at Gazala. There haven't been any near-mutinies or desertions. That was all disinformation. By now, Eighth Army will already have rallied: it will have been reinforced by divisions from Palestine. Claude Auchinleck will already be preparing to give Rommel the shock of his life. Eighth Army is strong, but the object of *Runefish* was to convince the enemy that it was weak, so that Rommel would be *drawn* into invading Egypt. He'll be defeated there. He's walking into a trap.'

Caine's mouth groped for words. 'But surely,' he said, 'Rommel would have done that anyway, without any help from you?'

Rose dimpled a smile, her beautiful overlapping teeth bone-white against the gore-dark face. 'No,' she said. 'The long-term strategy of Axis High Command was to take Tobruk, then invade Malta. Only after that, after they'd secured their supply base, would they go for Egypt. We had to make sure they went for Egypt first. Of course, Rommel might have *wanted* to invade Egypt all along. That's in his character, but he isn't top dog, he's under the orders of Axis High Command . . .'

Caine screwed up his face. 'I don't get it. Wouldn't the Auk have been *happy* if the Axis had gone for Malta first? Wouldn't it have taken the pressure off the Eighth Army?'

'Not at all,' Nolan said. She blinked and leaned forward, her face taking on the fervent expression of an evangelist. 'Tom, the North Africa campaign is a campaign of logistics. It'll be won, not by bravery or aggression, but by supplies. Auchinleck knows that. Malta is the key to the campaign, because from Malta our RAF boys can block Axis supply-lines, sinking their convoys at will. While we hold Malta, Rommel can't ever be sure of his supplies or reinforcements, and without them, he's done for. His strategy depends on external supply.'

Caine surveyed her silently, beginning to glimpse, at last, the far-away shadow of the truth.

'The Panzer Army was badly weakened by the Gazala battles. Rommel's in a bad way. He's down to a single infantry brigade and a handful of tanks. He's short of supplies, and as long as we hang on to Malta, he'll stay that way. The Axis can't invade both Malta and Egypt at once, because they don't have the air power. They can only do one *or* the other, and whatever happened, they had to be deterred from attacking Malta. The only way of doing it was to make Rommel think that he could take Egypt *despite* his weakened condition – that Eighth Army was in such a chaotic state that his few men and tanks would be able to swat us aside like flies. Yes, Claude Auchinleck guessed that Rommel would *want* to advance, even against the orders of his High Command. Our task was to encourage his recklessness. The *Runefish* mission furnished him with intelligence that would help him convince his top brass that they could get away with it.'

Caine saw a distant, almost euphoric look in her eyes. 'I was ready to die, Tom,' she said. 'The only thing I had left in life was to get back at the Hun for what they did to Peter, not just by bumping off a few Jerry soldiers, but by something big, something that would upset the whole Nazi applecart. "A" Force had the plan, but they needed someone to bring it off – someone who'd be conspicuous. A female courier would stand out like a lighthouse in a sea-storm. They needed someone convincing, who could play the role of a snooty British officer. I volunteered, and I got the part. I'm an actress, Tom. Before I came to Cairo and worked in a cabaret, I had some good parts – I've played Shakespeare. I knew I probably wouldn't survive the mission, but I didn't care. My life in exchange for scuppering the whole Nazi war effort in North Africa? After what those bastards did to Peter? It was a small price to pay. Of course, I didn't really know about you . . . about the side mission . . .'

'*Side mission*?' Caine gasped, shuffling backwards. 'What the hell do you mean you didn't *really* know? I was sent to rescue you or take you out . . .'

Nolan pursed her lips. 'No, Tom, that wasn't your real objective. They didn't want me taken out – at least, not before I passed my message to the Boche – and to rescue me wasn't part of the plan. You were sent to make it look more . . . more authentic. When the Hun clicked that GHQ had dispatched a unit to snatch me or silence me, it would make what I had to say *valuable*, don't you see? Your mission was a decoy: it was all part of the shill.'

Caine's eyes bugged out. 'Of course . . .' he said, like a man noticing the dawn for the first time. 'That's why you couldn't come with me at Biska – you still hadn't passed on the intelligence. If we'd snatched you then, you'd have failed . . .'

'You've got it,' Nolan smiled apologetically. 'I had no choice but to put you off. You see, I didn't know that anyone was coming for me. A decoy search-and-rescue op was broached as a possibility during my briefing, yes, but the idea was put up only as a means of upping the ante, not a genuine rescue-attempt. You were fed the *Assegai* story as a fragile cover.'

'What does that mean?'

'Look, Tom, I wasn't privy to this – I'm just speculating. A fragile cover is one that's meant to be broken – what the "A"-Force boys call a "shill". If you or any of your group talked under interrogation, the weakness of your cover story would be so glaring that it would look like it was attempting to conceal the *real* story. It would make my story look more bona fide. The "A" Force planners thought that a search-and-rescue unit would be wiped out or captured within a couple of days. No one ever expected a small outfit like yours to get through. The odds were about 5 per cent. What you achieved was incredible, Tom. It was against all the odds. When you walked into my cell at Biska, I just couldn't believe it. I was shocked. Maybe I over-reacted. Maybe I could have got you out before Rohde arrived, but

I doubt it, and anyway, if he'd noticed, it would have looked suspicious. What else could I do? My job wasn't done. I had to make sure you didn't pull me out, not at any price.'

Caine saw that her eyes were heavy with tears again. When she touched him, it was electric. 'I'm sorry about your friend at Biska, I really am,' she said. 'I'm sorry about all your men, but be certain of two things, Tom: their lives weren't sacrificed for nothing, and you didn't fail . . .'

Nolan felt for his hand, gazed into his face, her eyes green fire. 'I know it might have been wrong that you weren't given the choice – that you and your men were considered expendable. Maybe your brass should have told you, but I suppose they thought the less you knew, the more convincing it would seem. None of us is going to get out of this alive now, but that doesn't matter. What matters is that we *did* it, Tom. We brought it off. Rommel *is* going for Egypt, and he'll never get out in one piece. Rommel's an egotist when it comes to strategy, and we used his greatest flaw against him. He was sucked in by his own rashness, goaded into making the worst mistake of his career. Together, you, me, all of us, we've helped change the course of the campaign. We might even have changed the world.'

Caine felt himself carried away by her rhetoric. He puckered his brow, trying to block his elation, trying to decide what he felt. He and his men had been sacrificed, that was certain. St Aubin should have informed him – should have given him the choice. Yet he wasn't sure whether, after all, being ignorant of the truth hadn't been for the better. He stared at Nolan with new eyes: he'd believed that she'd thrown away the Allied war effort on a whim. Instead, she – a *woman* – had volunteered for the operation knowing full well that she wouldn't survive. He tried to grasp the astonishing devotion to the cause, the amazing courage it must have taken to step deliberately into the enemy's lair without any hope of coming back. 'I don't care what your name is,' he said. 'I don't care if you're an officer or a grunt or a civvie. All I know is, you're one bloody hell of a woman.'

She chuckled. 'So *the Voice* worked after all?'

Laughing, he threw his arms around her, enveloped her body, felt the warmth of it, felt her muscles tense and relax under the loose khakis. She shivered, gasped, closed her eyes, held on to him so strongly that Caine sensed she was feeling exactly as he had, that she was being carried away on a tidal wave, pulled in by some unstoppable magnetic force, so violent that it left you helpless and breathless. Their lips clenched: they melted into one another. They might have stayed that way all day if Wallace hadn't grunted, 'Hey, skipper. They're on their way.'

The German soft-skin wagons that had withdrawn from Murray's bombardment – five or six of them – were trolling cautiously through the burning wrecks on the wadi bed, following at least half a company of Brandenburgers in disciplined formation. The Jerries evidently knew that Caine and his comrades were there.

This time there were no mines, no daisy-chains, no support weapons: no mortars, no Vickers, no 20mm cannon. Caine knew it had to be a whites-of-the-eyes job. True, the Brens were effective to a thousand yards, but they had so little ammunition left that it would be pointless to engage the enemy at anything but close range.

Caine stuck a Player's Navy Cut in his mouth, passed his last few flattened, blood-stained cigarettes to the others. He lit the fag with his Zippo, cocked his Bren. There was a rattle of working-parts as the others followed suit. 'Stand fast,' he said. 'Wait till they're up close, then take as many

471

of the buggers with you as you can. Watch my tracer.' That, he thought, was the last order he was ever likely to give. He grinned as first Cope and Wallace, then Trubman and Pickney, flashed him the thumbs-up, their cigarettes clenched in their teeth. He felt overwhelmed: forced back sobs. He wanted to tell them how proud he was to have served with them, but they knew it anyway, and the time for speeches was done.

The enemy abandoned the trucks at the foot of the ridge. Caine surmised that the footsloggers might try to work round, to outflank his position, but they didn't – they came straight up the slope towards it. Traversing his barrel, Caine watched them coming on with grim, unhurried movements and felt a wave of admiration. *Good men*, he thought. *Steady.* If it weren't for those bloody Nazis . . . He stopped traversing; he backtracked. There, among the khaki ranks, he made out the tall, hood-eyed figure of Major Heinrich Rohde. He blinked and stared hard: it was too far to make out the Black Widow's features but there was something about the walk that was familiar – that sidling, feminine gait. It was Rohde all right. Caine thought of telling Copeland to take him out with his sniper-rifle, but no, this was personal. In any case, Rohde was only two hundred yards away – a snap shot for a Bren.

He lined up his sights on Rohde's torso, saw – or imagined he saw – the major's arrogant leer. He took the first pressure; he smiled, whispered, *This is for you, Moshe*, squeezed iron. The weapon burped twice. At precisely that moment a heavy-calibre field-gun bazookered behind him like a volcanic eruption – three sharp stabs of crumping ordnance clawed the air, stomped the ground like thunder. Caine heard shells frizzle, breathed in propellant, ducked, looked up to see three spirals of white spume and red dust sand-spouting among the enemy. He saw bodies tossed head over heels, saw the entire Jerry squad hit the deck.

The world went feral with noise – the rumpa-dumpa-dump of Vickers 'K's, the higher-pitched telegraphic ruckle of Lewis guns, the solid boxgrinding throb of Thompsons, the steady basso-profundo lump of a Bofors, the tuneless haw of mortar bombs. Caine dekkoed over his shoulder, and his mouth fell open. Behind them, a little to the left, no more than fifteen yards away, six stripped-down Ford trucks were raking through sand and gravel straight towards the escarpment edge, throbbing with automatic fire. One of the trucks was hefting a Bofors 20mm gun and a three-inch mortar on its back, but each of the others was manned by four or five men: all but the drivers were crouched intently over machine guns or SMGs, spitting tracer and ball. The men were wearing khaki shirts and shorts, and flowing Arab headcloths, and they looked mean, determined, deadly. There could be no doubt that they were Tommies.

'It's them,' Caine heard Copeland bawl. 'It's the LRDG.'

'I don't think much of the service,' Wallace roared.

The trucks screeched to a halt on the lip of the ridge and belted down fire at the Brandenburgers. The driver of the nearest Ford grinned through a mask of fine dust, beckoned to them – the most welcome gesture Caine had ever seen. It crossed his mind that, had the LRDG turned up on time, this whole last chapter of bloodshed might have been avoided, but a closer shufti showed him that the wagons were battered by shrapnel and peppered with bullet holes, and many of the men wounded. He didn't doubt that they'd risked their lives a dozen times over to get here. He was about to grab Nolan when he heard the drone of aero-engines directly above them. He drooped, thinking the Stukas that had bounced them earlier were back, but peering up, he got his second surprise. Only a thousand feet overhead, a brace of RAF Blenheim light bombers was gyring on thermals. They were identical to the bombers that had shot up his column – how many days ago, Caine couldn't recall. This time, though, the Brylcreem Boys knew their enemy: they were flattening out into a bombing configuration, reaming in with spine-chilling purpose.

Seconds later, Caine, Nolan, Copeland and Wallace were lifting the almost comatose Trubman and Pickney aboard the nearest wagon. A second truck pulled up near by and they helped each other to clamber in. Friendly hands pulled them aboard, English voices enveloped them in a bubble of cheeriness. Before they were even half in, the lorry had gone into a skeetering reverse. Clear of the edge, the driver did a racing three-point turn, and as the wagon spun, Caine saw that the other trucks were withdrawing in a blaze of covering fire. The lorry wobbled over stones, splashed up sandwaves, hit the serir: smiling LRDG men passed him a flagon of rum, pressed a cigarette into his mouth. Caine dekkoed back towards the ridge where he'd almost hung out his bones to bleach. The last thing he saw was the dark moths of RAF Blenheims dipping into attack mode, going in for the kill. He turned his back on them and took Nolan's small hand in his. By the time the flat crump of the bombs drifted to his ears the tiny column had already been eaten up by the Sahara.

46

Cairo had lost its bustle: shops were bolted and boarded up, offices shuttered. There was a curfew. The streetlights were out. The city was meant to be blacked out day and night, but was only dimmed. Barrage blimps were moored like captive dolphins over the city, ready to repel Axis air-attack. Except for queues outside the banks, the crowds had faded from the streets. Rommel was only two short hours from the Nile Delta, and Cairenes were hedging their bets. At GHQ quiet desperation was in the air. The desk-wallahs of Groppi's Horse and the Shepheard's Hotel Short Range Desert Group had already withdrawn tactically to Jerusalem, together with cook-and-bottlewasher units not required for the fight. From Alex, it was rumoured that the Royal Navy's entire Mediterranean fleet was about to weigh anchor.

If there was disquiet, though, Betty Nolan saw no panic. The Tommies on the streets retained an appearance of phlegmatic unconcern that was typically British. When she'd met Auchinleck at Grey Pillars, soon after their arrival, he'd seemed cool and confident. He'd kissed her, praised her courage, informed her that he was recommending her for the George Cross. Tom Caine was up for the Distinguished Conduct Medal, and Copeland, Wallace, Trubman and Pickney were all in line for a Military Medal apiece. Nolan was grateful for the honour, but her main concern was to discover when she could have her cyanide capsule pulled out.

When Caine, Wallace and Copeland had turned up at the LRDG rear echelon base at Abbassia barracks, they'd found it electric with activity: crews swarming like ants over scores of mint-new Sherman tanks, infantry reinforcements hotfoot from the Tenth Army in Palestine, whole convoys of trucks being loaded with tons of stores, hundreds of thousands of shells and mines for the Alamein front. St Aubin and his headquarters squadron had vanished without trace, and the camp's admin. staff had no time to deal with dislocated units. 'See,' Wallace had grumbled. 'If we'd holed up with Michele's lot, no one would have been any the wiser.'

Caine saw Harry Copeland's eyes fill with wistful yearning. He clapped him on the shoulder. 'Don't worry, mate,' he said. 'You'll find her.'

The far-away look vanished. '*Who?*' Cope enquired.

On a moonlit evening two days after their return, Caine and Nolan met for their long-planned celebration dinner at Shepheard's Hotel. Despite the dearth of regular bar-proppers, it was business at usual. They sat in wicker chairs on the mosaic terrace. They drank Rye highballs, they drank Scotches and soda. They nodded to the concierge, read unclaimed cables on the bulletin board. They marched into the dining room, were shown to a table decked with roses, covered in clean white linen. The other tables were crowded with men and a few women, most of them in Allied uniform. Waiters in brilliant white gallabiyyas and crimson cummerbunds worked silver service around them. Caine and Nolan polished off thick, juicy steaks. They drank wine. They basked in the hum of familiar voices – a luxury neither of them had thought to enjoy again. Outside, in gilded moonlight, the city's thoroughfares were crammed with tank-transporters and lorries moving up to Alamein.

The restaurant was 'officers only', but Caine was clad for the occasion in Sam Browne belt and service-dress, with lieutenant's pips on the shoulder-straps. He looked the part. So far, no one had found any reason to challenge him. Nolan looked charming in a sheer black evening dress that displayed her sleek hips, slim waist, deep cleavage, the alluring architecture of her bare shoulders. Her boyish quiff of golden hair had been trimmed: her long lashes tremored, her wide blue eyes prismed. She wore no jewellery but a pair of gold studs in her ears. Her wrists and ankles were still bandaged, and a silk scarf of the deepest blue disguised the dressing at the base of her neck.

'Did you hear what happened here the other day?' she asked, laughing. 'Apparently a group of Australian enlisted men broke into the Long Bar, which is reserved for senior officers. There was a general in there, and when he stepped up to explain the situation, they grabbed him and threw him out.'

'I bet that had the Redcaps swarming,' Caine chortled. 'Terrible people, those enlisted men.'

Nolan studied Caine's uniform, noticed that it was a tight fit around the shoulders. She giggled deliciously. 'Where did you dig that up?' she asked.

Caine watched her, entranced by the sultry red lips, the exotically crooked front teeth, the dreamy eyes. He'd become well acquainted with her face and body over the past couple of days, and his fascination with her had increased almost to an obsession. He didn't believe it would ever diminish. Despite the torture, the carnage, the stress, she continued to exude that waif-like air – that hint of dreamy vulnerability that he knew was so deceptive but found almost maddeningly seductive.

Caine pointed a burn-scarred finger at one of the lapel-badges on his tunic – an insignia that Nolan hadn't seen before. 'Looks like a flying dagger,' she commented.

'It does, but actually it's a flaming sword. I'm told it's meant to be Excalibur – you know, King Arthur, Knights of the Round Table?'

She nodded, peered closer at the scrolled motto. '*Who Dares Wins*,' she read. 'At least it's positive. Maybe it should read, '*Who Dares Wins If They're Lucky*, though.'

Caine's forehead crinkled. 'It's the only special-service mob left in the theatre, now Middle East Commando has broken up. It's officially "'L' Detachment of the Special Air Service Brigade", or SAS, but I gather that's just a propaganda exercise. They call it "Stirling's Parashots" after the chap who set it up: David Stirling, a Guardsman. They're all para-trained. The idea is to deploy them behind enemy lines as a sort of airborne commando. With our old outfit being disbanded, I've been told that the Parashots are taking on a bunch of our lads. I've been thinking about applying – it's either the SAS or RTU, and I don't fancy going back to the Sappers or returning to Blighty. Anyway, to answer your question, I borrowed these togs off a pal who transferred to the SAS.' He frowned and wiggled his right shoulder, still bandaged under the uniform. 'I admit that the shoulders are a bit tight.'

Nolan beamed, sipped wine. She took in Caine's tousled hair, the hard-core face, the steady, slate-grey eyes, the strong nose and jaw, the scarred, freckled features, the deep crescent of his chest. His way of talking – in enthusiastic bursts – was almost childlike, and very endearing. She felt a wave of tenderness, tilted her head to one side. 'You don't look quite at home in service dress,' she said.

Caine guffawed. 'Not surprising. Since I lost my commission, this is the first time I've ever worn it.'

On the ride back to Cairo with the LRDG, a bumpy, eventful journey of nearly a week, Caine had told her almost all there was to tell about himself. She had known he'd once held a commission in the Royal Engineers, but he'd never explained how he'd come to lose it. Now, Nolan's eyes sun-slitted, her lips parted, cheekily erotic. 'So how *did* you lose it? You promised to tell me.'

Caine took a sip of wine, put his glass down on the table. 'It's not that interesting,' he said. 'I suppose I should really be ashamed . . .'

She drummed the table, mock baby-like. 'Come on. Tell.'

'All right,' Caine sighed, rippling his shoulders uncomfortably under the tight jacket. He paused, composed himself, spoke hesitantly. 'About a year ago, we were being pushed out of Cyrenaica by Rommel. We were withdrawing fast, but we kept running helter-skelter into our own minefields. They were supposed to be mapped, but a lot of them had been laid in haste and no one had bothered. An armoured brigade was held up by an unmapped minefield west of Benghazi, and I was sent with my Sapper detachment to pull the mines. A few miles out of town we passed through an Italian colonial settlement – a bit like the one where we ran into Michele. The Itie civilians were still there – just peasant families – but the place was being looted by an Allied infantry mob, I won't say who they were.'

Nolan's face dropped in surprise. '*Looted?* That's not like our men.'

'Looting's bad enough, but these boys were also beating the Ities to a pulp for no good reason, and dragging women and young girls out and gang-raping them. It was disgusting. I tried to stop them, but they told me where to stick myself . . .'

He paused awkwardly and gazed back at her, saw that she was both enthralled and horrified.

'Go on,' she said.

He sighed. 'Look, it's not that I'm putting myself on a pedestal . . . I just couldn't stand it, that's all. War is war, all right, but what do women and kids have to do with it?' He took a deep breath. 'Anyway, I went to the CP to inform the battalion commander – a young half-colonel. He just waved me away as though it was nothing. Then I got mad.' An embarrassed smile crossed Caine's mouth as he recalled the incident. 'I pulled my Colt pistol, grabbed him by the throat, and told him that if he didn't order his boys to desist, and send his provost staff down to make sure they did, I'd blow his bloody block off . . .'

Nolan gasped, looked appalled. 'And did he?' she asked.

Caine blinked. 'Yes, he did, but by the time I got my detachment to the minefield, the armoured brigade I'd been sent to help had been bumped by the Hun. Oh, we got them through eventually, but not before they lost some men. I was blamed for that, and of course, I was guilty. I was lucky I only lost my commission: I could have been jankered for dereliction of duty. Then there was the business of threatening a superior officer. They went easy on me because they reckoned I'd acted with creditable motives.'

He furrowed his brow. 'They said I'd got my priorities wrong: protecting enemy civvies instead of our own boys. They reckoned that I'd treated my orders as a "basis for discussion". I suppose they were right in a way, but if I hadn't stepped in to protect those girls, who was going to? When I saw what our men – *our* men – were doing to them, something snapped. I had to stop them. I couldn't help it.'

He paused, his face flushed as though he'd just given away a big secret. Nolan studied him, nodded her golden head. 'That's it,' she said. 'That's why they roped you in for *Runefish*. Your record. I knew there had to be something . . .' She thought it over for a moment, drank some wine. Caine was looking uncertain, and his expression made her want to hold him, comfort him. Instead she covered his large hand with her smaller one. 'Some things are more important than orders,' she said. 'What you did showed real integrity – integrity as a human being, I mean. Deep down, your top brass knew it. You were ideal for the *Runefish* mission, because this time they didn't want blind obedience. They wanted someone who *would* second-guess his orders to take me out.'

They sat in silence for a moment, chewing it over. Caine's revelation of his past had reminded Nolan of recent news she'd acquired at GHQ. 'Julian Avery's dead,' she told him. 'That was the G(R) officer who trained me for the mission. He was tortured and shot by the same psychopath I came across in the act of raping and killing Lady Mary Goddard . . .'

'What?'

She nodded sadly. 'It turned out that the killer was a spy for the Abwehr – a Jerry brought up in Cairo. His real name is Johann Eisner, codename *Stürmer*. By chance, he picked up the spoof *Runefish* material Julian fed into the informer network. Apparently he tailed me and recognized me as Betty Nolan, cabaret dancer. He'd seen me that time I walked in on him and Mary Goddard, and he remembered my face. He even located my old flat on the Gezira, killed a Field Security NCO and a Sudanese doorman there, and kidnapped Julian. He tried to torture information out of him, then murdered him, too. Luckily for us, Field Security picked him up before he could do any real damage. It was a stroke of bad luck that might have sunk the whole operation.'

Caine attempted a smile. 'We should be grateful it didn't, then.'

'Yes, but there's something else. In the process of trying

to track down my real identity, he raped and murdered two other women. One was my friend Rachel Levi, a cabaret girl at Madame Badia's. The other was another female G(R) operator, Susan Arquette, whom I didn't know, but who was occupying my flat as my double.' The oceanborn eyes were distant now. 'I can't help feeling, in a way, that I was partly responsible for their deaths . . .'

Caine thought of the twenty good men he'd just left behind on *Runefish* – many of them hadn't even received a proper burial. 'I know how that feels,' he said. 'If Field Security have picked up this Eisner, though, he'll get the firing squad for certain . . .'

'No, he won't,' she said, lips pursed. 'That's the problem. A couple of days back, he escaped. They told me that he was being transferred from the Central Detention and Interrogation Camp to another location when his vehicle was ambushed by a band of about twenty Egyptians – bandits or gun-runner types. His MP escort were all killed or wounded, and he got away. He's on the loose out there.'

Caine absorbed this and nodded grimly. 'I expect they'll get him back soon enough.'

'I'm not so sure. He's obviously got access to a lot of help in Cairo. They say he speaks five languages fluently, and can easily pass as a native.'

Caine shook his head. 'A man like that – a nutter – he's bound to give himself away sooner or later.'

'I hope so,' Nolan said, forcing a bravado smirk, 'because he seems to have a personal grudge against me. Apparently, the last thing he said to his interrogator was, *I'll see that Nolan bitch in hell if it's the last thing I do.*'

For an instant Caine was shocked. 'He's probably long gone by now,' he said. 'I wouldn't waste your time worrying about him. Did you say he was Abwehr?'

'Yep.'

'One of our friend Rohde's men, no doubt. Birds of a feather and all that.'

This reminded Nolan of something else. 'You know that pot-shot you took at Rohde just before we were pulled out? Did you get him?'

Caine sighed. He'd already spent some time mulling over this question. 'I don't know,' he answered. 'Maybe I did, but I didn't follow through: I was distracted when the Bofors opened up. I never heard those LRDG trucks coming, did you?'

'No. The wind was in our faces, and we were totally focused on the enemy. They must have come up really fast.'

Caine nodded. 'Anyway, if I didn't get him, there's a good chance the Blenheims did. If not, he's still on the Axis orbat. I doubt he's in good odour with Rommel, though. He let you get away.'

Nolan shivered involuntarily. Caine knew she was remembering her ordeal at Biska. 'Look,' he said, 'if you – if the C-in-C, that is – was right in his assessment, the Axis are soon to go belly-up. Rommel will get his backside kicked at Alamein, and the Huns will be finished in North Africa. There are even rumours about a second front opening – Anglo-American forces landing in Morocco or Algeria or somewhere. It's soon going to be curtains, so I don't think you need to worry about sadists like Eisner or Rohde. As you told me back on the ridge, we *did* it: we succeeded. The *Runefish* mission might never be made public, but *we* know what we did – what *you* did. You paid them back for murdering your fiancé a thousand times over, a million times. That's why the Nazis will never win. Every atrocity hardens people against them: every Peter Fairfax murdered creates a Maddy Rose, ready to give her or his life to get even.'

Her eyes smiled at him. 'That's why you were right to stop our side committing atrocities. It creates resentment, starts a chain of revenge.'

Caine poured them both more wine and raised his glass. 'Here's to the lads who didn't make it, who gave their lives for freedom.'

She clinked his glass with hers. 'The ladies, too.'

'Yes, the ladies, too. Absent friends . . .'

Nolan was about to take a swig of wine when she noticed something that bothered her. At an adjacent table, slightly to her right, sat a tall, craggy-looking young major, puffing on a pipe. She hadn't noticed him before. He had a slightly amused expression and wary brown eyes, and he was staring at them both intently. What worried her most was the fact that his lapels bore the same 'flaming sword' insignia that Caine was wearing. She shot a warning glance at Caine, then gave the smallest of nods towards the major. 'Do you know that man?' she whispered.

Caine studied him discreetly. 'No,' he said softly, 'but I see what you mean. He's wearing SAS insignia. He must know I'm an impostor.'

He crossed his arms self-consciously over his lapel badges. He considered leaving, but decided that he wasn't going to be chased out. They'd planned this evening for a long time. They deserved it. He wasn't going to run away and spoil it now.

Nolan saw that he was resigned to staying, and let out a sigh. She forced a grin and lifted her glass again. 'Absent friends,' she said.

The words were hardly out of her mouth when there was an explosion of rage. Nolan jerked, spilling her wine, thinking that the noise must have come from the SAS major. Instead, a weasel-faced officer had appeared in front of their table – an officious-looking man in immaculate battle-dress and boots like polished glass. He had poisoned-berry eyes, very prominent front teeth and almost no chin. He was wearing a major's crowns, a black and scarlet 'MP' band on his right arm and carrying a scarlet-crowned field-cap smartly tucked under his left. Caine's heart sank. It was his former second-in-command, Captain – now evidently Major – Robin Sears-Beach: he was shaking with indignation. 'You've really crossed the line this time, Caine,' he roared, emitting tiny spats of saliva that landed on the table linen. 'I'm with the Central Provost Office now, and I'm going to throw the book at you. You managed to wriggle your way out of a court-martial last time – the CO's blue-eyed boy. I told you I'd be watching you. Well, there's no Middle East Commando any more, and there's no Colonel St Aubin here to let you off the hook . . .'

Caine stood up quickly, noticing that many of the guests at nearby tables had stopped eating and were glaring at him. The waiters were casting apprehensive glances in his direction. It wouldn't be the first time an enlisted man had been caught in Shepheard's with false insignia: they would enjoy the spectacle of seeing him dragged out by MPs. Sears-Beach was eyeing Nolan's cleavage, almost drooling. 'Who's this tart?' he demanded.

Caine's heart pumped: he saw red. '*Tart?*' he gasped, clenching his fists. 'I warned you once before about what I'd do if you ever . . .' He squared his massive shoulders and took a step towards Sears-Beach, who flinched and veered backwards. Caine glowered. He might have dropped the Redcap there and then, if Nolan hadn't cut in. 'Don't, Tom . . . he's not worth it.'

Caine made himself take deep breaths, forced his fists unclenched. Sears-Beach watched him, a hint of triumph on his face. 'Impersonating an officer is a very serious offence . . .'

'But not one that this man is guilty of, Major,' a slightly high-pitched, cultured voice cut in. 'You see, Lieutenant Caine here *is* an officer. As a matter of fact, he's under my command.'

Sears-Beach wheeled round in astonishment, saw that it was the craggy, pipe-smoking young major from the next table who had spoken. The man had risen to his feet, and Caine realized that he was very tall – a good six foot three. He wasn't much older than Caine himself – twenty-five or six perhaps – and there was a wild, unkempt look about him: his hair was well over regulation length, he had a day's stubble on his long chin, and his khaki drill bush jacket looked as though he'd slept in it. His manner was benignly eccentric, and there was a good-natured expression in his soft brown eyes. His pipe, empty now, was stuck in his mouth upside down.

Caine glanced at Nolan, trying to hide his bewilderment, but Sears-Beach was no longer paying attention to him. Instead, he was eyeing the officer's inverted pipe, the long hair, the unshaven face, the rumpled uniform. His eyes strayed from the major's crowns to the apparent youthfulness of his face. 'And who might *you* be?' he enquired, with only a soupçon more respect than he had reserved for Caine.

The tall major removed his pipe. 'Oh, how very rude of me,' he said in a mild, Oxbridge collegiate manner, 'I should have introduced myself. My name is David Stirling. I am the commanding officer of "L" Detachment, the Special Air Service Brigade.'

'"L" Detachment?' Sears-Beach chortled incredulously. 'You must be joking. There no such thing as the Special Air Service Brigade . . .'

Stirling's smile was deliberately patronizing. 'Indeed there is, Major. We are the main special-service troops in the theatre now, and we have absorbed many personnel from the disbanded Middle East Commando.'

Sears-Beach scowled, but looked just a smidgen unsure of himself.

'You may not be aware of this,' Stirling continued, 'but Lieutenant Caine here has just proved himself the most capable desert operator in the business.' He was staring at Caine directly, his eyes twinkling. 'If I may be so bold,' he said, 'I should say that he thoroughly deserves the decoration he's just been recommended for.'

'*Decoration?*' Sears-Beach's mouth gaped.

Caine and Nolan were watching Stirling with a surprise that was at least equal to Sears-Beach's. Stirling fixed his eyes on the Redcap officer again. 'Indeed,' he said, 'unless I am mistaken, this lady, too, has been cited for a decoration for the highest gallantry.'

'Lady?' Sears-Beach scoffed. 'What lady?'

Stirling's face lost its good humour abruptly, and even Sears-Beach noticed the hint of menace in the now hooded brown eyes. Stirling tilted his head slightly to one side. 'What would you call a woman who risked her life by going alone into the lion's den, endured capture and torture by the Hun, and personally took part in combat? Wouldn't you call her a lady?'

Sears-Beach caught the burning glare in Stirling's eyes, but ignored it. 'I'd call her an offender,' he said, sticking out his chin. 'Women are disbarred from combat: it's against King's Regulations.'

A flicker of exasperation crossed Stirling's face. 'Come, my dear Major. Surely, as a gentleman, you ought to apologize for casting aspersions on this lady's character.'

The tone remained silken. Sears-Beach was aware of the sting in it, but continued to bluster. 'Don't "dear Major" me,' he bristled, his mouth working indignantly. 'I'm assistant chief Provost Officer in this town and you have no right to tell me what to do. I mean, this is all utter hogwash. I was Middle East Commando myself: if this mob of yours is supposed to be recruiting ex-commandos, how come they never offered *me* a place?'

A thin smile played over Stirling's features. 'The answer to that is simple. You see, in the SAS, we have no time for the mediocre. We only accept the very best.'

He let the words sink in, caught Sears-Beach's eye with an expression that was insouciant and totally fearless. 'Lieutenant Caine is one of those excellent people,' he said. 'You, most unfortunately, are not.'

As Sears-Beach groped in soundless indignation, Stirling fumbled in his pocket for a calling-card. He pressed it into Caine's palm, his eyes sparkling with amusement. 'Come round and see me at my flat first thing tomorrow, will you, old chap?' he said casually. 'I think we have something of interest to discuss.'

He bowed deeply to Nolan. 'A very *great* honour, miss,' he said. He placed a dishevelled cap on his head, smiled admiringly at Caine, gave Sears-Beach an almost insolent nod, and with the eyes of the whole restaurant upon him, turned and swung off, elastic-legged, towards the door.